C...

BY
VICTORIA PADE

All the characters in this book have no existence outside the imagination of the author, and have no relation whatsoever to anyone bearing the same name or names. They are not even distantly inspired by any individual known or unknown to the author, and all the incidents are pure invention.

First published in Great Britain 2010
Harlequin Mills & Boon Limited,
Eton House, 18-24 Paradise Road, Richmond, Surrey TW9 1SR

© Harlequin Books S.A. 2009

Special thanks and acknowledgment are given to Victoria Pade for her contribution to The Foleys and the McCords mini-series.

ISBN: 978 0 263 88831 7

23-1010

Harlequin Mills & Boon policy is to use papers that are natural, renewable and recyclable products and made from wood grown in sustainable forests. The logging and manufacturing processes conform to the legal environmental regulations of the country of origin.

Printed and bound in Spain
by Litografía Rosés S.A., Barcelona

Victoria Pade is a native of Colorado, where she continues to live and work. Her passion—besides writing—is chocolate, which she indulges in frequently and in every form.

She loves romance novels and romantic movies—the more lighthearted the better—but she likes a good, juicy mystery now and then, too.

Dear Reader,

Tanya Kimbrough is not as trusting as Cinderella when Prince Charming presents himself in the form of Dr. Tate McCord. Tanya knows the score—she's merely the daughter of the McCords' housekeeper.

And this particular McCord heir is earmarked for Katie Whitcomb-Salgar, longtime friend of the family and Tate's on-again, off-again girlfriend since they were both teenagers. Tate and Katie may be off-again at the moment, but Tanya is convinced that that has more to do with the rough patch Tate has been going through since the death of his best friend in Iraq than with any permanent breakup. And there's no way she's willing to be nothing more than Tate's interim distraction. Even if he can put her on a slow simmer with just one glance. Will she be able to hold out? Or will she risk crossing social barriers to be with a McCord? Turn a few pages and find out... Here's hoping you'll all have happily-ever-afters.

Victoria Pade

Chapter One

"Sometimes I don't understand you, Blake. You open up enough to let me know the business is in a slump, that you think we really can find the Santa Magdalena diamond and use it to pull us out of the fire. But you bite off my head for asking how things are going."

Tanya Kimbrough froze.

It was nearly eleven o'clock on Friday night and she had no business doing what she was doing in the library of the Dallas mansion of the family her mother worked for. But her mother had gone to bed and Tanya had known the McCords were all at a charity symphony that should have kept them out much later than this. And she'd gotten nosy.

But now here she was, overhearing the raised voice of Tate McCord as he and his older brother came into the formal living room that was just beyond the library. The library where she'd turned on the overhead lights because she'd thought she would be in and out long before any of the McCords got home…

Make a run for it the way you came in, she advised herself.

She certainly couldn't turn off the library lights without drawing attention since the doors to the living room were ajar. But maybe Tate and Blake McCord would only think someone had forgotten to turn them off before they'd left the house tonight. And if she went out the way she'd come in, no one would guess that she'd used her mother's keys to let herself in through the French doors that opened to the rear grounds of the sprawling estate. If she just left right now…

But then Blake McCord answered his brother and she stayed where she was. What she was listening to suited her purposes so much better than what she'd already found on the library desk.

"Finding the Santa Magdalena and buying up canary diamonds for a related jewelry line are in the works," Blake was saying. "And we've launched the initial Once In A Lifetime promotional campaign in the stores to pamper customers and bring in more business. That's all you have to know since you—and everyone else—are on a need-to-know-only basis. Your time and interest might be better spent paying some attention to your fiancée, wouldn't you say?"

"What I'd say is that *that* isn't any of your business," Tate answered in a tone that surprised Tanya.

The sharp edge coming from Tate didn't sound anything like him. The brothers generally got along well, and Tate had always been the easygoing brother. Tanya's mother had said that Tate had changed since spending a year working in the Middle East and suddenly Tanya didn't doubt it.

"It may not be my business, but I'm telling you anyway because someone has to," Blake persisted. "You take Katie for granted, you neglect her, you don't pay her nearly enough attention. You may think you have her all sewed up with that engagement ring on her finger, but if you don't start giving her some indication that you know she's alive, she could end up throwing it in your face. And nobody would blame her if she did."

Katie was Katerina Whitcomb-Salgar, the daughter of the McCord family's longtime friends and the woman everyone had always assumed would end up as Mrs. Tate McCord long before their formal engagement was announced.

"You're going to lose Katie," Blake shouted, some heat in his voice now. "And if you do, it'll serve you right."

"Or it might be for the best," Tate countered, enough under his breath that Tanya barely made out what he'd said. Then more loudly again, he added, "Just keep your eye on finding that diamond and getting McCord's Jewelers and the family coffers healthy again. Since you want to carry all the weight for that yourself, you shouldn't have a lot of spare time to worry about my love life, too. But if I want your advice, I'll be sure to ask for it."

"You need someone's advice or you're going to blow the best thing that ever happened to you."

"Thanks for the heads-up," Tate said facetiously.

And then there were footsteps.

But only some of them moved away from the library.

The others were coming closer...

Too late to run.

Tanya ducked for cover, hoping that since she was behind the desk whoever was headed her way wouldn't be able to see her when he reached in and turned off the lights.

"Tate hasn't even been staying in the house since he got back. He's living in the guest cottage..."

Tanya's mother's words flashed through her mind just then and it struck her that merely having the lights turned off might not be what was about to happen. That Tate might use the library route to go to the guesthouse that was also out back....

Tanya's heart had begun to race the minute she'd heard the McCords' voices. Now it was pounding. Because while she might have been able to explain her presence in the library at this time of night, how would she ever explain crouching behind the desk?

Or holding the papers she'd been looking through—because until that minute she hadn't even realized she'd taken them with her when she'd ducked.

Please don't come in here....

"What the hell?"

Oh, no...

Tanya had tried to turn herself into a small ball but when Tate McCord's voice boomed from nearby, she raised her head to find him leaning over the front of the desk, clearly able to see her.

This was much, much worse than when she was six and had been caught with her fingers in the icing of his twin sisters' birthday cake. His mother Eleanor had been kind and understanding. But there was nothing kind or understanding in Tate McCord's face at that moment.

Summoning what little dignity she could—and with the papers still in hand—Tanya stood.

It was the first time she and Tate McCord had set eyes on each other in the seven years since Tanya had left for college. And even before that—when Tate had come home from his own university and medical school training for vacations or visits while Tanya still lived on the property with her mother—there weren't many occasions when the McCord heir had crossed paths with the housekeeper's daughter. Plus, Tanya had been very well aware of the fact that, more often than not, when any of the McCords had seen her, they'd looked through her rather than at her.

So she wasn't sure Tate McCord recognized her and, as if it would make this better, she said, "You probably don't remember me—"

"You're JoBeth's daughter—Tanya," he said bluntly. "What the hell are you doing in here at this hour and—"

He glanced down at the papers and held out his hand in a silent demand for her to give them to him.

She did and he looked over what—before she'd been interrupted—she'd discovered to be some sort of mock-ups for ads for a suggested line of jewelry using canary diamonds set in old Spanish designs.

Tanya had taken the papers from a file that was still open on the desk in front of her. After Tate McCord's initial look at them, he pulled the entire file toward him to see what else she might have gotten into.

While he sifted through what she already knew were similar pages, Tanya was wishing she wasn't dressed in a shabby, oversize, cut-up old sweatshirt and a pair of draw-string black pajama pants with cartoon robots printed on them. She also wished she wasn't completely makeupless and that her shoulder-length espresso-colored hair wasn't pulled up into a lopsided ponytail at the top of her head. Looking as if she were ready for bed made her feel all the more at a disadvantage. When she realized that the wide neck of the sweatshirt had fallen from her shoulder, she tugged it back into place.

It was something Tate McCord saw because just as she

did it, he raised his gaze from the file and eyes that were bluer than she remembered drifted momentarily in that direction.

Noticing did not, however, change his attitude toward her—his expression remained stern and angry.

"So, I repeat—JoBeth's-daughter-Tanya, what the hell are you doing in here, at this hour, going through things that you have no right to go through?" Tate McCord finished by tossing the papers he'd taken from Tanya back in the open file.

"I know this can't look good," she said.

But he definitely did look good! Better even than she remembered him.

Unlike her in-for-the-night apparel, he was dressed in a dark suit that accentuated the fact that he was tall and lean, with broad shoulders and a more toned, muscular physique than he'd had in his earlier years. His face had matured into sharply defined angles that gave him a decisive chin and high cheekbones. His mouth at that moment was a stern line beneath a strong, thin nose and his penetrating, clear blue eyes seemed to have taken a bead on her, which should have kept her from thinking that she liked his dark blond hair slightly longish, the way he was wearing it now....

But it was the expression that said he was waiting for an explanation that she knew she really had to address.

"My mother dropped her sweater when she came through here today after she finished work—" Tanya pointed to the plain white cardigan that had been her excuse for this foray. She'd picked it up from the floor where it had fallen and tossed it across the back of a chair before beginning her snooping. "Mom likes to wear it when she walks over from the bungalow in the mornings. She was just going to leave it and get it tomorrow, but I thought I'd come back for it tonight so she'd have it."

All true, but feeble at this point. Very feeble.

"And while you were here, you thought you'd take a look around, at things that you shouldn't look at, and then hide under the desk so you didn't get caught eavesdropping on what Blake and I were saying in the other room? Or are you going to pretend you didn't hear anything?"

There was that facetious tone again. It could be harsh. And it didn't help that his assumptions of what she'd done were right.

Maybe offense was the best form of defense....

"I heard enough to know that there's a whole lot going on. That all the suspicions about McCord's Jewelers' business being way down have some foundation. That the rumors that the McCords came into possession of the Santa Magdalena diamond when you all got the Foley's land and silver mines could also be the truth. I heard enough to know that your family does think the diamond can be found."

"So you heard plenty."

"And I'll admit," she continued, "that when I came for Mom's sweater and saw the file, I got curious, and since it was open I looked at those pages—" That was a lie, not only had she opened the file herself, but she'd come to get the sweater hoping that there might be something of interest to her in the library where business was sometimes conducted. "But now that I know things are popping here, it seems to me that there's a story in it that I could use."

"You're going to make me sorry I did what your mother asked and send your résumé over to my friend at WDGN, aren't you?"

WDGN was one of the local independent news stations.

"I didn't know which of you got me the interview, but thanks for it," she said as if that mattered at this point.

"Oh, believe me, you're welcome," he said snidely.

"But here's the thing—" she went on, ignoring his disapproval "—I've been making my living in the world of broadcast journalism for a while now and this is how it works—at least for me because I haven't made any kind of big splash yet—a new position means I start at the bottom. The bottom is filling in for other reporters or doing whatever the seasoned reporters have moved on from or refuse to do—"

"Was I supposed to see if I could have you hired at the top?"

"That's not what I'm getting at. What I'm getting at is that between the story of the diamond—whatever it might be and especially if you do actually find it—and the story of the McCords' feud with the Foleys, well, let's face it, if the McCords or the Foleys sneeze it makes the news so stuff like this could get me an anchor chair." Not to mention the other tidbit the staff was whispering about that *wasn't* public knowledge—that Tate's mother Eleanor had an affair with Rex Foley and that the youngest brother, Charlie, was Rex Foley's son....

If Tate's sky-blue eyes had had a bead on her before, it was nothing compared to the way they were boring into her now and it made Tanya's tension level rise another notch. Especially when she began to wonder if she'd gone too far. The McCords *were* her mother's employers after all....

Then Tate McCord said, "Or how about a story where the housekeeper's daughter gets arrested for breaking and entering, for trespassing, for who knows what else should something turn up missing...."

Tanya took issue with that last part. She might be willing to do a little nosing around for a story, but she wasn't a thief!

"Should something turn up missing?" she repeated. "Go ahead, look around. Take inventory. I haven't so much as touched anything but my mother's sweater and the papers in that file. I have done almost nothing wrong!"

"*Almost* nothing wrong?" Tate took a turn at parroting in the midst of a wry laugh. "Believe me, with the McCord connections, *almost* can still get you arrested. And how would your mother like to hear that you're using the trust we have in her to do something like this?"

"You're threatening to tell my mommy?" Tanya said with some sarcasm of her own even though the threat to tell JoBeth carried more weight than the threat to call the police.

Tate didn't respond to her flippancy. He merely glanced down at the file again, closing it and laying his hand flat on top of it as if that could seal it away from her.

Then those eyes pinned her in place again and he said, "I'll tell you what this family *doesn't* need right now—a traitor in our midst."

"I'm hardly that," Tanya countered, chafing under that comment more than anything he'd said yet.

"So it's loyalty that brought you in here tonight?"

There was that facetiousness again.

"I was just hoping for an inside story. The discovery of that sunken ship that the Santa Magdalena supposedly came from has renewed interest in the diamond and I thought—"

"That you'd use your mother's position here as a way to get the scoop."

Despite pretending not to take seriously his threat to bring her mother into this before, Tanya was becoming increasingly worried that she'd done damage to the position that her mother had held since Tanya was barely two years old. She definitely didn't want that.

"I'm sorry, okay?" she conceded. "I shouldn't have—"

"No, you shouldn't have. But now that you have—"

"Fine. If you want to have me arrested then do it. But leave my mother out of it. She doesn't have anything to do with this. She's sound asleep and doesn't even know I'm here or that I had any intention of coming over here."

He seemed to consider that and Tanya had started to wonder how the robot pants and *Flashdance* sweatshirt were going to go over in jail when he said, "I'll make a deal with you."

Tanya raised her eyebrows at him and waited.

"I'll keep your secret about this little escapade tonight if what you heard and saw here, stays here."

Jail in robot pants and a *Flashdance* sweatshirt was easier to accept.

"You want me to just sit on the fact that the McCords honestly *do* believe they have the Santa Magdalena diamond?" she said incredulously. "That you're so convinced of it that your brother is planning the family's business future around it?"

"That's exactly what I want you to do."

"I think *that's* unfair of you!" Tanya said with a little heat in her own tone now. "This is something that could make my career and you want me to do nothing with it when we both know it's going to come out sooner or later, and potentially be a coup for someone else? I'll grant you that I may have stepped over the line using my mother's position here, but I don't think I should be penalized because she works for you."

Tate McCord gave her the hard stare. But if he thought she was going to back down because of it, he was mistaken.

Maybe he saw that in the fact that she didn't waver in the stare down they were engaged in because he took his hand from the file, stood straight and said, "Okay, how about this—whether or not we do have the diamond and where it might be and if it can be found are all questions that have yet to be answered with any kind of certainty. What you think Blake is planning the business's future around is really—honestly—a gamble we're taking. But if—big *if*—we should end up finding the diamond and everything pans out, I'll promise you an exclusive."

"In other words, you want to buy some time," she said.

His eyebrows were well shaped and one of them rose in reply.

"My price is higher than that," Tanya said, deciding that if she was in for a penny, she might as well be in for a pound.

"Your *price?*" He was obviously astounded by her audacity.

But Tanya didn't let that daunt her. "I want the whole story—and I mean the *whole* story, so that if the diamond ends up being a bust, I'll still have something to launch me. Like I said before, if the Foleys or the McCords sneeze, it's news. But there are a lot of details and history and background that even I don't know. And if I don't have the complete picture after growing up here, I have to think not many other people do either. So it can give meat to the bigger story of the Santa Magdalena diamond finally, actually, being found. Or it can at least give me a well-rounded, juicy human-interest piece about Dallas's two most illustrious—and infamous—families. And why they hate each other."

"What kind of details, history and background are we talking about?" Tate said in a negotiator's voice.

"Inside information on the family—the personal things that haven't been in press releases. I want to know about the feud with the Foleys—the truth. I want to know all about the McCord jewelry empire—including if it's hurting. I want the full package, enough to make it inter- esting even if it turns out that the search for the diamond is nothing but a wild-goose chase."

"Meat," Tate repeated the word she'd used moments before. "You want to treat us like meat."

"I just want the truth and not what's already common knowledge. Think of it this way, you got me a job at an in- dependent news station that *isn't* owned by the Foleys so there won't be any pressure to make you guys look bad. My mom works for you, I grew up here—if anyone will do the story without painting you in a bad light, it's me."

"Or I could just have you arrested and fired and—"

"And then I could go to one of the Foley-owned stations or newspapers or what have you and do the story from their angle."

Once more Tate McCord stared at her long and hard.

"You know, I *like* your mother."

Meaning he *didn't* like her. Tanya had absolutely no idea why that bothered her. But it did.

Still, she wasn't about to show him so she merely raised her chin in challenge.

Then he surprised her and laughed. "And I'm assuming I get to be your source?"

"You're the one proposing we make a deal."

She wasn't sure if he liked that answer or if he had something up his sleeve, but he smiled and said, "All right. Deal—you keep quiet for now, I'll give you the inside story and the exclusive on the diamond if we find it."

He held out his hand for her to shake.

Tanya took it, clasping it firmly to let him know she wasn't intimidated by him.

But what she hadn't anticipated was how aware she would be of the way her hand felt in his. Of the strength emanating from his grip. Of the texture of his skin. Of the tiny goose bumps that skittered up her arm...

Then the handshake ended and something made her sorry it had.

But that couldn't be...

"For now I guess I'll just say good-night, then," Tanya said, thinking that in all that had happened since she'd first heard Tate McCord's voice this evening, she hadn't wanted to get out of there as much as she did at that moment, before anything else totally weird came over her. Or overcame her...

"Good idea," he confirmed.

So Tanya stepped from behind the desk, snatched her mother's sweater from the back of the chair on her way to the French doors and finally went back out into the night air.

And the entire time she held her head high, knowing that Tate McCord had followed her to the door to watch her go—probably to make sure she did, she thought.

But it also occurred to her, as she took the path that led through the woodsy grounds to the housekeeper's bungalow she was temporarily sharing with her mother, that she wasn't sure what her mother and the rest of the staff was talking about when it came to Tate. He didn't seem dark and brooding and withdrawn and dispirited to her.

To her, he seemed full of life, full of fire.

Fire enough to have nearly set her aflame with a simple handshake...

Chapter Two

A good night's sleep had been hard for Tate to come by in the last year and a half, and Friday night hadn't broken that pattern. He'd had trouble falling asleep and he was wide awake before the sun was even up on Saturday morning. And once he was awake there was no going back to sleep. Luckily he'd gotten used to functioning on only a few hours rest during internship, residency and surgery fellowship.

By 6:45 he'd made himself a pot of coffee and he took his first cup out of the guesthouse to sit at one of the poolside tables with the newspaper that Edward—the McCord's butler—hadn't failed to leave at his doorstep since he'd returned from the Middle East and opted to live outside of the main house for a while.

Tate didn't open the paper, though. He knew there would be articles on the war in Iraq, on situations in

Pakistan, Afghanistan and Lebanon. Unlike when Buzz had been over there and Tate had been anxious for any news, since Buzz's death, since spending the year in Baghdad himself, some days he just didn't want the reminders. He sure as hell never needed them....

Don't make me kick your ass!

He knew that's what Buzz would be saying to him if Buzz was around now. If Buzz saw him staring at that newspaper and wanting to toss it into the pool. There was no way Buzz would have stood for this damn black mood he'd been in since his best friend's death.

Bentley—Buzz—Adams. Like Katie, Tate's fiancée, Tate had known Buzz all his life, despite the fact that they'd come from different backgrounds. Politics and the military—that's where Buzz's roots were. His father, grandfather and great-grandfather had all been high-ranking army officers who each served as military advisors to presidents. But Buzz's own father hadn't wanted his family to live the nomadic military life, so Buzz had been raised at his grandparents' estate, just down the road.

Tate and Buzz had gone to private school together. They'd gone to college together. They'd even gone to medical school together and applied for residency at the same hospital. Their paths hadn't veered until residency was over and Tate had opted for a specialty in surgery while Buzz had followed his family's tradition and joined the army to serve as a doctor overseas.

Going to war was the first thing Tate and Buzz hadn't done together.

If only Buzz hadn't broken his tradition with Tate to follow his family's tradition....

But he had.

And everything else was water under the bridge now.

Everything but this funk Tate couldn't seem to shake.

He knew he was one hell of a downer these days, that everyone was wondering where the old Tate was. Most of the time he was wondering it himself. But the old Tate just didn't seem to be there anymore.

He also knew his lousy mood was going to factor in when the news about his engagement to Katie came out, and he regretted that. He didn't want people saying that Katie had bailed because he wasn't much fun anymore. Katie didn't deserve that.

She hadn't ended their engagement because he couldn't seem to lighten up. She'd made that clear and he didn't doubt it. That just wasn't Katie. In fact, he thought that if he'd put any effort into talking her out of breaking their engagement, the bad mood would have likely kept her around because she would have felt guilty for leaving him at a low point.

But he hadn't put any effort into keeping things going with her. Why should he have when she was right? She'd said that she'd been thinking that maybe long-term friend-ship and family pressure and the general belief that they'd end up together shouldn't, ultimately, be why they *did* end up together. That she didn't think she had the kind of feelings for him that she should have going into marriage. That she didn't feel passionate about him.

Maybe that should have been insulting, but it hadn't been. Instead, he'd understood it. His own feelings for Katie had never been all-consuming or particularly pas-sionate. Which was probably why calling things off just hadn't mattered a whole lot to him.

Of course, it also didn't really matter to him that Katie

wanted to keep the breakup a secret until she could see her parents in Florida and explain it to them.

It didn't matter to him that Katie wasn't head over heels for him.

It didn't matter to him that they'd broken up.

It didn't matter to him that he needed to maintain the pretense that they hadn't.

Since Buzz's death, and even more so in the six months since he'd been back from Baghdad, it had just been tough for things like that—for most of what mattered to the people around him—to have the importance they might have had before....

He took a drink of his coffee and then replaced the cup on the table, staring into the steaming beverage that still remained.

He liked his coffee strong and black, and looking into the brew now made him think of Tanya Kimbrough's eyes. They were the color of Italian espresso—dark, rich, liquid pools of espresso....

Recalling that made him think of one thing that had mattered to him—last night and finding Tanya Kimbrough in the library. That had definitely mattered.

When he'd found her there he'd taken a mental inventory of what he and Blake had said because what was going on with the business *did* matter. He'd recalled that they'd said the jewelry business was in a slump, that they believed they knew where the Santa Magdalena diamond was, that Blake was buying all the canary diamonds to use as a tie-in.

Then there were the papers Tanya had seen on the desk, too—Blake must have forgotten the file and while there hadn't been anything in it but preliminaries for the advertising campaign, it was still information they didn't want released.

And after cataloging what Tanya Kimbrough could have known, the wheels of Tate's mind had started to turn, imagining her prematurely revealing that they were looking for the Santa Magdalena diamond. No, he and Blake hadn't talked about the crucial clue Blake had discovered in the border of the deed to the land and silver mines they'd taken over from the Foleys decades ago. Still, if word leaked that there was a very real reason to suspect the diamond might be found? Any number of treasure hunters could descend on them to complicate the search. And possibly accidentally find the diamond before they did.

Not good.

Tate had considered what would happen if word leaked that Blake was cornering the market on canary diamonds and coming out with a new line of Spanish-influenced designs to coincide with the discovery of the Santa Magdalena. Their competitors would launch lines of their own to steal their thunder and undermine their sales and, potentially, leave Blake at a disadvantage in breathing new life into the business.

Also not good.

And let the world know that the renowned McCord's Jewelers was in a decline? That the family fortunes were compromised?

Certainly not good.

And since Blake was up to his eyeballs in the family's problems already and—as usual—trying to bear the burden as much on his own as he could, rotten mood or not, Tate had decided that it was better if he dealt with the housekeeper's daughter rather than dumping any more on his brother.

Which was why he'd struck that bargain with her for an insider's look at the McCords and an exclusive on the diamond if they found it. Left to her own devices, Tanya Kimbrough could cause trouble and he was going to do whatever he had to to prevent that. If that meant sticking to her like glue to keep a close eye on her for the time being, then that's what he was going to do.

It's a dirty job, but somebody has to do it....

Tate knew that's what Buzz would be saying to him if he told his friend he was only taking on Tanya Kimbrough to spare Blake.

Yeah, okay, it was hardly as dirty a job as studying a dusty deed or digging around in the dirt of a deserted old silver mine. Keeping an eye on a beautiful woman was definitely not drawing the short straw.

And Tanya *was* a beautiful woman.

The scrawny, funny-looking kid had grown into a knockout—there was no question about that.

Her hair was as dark as her eyes—coffee-nib brown—and so shiny it looked like satin. Coupled with those eyes against a fair, flawless complexion, she'd been the freshest-faced burglar in existence. Fresh-faced and beautiful even without any visible signs of makeup, with that thin nose and those pale pink lips, those high cheekbones and the slightly squarish jawline sweeping up from a chin that looked as if it could be a little sassy.

Unlike her taller, slightly stocky mother, Tanya was petite—no more than five-four he was guessing. She was thin, but not too thin, and she had curves in all the right places—at least he thought she did even though that chopped-up sweatshirt she'd had on had done more camouflaging than revealing.

Of course it *had* revealed one shoulder before she'd yanked the fabric back into place. And the mere sight of that creamy skin had made him suddenly aware of his own heartbeat. And the fact that it had sped up....

Only slightly.

But still, that was more than most things had done to him lately. A simple bare shoulder…

Hell, he was a doctor. He saw naked shoulders—and naked everything else—all the time. Why had a simple glimpse of Tanya Kimbrough's shoulder done anything at all to him?

Maybe it had been an adrenaline rush, he reasoned. He'd just had that argument with Blake and then spotted someone he'd initially thought to be a stranger lurking behind the desk. He hadn't actually been alarmed, but it wasn't beyond the realm of possibility that his subconscious had set off an alert response. After Baghdad, that seemed likely.

And if it had felt like something other than that?

He was likely only misinterpreting it.

He did know one thing, though—he wasn't hating the idea of keeping an eye on Tanya Kimbrough.

In fact, if he analyzed it, he'd say he might even be looking forward to it.

He might say he'd even gotten a small rush out of that back-and-forth with her last night. A small rush that he wouldn't mind having again…

But that *couldn't* matter, he told himself.

The charge he'd gotten out of their verbal exchange and the fact that she'd held her own with him, the smooth skin on a shoulder he'd been inclined to mold his hand around, the silky hair he'd wanted to see fall free, the lips he'd had a fleeting thought of tasting, the tight little body hidden behind funny-looking pants and a sweatshirt that someone had taken scissors to—none of that was as important as protecting his family, or as important as his promise to Katie to pretend they were still engaged until she told him otherwise.

But still…

He *was* looking forward to seeing the housekeeper's daughter again.

And continuing to see much more of her for a while to keep her contained?

That didn't feel like a hardship either.…

"What are you doing here?"

Tanya could see that Tate was surprised to find her waiting for him when he left the operating suite of Meridian General Hospital at eight o'clock Saturday night.

"I told you you were going to talk to me whether you liked it or not," she countered heatedly.

"When did you tell me that?"

"At the end of the sixteenth voice mail I left you today."

"I got called in for an emergency surgery early this morning. I've been standing at an operating table for the last—" he glanced at a clock on the wall "—eleven hours and twenty minutes. Not a lot of message checking goes on when I'm up to my elbows in a man's gut."

"Gross," Tanya said reflexively.

Tate merely raised an eyebrow at that, giving her the impression that that was the response he'd been going for.

But if he thought disgusting her was going to make her back down, he needed to think again.

"Eleven hours and twenty minutes of surgery or not, we're going to talk," she insisted.

"If I've inspired sixteen voice mails I guess we'll have to," he said sardonically but sounding weary nonetheless. "First I have to let the family know how my patient is—" he nodded in the direction of a group of people she hadn't noticed before but now realized were also waiting for him "—then I have to write orders to get this guy into recovery. After that my plan is for a quick bite to eat at the deli across the street before I have to operate on the other passenger from this car accident. So if you're determined that we talk right now, you can either wait for me here and go over to the deli with me, or go ahead of me to the deli— but one way or another there's only going to be a small window before my next patient is prepped and ready to be opened up."

It irked Tanya all the more to have him dictate to her, but she wouldn't let that stop her.

"Fine, I'll wait here," she said cuttingly.

Now that she'd finally found him, she had no intention of letting him slip away from her. After calling his cell phone all day, she'd questioned almost the entire house staff before finding someone who knew Tate was at the hospital. When she'd called the hospital she'd been told she couldn't speak to him because he was in surgery. That had prompted her to come here to ambush him as soon as he got out. But she'd been lying in wait for nearly two hours and was not willing to go ahead of him to the deli and risk him not showing up.

So she perched on the edge of the same seat she'd occupied for the last two hours and watched him intently.

When he was finished talking to his patient's family, they headed for the elevators and Tate moved to the nurses' station. He said something to the nurse there and while she went to do his bidding, Tanya continued to keep him in her sights.

As she did, it occurred to her that while, over the years, she'd seen Tate McCord in tennis whites, in tuxedos, in suits and ties and casual clothes of all kinds, she'd never seen him in scrubs. And that he looked too sexy to believe in the loose-fitting, teal blue cotton garments that resembled pajamas more than street clothing.

Then, adding to that sexiness he seemed unconscious of, he rolled his shoulders, arched his spine and raised his elbows to shoulder height to pull his arms back until even Tanya heard something crack—obviously working out the kinks that hours of surgery had left.

But regardless of the fact that she was overly aware of every little thing about him, she refused to let any of it influence her. She was steaming mad and she was going to let him know it. Nothing—including being one of the best-looking, sexiest men she'd ever seen—gave him license to mess with her career! Not even if she had overstepped her bounds the previous night.

The nurse brought him a metal clipboard then, and when he was done writing the orders for his patient, he handed the chart back to the nurse and finally turned to Tanya.

"Ready?"

"You don't need to change clothes?" she asked, hoping he would and that different clothes might help lessen the effect he was having on her in scrubs.

But he shook his head. "Hadn't planned on it. Like I said, I have another surgery scheduled tonight and the deli doesn't have a dress code. Unless it offends you in some way…"

"I couldn't care less what you're wearing," she lied.

"Then let's go get something to eat before I pass out from hunger."

The trip through the hospital and across the street was

filled with Tate greeting and exchanging quips with nurses, attendants, volunteers, other doctors and even the janitor. Then they reached the deli and he was right—there were more customers dressed the way he was than in anything that resembled the slacks and shirt Tanya was wearing.

Not that she felt out of place, but it did occur to her as she peered at the other men in scrubs that she didn't find any of *them* particularly attractive....

Still, she did everything she could to overlook Tate's appeal as he ordered his "usual." She rejected his offer of food and accepted only a lemonade before they went to one of the booths that lined the walls of the small restaurant.

Despite what he'd said, Tate seemed more tired than hungry. After setting his pastrami sandwich and iced tea on the table, he left them untouched while he sat lengthwise on his side of the booth to put his feet up. He also rested his head against the wall and closed his eyes— probably to wind down and relax the way he'd intended to do without her company.

But Tanya wasn't going to be ignored.

"So how did you have time to ruin my life if you were up to your elbows in someone's insides all day and most of tonight?" she demanded before she'd even sipped her lemonade.

Rather than add to Tate's stress, that actually brought an indication of amusement in a slight upward curl of the corners of his mouth even before he opened his eyes to look at her. "How did I *ruin* your life?"

"I got a call at nine o'clock this morning from the owner of WDGN—not the station manager who hired me, but the station *owner*—"

"Chad Burton."

"Your friend," Tanya said derisively.

"We're more acquaintances than close friends. I went through school with his son, Chad Junior. I helped Junior pass chemistry and physics, although he ended up an interior decorator, not a doctor the way Chad Senior had hoped. But Chad Senior has always been grateful. Chad Senior and I have also been on a lot of committees together, we play golf now and then—"

"You're friends enough to have called him sometime between last night and nine o'clock this morning to persuade him to put me on a leave of absence—"

"With pay," Tate pointed out, not bothering to pretend he hadn't been behind today's turn of events.

"With or without pay, from today forward—indefinitely—I'm on special assignment to work the McCord story. That means no on-air time, no other duties, no other stories, no other assignments, no chance to prove myself in any other way or gain any other ground after just two weeks of working there. I was told I'm not to show my face at the station until I have the whole McCord thing ready to be put together."

"But you're still on the payroll, so—"

"This isn't about money!" Tanya said, ferociously whispering to keep from shouting. "If I don't go back with something good—like the discovery of the Santa Magdalena diamond itself—I'll be *lucky* to be doing the agriculture reports on the predawn weekend newscasts. Plus they'll probably hire someone else to do my job in the meantime and that someone else could just replace me if the McCords don't come up with the diamond and all I have is a human-interest piece. You may have put in a good word for me to get this job, but my credentials and abilities actually got it for me, and you don't have the right to pull it out from under me just to suit your purposes!"

He sat up straight in the booth, putting his feet on the floor and finally unwrapping his sandwich to take a bite. Not until he'd chewed, swallowed and washed it down with a drink of his iced tea, did he say, "I had to make sure you didn't have the opportunity to go back on your word to keep quiet."

"I could still do that—I could go to a Foley-owned station."

He remained unruffled by her threat. "You could," he said. "But that talk about loyalty last night got me to thinking—your mom has worked for us for twenty-two years. She oversees the whole staff. She's my mom's right hand around the house. I'm not going to say we're all family, but there's a connection that you sure as hell don't have with our archrivals. You must feel *some* amount of loyalty."

"How much loyalty did you feel when you called Chad Burton?"

"Today or when I called him to say I was sending over your résumé?"

Tanya glared at him. "That was something my mother did without telling me until *after* it was done because she wanted me to move back here. The résumé you sent over wasn't even a recent one. It was the first one I did out of college—my mother found it in an old file. *I* faxed them the *real,* current résumé, which is what got me the interview."

Tate ignored all of that and merely went on to answer her question about his loyalty.

"I wasn't being disloyal. I was only playing it safe. And Chad was thrilled with the idea of getting an insider's view of the McCords. Plus, even though I didn't do anything but allude to the diamond, I let him know that there was the potential for big news to come along with the *human-interest* stuff, and he was nearly drooling over the chance for WDGN to be the one to break that big news. This really could put you on the map."

"I lose ground not being there, not having my face in front of a camera every chance I can get," she insisted. "There's no reason I couldn't still be doing my job there and compiling the McCord information."

"But now you don't have to do anything but focus on the McCords."

"Who are *not* the center of the universe, just in case you were wondering!" Tanya said, her voice raised enough to garner a glance from the couple at the nearest table.

"It's just a precaution," Tate said calmly.

"You're trying to control me," Tanya accused.

"Yes, I am. But only in this and only for the sake of the greater good."

"As if that makes it all right."

"Was it all right that you broke into my family's home last night to spy on us and try to get information to expose things that could hurt us if they got out at the wrong time?" he reasoned.

"So you're exacting revenge?"

"Nooo, not at all. You still have your job and your paycheck. You have the chance to do an exclusive story on the McCords and be the reporter who tells the world if we find the Santa Magdalena diamond. You just won't be doing anything *but* that for now."

Tanya narrowed her eyes at him. "You'd better give me a good story," she warned.

"And you'd better put all your energy into me and *getting* a good story," he countered.

"Into *you?* Why would I put my energy into *you?*"

He smiled. A slow, lazy, sexy smile. "I guess because I'm the teller-of-the-tale, and the happier I am, the better the tale-telling?"

"And what does that mean? That not only do I have to climb the mountain to get the answers from The Great One, but that I have to bring enticements, too?" she asked facetiously.

His smile stretched into a grin and he didn't at all look like the sad, somber, lackluster shadow of his former self that her mother and the rest of the staff described him as.

"Enticements?" he repeated as if he hadn't been thinking that until she suggested it. "I like the sound of that."

"Well, get over it," she advised bluntly, knowing he was merely having some fun at her expense. "There's no way I'm bringing *enticements* to get you to tell me about your family."

"Too bad," he pretended to lament.

"I'm serious, Tate," she said, using his name for the first time as an adult.

"Yes, you are, Tanya," he agreed, barely suppressing a smile. "You are *very* serious."

"I mean it—you'd better give me something good enough to make this *sabbatical* worth my while."

He seemed to take that in a different—and lascivious—vein than how she'd intended it because his smile appeared full force again and it was laced with wicked amusement.

But before he said anything else, the pager clipped to the bottom of his shirt went off, drawing his attention.

He glanced down at it. "I have to get back," he announced, grabbing another quick bite of his only half-eaten sandwich and then rewrapping the rest to take with him.

As he did, he returned to what they'd been talking about.

"All I meant when I said that you should put your energy into me was into *spending time* with me to get your story—as part of the job you really are still doing."

He stood, guzzled most of his iced tea and, after replacing the glass on the table, added, "And to that end, why don't we start with a real dinner tomorrow night? My treat and we can both eat."

"Since it's now my *job,* I guess so," Tanya conceded.

"Eight o'clock? I'll meet you at the pool and we'll go somewhere from there?"

Tanya nodded and that was all it took to send him rushing out of the deli.

As she watched him go her anger at him began to waver. Maybe it was the sight of him from behind in those scrubs that loosely covered his broad shoulders and barely grazed a derriere to die for.

But instead of thinking about the influence he'd used to keep her under his thumb, she was thinking more about the fact that her job now was essentially spending time with Tate McCord.

And how, as much as she should be resenting that, she was actually a little excited by the prospect....

Chapter Three

"I don't like it, Tanya. And I don't think it's a good idea."

"It'll be fine, JoBeth."

Calling her mother by name and in the special teasing, cajoling tone Tanya used usually made her mother laugh. Now it barely elicited a smile.

When Tanya hadn't gone in to do the early Sunday newscast, JoBeth had asked why. Tanya had had to tell her mother what was going on with Tate and the special assignment to do the McCord story—although she'd omitted the fact that it was the result of being caught snooping in the library on Friday night.

"The McCords have always been good to us, Tanya. When your father walked out and left me with a two-year-old and no money and no education and no skills, Mrs. McCord—"

"—not only gave you a job, but since the housekeeper at the time wasn't living here, she let us live in this bungalow when none of the other maids got that kind of accommodation," Tanya said, repeating what her mother had said many times as she'd grown up. Then she continued with what she knew JoBeth was going to say. "Mrs. McCord promoted you from maid to housekeeper to overseeing the whole staff. She gave you flexible hours whenever I was sick or you wanted to go to my school meetings and functions. She wrote my recommendation letter to college and to the scholarship committee that paid my tuition for four years. I haven't forgotten any of that."

"But now you'll try to dig up dirt on the McCords to get yourself more on-air time? That's not right."

They were at the kitchen table with coffee and toast, both of them in their bathrobes, not long out of bed. JoBeth had Sunday mornings off and Tanya regretted that rather than relaxing, her mother was stressed about this.

"I'm not going to *dig up dirt,*" she assured JoBeth, deciding to put a positive spin on the turn of events to ease her mother's mind. "Some of this even came at the *suggestion* of Tate, who also talked to the station owner—that's why I won't be doing anything but devoting myself to this for a while. Tate is going to be walking me through the family history, including the reasons why there's a problem with anyone named Foley—which I've never understood. Hopefully, he'll let me have an insider's look that will include finding the Santa Magdalena diamond—if they actually do—and it will all give me a leg up here in Dallas. So really, this is still a lot like the little extra help Mrs. McCord has given along the way—think of it like that."

But apparently Tanya's mother was not won over by that argument because JoBeth narrowed her dark eyes at Tanya, increasing the lines that fanned out from their corners. "These people are my *employers,* Tanya. I'm dependent on them for my *livelihood.* For my whole day-to-day existence."

"And I'm not going to do anything to jeopardize that." If what she'd done Friday night didn't count...

But suddenly Tanya took stock of JoBeth sitting across from her at the tiny table they'd eaten most of their meals on.

Her mother worked long hours that had aged her—something Tanya saw in the single shock of prematurely white hair at JoBeth's temple. But Tanya knew that her mother was not only grateful for the job, JoBeth enjoyed it and the camaraderie and closeness of the household staff that went with it.

And if that hair that was down now would soon be in a bun that was as tightly wound as her mother had always had to be, that control was something Tanya knew her mother took pride in. If the milkiness of JoBeth's skin was evidence that vacation sun rarely touched it, it wasn't for want of time off, it was because JoBeth preferred her routine here to sitting on a Caribbean beach. If JoBeth's slight pudginess came from caring for the McCords rather than paying attention to exercise or cautious eating for herself, Tanya knew that her mother would say it was a treat to get to taste the delicacies prepared by the McCords' chef.

And Tanya was also well aware of the fact that while the cottage with its two small bedrooms and this area that combined kitchen and living room was hardly luxury living, her mother loved the housekeeper's bungalow and considered it her home—a home she'd refused to leave even when Tanya had tried to persuade her to move to California with her.

Which all added up to more than a livelihood that

JoBeth didn't want to lose, it was the life her mother had made for herself. And Tanya realized even more than she had before that she had to be careful not to do anything that would compromise that or put it at risk.

"Who better to do this story?" she said to her mother then. "I'm obligated to report on any skeletons I might find in the McCord closets, but I won't sensationalize them. I'll do a fair and honest piece that will come primarily from information Tate relays—so you know there aren't going to *be* a lot of negatives in the mix—and I won't go searching for them the way someone else might. I'll take what Tate gives, hope it all leads to the bigger story of the discovery of the diamond and leave it at that."

"Tate," her mother echoed. "You shouldn't be imposing on him. He has too much on his mind as it is. Since his friend died in Iraq, since he came back from there himself, he's troubled, Tanya. You can't be bothering him to get yourself—"

"He offered, Mama. I won't be *bothering* him."

"He offered?" JoBeth parroted ominously.

"He volunteered," Tanya amended because she'd caught the sudden switch in her mother's concerns. Now it wasn't the McCords who JoBeth was worried about, it was Tanya. And that was a more fierce protectiveness.

"You're a beautiful girl, Tanya—"

"Says my mother." Tanya dismissed the compliment.

"Tate has eyes."

"And a fiancée," Tanya reminded. Then, in an attempt to calm her mother's fears, she said, "Tate is *engaged* to Katie Whitcomb-Salgar—the person he's been promised to since they played together in the sandbox. And it wouldn't matter even if they hadn't finally gotten engaged—I know better than to get involved with Tate McCord, of all people. This is strictly business. For both of us. He's going to walk me through some family history and give me the exclusive on the outcome of whatever it is that's going on with the Santa Magdalena diamond—that's all there is to it. There's nothing personal in it for either of us."

"For your own sake, you'd better make sure of that," JoBeth said, her round face reflecting the fact that Tanya had failed to ease her mind. "I don't want you getting hurt."

"I won't get hurt, Mama. I told you, it's strictly business."

JoBeth stared at her for a long moment as if she were hoping to be able to see the future in Tanya's face. Then, with no indication of whether or not she thought she had, she took her obvious concerns and her crossword puzzle into the living room.

Tanya interpreted that as a sign that her mother was tentatively accepting what she'd told her.

But while she stayed where she was at the kitchen table to finish her breakfast, Tanya was still thinking about it all.

This *was* strictly business between her and Tate—she hadn't said that simply to appease JoBeth. Tanya had outgrown wanting to be a McCord a long time ago. Yes, as a very young, starry-eyed girl she'd fantasized about being a part of what went on at the big house. But as soon as her mother had realized that was what she was doing, JoBeth had taken measures to keep Tanya's feet firmly planted on the ground. And ultimately—eventually—Tanya had come to see for herself that the McCords' life was not a life she wanted.

Of course mountains of money would be nice, but other than that? The McCords were under constant scrutiny, their every movement watched. They were talked about and criticized, envied and resented. And none of that appealed to Tanya.

Plus, the McCords existed in an insular world where everything remained the same from generation to generation. Where the names, the faces, the cliques never changed. Where new blood was seldom let in. Where some fight, started long, long ago for reasons Tanya wasn't sure even they knew, was still burning. It all just seemed so stagnant to her.

And in keeping with that, Tate *was* engaged to Katie Whitcomb-Salgar—the daughter of his mother's and late father's close friends and someone who had moved within that same small, insulated circle his entire life, too.

But Tanya understood why the fact that Tate was engaged didn't put her mother's mind to rest. Both Tanya and JoBeth had been around the McCords long enough to know that the relationship between Tate and Katie ran a pattern—together, not together, together again.

Just because they'd finally gotten formally engaged didn't mean this was the time they made it to the altar. One or the other of them could still decide to put the wedding off, to separate the way they had dozens of times in the past.

And if that happened and Tanya caught Tate's attention during the interim? He could be very persuasive. But in the end Tanya would only be a dalliance for Tate before he went back to Katie anyway. Which he always did.

That was what Tanya knew her mother was worried about.

But JoBeth didn't need to be. Not only would Tanya never knowingly get involved with anyone who was already involved with someone else, there was no way she would allow herself to be one of Tate McCord's fleeting detours from the woman his family had chosen for him.

No, the whole thing—what it meant to be a McCord and interrupting Tate's destiny to be with Katie Whitcomb-Salgar—was just not for Tanya.

Regardless of how terrific Tate might have looked in those scrubs last night.

But he *had* looked terrific....

Still, after a moment's indulgence in that mental image, Tanya shoved it aside.

That man was off-off-off-limits, as far as she was concerned. The only purpose he served was to provide her with a good story that she could use to boost her standing at the station and launch her career in Dallas.

And the fact that he was the drop-dead gorgeous, charming, smart, accomplished Tate McCord was merely something she needed to overlook in order to keep a professional and personal distance.

Which she had every intention of doing.

"Dinner with you meant the country club—I suppose I should have guessed, but I was thinking we were going somewhere low-key where we could get down to business," Tanya said as they left the club's fine-dining—and fanciest—restaurant.

The valet had Tate's sports car waiting for them. Tate went around to the driver's side. One valet opened the passenger door for Tanya, while another opened the driver's door for Tate. Only as their doors were closed for them and they were both fastening their seat belts did Tate say, "I can *get down to business,* if that's what you want. I just thought we were having a friendly dinner," he said with an innuendo-laden tone that purposely misinterpreted her words.

"What I want is to get down to the *business* I'm being

paid to do—a profile on you and your family," she quali-
fied, not taking his slightly flirtatious bait but also making
sure her tone was amiable. There had been confrontation
between them on the last two nights and that was not a
pattern she wanted to set.

Tate pulled out of the wrought-iron gates of the country
club and into traffic without responding.

"Nothing work related was accomplished at all,"
Tanya continued anyway. "You ended up talking more to
your cronies than giving me any useful information about
the McCords."

"My *cronies?*" Tate repeated as he headed for his
family's estate.

"The rest of the country-club set. Or was that the
purpose of dinner at the club—to avoid doing what you
agreed to do and at the same time show me that the
McCords hobnob with Dallas's richest, most famous, most
powerful and influential? And how even among the richest,
most famous, powerful and influential, it was still you who
was catered to to the point of the bartender counting the
number of ice cubes he put in your predinner private
reserve scotch?"

"Would I do something like that?" he said with no in-
flection at all, leaving her clueless as to whether or not that
had been his motive.

"And for future reference," she went on, still conversa-
tionally, "you should warn the person you're bringing to
the country club ahead of time. I was the only woman not
in pearls." In fact, she'd been underdressed in a pair of linen
slacks and simple camp shirt, while Tate was dressed more
appropriately in a cocoa-colored suit with an off-white
shirt and brown tie.

"Pearls are not mandatory," he informed her as they gained distance from the private club where memberships were primarily inherited and only the first names on the roster varied from decade to decade.

Tate took his eyes off the road to glance at her, his expression showing a hint of curiosity now. "So let me see if I have this straight—you're mad because we just had a nice dinner?"

"I'm not *mad*," she insisted. And she wasn't. "The food was fantastic and the waitstaff treated me like a queen." And in between the avalanche of obligatory hellos and small talk that had demanded Tate's attention while Tanya was barely given dismissive nods after her introductions, he'd been a perfectly pleasant dinner companion. "But I thought tonight would be the kickoff to my collecting information—or else why should we be together? And it's frustrating that nothing along those lines got done."

And as a result, she hadn't had work to keep her from noticing how easy it was to be with Tate.

"I don't need to see what a hotshot you are," she added.

"Ouch! Hotshot? That sounds bad."

"I'm just saying that the country-club side of you and of your family is not news. That kind of thing is in the society columns every day. You promised me the private side and that's not what tonight was."

"What tonight was," Tate said as they neared home, "was to make amends for costing you your on-air time and leaving you hanging yesterday. It's also Sunday and the club's regular chef takes Sundays off. His understudy—or whatever the guy who fills in for him is called—takes over in the kitchen on Sundays and the understudy goes all out to show his stuff when he gets that chance. I like to see what he comes up with. It's usually different and innovative and interesting. Like tonight—thin slices of Kobe beef that we cooked ourselves over a hot rock—so country club or not, why shouldn't we have gone there for dinner? Pearls notwithstanding?"

"Because that's all this turned out to be—a nice dinner—"

"And that's a crime?"

"I'm with you to do an assignment, not to go on a date," she said reasonably.

"This wasn't a date, it was just dinner," he said.

Which was part of what she knew she needed to guard against—what seemed like a really great date to her was nothing but an ordinary, everyday dinner to him....

"Or is that how this has to be?" he went on. "Strictly business? Do we need to sit on opposite sides of a desk, only between nine and five, and be formal and stuffy?"

Strictly business—that's what she'd told her mother this was. That was what she wanted it to be, what she needed it to be. But stuffy and formal? Sitting on opposite sides of a desk? Not only was that unlikely to get her the same kind of intimate portrait that came when an interviewee was relaxed and talking freely, but it definitely didn't appeal to her when it came to Tate McCord.

And that was another warning sign—the fact that Tate was striking a personal note in her that had nothing to do with work.

On the other hand, her first priority *was* getting the best story she could, and to that end, friendly and casual was the route to take.

"No, I don't want this to be done sitting opposite each other at a desk," she answered his question a little belatedly. "But I want to see the side of the McCords that isn't about being greeted by name by a state senator or where everyone in the place knows what you eat and drink—like tonight and last night, too. I'm well aware of the fact that the McCords are Texas royalty—even walking through the hospital with you was like being in a parade. What I'm hoping is that there's *something* else to you all. Something that gets you outside of your comfort zone and puts you in touch with the rest of the world—you know, those of us who are real?"

They'd reached the McCord estate but Tate hadn't pulled up to the garages. He'd gone around the other way to stop as near to the housekeeper's bungalow as he could get. When he turned off the engine he angled in his seat to look at Tanya.

"And just how far outside of your *comfort zone* have you ventured? How in touch with the rest of the world are you—as a *real* person? Because *worldly* is not how you strike me at the ripe old age of…what? Twenty-three?"

He was apparently not opposed to more confrontation tonight.

"Okay, I'm not *worldly,*" Tanya agreed. "But I think there's a huge portion of our society and the everyday life that most people live that you *are* out of touch with," she said, still calm but pulling no punches.

"*I'm* out of touch?" Tate said as if he were challenging her. But at the same time, something about this debate also seemed to have amused him because his eyes were bright and alive and he was barely suppressing a smile.

And as long as she wasn't alienating him, she didn't back down. "If you're talking about having gone to the Middle East like I've been told that you did, then no, that isn't an experience I've had or can relate to. And while I don't know why you went or where you were or how close to the war you got, or anything but that you spent a year somewhere over there, what I'm thinking is that you don't even have a concept of what life is like for the everyday person *here,* outside of your cushy existence. Given that, it's no wonder that what you must have encountered there was difficult for you to handle, and maybe if you hadn't been wrapped in cotton before—"

Tanya stopped herself because she realized suddenly that she was talking out of school. She was only guessing at what was going on with him, guessing that the reason he was so affected by his year away was because he'd gone from a virtual cocoon into something his life—of all lives—hadn't prepared him for. And she was doing that guessing based solely on what she'd heard from her mother and the other house staff.

"I'm sorry, that was out of line," she apologized in a hurry. "It's just that there's a lot of talk about you being depressed and changed and—"

She was getting in deeper and deeper.

"I should shut up," she concluded.

"And you think that because I spent my life *wrapped in cotton* that seeing what I saw in Iraq was more than I could take?"

Oh, she was sooo far over the line.…

"I'm not even sure how we got into this so let's back up. Even when I lived here as a kid what I saw was more the trappings of your family's money and status and what it allowed you all. But that isn't the story I want. Or the story I thought you agreed to give me. Whatever is going on with you—in your head—is your own business and none of mine. I shouldn't have shot off my mouth about it."

"But that's what everybody in your circle is saying? That I'm depressed?"

She wanted to kick herself. She also didn't want to get anyone into trouble and knew she had to do some damage control.

"Whether you realize it or not, people like my mom and some of the other staff who have been around a long time care about you. They're worried about you. They're only saying that you seem to have a lot on your mind, and my mom—in particular—doesn't like that I'm bothering you when you don't seem to be yourself. It's not like you're being gossiped about."

He stared at her for a long moment and beyond the fact that he still appeared entertained by her discomfort, she couldn't tell what he was thinking.

Then he said, "You can reassure everyone that I'm not depressed and that they don't need to worry."

"Good to know," Tanya said, not feeling at all relieved.

She was hoping for more from him that might let her know he wasn't going to make a big deal about this with the staff but there was no more to come.

Instead Tate pivoted in his seat again and got out, coming around to her side. But it seemed strange to wait for him to open her door. This *wasn't* a date, after all.

It also felt odd to have him walk her through the tree-lined path that led to her mother's cottage but that was what he did.

"Is living with your mom again a permanent arrangement?" he asked along the way, apparently returning to small talk.

"No, I'm just staying with her until I recoup some of my moving expenses and can find a place of my own."

"Do you have paper and something to write with?" he asked as they came through the trees on the other side and stepped onto the bungalow's front stoop.

Tanya didn't know what he was getting at, but she opened the small purse she was carrying and handed him a pen and a notepad she'd brought with her thinking that she was going to be working tonight.

He wrote an address on the paper and handed it back to her. Tanya assumed it was a lead on an apartment.

"Meet me there tomorrow morning at nine," he commanded.

Tanya looked from the paper to him, trying not to notice that the porch light illuminated the high spots of his handsome face and threw the hollows and angles into sharp shadows that only made him look dangerously attractive.

"I really won't be able to afford an apartment for a couple of months so it would be a waste of time—"

"It isn't an apartment."

"Oh. Then where am I going?" she asked.

"You'll see when you get there. No pearls. Come comfortable and ready to dig in."

"Shall I bring a shovel?" she joked.

"No pearls, no shovel," he answered but he obviously wanted to be mysterious and wasn't going to give her any other details.

"Oka-ay," she muttered. Then, rather than pursue a subject he wasn't going to expand on, she said, "Thanks for dinner."

That made him chuckle. "Even though it wasn't what you had in mind?"

"The food was still great. You're right, the understudy chef does do interesting things."

"Maybe next Sunday I'll just see if he'll do them takeout

so we can avoid the dreaded country club," Tate said wryly, making Tanya smile this time.

"Wow, you can do that," he mock marveled.

"What?"

"Smile. I was beginning to wonder. And it's nice, too. Who would have thought Miss Serious had a nice smile...."

"Miss Serious?"

"Well, there was nothing lighthearted about catching you in the library. You took me to task last night over stepping in with the news station. And tonight you've been all business even when business wasn't going on, and then you took me to task again on the way home. Plus you said yourself last night that you're serious—"

"That was a figure of speech. What I said was that I was serious about getting a substantial story out of this."

"Still, you're just plain serious, as far as I've seen. Maybe your mom and her cohorts should be worrying more about you than me."

Okay, so there hadn't been a whole lot of levity to any of the times they'd encountered each other since Friday night.

"This *is* business for me," she reminded him.

He smiled again, a pleased, warm smile that she liked entirely too much. "I'm glad you said business and not work. I don't think I like being *work* for anyone."

"Just make sure *business* gets done from here on," she pretended to chastise.

"Tomorrow, 9:00 a.m.," he countered.

She wondered if she was going to arrive at the address on the paper and find him sitting behind a desk. And if she would be expected to spend from then until five o'clock on the opposite side of that desk taking dictation on the story of his life.

She wouldn't put it past him.

But she knew better than to try to get any more information out of him about that, so she merely said, "Tomorrow, 9:00 a.m."

That seemed to satisfy him. It showed in his smile as he went on peering into her face for a moment more before he said, "You can tell your mother that you aren't."

"That I aren't what?"

He laughed. "That is some really rotten grammar for a journalist."

"That I'm *not* what?" she corrected the mistake she'd made on purpose, trying not to bask in the sound of his laugh or the fact that she'd inspired it.

"You're not bothering me. In fact, you're kind of a little spitfire and I'm getting a kick out of it."

"*Little spitfire?* You're aware that that's very condescending, aren't you?" she said even though it gave her a tiny rush to hear that she was rousing something in him.

"Hey, I'm just a sheltered, pampered, out-of-touch rich boy, what do I know?" he joked.

Again Tanya smiled, adding a hint of a laugh to it. And maybe her lighter side really was a novelty to him because several minutes lapsed while Tate just seemed to study her as if he couldn't quite figure her out.

Several minutes that made something else flash through Tanya's mind—that people in this position, saying goodnight at the door after having spent an evening together and sharing a nice dinner, very often kissed....

Which of course was not going to happen, she told herself in no uncertain terms.

And it didn't. Because then Tate said, "I'll see you at nine," and turned to retrace his steps to his car.

Tanya watched his retreating back, giving herself a silent but stern talking-to as she did.

There could not ever—*ever*—be thoughts of kissing when it came to Tate McCord.

That was absolutely, positively *un*thinkable.

Unthinkable and undoable.

Absolutely. Positively.

And if she was still standing there even after he was out of sight, even after she could hear his car engine restart, even after she'd heard him drive away?

It was because she was still silently lecturing herself about how she also—absolutely, positively—shouldn't be wondering what it would be like to kiss the mighty Tate McCord, either....

Chapter Four

"Rosa, this is Tanya Kimbrough. Tanya, this is Rosa Marsh—Rosa pretty much runs this place. Rosa, Tanya is going to pitch in for us today as a volunteer. I know you can use her," Tate said as he introduced Tanya to the heavyset nurse.

Then he leaned in close enough to Tanya's ear to whisper so only she could hear, "I thought I'd give you the chance to see how one McCord spends Mondays. And since *you're* so in touch with the *real* people, I figured you'd probably want to do more than just follow me around and take notes."

Tanya could tell that Tate was enjoying this—there was pure satisfaction on his handsome face as he left her to the woman named Rosa.

When Tanya had arrived at the address Tate had written in her notepad she definitely hadn't found a lead on an apartment for rent. She'd found a surgical clinic for the underprivileged in an extremely neglected portion of Dallas.

She'd also discovered that Tate was known there as Dr. Tate and that if anyone realized he was a McCord, it wasn't an issue. He was just Dr. Tate.

And Tanya was a volunteer for the day.

She didn't mind. It allowed her to watch him in action and pitching in was something she'd been taught to do even as a child. So Tanya followed Rosa's instructions and went to work herself.

She primarily did the nurses' bidding, performing cleanup and making sure patients were comfortable.

The small, inner-city facility was nothing at all like Meridian General Hospital. Sanitary conditions were met but that was about the best that could be said of it. Equipment was old, linens were clean but ragged, the linoleum floor was worn down to the cement beneath it in several places, and watermarks decorated the walls and ceiling.

Tanya would never have imagined Tate practicing there. Or fitting in with the two physician's assistants and four nurses who were all earthy, outspoken and irreverent. But there wasn't a single indication in anything she saw that made her think he held himself above any of them and they made it clear to her even when he wasn't around that they liked and respected him, and that they felt lucky to work with a surgeon of his caliber.

And the patients—some of them homeless, almost all of them lacking insurance or the ability to pay, many not English-speaking—were nothing like the majority of patients at Meridian General either.

Yet never did she see Tate treat any one of them without respect or compassion.

Plus it wasn't only their outpatient surgical needs—or even their general health needs—he met. He also seemed genuinely concerned for their well-being once they went beyond the peeling walls of the clinic. Numerous times Tanya overheard him ask if the patient had a home in which to recuperate. She saw him slip money to more than a few who clearly needed it. He even took the time to make phone calls to get additional assistance for two patients before he would release them.

She saw him go the extra mile over and over again, but not once did she have the sense that his actions were due to the fact that she was watching, or just to make himself look good. Most of the time he didn't even know she was anywhere near, and there were several instances when she learned what good deed he'd done through the nurses talking to each other. She also saw the nurses take many patients' nonmedical problems to him as if it were a common occurrence for them to enlist him, as if they knew from long before Monday that he was the person to go to.

By the end of the day Tanya wasn't ready to paint him as a saint—with people who weren't under his care he could be demanding and dictatorial. He could be outspoken about any slipups or oversights, and curt with patients' friends or family members who rubbed him wrong. But she had to admit that he wasn't what she'd expected. Or anything like what she'd known of him before. The image she'd had of him as she'd grown up on the peripheries of his life was suddenly altered.

Which didn't help her personally.

Because while finding him awesomely sexy in scrubs was one thing, being impressed by him, discovering that he might actually have some substance, some character, some depth, was much more of a bump in the road for her. It made him more the kind of man she liked, which also made him attractive to her on a whole other level.

Just when she didn't want him to be attractive to her at all...

The last patient wasn't ready to leave the clinic until nearly eight o'clock that night. Then the staff closed up and they all went out together.

Tate made sure his female coworkers got to their cars safely in the unsavory neighborhood. Once he had, he walked Tanya to hers.

"What do you say we meet at the guesthouse in an hour and I pay you for your services today with a little dinner?" he said as they reached her sedan.

It had been a long day and Tanya was tired, but that simple suggestion was enough to wipe it all away. Which she knew was a warning sign and yet she still said, "Dinner?"

"I'm thinking something quick and easy thrown into my wok after I shower. Are you up for it?"

Tate McCord owned a wok and knew how to use it?

"I can't believe you cook, so I guess I should see it for myself."

"Great. Be there in an hour, then," he ordered, opening her car door, waiting for her to get in then closing it.

Recalling her manners slightly late, Tanya started the engine in order to roll down her window and call to him as he went to his own car, "Can I bring anything?"

"Only yourself," he called back.

His tone, his attitude, were nothing but friendly. Completely aboveboard. There wasn't even the vaguest insinuation of anything else. So it was okay for her to have agreed to have dinner with him again, Tanya told herself as she rolled her window up.

And it was, after all, only for the sake of her story. Only to get to know him better—especially now that she'd learned there was more to know than she'd thought before.

And if she was instantly looking forward to what remained of this evening in a way she hadn't been until then?

It wasn't about the man. It was about the work and getting to the root of the McCords by getting to the root of Tate.

And maybe if she chanted that through the entire drive home, it might start to be true....

At the stroke of nine Tanya was knocking on the door to the guesthouse.

She'd showered. She'd shampooed the antiseptic smell out of her hair. She'd changed into a pair of white cotton pull-on pants and a peach-colored cap-sleeved T-shirt, scrunched her hair into waves and applied some blush, mascara and lip gloss to improve upon the haggard way she'd thought she looked when she'd arrived home.

But not because of Tate. Just because she'd wanted to. Or so she'd insisted both to herself and to her mother when JoBeth had voiced her concerns about another dinner with Tate and the fact that Tanya was primping for it.

"Right on time," Tate announced when he opened the door in answer to her knock.

She could tell that he'd showered, too. His hair was still slightly damp, the stubble that had shadowed his face when they'd left the clinic was gone and he smelled of a clean, fresh mountain-air cologne that Tanya couldn't resist breathing deeply of because the scent was too enticing.

He'd changed from his scrubs into a plain white T-shirt

and a pair of jeans Tanya knew her mother—and his—would consider ready for the ragbag because they were frayed and faded. But even so they looked fabulous on him, riding low on his hips and hugging his rear end like a dream.

And you have no business looking at his rear end! she reprimanded herself as she followed him into the guest-house in response to his invitation to come in.

"There's wine opened near the fridge over there," he informed her with a nod in that direction as he went straight to the island counter, obviously returning to what he'd been doing before her arrival—cutting vegetables.

And once more Tanya recognized the purely friendly overture that didn't smack of anything inappropriate or the slightest bit flirtatious.

Which was good. If they both stuck with that everything would be fine....

She glanced around at the guesthouse that was about the same size as her mother's bungalow and arranged the same way—the small kitchen space and living area were one wide open room divided by the island of cupboards with the granite countertop where Tate prepared their food. The place was equally as nice as her mother's cottage but no nicer and it seemed odd for Tate to be staying there when he had space of his own in the luxurious main house.

"So, you're living out here?" she fished as she poured herself a glass of wine and then joined him at the island counter.

"I have been for the last few months, yes," he confirmed.

"Why?" she asked bluntly since he hadn't offered more information.

He smiled a mystery-man smile and shrugged without taking his eyes off the peppers he was expertly slicing into strips. "Hard to explain," he said. "I suppose the easiest answer is that I'm not sleeping really well these days. I do a lot of getting up and walking around, trying to go back to sleep, getting up and walking around again. Out here I don't have to worry about disturbing anyone else. And I guess I just needed some time on my own."

He didn't seem to want to say any more about it because he pointed with his chin toward the vegetables still piled in a colander and said, "Dry those for me, will you?"

"Sure," she agreed, setting down her glass of very mellow red wine and using a paper towel to do as he'd asked.

"Where did you learn to cook?" she asked then, attempting a new subject.

"Trial and error. During residency, Buzz—do you remember Buzz?"

"I do. From what I recall, the two of you were inseparable, closer even than you were with your own brother. And I know he was killed in action in Iraq. I was sorry to hear it."

Tate nodded but he didn't remark on her condolences. Instead he went on with what he'd been about to say.

"During residency, Buzz and I got an apartment across the street from the hospital—we were working insane hours, we were on call more than off, and never getting enough sleep. We decided that it might help if we didn't have to commute. But losing the commute also cost me having a chef to fix my meals and Buzz having his grandmother to cook for him. We got sick of frozen dinners and takeout, and that was when we both learned how to make a few quick and easy dishes to get us through."

Tanya had the impression that talking about his late friend raised a mixed bag of emotions in him so she didn't encourage him to say more.

She didn't have the burden of keeping the conversation going, though, because then Tate said, "What about you? Do you cook?"

"Some. As soon as I could, I moved out of the dorm at college. I couldn't afford takeout or anything fancy, but I got my fill of tuna and canned soup in a hurry and I had to figure something else out. Plus I put in some time working in the restaurant industry—I came away from that with a few tips."

"College was where?"

"Los Angeles. I went to the University of Southern California—your mother actually wrote one of my letters of recommendation and helped me get a scholarship."

"I didn't know," he admitted. "What's your degree in?"

"Broadcast journalism."

He took more vegetables to slice. "Putting your energy into a degree like that is kind of risky, isn't it? What do you do with it if—"

"If someone does something underhanded and gets me taken off air?" she challenged.

He had the good grace to smile with some contrition. "Let's say, what if you grow a huge, unsightly, unremovable wart on the side of your nose and no news station on the planet will put your face on camera—what do you do with a broadcast journalism degree then?"

"There are jobs behind the camera that I could still do, but it's on-air time I'm after," she said, emphasizing each word to bring home her point.

He apparently decided to ignore her second jab because rather than respond to it, he said, "Why did you decide to come back here to work? Dallas is a big market for everything, but I'd think it would be flashier and more impressive to do the news in L.A. or New York or Washington."

"I interned in L.A. and worked there after I graduated. But the flashier, more impressive markets are also harder to break into and I didn't feel like I was on the fast track. Plus Mom never liked my living out of state or that far away from her, but she wouldn't move to where I was, so I finally decided to come back here. There's still the potential for climbing the ladder from a local independent station to a local network affiliate to one of the bigger markets, and maybe if that happens I'll be able to persuade her to come with me then. But the potential isn't there at all when…I'm…banned…from…even…the…local…independent…station," she said, speaking with even more exaggeration.

"I get the idea—I'm a low-down, dirty dog for sabotaging your big chance here. But let's not forget that what prompted *my* actions were *your* actions."

"All right, we'll call it a draw," she said as if she were being the bigger person.

It made him smile again as he finished with the vegetables and brought a plate of already-sliced beef from the refrigerator.

He tossed everything into the preheated wok where the sound of sizzling was loud enough to make it difficult to talk. Tanya didn't try and merely enjoyed the sight of Tate cooking.

He was as adept with that as he'd been with everything she'd seen him do at the clinic, and as she watched him it occurred to her that all the way around today she was getting a glimpse of him as not just someone born with a silver spoon in his mouth.

When he judged their meal ready he urged her to the small table nearby where two places were set. There was also a rice cooker and a plate that displayed three small bowls of what appeared to be sauces.

"Sweet, hot and spicy, not so hot," he described the sauces, aiming a long middle finger at each one and for some inexplicable reason, causing Tanya's focus to be on that finger rather than on the sauces. Or that finger and the thought of how even that was somehow sexy....

Then he retrieved the bottle of wine from where she'd left it after pouring her glass, and as they both sat down to eat Tanya determinedly reined in her mental wanderings.

"Did you wait tables or work in a fast-food place or a diner—or what—through college?" he asked after they'd tasted the food and Tanya had complimented his culinary skills.

She was a little surprised that he'd listened closely enough to what she'd said to recall her comment about having worked in the restaurant industry.

"We're supposed to be talking McCords and the jewelry business and the diamond, remember?" she reminded him before she got carried away thinking the fact that he was paying attention to what she said was anything special.

"The whole day was stuff you can use—the clinic is funded by my mother's charities and donations from McCord's Jewelers. I work there and oversee the rest of the staff to make sure the quality of care is the best that it can be. Now work is over for both of us," he decreed.

Tanya supposed she could concede to that. His small talk *was* staying within the bounds of propriety—it was only her own thoughts that had strayed. And while she would have liked to go on gathering material, she'd seen the day he'd put in and she had the sense that he needed a plain, ordinary, small talk–filled dinner, so she let him have it his way.

"Okay," she said, after another bite of the Asian-influenced cuisine. "Yes, I worked in a fast-food place—I was the bagel butterer on an assembly line at a sandwich shop. I also waited tables at one of those places that only serve breakfast—but I don't think you could call it a diner. And there was an upscale, fancy restaurant where I did some hostessing."

"So basically, you worked your way through college completely in the food industry."

"Basically, but not entirely. I also worked as a motel maid before I did any of that. But only for three days—"

"Three days?"

"That was all I could take. You can't imagine what kind of mess some people will leave in a motel room and the morning I found a dead guy was the day I quit—"

"You found a dead guy?" he asked, trying not to be amused.

"He'd died in his sleep, of a heart attack. But that was it for me—that was when I went with the restaurant work. Then, as soon as I could get on with a news station even just running errands, I grabbed it."

"I take it the scholarship wasn't all that great?" he said apologetically.

"No, it was," she assured him, not wanting to sound ungrateful. "I wasn't complaining. The scholarship paid my full tuition. But I had to earn money for books and fees and living expenses."

"I know you weren't complaining. I think I was just feeling guilty because I partied and played my way through college."

"You partied and played your way through middle school and high school, too," she reminded him.

He smiled sheepishly. "That I did. In fact, I was thinking

about you last night—about what I remembered of you growing up—"

"Not much, I'll bet," Tanya said, pushing away her plate because she'd eaten all she could.

His smile widened as he sat back, apparently finished eating as well. "Actually, I remembered that you were the you-shouldn't-do-that kid."

"You've lost me," she said, not sure what he was talking about.

"My most vivid memories of you are of looking up from something Buzz and I were about to do and seeing this big-eyed kid who had appeared out of nowhere to stand on the sidelines, very stoically shaking her head at me, and saying, *you shouldn't do that....*"

Tanya laughed. "I don't remember that."

"Oh, yeah. I remember because you were usually right. Of course I just thought you were some annoying little kid sticking her nose in where it didn't belong. But you were still right. The day Buzz and I tried out our dirt bikes on the front lawn—we were thirteen so you had to be—"

"Six."

"And you said, *you shouldn't do that, the gardener will get mad....*"

"And you did it anyway."

"And tore up the lawn. And the gardener *did* get mad, and so did my parents. I was grounded for two weeks. Then there was the time when we set up a ramp at the edge of the pool. We had new scooters and we were sure that with enough height we could jump the shallow end. There you were, doing your *you-shouldn't-do-that* thing again. I'm pretty sure I said something rude to you and told you to go away. You wouldn't go away and I figured I'd show you that you were nothing but a dumb kid. I ended up in the pool, destroyed the scooter and broke my leg. That cost me another two weeks of grounding."

Tanya laughed. "I honestly don't remember ever saying you shouldn't do anything."

"Then there was my party—"

"I remember the party. You were seventeen, I was ten. I watched from the bushes until my mom caught me. But I still don't recall a 'you shouldn't do that.'"

"Oh, yeah. I had permission to have twelve people over to swim that night. But nobody was going to be home so Buzz and I handed out flyers to everyone we knew and some people we didn't. We paid an older guy to buy beer and we were sneaking the kegs in the back and talking about what a huge, blowout bash the party was going to be. And again you appeared from out of nowhere to say—"

"You shouldn't do that?"

He pointed an index finger at her. "The you-shouldn't-do-that kid."

They both laughed.

"That one cost me a month out of my summer—I was going to get to stay home while my family vacationed in Italy but because of the party, my parents decided I couldn't be trusted and made me go with them."

Tanya shrugged. "Guess you shouldn't have done that," she joked as she stood and began to clear the table.

She half expected Tate to remain seated there while she did the work but he got up, too, and, side by side, they cleaned the dinner mess.

"What about you?" he asked as they did. "Did you go through your teens toeing the line like you thought I should have?"

"I kind of did, actually," she answered. "We might have grown up in the same general vicinity for the most part but, believe me, my life was completely different than yours. From the minute I was old enough to work I was expected to show responsibility by getting a job. So when I was here I worked in the ice cream shop—more food service. When I was with my grandparents I worked—"

"When you were with your grandparents? I didn't know you spent time away from here."

"Quite a bit of time. But that's a whole other story." And since the dishes were loaded into the dishwasher, his kitchen was in order again and it was getting late, she said, "A whole other story I'll save so we can call it a night—I promised my mother I'd be back before she went to bed and you must be tired yourself."

"Trouble sleeping, remember? But I wouldn't want you to keep JoBeth up waiting for you."

And worrying that she was staying any later than was necessary…

Tate walked Tanya to the door and put his hand on the knob to open it for her. But rather than doing that, he stayed in that position while pausing to look at her with the door still closed.

"This was nice," he said as if that surprised him.

"It was. Thanks for dinner. You get points for today and points for your cooking talents, too."

"Points? I didn't know there was a scorecard."

"Not literally."

"And why did I get points for today?"

"Because what I saw of you was so eye-opening."

"In what way?"

"I don't remember the 'you shouldn't do thats.' But I

do remember you doing some wild and reckless things in pursuit of fun and frolic—which was all I thought you were about. Mr. Good-Time. But today I saw for myself that there *is* more to you...."

Why had her voice gotten softer by the end of that? Why had it sounded almost intimate? And why was she staring up at him and thinking that she really was seeing him through new eyes? And that she liked what she was seeing so much more than when she'd thought he was just a handsome face....

"Anyway," she said, trying for a more normal tone and to halt the thoughts and feelings that were suddenly running through her. "I admired what I saw of what you did today and it will definitely be a part of the collage of the McCords."

He smiled. "I was impressed with you today, too," he said. "I wasn't sure if you were all talk or not, but you dug right in. And you didn't even flinch when old Nesbit came wandering out of recovery in the buff."

Tanya laughed. "*That* I won't be reporting on," she said. "Though you were really quick with that chart you held in front of his dangling participles so the lady I was giving juice to didn't see much."

"Dangling participles? Things were definitely dangling...." he said wryly, laughing too.

Tanya was having a much better time than she wished she was. It made it hard for her to make herself leave. And Tate wasn't encouraging it—he was still standing there with the door closed, looking down at her.

And it wasn't just *any* look in those clear blue eyes. He was looking at her in a way other men had looked at her. Just before they'd kissed her...

Was he thinking about it? Tanya wondered.

Because she was…

You shouldn't do that—the phrase that had been repeated so much tonight echoed through her head. And she knew it was true, that kissing him wasn't what she should do. Or let him do.

Even if something in her was shouting for him to go ahead and do it.…

Then he cocked his head just a bit to one side. But Tanya couldn't tell if he was even aware that he'd done it because he was staring so intently, so deeply into her eyes.

He leaned forward. Barely. Almost not at all.

Her chin went up about the same amount, on its own.

Shouldn't do that…

Except that she wanted to.

She really, really wanted to.…

But maybe the mere thought that they shouldn't do that somehow transmitted to Tate, who finally took heed of it. He straightened up again and turned the handle to open the door so she could go out.

Which was exactly what she knew she had to do. She had to get out of there before she did something stupid.…

"Tomorrow?" she said as she stepped across the threshold, stopping only when she felt the cooler night air on her face to turn and look at him from a greater distance than had separated them in the house.

"I have surgeries scheduled all day and dinner with the family tomorrow evening. But I've left orders for all the family albums to be dragged out of storage—I thought maybe we could go through them tomorrow night after dinner. That should give you a fairly decent family history."

Why did tomorrow night seem so far away? And why

was she thinking about how endlessly the hours would drag on instead of being aggravated by the fact that the entire next day would be wasted?

But that was how it was and she couldn't help it. She could only hope the time would pass quickly....

"Okay," she heard herself say compliantly. "If that's how it has to be."

"Unfortunately..." he said so quietly that she had the feeling he regretted having to wait, too.

But that couldn't be, Tanya told herself. *He's engaged— don't forget that....*

She said good-night then and headed in the direction of her mother's bungalow. But since she hadn't heard the guesthouse door close, just before she stepped onto the path that led through trees and bushes and would take her out of sight, she glanced over her shoulder.

There was Tate, standing in the doorway watching her.

And thinking what? About kissing her?

Had he almost kissed her or had she been wrong about that?

She must have been wrong.

But right or wrong, there would be no kissing of Tate McCord! she told herself.

Still, she thought he *had* almost kissed her.

And even though she knew it would have been a mistake, even though she knew it couldn't happen, as she slipped out of his sight down the path to the bungalow, she was wishing that this might have been one of those times— like all those others—when he'd ignored the you-shouldn't-do-that and done it anyway....

Chapter Five

"Katie. Hi," Tate said into his cell phone when it rang on his way to work Tuesday morning and the display let him know in advance who his caller was.

"I hope I didn't wake you," Katie replied to his greeting.

"No, I'm about five minutes away from the hospital. How's everything?"

"Okay. As well as could be expected, I suppose," Katie said.

Tate had known her long enough to think he knew all of her moods, but he couldn't pinpoint this one. Trying to, he said, "You sound tired."

"I didn't have the chance to tell my parents that the engagement is off until last night. You know how it is—there have been dinners and parties and people around since I got to Key West and I had to wait for a moment alone with them."

"And I don't imagine that they welcomed the news," Tate guessed, not eager to tell his own family for just that reason.

"No, they certainly didn't *welcome* it. They were actually very impatient with me."

"I'm sorry," Tate said sympathetically.

"It was no worse than I thought it would be, but still…" Katie sighed. "After all this time they were sure their dreams were finally coming true. I knew they weren't going to be happy to have me wake them up."

"What about you?" Tate asked point-blank because he still wasn't getting a clear read on Katie's feelings. And while he knew breaking up was for the best, he was concerned about her.

"Well, I *am* tired—you were right about that. We were up arguing until very late and I had an early hair appointment this morning so I couldn't sleep in. But otherwise…"

There was a pause that didn't convince Tate that Katie was merely worn out.

Then she continued. "I'm a little at loose ends. You *were* always sort of my guy," she said with a laugh that helped him believe she wasn't doing too badly despite the fact that she might be a little down in the dumps over the way things had turned out.

"Even when we weren't together," she went on, "there was always just that thought that we'd probably end up with each other some day. And it isn't as if I don't care about you, Tate—"

"Same here."

"But I truly do think there's more out there for both of us."

Why did Tanya pop into his mind at that exact moment?

But Katie was still talking and he forced himself to pay attention.

"—it just isn't easy to start over. I keep thinking that I haven't ever been in a single, long-term, committed relationship with anyone of my own choosing. That was part of the argument last night—I said I needed to be able to decide who the man for me would be. But just between us, the whole time I was wondering if I'll know *how* to choose someone for myself."

Tate laughed. "I'm pretty sure you just go with whoever you have the strongest feelings for," he said. And again—for no reason that made sense—Tanya came to mind.

"What about you?" Katie asked then. "How are you?"

"I'm doing all right," he said.

"You sound better than *all right*. You sound a little more like your old self. Were you that glad to get rid of me?"

"Come on, you know better than that," he chastised. "And I didn't *get rid* of you. If anybody got rid of anybody—"

"I'm saying it was a mutual decision. And now you can, too—that's why I wanted to talk to you first thing this morning. My mother is threatening to call yours. I asked her to wait but I don't know how long she will. So don't put off telling Eleanor or it'll be my mother who does."

"I'm having dinner with the family tonight. I'll tell them then."

"I hope it goes smoother with yours than it did with mine."

"Even if it doesn't, it'll all blow over before long," Tate assured her as he pulled into the doctors' parking lot of Meridian General.

"It's nice that we can still chat like this, though," Katie said then. "And be friends…"

"That isn't going to change—we've always been friends, we always will be friends. You know if there's anything you need from me you just have to ask, right?"

"Same here," she echoed his earlier words. "I should let you go, though, I just heard the parking lot attendant say good morning to you so you must be at the hospital. I'll try to keep my mother from calling yours at least until tomorrow."

"Thanks."

"And I'll see you at the Labor Day party—I should probably apologize to you ahead of time for anything my parents might say to you at that."

The McCords were throwing one of their lavish soirees to mark the end of the summer season and Katie's family was always at the top of the guest list.

"Don't worry about it. It'll be fine," Tate assured her once more.

"I hope so," Katie said. "I hope everything will be fine for us both."

"It will be."

"Well, one way or another, I just wanted you to know that you're free to tell whoever you want now. And thanks for letting me go first with the families."

"Sure."

They said their goodbyes then and Tate turned off his phone as he parked in his assigned spot.

But the freedom he now had to get the word out that he was no longer engaged to Katie was still on his mind.

Of course it was his family who had to be next to know.

But right after that?

For the third time it was Tanya who made an instant appearance in his head.

Because Tanya was really the only person he *wanted* to tell....

"The engagement is off? Oh, Tate…"

Tate had waited until everyone was finishing dessert

Tuesday evening to make his announcement. Not that *everyone* was there. His mother, Eleanor, was at the head of the table and her response to the news was rife with disappointment and disapproval. His older brother Blake was sitting across from him, and one of his younger twin sisters, Penny, was to his right. But even without the rest of the family there, Tate knew word would spread to Penny's twin, Paige, and to his youngest brother, Charlie, and he hadn't wanted to delay telling his mother until Paige and Charlie were around, as well.

"These breakups are never for good," Blake said with an annoyed sigh.

"It's time the *breakups* stop," Eleanor said. "I know you've been in a bad way since we lost Buzz, Tate. But I honestly think the path out of it is to finally do what you should have done long ago—stop this seesaw you and Katie have always been on and take a definitive step into your future with the woman you know you're going to end up with eventually."

"In other words, little brother," Blake said, "it's time for you to grow up."

Tate could have taken issue with that but he didn't. "What it is time for," he said instead, "is for Katie and me to get off the seesaw once and for all."

"What can you possibly be thinking?" Blake demanded, surprising Tate with a reaction that was stronger than Tate had expected from his brother. Blake should have had enough on his mind with the current business problems and trying to find the Santa Magdalena diamond to make this low on his list of concerns. "Why don't you open your eyes and take a look at what you have in Katie?" Blake continued. "You keep going back to her—you must recognize on some level how terrific she is. What will it take for you to just accept that you aren't going to do better?"

"You don't know what you're talking about, Blake," Tate said calmly. "I do know how terrific Katie is. But when there isn't that…certain something…between two people, you can be terrific, she can be terrific, it just doesn't make any difference. And I'm sure you think this was my idea, but the truth is, it came about at her instigation."

"Isn't that exactly what I told you the other night?" Blake said with disgust. "You took her for granted, you neglected her and now she's called things off."

"Ultimately, it was a mutual decision," Tate said, borrowing from Katie. "At her instigation, but a mutual decision. We both agreed that all these years have been more about what the families wanted, what the families pressured us into, and not about our feelings for each other. But the bottom line—" Tate said, thinking that his brother was a bottom-line kind of person "—is that we don't have the kind of feelings that end in marriage. At least not a happy, lasting marriage. And since—for some reason—you seem to have adopted the role of Katie's champion, isn't that what you'd want for her? To be married to someone she's actually in love with and has a chance to be happy with for the rest of her life?"

"It goes without saying that that's what I'd want for her. For you both," Blake added impatiently.

"Well, we've come to the conclusion that that isn't what we'd have together."

"That's the conclusion you've come to this week. Or this month," Eleanor said as if she was at her wits' end with him. "But next week or next month, you'll be telling us you're back together again. Just stop this on and off!"

"We have stopped it, only we've stopped it at *off*,"

Tate said, concealing how much he wanted this to end because he was itching to get to Tanya to go through the family albums the way they'd planned. "This is it for Katie and me, whether the families like it or not," he concluded firmly.

"And *families* shouldn't enter into a person's relationships," Penny said then, chiming in for the first time.

Tate appreciated his younger sister's support but it surprised him, too. Penny was the quieter, more introverted of the twins. She didn't often venture into a family fray unless she had to.

"Talk to us when you have a *relationship* that the family enters into, Penny," Blake said sardonically.

"That's what I'm worried about—the family entering into *my* relationship," Penny muttered under her breath and with some defensiveness that seemed out of place.

"What does *that* mean?" Blake asked with a chuckle, as if Penny were six years old rather than twenty-six.

Tate saw how much that irked Penny—she sat up straighter, her lips pursed. Then she said, "I've…"

She stopped herself as if to gauge her words.

"It's okay, Penny," Tate said. "I appreciate that you're on my side, but you don't have to fight my battles."

"It isn't only your battle," his sister answered as if she'd just that moment come to some kind of decision.

Then she made an announcement of her own. "I've been seeing Jason Foley."

That came as far, far more of a shock than Tate's broken engagement and brought several moments of stunned silence before Blake broke it.

"Jason Foley?" he repeated in disbelief.

"What do you mean you're seeing him? As a friend?" Eleanor asked in a controlled tone.

"More than friends," Penny said.

"You're *dating?*" their mother pressed, beginning to sound alarmed.

Penny hesitated. She was a private person and Tate realized this wasn't easy for her.

But then she said, "Yes, we're dating."

"That's bad, Penny," Blake decreed. "You know the Foleys hate us, that they've been convinced for decades that we cheated them out of the land, and now with the potential that the diamond could be—"

"This doesn't have anything to do with that," Penny insisted.

"Don't kid yourself!" Blake said in a louder voice. "Don't you think it's just a little suspicious that now—of *all* times—there's a Foley sniffing around? They're looking for a way in, Penny! For information about the diamond!"

"You haven't actually given me any information about the diamond except to enlist me to design jewelry that will tie into it if you find it."

"I don't want the Foleys knowing even that much. That's what they're after—any crumb they can get their hands on and use!" Blake shouted.

Tate was aware of how invested Blake was in the business, in finding the diamond, in using it to salvage McCord's Jewelers. He knew his brother was under pressure he wasn't willing to share unless it was absolutely necessary because Blake always believed he was the best person to shoulder the load. And Tate thought that because of all that, it didn't occur to Blake how insulting to Penny it was to imply that Jason Foley was interested in her only as some kind of ploy. Even though Tate agreed that it was a possibility.

"We don't know that that's why Jason Foley is seeing Penny, Blake," he said.

"I know nothing good can come of a McCord getting involved with a Foley."

"Charlie came of it," Penny said, using the information their mother had only recently shared with them that the youngest McCord was the result of an affair Eleanor had had with Rex Foley twenty-two years earlier.

But it was information that had caused all of Eleanor's children to give her a wide berth ever since. To Tate's knowledge, none of them had discussed it with their mother in any depth, even since Eleanor's return that morning to take care of the last details of the Labor Day party. So Tate could hardly believe his ears when Penny used that information for her own purposes now.

Glancing at his mother, Tate found her unruffled by it, though. Instead, venturing delicately into the subject that still wasn't easy for any of them to accept, Eleanor said, "Yes, Penny, Charlie *did* come of my involvement with a Foley. But that's why I can speak from experience and tell you that a tie between a Foley and a McCord is a rocky road."

"We just don't want you to get hurt, Penny," Tate added.

"That's true," Eleanor confirmed.

"What's *true*," Penny countered, "is that whatever is between two *families* shouldn't interfere with what might—or might not—be between two individual people. Not when it comes to you and Katie, Tate, and not when it comes to whoever I'm with, either. Jason and I are seeing each other and it doesn't have anything to do with the fact that I'm a McCord and he's a Foley. It doesn't have anything to do with an old feud, or with land that changed hands a gazillion years ago, or with a diamond. It's *in spite* of all that and it's only about Jason and me."

"I hope you're right," Eleanor said with worry lines creasing her brow.

"I'm telling you," Blake seemed unable to keep from re-iterating, "you don't know what the Foleys could be up to."

"It may be perfectly innocent," Tate contributed. "Jason Foley may just be carried away by how terrific *you* are. But be careful—that's all we're asking. When it comes to a Foley, be really careful...."

Chapter Six

Tate was sitting at one of the poolside tables when Tanya came out from the wooded path after leaving her mother's cottage Tuesday night. The moment she stepped through the clearing in the bushes and magnolia trees she saw that he was watching for her and a small smile turned up the corners of his mouth.

Why *that* sent something gooshy through her, she didn't know, but that bare hint of him being pleased to see her was all it took to heat her from the inside out.

Then his gaze went from her free-falling hair, down the teal T-shirt she was wearing to her flowing wide-leg slacks as she crossed to him. His smile grew bigger. And that internal heat took on a rosy, sensual glow.

Stop it! she ordered herself, trying to keep uppermost in her mind that in spite of the fact that it was late evening, that they were suddenly together again, under a clear moonlit sky, this was about work. *Only* work...

"Finally!" Tate muttered when she reached him, before she'd even said hello.

"You just called me five minutes ago to tell me to come over," she said, thinking he was making a comment about having to wait for her.

He shook his head. *"Finally* we can get to what we had planned tonight."

"Ah," Tanya said as she took the chair nearest him.

What they had planned tonight was to look through his family albums. And since there was a stack of them on the table, she sat where they would each be able to see them. It didn't have anything to do with the fact that she *wanted* to sit close to him. Want to or not, she swore that she wasn't going to let this evolve into anything more than doing her job tonight.

"I brought the wine I started on at dinner. Will you have some?" Tate asked then, picking up the open bottle and refreshing his own glass while he indicated the clean glass beside it.

"This is supposed to be work for me," Tanya reminded them both, holding up her notepad and pen to prove it.

"Sometimes mixing business and pleasure is a good thing," he enticed.

"I hope that isn't your philosophy when you do surgery," she countered.

That merely made him laugh and question her again by holding the bottle higher.

She shouldn't. This *was* work.

And yet she heard herself say "Maybe just one glass."

She set her pad and pen on the table as he poured,

using his averted glance as an opportunity to give him the once-over. The pool area where they were sitting was well lit and she could tell that he'd dressed for dinner and then undone some of it for this. There wasn't a suitcoat or tie anywhere around, but he had on gray slacks and a crisp white shirt with the long sleeves rolled to his elbows. He was also clean shaven, the scent of his cologne just barely wafted to her and his slightly longish hair was neatly combed.

Would it have helped if he'd looked grungy? she asked herself, knowing her vow to keep this out of the realm of another datelike evening with him was already weakening.

But somehow she doubted that the way he was dressed made any difference. The man just seemed to hold an appeal for her that she didn't fully understand. Maybe he'd unearthed some kind of deep-seated attraction to unavailable men that she hadn't known she possessed.

But he *was* unavailable—in so many ways—and she told herself not to forget that.

When the wine was poured and the bottle replaced on the table, Tate handed her her glass and lounged back in his chair with a deep sigh of what sounded like relief.

"Rough day?" Tanya asked as she took a sip of the wine.

"Rough dinner," he amended.

There was talk among the staff about the tense state the family had been in since rumors had begun to surface that Tate's mother had announced that her youngest son, Charlie, was a Foley. None of the staff knew any of the details, but they did know that Charlie had almost instantly gone off to settle back into college early, and that Eleanor had taken some time away herself.

Tanya assumed that tensions over Charlie's paternity

were still the cause of the rough dinner, but Tate didn't offer her any explanation as she took another sip of wine.

"So, how far back would you like to go?" Tate asked with a nod toward the albums.

Good, he is getting right down to business, Tanya told herself to ward off a ridiculous sense of disappointment that he wasn't bothering with small talk tonight.

"I did some background research today and thought about how I'd like to do this," she said, trying to sound purely professional. "I'd like a clear picture of the McCords and your family history first. Once that's accomplished, I can get into the story of the diamond and the treasure and of the feud with the Foleys, and the land and silver mines that changed hands, too. But for tonight, how about starting with just the family stuff?"

"Whatever you want."

"And since it looks as though the feud between the Foleys and the McCords began with Gavin Foley and Harry McCord—"

"My grandfather."

"—that seems like the furthest we need to go in McCord family history."

"Okay, Harry McCord it is," Tate said, sitting up and reaching for the albums. He discarded two of the more ragged ones before settling on one that displayed old, poor-quality black-and-white photographs of a man who bore a clear resemblance to him. "These are of my grandfather in front of the silver mines that launched the McCord fortune and, ultimately, McCord's Jewelers," he informed her.

Tanya flipped through page after page, noting that there were five mines, all of them with a large stone at their entrance, each with a petroglyph carved into it to name it. The Turtle mine. The Eagle mine. The Lizard. The Tree. The Bow.

"Can I have a few of these pictures to use? I'll make sure they're returned," Tanya said when she'd reached the end of that album.

"I don't see why not," Tate agreed, taking them out and giving them to her.

"So, was your father Harry McCord's only child?" Tanya asked then.

"No. My father was the oldest son. The younger—my Uncle Joseph—lives in Italy. You must know Gabby? My cousin?"

Gabriella McCord was a famous model and it was nearly impossible to pick up any magazine, newspaper or tabloid and not find her face on the cover. So Tanya felt a little stupid for not having considered from where on the family tree Gabby McCord had sprouted. She didn't admit it, though.

"I know *of* her," Tanya said. "The whole world knows *of* her. But it isn't as if she was ever introduced to the housekeeper's daughter on one of her visits, and I had no idea how she fit into the family—I guess I'd never really thought about it."

"Well, Gabby's father is Joseph. Joseph married an Italian actress descended from royalty over there. They made their home in Italy, and Joseph oversees and manages the European branches of McCord's Jewelers. My grandmother died in childbirth with Joseph." Tate found a picture of his grandmother and a few of Joseph growing up and as an adult, showing them to Tanya.

"So Harry McCord raised Devon—your father—and your uncle on his own?"

"That's the story. My father said one of his earliest memories was of going out to the mines with my grandfather, and that was where he and Joseph spent most of their time growing up—if they weren't in school, they were working alongside my grandfather."

Tate moved on to the next album, flipping through more shots of the brothers Devon and Joseph until he reached one of them with Harry McCord, standing outside of McCord's Jewelers.

"That was the first store," Tate said.

Tanya took a close look at the nondescript glass storefront that could hardly compare to the current McCord's Jewelers. Now they were known for their marble entrances, their plush lavender and gray carpeting, their mirrored cases and velvet displays, their leather club chairs for shopping in comfort. And their new customer-pampering campaign had only increased the level of luxury that was a world of difference from that initial jewelry shop.

"You've come a long way," she observed.

"That was my father's doing. And Blake's. I take no credit for what goes on with the jewelry business."

"I'd like to use this picture of the original store."

"Go ahead."

Tanya took it to put with the others she was collecting. Then they moved on to the next album. It contained pictures of Devon McCord's wedding to Tate's mother, the beautiful, blond Eleanor Holden.

"Huh," Tanya said as she glanced through them.

"What?"

"Your mother is the most somber-looking bride I think I've ever seen, and your father looks more victorious than smitten."

"That seems about right," Tate said, leaning in for a closer look and giving Tanya a better whiff of his cologne that was more heady than the wine she was slowly sipping.

"Why does that seem about right?" she asked.

"That my father looked victorious? That was always how he was when it came to my mother."

Devon McCord had only died a year ago but while Tanya remembered the man, she had never paid any attention to his relationship with his wife, so this was news to her.

"What do you mean?" she said.

"Some of it goes back to the problems with the Foleys—my mother dated both my father and Rex Foley, you know?"

"No, I didn't know that," Tanya said, her interest sparked.

"I don't really know much about it except that she did. The only thing I know is that my father would say—*Rex Foley wanted her but I got her.* Only he didn't say it as if it made him a lucky man—which was how I always thought he *should* have said it. He'd say it as if she were the spoils of war. Just one more thing he'd won out over the Foleys, as if it wasn't my mother who mattered as much as his victory over Rex Foley."

"And now your dad is gone and you find out that Rex Foley is Charlie's father...."

Tanya knew her mother would be furious with her if JoBeth found out she was taking such a liberty with a McCord. The McCords probably didn't even realize that the staff was aware of what was going on within the family, and certainly no employee—or employee's daughter—was at liberty to inquire about it.

But at that moment Tanya wasn't there as the housekeeper's daughter. She was there as an investigative reporter. And that meant asking even the probing, off-limits questions.

Tate didn't answer it readily. He sat back, he took a drink of his wine, he raised a single eyebrow at her. "Hard to keep a secret from the staff," he said.

Tanya raised both of her eyebrows back at him, committing blame to no one.

"It's a private matter," he said then in a tone that warned her not to pursue the subject. "We're all still trying to come to grips with it. We definitely don't want it announced in a news report. But then, that seems to fall more into the category of gossip than what you said you want to do."

Tanya had to smile at his attempt to manipulate her. "I don't know—two of Dallas's preeminent families who have been in a long-standing feud, now connected by blood because the head of one of the families had an affair with the head of the other? That makes for a thin line between gossip and news. Especially in a piece like this."

"*Affair?*" Tate repeated as if she were overstating.

"It *wasn't* an affair?"

Tate's sky-blue eyes bored into her for a moment as if he were sizing her up. Or judging just how much of a problem she could be for him. Gone was the openness she'd seen more of recently, replaced by a cool aloofness and the much harder edge she'd seen in him on Friday night in the library.

Then he sighed again and said, "I'm going to be straight with you—I don't really know what went on between my mother and Rex Foley. I know—have always known—that she *dated* Rex Foley when they were teenagers. I don't think there was anything between them once she married my father, and how they got together again is a mystery to me. I know—hell, you might even remember—that my parents' marriage hit a rough patch and they separated.

Charlie was conceived during that separation so obviously my mother turned to Rex Foley then, but I have no idea how that came about. Has she been involved with Rex Foley since then? I don't know and to tell you the truth, I don't want to know. Whatever happened is my mother's business."

There was no question in Tanya's mind that she'd just poured salt into an open wound. And what that had done was reawaken the new—and not necessarily improved—Tate, just when she'd been getting a little more of the old.

Tanya had to admit that the new Tate was far more daunting. But it was her job to be undaunted.

"How is the fact that your mother had—or has—a relationship with Rex Foley affecting your family?"

"Right now, I'd say that we're all just a little dumbfounded. Who knows what will happen in the future?"

"Have feelings changed toward Charlie?"

"No. Charlie is what he's always been—our brother."

"Now he's also brother to the Foleys...."

Tate didn't like this direction. He frowned at her. "We all have our flaws," he said in a clipped voice she'd never heard him use before.

"Being half Foley is a flaw?" she ventured anyway.

"Are you going to make me sorry I agreed to do this?" Tate demanded suddenly.

"Probably."

There was a moment of silence during which Tate gave her the hardest stare she'd ever had. Tanya actually thought he might get up, walk away and let her suffer the consequences of snooping through the library on Friday night. She thought it was a very real possibility that he might just have her fired from the studio, fire her mother as housekeeper and generally wreak havoc on her life rather than continue this.

But then his handsome face eased into an unexpected smile again and he shook his head. "I don't know if being half Foley is a flaw or not," he finally answered. "Right now it's confusing for us all—especially for Charlie—and I think we just have to wait and see how it plays out."

He said that with enough finality to let her know he wasn't going to say any more on this topic.

So Tanya switched gears.

"I suppose McCord's Jewelers' financial woes are more of a priority than Charlie's parentage at this point, anyway," she said.

"Strike two! You really are aiming to tick me off tonight, aren't you?" Tate said, though with a hint of humor infusing his words.

"Just doing my job. There *are* rumors that the family business is floundering and from what I overheard Friday night, the rumors have some foundation in truth—that makes it part of the story," she insisted.

"The jewelry business is Blake's bailiwick and the only thing I'll say, the only thing I know to report, is that he's working to increase sales the way any number of businesses do—with new advertising or new packaging or new whatever. That doesn't mean anything is *floundering*."

"I've seen the ads—A Once In A Lifetime Experience," Tanya said. "Coffee and pastries for morning shoppers. Champagne and hors d'oeuvres later in the day. One-on-one customer service—"

"And Gabby—don't forget Gabby is available by e-mail for personal shopping advice for certain clients who want to know what a high-profile trendsetter would buy."

"That sounds like you're putting in a plug for Blake's new public relations campaign."

Tate merely smiled as if that was exactly what he was doing and was pleased to be able to again control the information that would go into her story.

But she couldn't let him get too comfortable. "And I heard you and Blake talk about him stockpiling canary diamonds to use as a tie-in with the Santa Magdalena diamond *when* he finds it."

Tate sobered and sighed again. "You're just digging around all over the place, aren't you?"

Tanya gave him the that's-my-job shrug.

"Let's just say," Tate said, "that it wouldn't do any harm to have the Santa Magdalena diamond appear. And I *hope* that that happens and the focus of your report leans more in that direction—in a direction that can *help* rather than hurt."

"In other words, you'd like it if my report could be more in the way of free advertisement than anything really revealing."

He just grinned.

"So you're using me? Is that why your fiancée isn't putting the kibosh on your spending so much time with me?"

"My *fiancée*..." He took a drink of his wine, looked at the glass as he set it back on the table then said, "No more fiancée. No more engagement."

"Oh..." she said, not impressed by the announcement.

He cocked his head at her. "You don't believe me?"

"Oh, sure," she said flimsily.

"You *don't* believe me."

"Believe you, don't believe you—it isn't really a matter of that. If the engagement was on yesterday and off today, it'll just be on again tomorrow."

"Even the staff—and the staff's family—has been keeping track of that?"

"Hard not to. One day you're an item, the next you aren't."

He shook his head. "Well, I hate to switch things up, but it's not the same this time. The engagement is definitely off."

Something about the way he said that gave Tanya a strange moment of elation that she tempered in a hurry. Then she shook her head at him, denying her own response and his claim all at once.

"You *still* don't believe me?" Tate interpreted that part of the head shake.

"It doesn't matter. This is how things go with you two. It stands to reason that you wouldn't make it to the altar the first time around. There will probably be a couple of engagements and breakups before that will happen. But do I think it will *eventually* happen? Sure."

Tate rolled his eyes. "This is tonight's dinner all over again."

So the subject that had made his family meal rough hadn't been the Charlie issue, it had been Tate's broken engagement....

"Your family didn't take it seriously either?" Tanya asked.

"Only seriously enough to be annoyed. But I *am* serious—Katie and I are—"

"I know, broken up."

"Once and for all."

Why was there that part of her that wanted so much to buy the finality he was selling? To think that it was even a possibility that Tate McCord and Katie Whitcomb-Salgar could be no more for real? It shouldn't have any impact on her at all, one way or another.

And yet it did. It raised a hope in her that was completely out of place. That shouldn't have been there. That she didn't *want* there. It made her feel as if she were walking a tightrope and had just discovered she didn't have a safety net. It shook her.

And she suddenly felt the need to get out of there. To get some distance in which to gather her wits and regain some balance. Some distance that would take her where Tate wasn't right there beside her, smelling so good, looking so good, and now not engaged....

"I think we've done enough here tonight," she said, getting to her feet. "We've laid the groundwork. We can probably call it quits."

She knew that had come out of the blue and the hastiness of it had obviously confused Tate. "We haven't even talked about the present-day McCords—with the exception of Gabby," he pointed out.

"I know about the present-day McCords," Tanya said as she closed her notebook, clipped her pen to it and began to make a pile of the photographs she was taking. "Your mother looks after the household and family and does charity work. Blake is the CEO of McCord's Jewelers. You're a surgeon. There's the twins, Penny and Paige— Penny is a jewelry designer, Paige is a geologist and gemologist. And there's Charlie, who's a student at Southern Methodist University and who we've also talked about tonight. Did I leave anyone out?"

"No, that's the lot of us," Tate confirmed, his tone still perplexed.

He stood then, too. And while Tanya hoped it was just a polite acknowledgment that she was about to leave, instead he said, "I'll walk you back to your mother's place."

"That's okay, you don't have to," she said, wishing it hadn't sounded so panicky.

"I want to," he assured her.

"Whatever," Tanya said, trying for aloofness and failing as she picked up everything and held it in front of her like a schoolgirl carrying books. Carrying books close and tight and protectively.

"Did I tick *you* off somehow?" Tate asked as they headed for the path that wound away from the pool.

"No. I don't know why you would think that."

"Maybe because you're acting as if I just grew fangs or something. Is my *not* being engaged scary to you?"

Terrifying. Although she wasn't exactly sure why, except possibly that she was terrified that she might give in to that wave of elation that had washed through her when he'd told her his engagement was off and let down her guard with him.

But if she let down her guard, then what? She could end up just another person he occupied his time with while he was on one of his innumerable breaks from Katie Whitcomb-Salgar. And all Tanya could think was, *Oh, no, not me.*

She just wasn't sure she could stick to it.

Although there *was* still the issue of her mother and her mother's job, and the fact that Tate was her mother's employer....

Reminding herself of that helped. It actually allowed her to begin to relax again.

Even if Tate wasn't engaged any longer, there was still a good—a *very* good—reason why she absolutely couldn't and wouldn't let anything happen with him. Anything even like last night when she'd thought he might be on the verge of kissing her.

Then something else that seemed completely unlikely occurred to her and compelled her to say, "When did this particular breakup come about? I didn't think Katie was even in Dallas."

"We broke up about a week ago but she wanted to tell her parents before word got out and I agreed to that. She is in Florida with them. She called this morning to let me know our private gag order was lifted and I could tell whoever I wanted."

So the engagement had been axed before Tate had found Tanya in the library on Friday night. It didn't have anything to do with the fact that he might be entertaining some notion of diddling the help's daughter.

Tanya was relieved that that hadn't been the case. That she hadn't had anything to do with this particular breakup. She was also glad that she hadn't said anything along those lines that would have embarrassed her. She was a little embarrassed anyway that she'd even had such a thought. Which was probably—like her thoughts of him kissing her—nothing but some kind of flight of fancy that she wasn't even sure why she was having.

And she should just stop it, she told herself. Stop the flights of fancy, stop thinking anything was going on between them. And while she was at it, stop thinking about him every minute of the day and night, the way she had been!

They'd reached her front door when Tate said, "We haven't talked about tomorrow."

"No, we haven't," Tanya answered glibly, slowly settling down and coming to grips with herself and his news.

"I have to make my rounds in the morning, but I'm free in the afternoon. I thought I'd give you a tour of the McCord contributions to the city and end with an evening under the stars."

Tanya glanced up to the sky and then dropped her gaze to blue eyes that were watching her intently. "Isn't that what we just had? An evening under the stars?"

"I have something a *little* bit different in mind. What do you say?"

"Is it all for my report?" she asked to make it clear that that was the only thing she would agree to.

"Every bit of it," he assured without hesitation.

"Then okay."

"You still haven't answered my question about if my being *un*-engaged is somehow scary, though," he said then, smiling slightly.

"No, you're being un-engaged is not scary," she said as if the question itself was silly.

"You honestly did just decide on the spur of the moment that it was time to stop working tonight?"

"Yes. Why would I care if you're engaged or not?"

Okay, she'd been doing so well and then she'd gone and taken it too far by sounding defensive.

"I care," he said quietly, pointedly, continuing to gaze into her eyes.

And then she felt rotten. If he had been anyone else and this had been any other situation, she wouldn't have reacted the way she had to the revelation that he and the woman he'd intended to marry had ended things. She would have been more caring, more compassionate. She wouldn't have thought about herself.

"I'm sorry," she apologized. "I guess I was kind of callous. Even if you have had a lot of ups and downs in your relationship, that doesn't mean that you wouldn't be upset—"

"I'm not upset," he said. "And I don't mean to sound callous either, and maybe sometime I'll tell you why this *didn't* upset me, but what I do care about is that now I don't have to pretend that I'm committed to something—or someone—I'm not committed to."

"Because you're a bad secret-keeper?"

"Because I wanted to do this and I couldn't," he said, surprising her by coming in for the briefest, lightest, faintest of kisses.

A kiss Tanya didn't even have time to close her eyes for or respond to. And yet, a kiss that still managed to leave her lips tingling and her pulse racing.

But in spite of that, when it was over she shook her head at him. "Engaged or not, you can't do that," she said firmly.

"Why not?" he asked, smiling as if it was him who wasn't taking her seriously now.

"My mother works for you."

"I know that doesn't make for the most ideal situation, but—"

"But nothing," Tanya managed to sound so much stronger in her convictions than she felt. Especially since she was willing him with every ounce of her being to kiss her again...

Tate's smile went crooked—and almost too sexy and endearing to resist—before he said, "I do love a challenge."

"I'm not a challenge, I'm the housekeeper's daughter."

He nodded but she wasn't convinced that their very different social positions meant as much to him as it needed to.

Then, rather than address it again, he merely said, "I'll call you when I finish with rounds tomorrow. Plan on all afternoon and evening."

"To compile data for my report and that's it?" she said with a warning note in her voice.

"Nose to the grindstone all the way," he assured her.

"Okay," Tanya agreed a second time.

"See you then," he said.

Tanya nodded and watched him go, trying not to drink in every detail of his backside, of the confident swagger to his walk. Trying not to wish he was still standing in front of her instead, kissing her again. Kissing her more thoroughly than he had. His arms around her. Hers around him. Her hands slipping down to that very, very fine derriere she watched disappear into the shadows of the trees.

He's not engaged anymore....

The thought ran through her head like a wood nymph, taunting her. Tantalizing her.

But she chased it away.

Engaged, not engaged, it was all the same to her. She had more reasons than that not to give in to the attraction that kept sneaking in and taking over.

But it *did* keep sneaking in.

And taking over.

And the only way she had to combat it at that moment was to also remind herself that the odds of his not-engaged status lasting were slim to none.

And there was no way she was going to let herself be his hiatus-honey.

Chapter Seven

Tate was still thinking about Tuesday night—and Tanya—on Wednesday as he drove home from making rounds at the hospital.

Not that it was unusual these days for him to be thinking about Tanya. But what had her on his mind today was trying to figure out what had happened last night. One minute they'd been talking and—he'd thought—having a good time, and the next minute the tone had changed and she was up and out of there. In a hurry.

It had been obvious that it was the news about his broken engagement that had put a damper on things. But why? Why should that have caused her to shy away?

Certainly there was nothing about it that *should* have sent her running into the night. Or reacting like his family, either.

He had no idea what would put Tanya's response in the

same category as his mother's and Blake's, but even if it was just in the same general ballpark—even if Tanya had felt some kind of affront to all of womankind—he hated the thought that something about him or something that he'd done had put her off like that.

It didn't bother him that his family might be disgusted that he was once again not following through with Katie. But Tanya? That was something else entirely. It bothered him that Tanya might think badly of him.

It bothered the hell out of him....

And that was new.

Caring what someone thought of him? He'd gone through his life not really considering what anyone thought about him. Let alone what the staff had thought about him. Or a member of the staff's family—most of whom he'd never so much as met or heard about.

Yet here he was, being eaten up by the thought that the housekeeper's daughter might think he was a jerk.

The housekeeper's daughter—that had been Tanya's sticking point last night, that he couldn't kiss her *because* she was JoBeth's daughter. But while that was also what he'd been raised to believe—that there was to be no fraternizing with the help and, certainly, not with the help's daughter—he was wondering now if Tanya had only used that as an excuse. If the real reason had been that she didn't think much of him and so didn't want him kissing her. Or doing anything that might make things more personal between them. If the real reason was that her opinion of him was that low....

Oh, yeah, he definitely hated that thought. It was actually something he'd considered to be a possibility earlier, too—when she'd slipped and let him know she thought he'd lived his life wrapped in cotton he'd had the impression that she didn't think too highly of him then—but he liked it even less now.

So much less that he decided he couldn't just let it slide. He was going to have to talk to her about it. And if that meant trotting out details of his and Katie's private relationship to the help's daughter?

He knew no one would approve of that.

But this was his business and it was important to him.

Although why it was so important he still wasn't sure.

He wasn't sure why it was so important. He wasn't sure if he should let anything personal develop between them. He wasn't sure what was going on with him when it came to Tanya.

He was only sure of one thing—that kissing her last night had been something he'd been wanting to do and denying himself because of his agreement with Katie to go on pretending they were engaged until she gave him the go-ahead to stop. And last night, when he'd been given the go-ahead, kissing Tanya had been uppermost in his mind the whole time they'd been looking at those old family photos.

Only the fact that he *had* kissed her hadn't left him rid of the desire. It had only made him want to kiss her again. And better.

Which she'd told him not to do. And if she'd told him not to do it because she thought he'd been a jerk to Katie, he needed to amend that impression.

Of course if she'd told him not to kiss her again because she just didn't like him...

It was probably better to find that out sooner rather than later.

But simply telling himself that brought back the caring-what-someone-thought-of-him thing.

Because damn it all, housekeeper's daughter or not, he *did* care what Tanya thought of him, and he cared so much it was unsettling.

He'd lost his best friend to war. He'd spent a miserable year himself in the Middle East. He'd come home unable to look at anything the way he had before. But today *this* was what was bothering him?

Regardless of how he tried to dismiss it, though, yes, *this* was what was bothering him. Over and above everything else, he couldn't shed the idea that Tanya Kimbrough, the housekeeper's daughter, might not like him.

That was the long and the short of it.

Unfortunately, coming to that conclusion didn't get him any closer to understanding it.

Or to understanding why it seemed as though Tanya's effect on him was growing by the day....

"Okay, okay, I get it—the McCords are generous, civic-minded, caring people who have funded, or partially funded, or raised money for, or sponsored innumerable things that all benefit the citizens of Dallas!" Tanya said, crying uncle as Tate pulled into the parking lot of a plane-tarium that was named for the McCords.

He'd called at one that afternoon to let her know he was back from the hospital. By two they were on a tour of the city. They'd been to the zoo, where the McCords were responsible for a new aviary. They'd been to Meridian Hospital, where an entire surgical suite owed its existence to the prominent family. They'd been to the historical museum, where a new wing was being built by them.

They'd driven by two shelters—one for families, another for women and children. They'd been to or driven past a number of other, smaller beneficiaries of the McCord generosity and energies, and it was nearly nine o'clock Wednesday night when they arrived at the planetarium.

"This is where we're having dinner," Tate told her.

"I'm not sure Gummi bears are going to do it for me," Tanya said. "Besides, I think we're too late—there's only that truck in the lot and the sign says closed."

Tate turned off the engine anyway, giving her that mystery-man smile he flashed to intrigue her. Then he got out.

Tanya wasn't sure what he had up the sleeve of the pale blue shirt he was wearing with a pair of darker blue slacks that fit him like a dream, but she also wasn't sure she was going to go along with it. So she stayed where she was, watching him come around to open her door.

"Honestly," she said from her seat, laying a hand on the notebook she'd been writing in for the last several hours. "I have a complete picture of the McCord good deeds. I don't need to see the stars you provide, too. I'll just add the planetarium to the list, I promise."

He didn't say a word. He merely crooked a long, upturned index finger, motioning for her to get out.

Tanya sighed, took hold of her notebook and pen and complied, hoping he wasn't thinking that snack food at the planetarium was a meal. She'd been so unreasonably excited about seeing him today that she hadn't been hungry for lunch and had literally just waited by the phone for his call. But with only a single pancake to tide her over for the entire day, she was starving and worried that her stomach was going to begin growling at any moment.

Once she was out of the car Tate closed the door and led

the way to the planetarium's entrance. When they reached it he didn't even try the door. He just tapped on it—three quick raps of his knuckles.

In answer, it was opened from inside by a man who knew Tate on sight. He said, "Nice to see you, Doctor McCord."

"You, too, Andrew."

The man stepped aside and Tate ushered Tanya in ahead of him, following behind.

Once they were in the planetarium's lobby, Andrew closed the doors and Tate again addressed him. "Are we all set?"

"Yes, sir," the man answered. "You can go right in."

Tate swept an arm toward the theater and that was where he and Tanya went while Andrew quietly brought up the rear as far as the theater doors.

There was already a night sky projected overhead when Tanya and Tate alone entered the large domed room.

"I give you Paris under a full moon," Tate said then, pointing to the Eiffel Tower silhouetted on the horizon line.

Andrew closed the theater doors, leaving them bathed in the glow of that moon and the dim, milky illumination of the mock streetlights that also dotted the horizon line, surrounding them as if they were on a Parisian avenue.

They were standing in a clear space at the rear of the auditorium seats that descended around the projection platform. Nearby were two chairs positioned at a linen-covered bistro table that was set with china and silver. A small bouquet of white roses and lit candles drew Tanya there just as soft music began to play over the speaker system.

"Wow" was all she said.

Tate joined her at the table. "You'll notice that we have French wine, French bread and French cheeses to start," he said, pointing to the wine that was opened and waiting for them, and at the artfully arranged platter of appetizers. Then he indicated the smaller table nearby and the covered dishes that it held. "When we're ready, we have roasted pork with fennel and herbs, green salad with mustard vinaigrette, flageolet beans with chervil and butter and—for dessert—*pots de crème au chocolat.*"

"Let's start with that," Tanya joked.

"The chocolate?"

"I'm kidding. Sort of…"

He smiled. "We can if you want."

"No. But what are those beans?" she asked, feeling uncultured because she didn't have any idea what they were.

Tate leaned near enough to confide and make her pulse quicken. "I called the best French restaurant I know, took their recommendation and memorized the name but I'd never heard of them before, either. Apparently it's some kind of light-green bean."

Tanya laughed, feeling better about her ignorance, and tried very, very hard not to appear as impressed as she was by all the trouble he'd gone to.

"Is this supposed to be a part of my report?" she asked then.

"The planetarium is. But the dinner is just for us."

"There is no *us*," she said reflexively, maybe to counteract the fact that she'd liked hearing it.

"There's you. There's me. We have to eat and there's food. We've just put in a full eight-hour workday that's finally finished. And now we can have dinner. That's all there is to it," he assured her.

It didn't seem as if that was all there was to it. It seemed very datelike and incredibly romantic. Which meant that, under the circumstances, she should put up a fuss.

"You wouldn't be trying to compromise my journalistic integrity, would you?" she asked.

"Not my intention."

"What *is* your intention?" she challenged.

He smiled that mystery-man smile once more. "To have dinner after a long day," he insisted, holding out one of the chairs for her.

She still thought he had something up his sleeve but she didn't know what it could be and she *was* starving, and this was all just too appealing for her to turn down.

So she sat in the chair and slipped the linen napkin from the table to the lap of her khaki slacks while Tate went around and took the other chair for himself.

"This *could* actually look bad for you," she goaded him as he poured them both wine and offered her the cheese and bread first.

"Why is that?"

"Well, first you spend the day showing me all the things you and your family do to benefit other people, then you shut down this whole planetarium just to suit yourself. How many small children who need to know where Orion's Belt is for school tomorrow could fail because they came here tonight and found the place closed just for you?"

"It's always closed on Wednesday night," he told her. "And I'm paying Andrew overtime for this, along with getting him seats to some sold-out concert his daughter wants to go to. No one is being hurt, and the only inconvenience is voluntary and well compensated."

"So all in all, today and tonight were to convince me that you're perfect. There are no flaws in the McCords," she teased him slightly as they ate their appetizers and sipped their wine.

"Nobody's perfect. But I know it's easy for people with the kind of life we lead to seem shallow and I wanted to show you that we aren't."

He paused a split second and then said, "Well, to be honest, shallowness has been true of me to some extent. At least it was. I hope it isn't anymore, and I wanted to be sure it was clear that it isn't the case with the McCords in general."

"Is that why you became a doctor—to stop being shallow?" Tanya asked.

"Actually, it was part of being shallow that *led* me to be a doctor."

"How so?"

"I didn't do it because I was being altruistic or had some higher calling to help humanity," he said as if he disapproved of his own motivation now. "I did it partly because Buzz was going to do it—I told you, his whole family for generations had been in the military, but Buzz didn't want to be in combat. He thought becoming a doctor would give him a better way to do his part. My earliest thought was that I'd give medical school a shot so we could party through that the way we had through college."

"You thought *medical* school was going to be a party?"

"Buzz and I had a knack for making *everything* a party. But my next thought about medicine was that I needed my own thing—Blake had the family business, that was *his* thing. I hated business and didn't want to share his spotlight. So I figured I'd be a doctor—plenty of splash and sparkle and status and respect in that. Then I went all the way to becoming a surgeon because I liked that it was one of the least personal of the specialties—I could stroll in, cut, stroll out."

"That's quite an admission," Tanya said, surprised that he'd made it.

"I don't feel that way now or maybe I wouldn't admit it."

They moved on to their meal with Tate serving her as she said, "You don't regret becoming a doctor, then?"

"No. In fact, I think that if I hadn't, I wouldn't have been able to get through the last year and a half. It's the only thing that's kept me going, that's let me feel as if I could contribute something."

There were two questions that popped into Tanya's mind in response to that. But the most obvious went in the direction of his feelings since his friend's death. And she could already see shadows forming around his mood just at the mention of Buzz, dampening the more lighthearted tone that had followed them through the day and evening. She was loath to explore that and cause those shadows to cover everything. So instead she asked the other question his comment had raised.

"It wasn't Katie who kept you going during the last year and a half?"

Tate shook his handsome head. "Katie is great, don't get me wrong. I think the world of her."

Which was why he'd likely get back with her, Tanya reminded herself to keep this romantic dinner from swaying her too much.

"But the truth is," Tate continued, "what was between Katie and me was just not enough to make Buzz's death any easier."

"Is that why you ended the engagement?" That was private and personal and off-limits for a McCord staff member or a staff member's daughter to ask—again Tanya knew her mother would be appalled. But she was doing it anyway

because she just couldn't stop herself. Even though this information was not anything she would include in her story
and it was purely her own curiosity that had a hold of her.

"*I* didn't end the engagement," Tate said. "It started out
as Katie's idea."

"It *started out* as her idea?"

"It wasn't a big dramatic breakup. There wasn't a fight
or an argument that made her throw the ring in my face, or
had me demanding it back. It was like everything has
always been between Katie and me—civilized." Tate
laughed a wry chuckle. "That was the problem—not a lot
of passion. She came to me—when we could work it into
our schedules—and said she'd been feeling like our getting
married might be a mistake because there *wasn't* any kind
of overwhelming passion between us. That we both might
deserve more. And I had to agree with her."

"That *is* civilized," Tanya said a bit facetiously,
thinking that such civility was reason enough for her not
to take the breakup seriously. If Tate and Katie had had
a knock-down, drag-out, relationship-killing fight, it
might be easier for her to believe they wouldn't get back
together. But as it was, this sounded like what she knew
of their other breakups—a no-harm, no-foul split that
was easily repaired.

"Like I said, there was a shortage of passion. Without
it, it's easy to be *civilized*," Tate said, apparently not
offended by her gentle sarcasm. "I think that's also why it
didn't upset me to any great degree—once Katie brought
it up, not getting married seemed to make more sense than
getting married did. I thought she was right—people
should get married because they can't stand to be apart, and
that was definitely not Katie and me. I just don't want you

to think that the engagement ended because I treated Katie badly or dumped her on some kind of stupid whim—"

"Like in the past?" Tanya teased him as he served their desserts.

"We never separated because I treated Katie badly," he defended himself. "That isn't my style."

Tanya smiled, pleased that he seemed so concerned that she might think that of him. She didn't. She knew his success with women had always been in his good treatment of them. But rather than let him off the hook, she said, "But there *were* times when you dumped her on a whim?"

"Katie and I have a long history. Sure, there was a time or two when my reasons for breaking it off with her were pretty shallow—I told you I could be that way before. But to be fair, there was once when Katie dumped me to take a guy with better hair to a country-club dance."

Tanya couldn't imagine anyone with better hair, but she didn't say it. Instead she said, "I don't know, this breakup doesn't sound too much more serious than that."

"It is," Tate insisted as they finished their desserts. "I guarantee that hair was not an issue. I just want you to know that me being some kind of creep *also* wasn't the issue."

Tanya looked more closely at him, seeing just how important it was to him that she not have a negative impression. She was surprised by it.

"Why is what I think such a big deal to you all of a sudden? Even if I refer to you in my report as the family playboy it wouldn't come as news to anyone."

"It's not your *report* that worries me," he said seriously, meeting her eyes to lend weight to his words.

"What *does* worry you?"

He studied her for a moment but somehow in that moment

he apparently decided not to answer her question because he smiled a slow, small smile and said, "I'm a little worried right now that maybe you didn't get enough dessert."

Okay, so she *was* trying to spoon out every last creamy drop of that *pots de crème*. She'd just hoped he hadn't noticed.

She smiled sheepishly back at him. "It was fabulous."

Just when Tanya was about to repeat the question he'd dodged, there was a knock on the theater door, and Andrew poked his head in. "The night cleaning crew is here, Doctor McCord."

"Okay, thanks, Andrew," Tate answered. Glancing at Tanya once more he said, "I'm afraid that's our cue—I promised we'd leave so we didn't hold up the cleaning crew."

"Ah, Paris, it was nice while it lasted," Tanya joked as she set her napkin on the table and stood to go.

The opportunity to explore his concerns seemed to have escaped her by the time they got to the car. Tanya used the drive back to the mansion as an opportunity to get a few facts straight about the McCord philanthropies. Then they were home again and Tate was once more walking her to the bungalow's door.

"On Friday night there's a formal dinner, dance and silent auction at the country club—technically, it's a charity ball. Anyway, my family is sponsoring it to raise money for IMC—the International Medical Corps. It's the group I worked with in Iraq. What do you say to going with me? I'm sure you'll want to sample some of the glitz that goes into being a McCord so you can report on that, too," Tate said as they reached the porch and stepped into the glow of the light her mother had left on for her.

"Formal—as in tuxedos and prom dresses?" Tanya asked.

"I'll be in a tuxedo, yes. But I've never thought of what the women wear as *prom* dresses. Fancy, yes, but—"

"Either way, I don't own anything like that. I'll probably be able to pick up photographs of the event from the society pages to include that element."

"How about this, then," he said as if he didn't intend to take no for an answer. "I have surgeries scheduled all day tomorrow, but what if I take you on a little shopping trip in the evening to outfit you?"

"With a fancy dress?" Tanya said, excited and a little put off by the idea all at once.

"A dress, shoes, whatever it takes to get you there."

"Is this a case of charity beginning at home?" she asked with some distaste.

"Absolutely not. It's a case of my having to go on Friday night because my family initiated it on my behalf. I haven't been doing many of these things since I got back from Baghdad but I have to go to this one and I've been dreading it. Then I started thinking about getting you to go with me, and…no more dread. And since you'd be doing me a favor, it wouldn't be right for you to have to foot the bill for new clothes to do it."

Memories of peeking through the bushes as a child and seeing McCord women dressed in elaborate gowns, the men in tuxedos, flashed through Tanya's mind. It had seemed more like a fantasy than anything real and while some of the events had been held at the mansion, she'd always wondered what the ones held at other places were like.

And now Tate was offering her the opportunity to step into the fantasy.

Actually, he was asking her to do it for him, as a favor.

And it *would* be something she could use for her story....

"Say yes," he urged as if he knew she was weakening. "I'll call and make sure there's an endless supply of *pots de crème* there just for you."

That made her laugh.

"An insider's look," he reminded, "that's what you signed on for. Friday night will be that."

"Okay..." she said tentatively because she really wasn't sure this was a good idea.

Tentative or not, it was enough to make him smile. "Great!"

"But the only thing I'll accept from you is advice on a dress. I'll buy it myself," she added, her pride taking the forefront.

"No way," he said firmly. "You're doing me the favor, so the dress is my treat."

Pride notwithstanding, as the image of the kind of gowns she'd seen worn for these events became clearer in her mind, she began to fear she might be biting off more than she could chew financially. But rather than completely concede yet, she said, "I'll make a deal with you. Tomorrow I'll call the station and see if they'll buy the dress as a business expense. If they won't—"

"Then you'll let me. Deal. But either way, keep tomorrow night open for shopping."

An evening of shopping for a fairy-tale gown with Tate—as much as Tanya told herself she was wading into risky waters, she couldn't help the little thrill that went through her at the prospect.

"All right, all right, all right," she said as if she were conceding to something against her will.

And then there was no more to be said except good-night. Only she discovered that she wasn't eager to end her time with him despite the fact that there had been several hours of it.

Maybe he felt the same way because he didn't seem in any hurry to go. She did have the sense that he had something else on his mind, though. She just couldn't guess what it was.

Then, in a hushed voice that let her know that what he was confiding wasn't easy for him to reveal, he said, "Since Buzz died, since coming back from Iraq, things haven't been the same for me. They haven't been as…I don't know, as much fun, I guess. Then I found you in the library Friday night and…" He shrugged. "Things are somehow looking better and better.…"

Tanya didn't know what *things* he was talking about but before she could ask, he added, "I can't stand the idea that you might think the worst of me when you seem more and more like the best thing that's happened to me in a long time.…"

"It makes a difference what the housekeeper's daughter thinks of you?" she asked.

"It makes a difference what *you* think about me," he said, staring deeply into her eyes.

Then he leaned forward and it was obvious he wanted to kiss her. But rather than doing it, he waited, poised, giving her the chance not to let it happen.

And she knew she shouldn't let it happen. She'd even told him point-blank the night before not to do it again.

But there he was, the man who—in the last few days— had let her see past the charm, the arrogance, the entitlement she'd known of him before, into the vulnerable part of him now. There he was, his starkly chiseled face only inches above hers, *wanting* to kiss her. And she wanted him to.

So she didn't say no. She didn't even shake her head. She just tipped her chin....

It was go-ahead enough.

Tate came the rest of the way, pressing his mouth to hers in a kiss that wasn't quick or brief or offhand like the one the night before. It was a thoughtful, studied kiss with lips parted just slightly and his breath warm and sweet against her skin. It was a kiss that lasted long enough for Tanya to kiss him in return—heaven help her....

Then it ended and Tate straightened to his full height again, smiling a soft, quiet smile.

"Tomorrow night," he said.

Tanya merely nodded and watched him turn and walk away because she was still a little stunned at the thought that he'd just allowed her a glimpse of himself that was unveiled, undisguised.

And that it was that man—the man behind the McCord veneer—who had kissed her....

Chapter Eight

"You're not Cinderella, Tanya."

"I know, Mama." Tanya had probably told her mother more than she should have. She hadn't told her about how Tate had been uncommonly open with her at the end of the previous evening or about the kiss. But she *had* told JoBeth about the charity ball and the dress she was scheduled to go out and shop for with Tate in twenty minutes.

"You're not Cinderella and Tate McCord isn't Prince Charming—or even Doctor Charming—who will whisk you away to the castle to live happily ever after. Not that you *couldn't* be whisked away to something wonderful," her mother added. "It's just that I would want you whisked away to something wonderful by someone better for you than a McCord."

That made Tanya's hairbrush pause in midstroke. "*Better* than a McCord?" she said as she went on to sweep her hair into a twist up the back of her head, leaving curls to cascade at her crown. "I thought you were the McCords' biggest fan."

"I am. But so much money and power sometimes brings the weight of the world down on their shoulders—like Tate seems to be feeling now. It makes them complicated people with complicated lives. And sometimes all that leads them to look outside of their own circle to escape for a while. But not forever, Tanya. Never forever. I've been around here long enough, I have eyes and ears, I know what goes on. And they always end up right back in the middle of that circle. With the same people who have always been there...."

"I know, Mama," Tanya repeated. "I'm going to the charity ball to see firsthand what goes on in that circle of theirs for my report. I have to let Tate pay for the dress because the station I work for doesn't have that kind of budget, and *I* certainly can't afford it. But afterward I'll have the dress cleaned, wrap it up and give it back to him. And I'm not letting any of this go to my head. I promise."

JoBeth didn't look reassured as she stood in the doorway of Tanya's bedroom watching Tanya zip the side zipper of the short-sleeved, black-and-white checked sundress she'd opted to wear because it was easy to get on and off when she tried on gowns.

It was also extremely formfitting and boosted her breasts just a little above the scoop neck. But it was the easy on-and-off that had made her choose it, not the hint of cleavage it exposed. Or so she told herself....

"Don't let it go to your head, don't let it go anywhere else, either," JoBeth cautioned. "It's dangerous for you to start wanting to live the way they live. To want what they have. To want to be one of them..."

"Everyone wants what they have and to live the way they live—that's why their every move makes news. But I *don't* want to be *one* of them."

"It's even more dangerous to want one of them for yourself. Or to want one of them to want you…"

"I don't want that, either," Tanya swore as she applied a light dusting of blush, a second layer of mascara and some lip gloss to finish getting ready.

When she had—and with Tate due any minute—she grabbed her purse and went to meet her mother face-to-face at the bedroom doorway, uncertain if JoBeth was going to go on blocking it or let her through.

"It's just a job, Mama," Tanya said. "Work. A news report I'm doing. When I have all the material I need I'll go my way and Tate will go his, and that will be it."

Her mother stared at her, frowning.

But when the doorbell rang and they both knew it was Tate there to pick Tanya up, JoBeth did step back and let Tanya out.

Tanya kissed her mother's cheek as she went around her and said, "Don't wait up—I know you have an early day tomorrow." Then she headed for the front door.

And as she did, she thought that she might have just lied a little when she'd told her mother that she didn't want Tate for herself.

She was definitely *trying* not to want him—that much was true.

But was she succeeding?

Almost not at all…

Shopping McCord-style was not like any other shopping Tanya had ever done. Tate didn't take her to a mall or a department store where there were racks or shelves or displays of clothes for her to pick from. He took her to a shop she'd never even heard of called Dana and Delaney's.

From the outside it looked more like a well-appointed doctor's office and even when they went inside they were welcomed by a woman who stood and came out from behind an antique reception desk to greet Tate by name.

After amenities were exchanged and Tanya was introduced, she and Tate were taken to a private sitting room where they were handed over to Hildy, their fashion advisor.

Hildy invited them to sit on the plush velvet settee, offered them glasses of champagne and then presented them with an array of the kind of gowns Tanya had only seen for herself when spying on McCord social events—all of them a very long way from prom dresses.

Tanya narrowed the field down to five and then she and Hildy adjourned to an equally elaborate dressing room to try on the gowns. She refused to model them for Tate and chose for herself which she liked best, accepting Hildy's confirmation that the ruby-red silk taffeta strapless gown that followed her every curve in perfectly petaled tiers to the floor was The One.

Tanya took Hildy's recommendation for shoes and a matching clutch, stood still while the seamstress pinned it for alterations and hemming and then was assured the dress would be delivered to the McCord mansion the next afternoon. Never did she get so much as an inkling of how much she'd spent, even when Tate instructed Hildy to have the bill sent to his office. But whatever the ensemble had cost, Tanya had never worn anything as sophisticated or elegant and was as excited to wear it again as she had been to wear her Halloween costumes as a small child.

Since Tate hadn't been able to pick her up until nearly eight o'clock, it was after eleven by the time they left Dana and Delaney's—long after the shop had closed to the public or anyone else who didn't receive the special attention allotted the McCords. But just when Tanya was silently lamenting the fact that the evening would end so soon, Tate said, "I was in one surgery after another all day and never had a chance to eat—I'm starving. Are you hungry?"

"No, but I don't mind if you want to stop and have something." In fact, she was far more pleased with the prospect of tacking on any amount of time she could to this evening than she should have been, but she didn't let it show.

Tate chose a small sandwich shop only blocks from home. Tanya declined a sandwich but didn't require much persuasion to agree to a warm chocolate chip cookie and a glass of iced tea.

They took the food to a booth in the rear of the deserted restaurant and sat down.

"So," Tate said as he unwrapped his sandwich, "when we were thirteen Buzz and I wanted to learn to surf."

Tanya had no idea where that remark had come from but assuming he was merely making conversation, she said, "Uh-huh…"

"After school one day we decided to practice down the entrance stairs. Dumb idea, I know. Of course it didn't work, my surfboard got away from me and went through a window. Your mom never said a word—she had the mess cleaned up and the glass replaced before my parents got home and they never knew anything had happened. But the look your mother gave me…" Tate shook his head. "She didn't have to say anything. I knew better than to ever try that in the house again. How come she was giving me that same look from behind you when I picked you up tonight?"

Ah, *that* was where this was going....

Tanya didn't see any reason to beat around the bush. "She's worried about me seeing so much of you."

"Am I a bad influence?" he half joked as he took a bite of his sandwich.

"Yes," she said with a laugh. "But that's not what Mama is upset about. There was a time—I was seven or eight—when my mother realized that I was pressing my nose up against the window of the McCord life, so to speak, and dreaming that that was where I belonged. Mom wanted to snap me out of it to make sure I knew that your lifestyle wasn't the reality for me. Or for most people. But now she's afraid I might slip back into the fantasy again if I hang out with you too much."

"How did she snap you out of it?" he asked.

Tanya smiled slightly—as much at the thought of her mother's wisdom as at the sight of his angular features shadowed by a hint of the beard he apparently hadn't had the chance to shave between surgery and getting her to the dress shop. It made him look rugged and scruffily handsome and so sexy that it did make him a danger to her— dangerously attractive....

"How did my mother snap me out of it...." Tanya repeated because she'd been a little lost in admiring him and needed to catch up. "She sent me to the real world," she said.

"*Real* people, *real* world—I think I'm detecting a theme," he joked.

Tanya didn't respond to that. She merely went on explaining how her mother had focused her. "The way you live may be the real world for you, but it isn't the real world for most people—the world that my mom knew I would have to live and work and function and survive in— and it was important to her that I be aware of that. So she started to send me for most weekends, holidays and vacations to stay with my grandparents whether she could get away or not."

"I take it your grandparents *do* live in the real world?"

"They're regular working people—before they retired my grandfather was in construction, my grandmother was an elementary school custodian. And I saw firsthand through them what I didn't see living with my mom inside the walls of your world even if I wasn't a part of your world."

"What did you see?" Tate asked as if he were genuinely interested.

"I saw firsthand what it was like for people to have to stretch a dollar to make ends meet when they didn't have leftovers from the McCord kitchen to supplement their groceries, for one," she said, trying not to bask in the intensity of his interest in her at that moment—even though it *was* nice to have such undivided attention from him.... "I saw firsthand what can happen when someone gets hurt on the job and loses income," she continued. "I saw how medical expenses can cost people their savings, their house, everything, and how those people might not know where to turn—"

"Did that happen to your grandparents?" he asked with what sounded like alarm.

"Some of it. Some happened to their good friends, to their next-door neighbors who ended up having to move in with their son when hard times hit. It was all heart-wrenching no matter who it was happening to. I just saw what it is to live the life *I* was born to, not the life you were.

My grandparents also made sure I knew things my mom had protected me from—"

"Such as?"

"How hard it had been for Mama to have my father walk out on her and leave her with a kid and no child support. My mom didn't want to burden me with her own problems, and I was only two when my father took a hike, so my earliest memories are of living in the housekeeper's cottage, playing in your kitchen or on the grounds of your house while my mother worked. I didn't have any idea what my mom had been through or how tough it had been for her, or how easy it was for a man to dump his family, not support his kid and get away with it."

Tate had finished eating and he wadded up his sandwich wrapper. But then he sat back, laid a long arm across the back of the bench on his side of the booth and seemed in no hurry to move on. Instead, his attention was still on her, studying her.

"It's strange, it seems as if you've always been around and because of that I thought I knew you—*some,* anyway. But I really don't, do I?"

"I guess you're getting to," Tanya pointed out. "Although I don't know why knowing me would be one of your priorities."

"Because you're an interesting person?"

"Oh, I know," she said facetiously, laughing. "I'm fascinating."

Tate ignored that. He went on watching her as if she was intriguing him regardless of what she thought. "So your mom sent you out to learn what the real world is like but now she's thinking you might get sucked into my world after all?"

"Into wanting to be a part of your world," Tanya amended. "What she doesn't realize is that since she made sure I *did* grow up seeing the real world, I also grew up feeling strongly that I should do something to shine a light on all the things that make the real world harder for people."

"That's why you went into the news business?"

"I'll grant you that it isn't saving someone's life on an operating table. Or doing the everyday work at the shelters—although I have volunteered and will again once I'm completely settled in in Dallas again. But through broadcast journalism I have the chance to air wrongs when I find them, to announce to a whole lot of people at once that there's help to be had and where to find it. I believe that that kind of guidance, that kind of exposure can make things change—"

"Exposure can make people change all right," Tate said, again as if it held meaning for him.

But before Tanya could explore it, he said, "A story about a rare diamond is hardly shining a light on the plight of the working man, though."

"Or the working woman," she added. "But I'm hoping it's my ticket to a position where that's what I can do. As it is now, standing in an ice storm reporting on slick roads doesn't make much of a difference. The diamond, the McCords, the feud with the Foleys—I'm just hoping it will earn me an anchor chair where I can do more."

Those clear, sky-blue eyes of his seemed to be boring into her. "I admire that drive to help. And you for being so determined."

That was gracious. And cordial. It wasn't *you're so hot I can hardly stand not to pull you under this table right now and make you mine.* But it still should have been gratifying.

And definitely the way things *should* have been between them.

It was just that she felt slightly disappointed by the impersonal sentiment it seemed to convey.

"It's not admirable, it's just why I became what I became and what I'm trying to do," she said. "It's also probably more than you wanted to hear and boring you to tears."

It was her own misplaced dejection that she was dodging when she gathered up the debris of his dinner and her own dessert and took it to the trash. She just didn't want to want anything more personal from him. She didn't want to want him....

And she had to nip it in the bud.

"We should probably get going," she announced when she returned to the table and found Tate still sitting where he had been before.

"It wasn't more than I wanted to hear," he said as if she'd just made that comment.

"Why? Because you're trying to get in touch with your employees and their families?"

She knew she was doing the same thing she had the night he'd told her he wasn't engaged anymore—being curt and somewhat abrasive to protect herself, to put distance between them.

But tonight he didn't seem to let it get to him. Very patiently, he said, "One thing I *never* am when I'm with you, Tanya, is bored. I like talking to you. Listening to you. Being with you."

Oh, that just made it worse....

"You don't have to—"

He laughed. "No one said I did. I just do."

He did stand, however, motioning toward the door to let

her know he'd leave because she'd made it so obvious that was what she was ready to do.

As he opened the shop door and then the passenger door of his car for her he said, "I'm betting the next thing you're going to say is that the only reason we're spending time together is for your job, and that's what we need to do—get back to business."

That *had* been what she was going to say. Basically.

"Well, my mom was right about tonight—it would be hard to sell what we've been doing as work."

"Think of it as being fitted for your uniform and then taking a lunch hour," he said wryly before he closed her door and went around to get in behind the wheel.

It was a short drive home and neither of them said anything during the trip.

Tanya had no idea what was on Tate's mind as he drove, but she was trying like mad not to be as aware as she was of every little detail—from the faint scent of his cologne, to the way his longish hair grazed the collar of his shirt, to his big, masculine hands on the steering wheel.

Her mother was right, she kept telling herself. To him, she was nothing but a brief stepping-outside-of-his-circle that he seemed to need right now. When that need passed, he'd go back inside the circle. Without her. And likely *with* Katie Whitcomb-Salgar.

No matter what he said....

When they got home Tate didn't immediately get out of the car. After turning off the engine he pivoted and stretched his arm across the top of her seat the way he'd been sitting at the restaurant, and said, "I have to make rounds in the morning but I'll be home by noon or so. Would you like to use the afternoon for Foley feud facts and diamond lore?"

The way he said that made Tanya smile in spite of herself. "Okay."

"When would you like to do it?"

Without thinking about it, she'd angled in her seat, too, and was looking at his traffic-stopping face and supple mouth, and suddenly remembering all too vividly that kiss of the night before.

"Why don't you come to the cottage?" she suggested. "Mama said she has electricians stringing the lights for the Labor Day party around the pool and the grounds tomorrow. The caterers are coming to put the final touches on the menu, and I think the tent people might be starting the set-up on top of everything else. So it seems like there will be too much going on to get any work done in the middle of all that."

"You know more about what's happening at my house than I do."

"That's my mother's job," she reminded him. "But if you come to the cottage I'll make lunch and we can sit on the patio back here, away from the fray."

Tate smiled a slow smile. "You're going to make me lunch?"

"It's the least I can do since you keep buying me dinner…and tonight's cookie. Don't expect anything fancy—just something we can munch on while you tell me about the skeletons in the McCord closet."

"Ah, yes, the skeletons…" he said with a comical wiggle of his eyebrows.

But even with their plans for the next day set, he didn't move. He merely went on looking at her for a moment longer before he said, "I keep wondering if things would be different if you and I had just met. If I was just Joe

Somebody and you were just Fledgling Newscaster, and our paths crossed—"

"You mean if you weren't a *McCord* and a member of the family that employs my mother, and I wasn't the housekeeper's daughter?" Another reminder to him.

"If we maybe met in the E.R. when you had a hot appendix that I had to remove—"

"Or we could meet because I was doing a story on up-and-coming surgeons in Dallas—at least then no blood would have to be spilled."

He laughed. "Okay, no blood. But then if I asked about your background, your family, where you grew up, you'd just think I wanted to know."

"No excess baggage," Tanya said.

"It might be nice...."

"Mmm," she agreed, thinking that it would be very, very nice. And make all of this so much different.

"Would you spend time with me then, just because I asked you to?" he probed.

"Not if your goal was to cut me open," she joked because she was leery of admitting too much.

"How about if my goal was just to be with you? Would you give me a chance?"

Should she lie and say no? Or should she go out on a limb with the truth?

"I'd probably give you a chance," she said tentatively. "But that isn't how things are."

He moved his hand from the back of her seat to her nape, toying with the stray wisps of hair that were free of the twist that held the rest, sending goose bumps down her spine.

"Still," he said, "if we'd have a chance under different

circumstances, it seems as if we should have a chance under these."

"Different circumstances would change things," she said, wondering how her voice could have been so soft when she'd wanted it to be firm.

He nodded, agreeing with her. But as his eyes held hers she didn't have the sense that he completely concurred. "It's hard to care about circumstances, sometimes, when they seem so far removed from what's here and now...."

"They aren't *so* far," Tanya said with a glance in the direction of the bungalow.

"Seems pretty far," he nearly whispered, compelling her to look at him again, to let him peer into her face, search her eyes with his.

His hand went from her nape to brush her cheek with the backs of his fingers and it felt so good she knew she should run. That she should open that car door, get out and just plain flee before this went any further.

But she didn't. Instead, somewhere along the way, she'd tipped her head into his caress.

She tipped it enough so that when he leaned forward to press his mouth to hers, she didn't even have to make an adjustment for it to happen.

And then there they were, kissing again. With a little familiarity tonight. With lips that were parted, with breath mingled, and nothing else seemed to matter from the moment it began.

Tate's hand returned to the back of her neck, cradling her head as he deepened the kiss, as his lips parted even more.

His other hand came to the side of her face then, while his mouth opened wider and his tongue made an appearance. Just the tip at first, testing the inner edge of her teeth, urging her to give him more leeway so he could meet and greet her tongue.

And her tongue seemed to have a mind of its own when he did, because the very second it encountered his it was just plain wanton. She gave as good as she got, every bit as adroitly, as adeptly, as aggressively until mouths were open wide and that kiss had turned wild and untamed.

Mouths clung and his arms came around her and pulled her to him. She let hers circle him, too, her breasts straining for his chest, their tips only barely finding him in the awkwardness of being separated by a gearshift. If only he'd waited until he'd walked her to the door tonight!

But then her mother might have seen this....

The thought of her mother cooled things for Tanya. Even though there was nothing in her that wanted it cooled. Even though everything in her was urging her on to more.

But this time her reminder was to herself—these weren't different circumstances. He wasn't Joe Somebody. Things were what they were and losing sight of that was not wise.

Tanya slipped her arms from around him and pressed her hands against his chest to push just enough to let him know this couldn't go on.

And yet she didn't push so much that she ended the kiss, it was Tate who had to do that—in stages, slowly, reluctantly.

But he did it, sighing softly when he had.

"We need to remember—" Tanya said, her voice a much sexier whisper than it should have been "—that I'm the housekeeper's daughter and that you're—"

"The guy who doesn't want any of that to matter."

"But it does," Tanya insisted.

He shook his head, denying it, but still Tanya moved the

rest of the way away from him to make it clear she meant what she said.

"Don't walk me to the door," she commanded because in her mind she could see them there—him kissing her again, her up against him in a seamless meeting of their bodies while mouths renewed what she was craving so much she could hardly stand it. She knew it would only make it more difficult to put the brakes on again. "Call me when you leave the hospital tomorrow so I'll know when to expect you," she added just before she opened the car door and left Tate behind. All without another word from him, only a frown that said he didn't like that she was going.

But Tanya went anyway, not glancing back, making a beeline for her mother's tiny house, feeling Tate's eyes on her the whole way.

Tate who would leave and return to his so, so much bigger house.

Where he belonged.

Where she didn't.

But that kiss? When their mouths met it was definitely in some no-man's-land in the middle, between his world and hers.

And as Tanya let herself into her mother's place she couldn't help wishing that there was some way to stake a claim of her own on a little of that no-man's-land.

Where she might actually be able to have something with Tate…

Chapter Nine

"I know I said that I was going to start my report with your grandfather Harry and Gavin Foley because the feud began with them, but after doing more research I think I have to take it a generation back from there—at least on the Foley side—to get the diamond in," Tanya said.

It was Friday afternoon and she and Tate were sitting at her mother's patio table outside the bungalow's back door. They were eating shepherd's pie and salads that Tanya had made. There were also two glasses of iced tea and a pitcher nearby for refills. But Tanya was less interested in the food than in trying to keep her mind off of Tate in order to concentrate on her work.

It wasn't easy. The table was small and even sitting across from each other their knees kept brushing together under it. And every contact caused those same little goose bumps that had gone down her spine when his hand had closed around the nape of her neck last night.

"The Santa Magdalena diamond goes back to Elwin Foley—Gavin's father," Tate supplied, obviously unaware of what merely being near him did to her.

Tanya picked up the story from there, reciting what she'd learned on the Internet. "And it was Elwin who—so the story goes—was sailing on the ship that was possibly a ship of thieves. The ship was carrying the diamond and other treasures of some sort when it went down. Not many of the crew survived but Elwin did, and rumor had it that he somehow made off with the diamond and a jewel-encrusted chest of coins."

"That's what I've always heard," Tate confirmed between bites.

"But according to my research," Tanya continued, "it wasn't verified that anything *but* the few crew members had made it off the ship until divers located the ship a few months ago. When no jewel-encrusted chest of coins and no Santa Magdalena diamond were found on it, the possibility that Foley *could* have made off with them increased."

"Or the diamond and the treasure weren't ever on board in the first place and the whole thing was a tall tale," Tate said.

Tanya had to glance up from her notes to look at him. She'd been trying to avoid too much eye contact because every time it happened she flashed back to that kiss they'd shared in his car the night before and all she really wanted to do was jump the man's bones. But she wasn't going to let him get away with pretending that there was no foundation to any of what she was hoping would be the pinnacle of her report—the Santa Magdalena diamond and its discovery.

"I've read the history of the stone," she said. "It was

mined in India. It's a flawless forty-eight-carat canary diamond with perfect clarity, and it's said to be even more beautiful than the Hope Diamond. There's no question that it exists—in case your next move is to try to convince me that even *that* was never any more than legend. There's also no question that the diamond's last known location was on that same ship that Elwin Foley was on. It's now known that the diamond hasn't been at the bottom of the ocean all this time, which means the likelihood that Foley got away with it is all the greater. And since the McCords ended up with the only Foley assets years ago…" Tanya let that conclude itself. But she did add, "And—supposedly—the diamond has also brought only bad luck to any hands it's fallen into and is believed to be cursed. Maybe a curse that's responsible for the McCord empire hitting its current slump?"

Tate grinned. "Cursed? Now *that* sounds more like myth or folklore than fact."

He was hedging and she knew it as surely as she knew she wanted to run her hands through his hair.

"The cursed part may be myth or folklore, but none of the rest of this is," Tanya said, standing her ground. "What you and Blake were talking about on Friday night came through loud and clear in the library—I know that your family is looking for the diamond. And with reason to believe that it can be found. So don't waste my time trying to make me think for a minute that we're talking fiction rather than fact."

"You'll never just roll over and make it easy for me, will you?" he said with more of that grin that let her know he liked the challenge.

Had Katie Whitcomb-Salgar not provided that for him? Tanya wondered. Or would not getting his own way with her be what drove him back to the heiress?

Not that it made any difference to Tanya. She wasn't changing her position regardless. Although the image of *rolling over* for him did have its own appeal…

Then Tate said, "I thought we were talking history."

"In other words, let's stick to the safe subject of the past."

Tate's smile turned very Cheshire cat and it was so sexy it blew her away.

She took a bite of her lunch and used the moment to get a grip on herself so she could redevote her attention to her work.

"All right, that's the diamond's background," she said then. "Let's get into the feud and how the McCords became the owners of Foley land and silver mines."

"Fairly," Tate said defensively. "But that's not the way Gavin Foley saw it."

"How did Gavin Foley see it?"

"He and my grandfather—Harry McCord—were playing poker. Gavin put up the deed to his land and the five mines on it—mines that *his* family had started and never stuck with long enough to make them pay out. Gavin lost, my grandfather won the hand and the deed."

"Fair and square," Tanya said.

"Only Gavin figured he couldn't have lost unless my grandfather cheated. Which he didn't. But Gavin swore to his dying day that the game was fixed."

"His dying day was when?" Tanya asked, taking notes.

"I'm not sure. A while ago—eight, nine, ten years—you'll have to get the exact date from somewhere else if you need it. I know it was after my mother persuaded my father to offer the Foleys the opportunity to lease the land from us."

"Why did your mother do that?"

"She was hoping it would end the feud that started with

that card game. It was always Gavin Foley's goal to get back on that land, and while the lease didn't return ownership to him, it did give him the chance to start a ranch there. He was pretty old by then but the family pitched in to start it up for him, and his grandson—Travis—helped him run it until he died. Travis Foley still runs it now."

"But lease or no lease, the feud didn't end?"

Tate shook his head. "The Foleys—being the *Foleys*—took the lease and just went on acting as if we'd done something wrong."

"Did Elwin Foley hide the diamond somewhere on the land? Is that why Gavin was so determined to get back onto it—to look for the stone and the treasure?" Tanya asked.

The Cheshire cat smile came out again. "Do I look like a mind reader? All I know is that Gavin Foley wanted back on the land but getting there through leasing it didn't appease him. He still said the land was rightfully his and he still hated us because it wasn't. He apparently kept his family fired up about it, too, and the lease didn't end the Foleys' dislike of us."

"Or the McCords' dislike of the Foleys," Tanya pointed out.

Tate's only answer was to raise his iced tea glass as if in toast before he took a drink.

"Did the lease essentially give the land back to the Foleys indefinitely?" Tanya asked.

Tate shook his head. "It's a fifty-year lease—it'll be up in thirty years or so—"

"Then—doing the math—your mother pushed for the lease for the Foleys right about the time she was pregnant with your brother Charlie, Rex Foley's son...."

Tate had a mouthful of shepherd's pie when she said that

and he chewed very, very slowly, all the while staring at her in a way that made it obvious he hadn't liked her figuring that out.

When he'd swallowed he went on as if she hadn't said it.

"So in thirty years when the lease is up we could just kick Travis off the ranch and the land if we wanted to. And the lease is for the land only—we retained the mineral rights to the mines—the Foleys have no business anywhere near any of them."

Message received—he was not going to talk about his younger brother's parentage.

Since that wasn't her focus today anyway, Tanya conceded and stuck to the subject at hand.

"Are you still taking silver out of the mines?"

"No. It was my family who ended up digging deep enough to actually strike substantial silver. But the five mines themselves were played out years ago. They were the foundation for the jewelry business. Retaining the mineral rights is more on principle than anything. The mines don't do us any good anymore and they wouldn't do the Foleys any good either."

"Besides, the Foleys made their money in oil, didn't they?"

"That they did."

Tanya had barely touched her lunch but Tate was finished with his and sat back in his chair. It didn't help her to now have his penetrating eyes so steadily on her. It did improve her posture, though....

Work—just stick with work, she commanded herself.

"So, I'm not sure I understand how the feud has been fueled over the years," she said. "It seems as if when the Foleys made their own fortune in oil they should have stopped resenting the McCords."

"That's where it gets more personal," Tate said.

"Because of your mother originally dating both your father and Rex Foley?" Tanya guessed, referring to what Tate had told her when they'd looked through his family albums.

"There was definitely bad blood over that," Tate admitted. "Like I said before, I don't know much about it, but I do know that there was a rivalry that breathed new life into the feud. I also know that my mother dated Rex Foley all through high school and thought he was the man she would marry, and that my father was jealous of that. I don't have any idea what happened for her and Rex to break up, but that was when she got together with my father."

Tanya hesitated, wondering if what she wanted to explore next was going to make Tate angry. But she ventured it despite the risk.

"In my research I made note of some dates. Blake was born less than nine months after your parents married...."

"Is that right?" Tate said but in a way that made it clear it was no news to him.

"So...the union of your parents was a shotgun wedding?"

"I've never been told there were weapons involved. And to be honest, it isn't something I've ever had a heart-to-heart talk about with my mother. I'm sure it isn't something she'd want on the news, though."

Second message received—the advantage of having Tanya do the story was that that was a tidbit that should be omitted as a courtesy.

But she wasn't interested in doing a sleazy tabloid-type report so Tanya didn't pursue that, either.

She did say, "It's strange, isn't it, how intertwined the Foleys and the McCords are even though you all hate each other? Especially now with Charlie being a Foley...."

Tate gave her that glare again to warn her away from talking about Charlie.

"Okay, I know you're probably protective of him," Tanya said. "I respect that, and I'm not going to put any of that too-personal stuff in, so you can relax."

That must have eased his mind because he seemed to have let down his guard when he said, "You're right, though, about how intertwined we always are with the Foleys. I just found out that Penny is involved with Jason Foley."

"Really?" Tanya said. She had the sense that they had just somehow stopped working, that Tate was actually confiding in her. And being offered that kind of trust from him gave her an entirely new kind of rush.

"That's what Penny said at dinner the other night," he confirmed. "I'm not sure to what extent she's involved with Foley, but you're right, there does always seem to be some *intertwining.*"

"Your family can't be happy about a relationship between Penny and a Foley," Tanya observed.

"Definitely not happy about it, no. Decidedly leery of it. Unanimously worried for her. For my part, I'd like to be happy for her but a Foley coming into the picture right now just seems a little *too* convenient to me."

"Right now when it looks as if their ancestor really did get away with the diamond and probably stashed it on the land they lost to you. At a time when the diamond could be up for grabs to the first person to find it," Tanya summarized.

Tate answered only with an arch of his eyebrows.

"Still," Tanya said, "Penny has a lot to offer—it's possible that Jason Foley just likes her, isn't it?"

Tate looked as though he wanted to believe that but wasn't convinced.

There was no opportunity for him to answer her question, however, because just then Edward, the McCords' butler, appeared from around the side of the bungalow carrying a garment bag.

"Excuse me for interrupting. But Tanya, this just arrived from Mrs. McCord's favorite shop. The deliveryman insisted it was for you. I told him he must be mistaken, especially since he also said the bill that goes with it is for you, Doctor McCord. But it *is* your name on the ticket, Tanya, and the envelope is addressed to Doctor McCord. Can that be right?"

And just like that Tanya went from feeling perfectly fine to feeling awkward and uncomfortable and humbled....

"It's right, Edward," Tate said. "The dress is for Tanya. The bill was supposed to go to my office but it's for me regardless. You can leave it on my desk."

Tanya sat there frozen and speechless, looking up at the man who had worked for the McCords as long as her mother had, knowing that reality was staring back at her from his questioning eyes.

She was well aware of what the staff said—and thought—about any employee who foolishly tried to step from the oven or the dust cloth or the garden shears into the McCord family ranks. And as Edward stood there with that garment bag, she knew he was wondering if she had become one of them.

No pride, no dignity, no brains because it never actually happened—that was what was said of those who hadn't known their place and had attempted to climb that particular social ladder.

Now, for sure, there would be gossip about her, whispers. Her mother would be embarrassed to have to admit that Tate McCord had bought her a dress that likely cost more than any one of the staff earned in a month's salary. And Tanya wanted to crawl into a hole and hide from the shocked expression of a man she was fond of and respected and didn't want thinking badly of her.

But sitting there like a statue wasn't helping anything so she got up to take the garment bag.

"Thanks, Edward," she muttered as she did, unable to meet him eye to eye, wishing she could say *it isn't what you think.* Suffering some guilt over the fact that the kisses she and Tate had shared didn't make her altogether innocent, either....

"I'll leave this other on your desk, Doctor," Edward said then, leaving.

For Tanya there was so much tension in the air it seemed palpable, but if Tate picked up on it, it didn't show. And he didn't have a chance to say anything because his cell phone rang just then.

"It's one of my nurses, I'll have to take this," he said after checking the display. Then he flipped the phone open to answer it.

While he did, Tanya gave him some privacy by carrying the garment bag into the house.

In spite of the negatives that had just come of it, once she'd hung the bag over the top of the pantry door she couldn't resist unzipping the zipper to look at the dress.

It was even more beautiful than she remembered. Too beautiful to have caused such ugly feelings.

But now there were both the negatives and the positives churning inside of her.

"I have to go back to the hospital—"

Tanya jumped at the sound of Tate's voice coming from

behind her where he was poking his head through the screen door. "One of my patients is having some problems. But I should be back in time for tonight."

Tanya nodded, thinking that as she stood there, with the beautiful dress on one side and Tate's handsome face on the other, it just seemed so unfair that there had to be any negatives at all.

But the lingering sense that she was somehow doing something to be ashamed of remained just the same.

"Thanks for lunch," Tate said then.

"You're welcome," Tanya answered even as doubt washed over her about whether she should wear the dress and go with him tonight.

Or stay at home in the housekeeper's bungalow with her mother.

Where she belonged…

Tanya and what they'd talked about over lunch was still on Tate's mind as he drove to the hospital.

He'd made sure he told her only what wouldn't do any harm for her to know, what was common knowledge. He hadn't told her that at about the same time the sunken ship had been discovered and it was confirmed that the diamond wasn't on it, Blake had been going through their father's personal papers hoping for ideas to help boost the business. In the process of that, Blake had found the deed their grandfather had won from Gavin Foley.

Tate hadn't told Tanya that in looking at that deed, Blake's memory had been triggered from his boyhood spent exploring those played out mines on the land. That Blake had realized that there could well be a clue in the drawings that decorated the deed's border. That the mines themselves were each marked by a stone bearing a petro-glyph of its name—the Turtle mine, the Eagle, the Bow, the Lizard, the Tree—and that images of those petroglyphs were drawn on the border.

Tate hadn't told Tanya that all but one of the drawings were identical to the petroglyphs that Blake knew well. But that in the drawing of the eagle there was a diamond in the bird's talons. A diamond that wasn't on the petroglyph itself.

Tate certainly hadn't told Tanya that because of that one tiny discrepancy, Blake was banking on the Santa Magdalena diamond and the treasure chest of coins being hidden in the Eagle mine. Or that Blake had enlisted their sister Paige to secretly find the diamond—which she was about to try to do—in the deserted mine that was now a part of the ranch the McCords had leased to Travis Foley.

It wasn't that he wouldn't give Tanya all of that infor-mation when the diamond and the treasure were safely in McCord hands—in fact he was hoping it would make not only a career-building revelation for her, but would generate the publicity McCord's Jewelers needed to rebound from the current slump. He just couldn't tell her any of that now.

He also hadn't gotten into the more personal aspects of his family's history, but those he might never give her. He certainly wasn't going to tell her that not only had his mother been pregnant with Blake when she'd married his father, but that it was relatively clear to the whole family that their parents' marriage had never been a love match. Or that his mother had always treated Blake differently, that she'd never seemed to bond with him the way she had with Tate, the twins or certainly with Charlie, whom she doted on.

That was just not information that needed airing.

And yet he *had* told her about Penny and Jason Foley....

Not that he'd told her that with any forethought—the words had just come out.

His sister being involved with a Foley had been weighing on him and he'd felt the urge to get it off his chest. And all of a sudden he had. To Tanya.

But not in terms of giving her information for her news report. Just because she was who he'd felt inclined to tell. The one person he'd had the urge to open up to. The first person since Buzz...

Was he honestly finding similarity between his relationship with Tanya and his friendship with Buzz?

That didn't seem possible.

And yet there *was* something similar in how easy it was to be with Tanya. To be himself with her.

Of course the other things she stirred in him couldn't have been more *un*like his friendship with Buzz. But still, what was there about Tanya that seemed to draw him out of himself?

He couldn't explain it even after trying for several miles to figure it out.

He just knew that he liked the way he felt when he was with her.

More than liked it—he was beginning to crave it.

And it was over and above the fact that he liked her. That he craved her in so many other ways....

But liking her, craving time with her, craving *her,* was all there, too. And growing so much, so fast that last night's sleeplessness had been solely due to that kiss ending too soon and forcing him to go home more frustrated than he'd been since puberty.

And all through lunch today? He might have been

talking poker games and lost diamonds and feuds, but what he'd been thinking about was the reddish streaks glistening in her shiny hair. About the way her skin turned nearly translucent in the sunshine. About how natural light let him see tiny lines of topaz in her dark eyes. And how when she sat up straight her breasts pressed against her tank top the way he'd wanted them pressed against him last night.

What he'd been thinking about was how he'd just wanted to pull her over that table and onto his lap and kiss her again....

That had been about when Edward had shown up with the dress.

Everything had changed then.

Tanya had seemed so uncomfortable. So self-conscious. Her face had turned the color of the stoplight he was paused at at this very moment.

Did she think the butler was judging her? Disapproving?

Was Edward judging her?

The butler hadn't liked that the dress did belong to Tanya or that Tate had paid for it—Tate *had* gotten that impression. And as for disapproving? There had been that, too, he thought.

Damn.

He regretted that he'd inadvertently put Tanya in that position.

So take her out of it, he told himself.

But taking her out of the position she was in meant delegating her back to the staff side of things while he stayed firmly on the other side of the line that divided them.

And while he knew intellectually that that was probably what he *should* do, he also knew he couldn't. Not when it could cost him nights like last night and afternoons like today. Not when it would cost him having Tanya by his side tonight at the damn charity ball he didn't want to go to.

Because the only thing that was making him look forward to tonight was the thought that he was going to be with her.

And more than that, what was helping him to increasingly see daylight through the darkness was Tanya.

And he just couldn't give that up.

At least not before he had to…

Chapter Ten

Everything about Friday evening fell just short of being perfect.

Tanya's dress was even more fabulous than she remembered it—or maybe it was the minor alterations that had made it even better. Her hair worked exactly the way she wanted it to—it was just full enough, just wavy enough, and it cascaded around her shoulders just the way she wanted it to. She did on-camera makeup to make sure she didn't look washed-out, and yet the only thing her mother said when JoBeth took in the complete picture was a very flat, "You look nice," before reminding Tanya that she didn't think this was a good idea and warning her to be careful in a tone as dire as she might have used if Tanya was about to walk through a field of land mines.

Not the most perfect of send-offs.

When Tate picked her up he seemed duly impressed by

his initial look at her—his eyebrows shot up, he breathed an appreciative breath that would have blown out a birthday candle and said, "Wow!" And he looked dashing and sophisticated in a black peak-lapel tuxedo with a shadow stripe, a white shirt and a tie that was also white but with a silver cast to it.

Yet there was something subdued about him that Tanya thought was an example of what her mother and the rest of the staff had said about his recent moods—he was quieter than he'd been at any time since he'd discovered Tanya in the library a week ago, and he seemed somehow removed, distant.

Again, not quite perfect.

The charity ball was everything Tanya had imagined as a child. The country club's ballroom was large and elegantly decorated. Crystal chandeliers hung overhead. The tables were linen covered and set with fine china and silver and adorned with an abundance of roses.

The women were all dressed impeccably in gowns as fine as Tanya's, the men in tuxedos as well tailored as Tate's. There was subtle music being played by a twelve-piece orchestra, and the food was some of the best Tanya had ever eaten. Tate introduced her to more people than she could keep track of, and Tanya was relieved that his former fiancée hadn't yet returned to Dallas and so wasn't there.

His family was courteous and friendly in an awkward sort of way. But despite the fact that not everyone knew she was the housekeeper's daughter, at no time during the evening did Tanya feel warmly welcomed into Tate's social circle. Instead, she was acutely aware of the fact that she was a fish out of water. It made her wonder if she should have let the afternoon's doubts prevail over her desire to be with Tate.

Once more, not exactly perfect.

And maybe that had as much to do with Tate as it did with Tanya's acceptance—or lack of it—with his peers. Because all through the evening she continued to be aware of that "something different" about him that she couldn't completely pinpoint. Or explain.

He was flawlessly attentive and considerate of her, but he was somber and he made only minimal effort to mingle with anyone else. Plus he seemed barely able to tolerate the many, many people who approached him to welcome him home from the Middle East, to applaud him for the year he'd spent there, to let him know they were happy to be contributing to his cause. It was as if with each time that happened, Tate became more stiff, and Tanya could sense the tension in him was growing.

So no, not quite the perfect evening.

After dinner and several people taking the podium to applaud Tate for his war efforts and to talk about the silent auction and where the proceeds would go, the orchestra began playing music to dance to. That was when Tate leaned close to Tanya's ear and said, "My family will stay to the end but I think my obligations here are about done. Would you mind if we cut this short and left?"

Because it *wasn't* quite the perfect evening, Tanya assured him that she wouldn't mind at all and let him guide her from the ballroom without a backward glance.

On the drive home she was still trying to figure out what was going on with him so once they were well on their way she said, "That patient you had to go back to the hospital for today—did they do okay?"

"Fine," he answered, still sounding as if his mind was elsewhere. "He just needed an increase in his pain meds."

"And what about you? Do you feel okay?"

"I'm fine, too," he said without taking his eyes off the road.

But he didn't offer her any more than that and in this mood, she was slightly wary of pushing him. She left him to his silence, recalling what her mother had said about the McCords having the weight of the world on their shoulders. Looking at Tate and how troubled he seemed, Tanya thought her mother might be right.

Tonight when they reached the estate Tate pulled up to the front of the main house rather than going nearer to the housekeeper's bungalow.

He still didn't say anything and had opened her door by the time Tanya had gathered her purse and tugged on her skirt to make sure she didn't catch a heel in the hem when she got out.

Then Tate closed a strong hand around her elbow and steered her through the mansion's front door.

It was not a door Tanya had gone through more than a few times in her life, and never with a McCord. And it made her think that he really *was* distracted.

Maybe he'd forgotten where she lived. Or that she *wasn't* Katie Whitcomb-Salgar.

Or maybe tonight he was so enmeshed in his own doldrums that it was just up to her to make her way through the house and let herself out the back to get home on her own....

But once they were inside, Tate took a right turn at the far end of the foyer and suddenly Tanya found herself in the den with only a single desk light on to cast a dim glow in the large room.

"How about a drink?" he asked.

Tanya had had champagne at the ball, while Tate had nursed nothing but sparkling water. "I get sick if I mix liquors so I think I'll pass. But you go ahead—you haven't had anything all night."

He just shook his head as if he'd changed his mind and a drink didn't appeal to him after all.

Then he surprised her by taking her hand and giving her an endearingly shamefaced smile. "Come and sit with me and let me apologize to you," he said, pulling her along with him to the sofa.

Every other time he'd touched her throughout the evening it had been the lightest of contacts—on her back, her arm—all absolutely appropriate and proper, and still each one had set off those goose bumps again. But none of it had been anything like the warmth that flooded her at having his big hand close completely around hers as if it was something he'd done a million times before.

She tried not to let it be such a big deal to her.

But then they reached the couch and after urging her to sit he released her hand and she felt disappointment.

There was some compensation for the loss in watching him shrug out of his tie, though, and toss it aside. In watching him open his collar button as if he needed air and take off the tuxedo jacket—rolling the tension out of his broad shoulders in a way that made her mouth go dry before he draped the coat over the sofa's arm.

Where her mother or one of the other staff would probably find it and have to pick it up tomorrow morning....

Tanya had no idea why that crossed her mind.

But it was fleeting because then Tate sat down, leaving only enough space between them to angle toward her and stretch his left arm along the sofa back, faintly brushing her bare shoulder. That brought out the goose bumps again and made her wish he would curve that arm around her instead and pull her close....

"I'm sorry about tonight," he said then, drawing her out of her mental wanderings.

"I don't know what there is to be sorry for."

"I know I was lousy company."

"You weren't *lousy* company. Just... Well, it didn't seem as if you were enjoying yourself," she answered.

"I was enjoying being with you. Just not there."

"At the country club? You didn't mind it when we had dinner there," she pointed out.

"It's these big splashy affairs. I haven't had a lot of patience for them since—" he cut himself off, then "—in a while."

"Since your friend Buzz's death?" she asked. She hadn't pushed him on this before because she'd known it would bring down his spirits. Tonight they were already down and she thought it might do him some good to talk about it.

But once she'd asked that question she held her breath, unsure what his reaction would be.

"Actually," he said without any anger or compunction that she could see, "after Buzz died I didn't go to anything like this. I wasn't into socializing. It's just been since I got back from the Middle East that I've been expected to do it all again. And I'm finding it grating."

"Why is that?"

"A lot of reasons, I guess."

"You miss your friend all the more in places where you would have ordinarily seen him? Like tonight?" she guessed.

"Sure, there's some of that."

He made it sound as if missing his friend was not the

major component but since he seemed to be willing to talk about Buzz, Tanya opted for going in that direction.

"His death must have been awful for you."

"It was a nightmare all the way around," Tate confirmed.

He swallowed hard enough for his Adam's apple to bob and Tanya was sorry she hadn't accepted that drink he'd offered earlier. She thought if she had, he might have had one, too, and she thought he could use it now.

But when she asked if he wanted one, he still declined.

"I can't imagine what it must have been like to see someone who was as close to you as a brother hurt so badly," she said, because she didn't know what else to say and she *couldn't* imagine it.

"It was...something," he said as if it had been too horrible to put into words.

"What made you want to go from that to the place where it had happened to him?" she asked because she was baffled by it.

"My family made the same argument. And I'm not sure I can explain it any better now than I could to them then. The contact I had with Buzz while he was over there was through letters and e-mails, an occasional phone call. But in every one of them he said he was glad he'd gone. That he thought he was helping and that was important. After he died...I don't know, I just had this *drive* to contribute something—something more than money—to what had been worthwhile to him at the end of his life. He'd said a lot about how much need there was outside of the military for medical care. That most of the organizations that go in and give aid weren't doing it—either because it was too dangerous or because the countries those organizations came out of didn't agree with what was going on. And when he died I wanted to do what he'd felt needed doing."

"In honor of him," Tanya said, feeling tears flood her own eyes.

But he hadn't let any fall and she didn't either. Blinking them back, she said, "So you joined the International Medical Corps—where the money from tonight's silent auction will go."

"The IMC, right."

"And you spent a year in Baghdad?" Tanya asked because she didn't know if she had the details straight.

"Primarily Baghdad, yes."

"What was it like?"

"Nothing like tonight," he said with a hint of distaste echoing in his tone. "It was intense. Eye-opening. There's nothing here to compare it to, that's for sure."

He went on to describe working until he dropped day after day under less-than-ideal conditions. Seeing patients injured in bombings and in the destruction that came with war. Operating on small children who would suffer a lifetime of infirmity due to their injuries.

He told her about what he'd seen of the hardships there, of his own rudimentary living arrangements, of eating food that was hardly country-club fare.

"If you want a rude awakening, I recommend it," he concluded.

"Being a war correspondent isn't really what I aspire to," she said. "I think I'll stick to the problems at home and trying to do what I can here. But it's no wonder you came back affected by it all."

His tight smile this time was more knowing. "But not *affected* the way everyone seems to think," he said. "I'm not depressed. I'm not suffering post-traumatic stress disorder. But I am…different."

"You don't like parties anymore…" she said, attempting to inject some levity.

"It isn't that I don't like them. I'm just having some trouble…feeling as if I fit in the way I did before. Embracing the excess after being where I've been and seeing what I've seen. It wasn't that spending my life wrapped in cotton—as you so colorfully put it the other night—made experiencing what I experienced in Iraq more than I could handle. It's that now I can't just roll myself back up in the cotton and go blithely on."

"Ohhh…" Tanya said as she finally understood what was happening with him. "Iraq was for you what living with my grandparents was for me—it took you out of the comfort of the cocoon and put you face-to-face with the real side of things."

"Exactly."

"And now you work in the clinic for the underprivileged and don't just *stroll in, cut and stroll out,*" she said, repeating what he'd given as one of the reasons he'd chosen surgery as his specialty. "Now you get involved with your patients—I know you made sure the ones who needed more help on Monday got it whether from other organizations or even by taking money out of your own pocket. You're hands-on."

He didn't seem to want his good deeds talked about because he shrugged all of that away and instead said, "Now I'm having trouble with all of this—" he motioned to the well-appointed room around them.

"Is that why you're staying in the guesthouse?" she said as another light dawned for her.

"That's certainly part of it." He used an index finger to move her hair over her shoulder, brushing her bare skin in the process before he put his hand on the sofa back again.

"So how do you do it?" he asked then.

"How do I do what?"

"How do you go from reporting on people sleeping on the street to sleeping peacefully in your own warm, comfortable bed?"

"Is it guilt you're feeling?"

"Hey, you're the one who rubbed in the fact that I've led a pampered, useless life—are you going to tell me now that you don't think I *should* feel guilty?"

"Okay, I was basing that on the Tate I knew before. But that isn't who you are now," she said, meaning it because tonight he'd let her see just how true that was and why. "If you ask me, this Tate is a better one than the old, good-time-Charlie Tate. I believe you when you say you aren't depressed or suffering PTSD. I think you've just grown up. Matured. Developed a third dimension. Only now you have to learn to strike a balance—a middle ground between constant good-time-Charlie and the guy who has so much conscience—not guilt, conscience—that he can't go to a party and enjoy it. And yes, what I think is that guilt is the wrong label, I think it's *conscience,* and that developing a conscience that might not have been too evolved before is a good thing."

"And how do *you* strike that balance?" he challenged.

"When you went to the Middle East you didn't think you'd stop the war or be able to bring back your friend, did you?" she asked him rather than answering his question directly.

"Of course not."

"You just wanted to do what you could, right?"

"Right."

"And that's something. Even a drop in the bucket is still a drop. That's how I see it. You do what you can for others, then you take comfort where you can for yourself. It's like money in the bank—you spend some, you put some back. You can't feel guilty for replenishing, replenishing is what allows you to go on giving. If you *only* spend, after a while you're spent and you can't do any good at all because you don't have anything left to give. It's just that *your* replenishment is more lavish than most."

That made him laugh slightly, the way she'd hoped it would to ease a bit of the tension.

"In other words, I should just shut up and accept what I have?" he joked in return.

"As long as that isn't *all* you do—the way I think it was for you before. But from what I've seen of you this week, that *isn't* all you do now. I just don't think that means you can't go to a fancy country-club party or live in this house. Appreciate what you have. Share and do what you can. Balance."

"I appreciate you in that dress," he said, dropping his glance downward for a split second.

Did his change of subject mean he didn't want to talk about the more serious things anymore or that his spirits had lifted?

Tanya wasn't sensing the low spirits so much in him now but she didn't want to take credit for that, so she told herself Tate was just ready to talk about something else.

Which he continued to do when he said, "Did I tell you how fantastic you look?"

"I believe there was a *wow* involved."

"Looking at you, being there with you tonight was the only thing that got me through it. Thanks for coming with me."

"It was nice," she said, because while it might not have been perfect, it *had* been nice enough.

"Say you'll come to the Labor Day party on Monday night, too, so I can start appreciating that."

Tanya laughed. "I don't know...."

"All you *need* to know is that I want you there," he said.

His eyes were searching her face the way an art lover might look at a portrait—studying it as intently as if he were memorizing it. Things had changed in the atmosphere around them—calmed, quieted, turned somehow sensual— and that was so much better than before that Tanya just breathed a silent sigh of relief.

"Sometimes it seems like you're the older and wiser of the two of us," Tate said then, with an engaging smile.

"Oh, that's always what a girl wants to hear," Tanya joked, getting lost in the heat of that sky-blue gaze, in staring back into the face she couldn't seem to get enough of.

He grinned and slid his hand from the sofa back to mold his palm to the side of her neck. His fingertips were at her nape, his thumb was just behind her jaw and there was a nearly infinitesimal urging for her to tip her head up to him.

Tanya didn't resist, making it easy for him to lean forward and find her lips with his.

And that kiss was where the pattern of not-quite perfects ended, because it *was* perfect. So perfect that the moment it began, everything else seemed to fall away and leave nothing but the two of them.

How they'd achieved that kind of harmony so soon, Tanya couldn't fathom, but his mouth on hers felt absolutely natural, and she thought what she'd thought when he'd held her hand earlier—that it was as if they'd been doing it forever.

Lips parted in unison, breaths mingled and when his tongue came to hers it was like a secret only they could share.

Tate's right arm slipped under her thighs, bringing them over his so they could be closer still. Then that arm went around her, holding her while tongues cavorted, claiming each other with abandon.

Tanya's hands went to Tate's chest—a solid wall of steel that was nothing like her own breasts burgeoning from the tight, strapless dress and yearning for his touch.

No, no, no—that couldn't happen, she told herself. She wouldn't go that far.

But the craving was stubborn and stayed. Grew, in fact, as both his hands coursed around to the exposed flesh of her back and inspired more goose bumps.

Big, warm, adept hands that she knew would work magic on her far more sensitive front if only that was where they were....

Their kiss was deepening, mouths were open even wider, tongues were engaged in a sexy skirmish, things were awakening in Tanya that were wiping away rational thought and replacing it with pure, raw desire.

She felt her nipples harden and strain against the near prison they were bound in, and as she ran her hands around to Tate's back and pressed her fingers into the expanse of muscle there she wondered if she took a deep enough breath and arched her spine a little, if her breasts might just escape on their own....

But it didn't take anything quite that outrageous to draw Tate's attention in that direction as one of his hands began a slow path from her back to her side, and then to her breast. Cupping it, molding his palm around it the way he'd molded it to her neck before, he kneaded and caressed, pushed and pulled and tormented her by making her just want more.

But popping out of her dress apparently wouldn't have been as easy as a deep breath and an arch because Tate's hold was firm and even when he lifted more than she could have, the dress held tight.

Damn designer dress!

And oh, how she was dying to feel his touch on her bare breast!

She pulsed into his massaging hand, sighing softly when he let a single fingertip trail along the bodice's edge to tantalize the naked flesh above it.

But still she wanted more. Especially when she felt him harden at her thigh…

His mouth abandoned hers, kissing the hollow of her throat, the center of her breastbone, reaching the swell of one breast with the tip of his tongue as he hooked a finger between her cleavage and the dress and tried to make some headway like that.

Her nipples were both hard little gems of need but the dress offered no leeway and after a few attempts, Tate gave up on that route and reached for the zipper that ran from under her arm to her hip.

He discovered the hook that was at the top of it and unfastened that without too much trouble.

And Tanya thought, what would happen if she just gave in to this…

The dress would come off. Here in the den of the McCord mansion. His family's home. The house where she had rarely been allowed past the kitchen. The house her mother had spent years and years cleaning.…

Tate eased the zipper down a scant inch.

And Tanya thought, what about the morning? Would one of the staff come in and find some tiny remnant that would give her away? Even just a bright red string from this dress she was itching to get out of now. Then everyone would know that she'd been in the house, with Tate....

Tate eased the zipper down another inch and by then she really could have freed herself from the boned bodice with only a deep breath.

But instead she thought again what she'd thought at saner moments than this, what if she *was* only a distraction for Tate tonight, an escape from his dark mood....

And then, it was as if there were two of her. While half of her was still in his arms, wanting every bit of what he was clearly going to do, there was another part of her that was pulling away from his kiss, dragging her hands from his back and stopping him from unzipping that zipper any more.

"No, I can't. Not here or now or... I can't."

"We can go out to the guesthouse," he suggested, kissing her neck.

And it felt so good....

But she shook her head. "No. Not only not here. Not now—"

"Why not now?"

"It hasn't been a good night for you. I don't want to be...a diversion." Not from his feelings about losing his friend, not from his adjusting to his new vision of life, not from Katie Whitcomb-Salgar, who he could well end up with after all....

He sat up straight and looked at Tanya. "You are very diverting, though. How could you be anything else looking like that?" he said with a smile that spread languidly across his handsome face.

But she wouldn't allow herself to be *only* that and tonight she was too worried that that might be the case. So she again shook her head and merely repeated, "No."

He kissed her once more—softly, sweetly, enticingly, weakening her willpower and making it all the more difficult for her to stick with her decision.

Before she caved, though, he ended that kiss and she tried to strengthen her resolve by rezipping her dress.

Then Tate gallantly replaced her feet on the floor and stood, taking her hand and tugging her to stand.

"Come on, I'll walk you home," he said, continuing to hold her hand.

Tanya had just stepped away from the sofa when she remembered her evening bag.

"Wait," she said, reaching for it where it was being almost swallowed by the couch cushion, where her mother or one of the maids or Edward might have found it and begun to wonder....

Relieved that that possibility had been avoided, she told herself it was better that she hadn't let anything else happen to put her at risk.

If only her body agreed....

Tate led her through the house and out one of the rear doors. Neither of them said anything as they went to the housekeeper's cottage, and Tanya tried to be content with having her hand nestled in his for the trip.

Then they reached the bungalow and under the porch light Tate faced her again, laying a gentle palm on her cheek and looking deeply into her eyes.

"I'll do whatever you want. Or I won't do whatever it is you don't want me to do," he said in a deep voice that was for her ears alone. "But *I* want one thing clear—you aren't just a diversion to me. You're much, much more. So much more that I'm not even sure what, exactly. Something unlike what anyone else has ever been to me. Something special, I know that...."

He kissed her once more, softly, lingering, making her light-headed with wanting him all over again.

Then his hand slid from her face, his other hand let go of hers and he turned and walked away.

It took Tanya a very long while to recall why it was that she'd stopped what she'd stopped in the den.

And even after she'd recalled it, there was still that part of her that wished she hadn't stopped it at all.

That part of her that just wanted to be anywhere, at anytime, if she could be with him....

Chapter Eleven

Katie Whitcomb-Salgar was back.

Actually, when JoBeth had told Tanya that, JoBeth had called her young Miss Whitcomb-Salgar because that was how JoBeth referred to the daughter of the McCords' friends. But in Tanya's mind—as it repeated itself over and over again to torture her—Tanya kept thinking *Katie Whitcomb-Salgar is back....*

And it *had* repeated itself over and over, and tortured her. All day and all evening, and it was keeping her from going to bed as midnight on Saturday night approached.

Of course it didn't help that her mother had relayed the information at breakfast and that even though Tanya had gone looking for Tate repeatedly throughout the day and evening, he was nowhere to be found.

No, he and Tanya hadn't prearranged any time together today or tonight, and possibly he hadn't brought it up because he'd had other plans. Ordinary, everyday, innocent, other plans. But what if those other plans hadn't been so innocent? What if those other plans had been to see his longtime girlfriend on her first day home—that's what had troubled Tanya. What was still troubling her. What if he was off rekindling his romance with the heiress his family had handpicked for him?

Not that I should care, Tanya told herself.

But she *did* care. Too much to sleep, and so she decided that maybe a walk in the fresh night air might help. That maybe all the thoughts of Tate and all the thoughts of Tate reconciling with Katie Whitcomb-Salgar would just drift away....

Tanya made sure to leave the bungalow silently so she didn't wake her mother. Once she was outside she knew she should take her walk *away* from the McCord mansion, especially if she had any hope of walking off thoughts of Tate. But at dinner her mother had talked about the fact that the lights for the Labor Day party were all up and how the lighting people had outdone themselves. Tanya could tell by the glow coming through the trees and shrubbery that the lights were lit. And she wanted to see them. *That* was why she went in that direction, she told herself, to see the lights. Not to see if Tate had ever come home.

Because it's none of my business...

Even if things had been heating up between them.

Even if he had said what he'd said the night before about her being more than a diversion to him. About her being special.

He could have just been trying to get her out of that dress she'd already taken to the dry cleaners so she could return it to him the way she'd told her mother she would.

As she stepped through the clearing into the backyard of the mansion it *was* the lights she was looking at. Hundreds and hundreds of tiny white lights wrapped all the tree trunks and lower branches and then canopied from there to the house itself. They spiraled up the poles that held the white tents where food and beverages would be served, they outlined the entire rear of the house and adorned the covered patio to cast a beautiful bright glow on the entire area.

It was only after a moment of enjoying the spectacle that Tanya realized there was someone gliding soundlessly through the pool water, doing laps.

It could have been Blake—he and Tate were about the same height, they had similar body types and coloring, and the swimmer's face was in the water so that even when he raised it to take a breath he was swimming away from her and she couldn't see it. But despite not having a clear view, it took only a moment for her to be sure it wasn't Tate's older brother. That it was Tate. And that he was alone.

Of course that didn't mean that he hadn't just come from hours and hours with Katie Whitcomb-Salgar, and Tanya knew she should turn and duck into the camouflage of the bushes once more before Tate saw her. That she should distance herself from him before he did get together with the other woman yet again, even if that hadn't already happened.

But there he was, moving through the water by the power of his long, muscular arms, his shoulder blades glistening in the light, flexing with each stroke, and she was riveted to that spot, watching him, appreciating the view....

He reached the opposite end of the Olympic-size pool, disappeared under the water for a minute and then resurfaced for the return lap.

It was definitely Tate—now he was coming in her direction, and each time his face turned out of the drink Tanya could see it in all its chiseled glory. But he wasn't yet aware of her, so she could still sneak away.

But she didn't. She just had to know if he'd been with Katie Whitcomb-Salgar today....

Tanya took a few more steps toward the pool and by the time Tate reached the end nearest to her, something—her movement probably—had caught his attention. He stopped rather than making a blind turn the way he had at the other end, and stood so that his shoulders rose out of the chest-high water. He ran his massive surgeon's hands up his face and into his hair to slick it back. Then he opened eyes that were the same color as the pool tiles and took in the sight of Tanya.

He smiled.

"Hi," he greeted simply.

"Hi," Tanya responded, sticking with simple even though there was nothing simple about what she was thinking and feeling at that moment.

"How about a swim?" he invited, spreading his arms wide and fanning his hands through the shimmering liquid around him.

"My suit's packed in a storage box somewhere," she said by way of declining.

His smile grew and one eyebrow arched devilishly as his gaze dropped to the tight tank top and blousy elastic-waisted short shorts she had on. "How about a clothes-optional swim?"

"I don't think so," Tanya said, hoping that he hadn't come from the other woman only to flirt with her the way he had been most of the last week. Worse than being a diversion to fill his time until he patched things up with his fiancée would be to be juggled along with Katie Whitcomb-Salgar....

"I just heard on the car radio that it's still ninety-two degrees. The water feels good," he persisted.

"Where were you coming from?" Tanya asked before she realized she was going to, wishing she'd managed more subtlety.

"The hospital. I got called in to do an emergency surgery this morning. I've been in the O.R. for the last sixteen hours."

Not with Katie Whitcomb-Salgar....

Tanya couldn't help smiling. Grinning from ear to ear as relief washed over her and left her in an entirely different mood than she'd been in.

"What about you?" Tate asked. "I was going to whisk you away to take a look at some of the Foley oil wells for your report but since I didn't get to do that, what were you up to today?"

So it was her he'd planned to see today, even if he hadn't told her ahead of time....

Tanya went the rest of the way to the poolside, sat down on the edge and dangled her feet in the water, knowing she shouldn't feel as good as she did, that the very fact that she did was an indication of just how hard it would have hit her if Tate *had* been with the other woman during the last several hours. But she felt so good she just had to go with it.

"I worked," she answered his question about how she'd spent the day. "I organized my notes and did some research on the Internet—apparently the Foleys were destined to be on the docket today no matter what because it was Foley research I did."

"Did you find out anything interesting?"

"To me, because I didn't really know much about them.

I don't know if it's interesting to you. All I learned was that Rex Foley is the patriarch of the family and he recently left Foley Industries to start a consultancy. He has three kids. Zane, who *now* heads Foley Industries, Jason, who is the chief operating officer and a ladies' man—so no wonder you're worried about his involvement with Penny—and Travis, who's the rancher in the family. There's also one grandchild—Olivia—who is Zane's six-year-old daughter by his late wife," Tanya recited.

"Nothing new there for me," Tate decreed. And he didn't seem inclined to talk about his family's archenemies because then he said, "What about your evening? You didn't work tonight, too, did you?"

"Oh, tonight I had a hot date."

She'd only been joking but his frown said that wasn't how he'd taken it.

"Really? With an old boyfriend? Someone you knew before you moved away? Someone new?"

He was grilling her as if it was something he needed to know. Was that because he didn't like the idea of her being with someone else any more than she'd liked the possibility that he might have been with his former fiancée?

The mere chance that that was the case made Tanya feel better and better. She had to suppress a smile as she considered torturing him a little by drawing the joke out, but then she decided against it.

"I was kidding," she said. "I haven't met anyone since I've been back and as for someone from my past, I don't think Kevin—my high school sweetheart—would be interested in rekindling anything even if he *was* in Dallas—which he isn't."

Tate's smile made a reappearance. "That's it? *One* high school sweetheart? That's all you had?" he teased.

"Kevin Narcy," Tanya confirmed. "We went steady from ninth grade through graduation."

"Sounds serious."

"It was. As high school romances go. Just not serious enough to change either of our plans for after high school—Kevin dreamed of moving to Alaska and living some rustic, he-man lumberjack kind of life. I had no intention of doing *that*."

"Understandably. Did you part friends, and did he move to Alaska?"

"Yes on both counts—we parted friends and I wished him well when he climbed on the bus north. We even kept in contact for a while—as much as we could with him living in a cabin somewhere in the middle of nowhere, doing maintenance on the oil pipeline. But then he met a girl up there and got involved with her. I was invited to their wedding two years ago but I couldn't swing it, and since then I've just had Christmas cards."

"*He* got involved with someone else but you didn't?" Tate asked, obviously interested in her romantic history.

"Of course I did, too."

"Just one guy all the way through college?"

Tanya put her fingertips in the water and flicked a little at him because he made her sound so boring. "No, not *just one guy all the way through college,*" she repeated. "Although there was only one *serious guy*—I started going out with him my junior year and it lasted until about eight months ago."

"How serious?"

"Serious enough to talk marriage."

"That's all? You just talked about it?" Tate asked.

"And talked and talked and talked..."

"Why so much talk and no action?"

"Jordan just couldn't make up his mind—he kept going back and forth, back and forth. It seems like that's something you might be familiar with," Tanya goaded him.

"I don't know what you're talking about. I've never had any problem making up my mind—it's just that sometimes, when it's been about Katie, it might have *seemed* as if I made it up one way, then made it up another way, then made it up back to the first way again," he joked with some self-deprecation.

"Umm-hmm. Well, Jordan couldn't make up his mind about anything," Tanya continued. "He would order two full meals at dinner because he couldn't decide between them, and then have to eat part of my food, too, because it would look better to him and he'd think he should have ordered that instead. He is four years older than I am and had been in college long enough to have a degree by the time I started, but even after I'd finished my degree, he still didn't have one—"

"Not too smart?"

"It wasn't that. In fact, he had a nearly four-point grade average. He *could* have done anything he wanted. The problem was that he changed his major and what he wanted to be almost every semester. And when he did that, most of the credits he'd accumulated wouldn't count toward the new degree and he'd basically have to start over. He's up to his eyeballs in school loans and still hasn't graduated the last I heard. He can't vote because he can't settle on a candidate or a side on any issue. And he certainly couldn't commit completely to me or marriage or having kids."

"What if you had made the decision that he was going

WITHDRAWN

to marry you and just told him that was the way it was—
so it wasn't a choice he had to make?"

"Right—that's just how I want someone to be with me—
because I order them to and don't give them a choice. No
thanks," Tanya said facetiously. "I finally decided enough was
enough, I was sick of his back-and-forth, and I broke up with
him—again, something you might have experienced...."

"I have not experienced just two serious relationships
in my life," he said with a sly half smile that let her know
he was purposely misunderstanding her.

"No, *you've* only had *one* serious relationship. That's on
and off and on and off and on and off...."

"I beg your pardon. I've had several serious relationships."

Tanya rolled her eyes. "Who besides young Miss
Whitcomb-Salgar?" she challenged in disbelief.

"There was Heather McGinnley," he said with an exag-
geratedly rapturous expression and tone. "She was my sev-
enteen-year-old camp counselor when I was fifteen. I gave
her my virginity and a marriage proposal."

Tanya laughed. "Wow, you were really grateful."

"Hey!" Tate chastised, laughing too. "It wasn't grati-
tude, it was love."

"But then you came home from camp and—"

"Yes, then I came home from camp and there was
Katie," he acknowledged, "and I had to honor my obligation to escort her to Junior Cotillion. But Heather had
turned me down, anyway, so what's a guy to do? But that
doesn't mean I was any less *seriously* head over heels with
Heather before she rejected me."

"So, two serious relationships—sort of," Tanya allowed.
"That's the same as me."

"Then there was Marnie Wilson, the lifeguard at the

country-club pool," Tate added. "We had three very serious summers together and might have had more than the summers except that she spent the rest of the time away at boarding school."

"And in between there was—"

"Yes, Katie," he granted. "But I was still serious about Marnie when I was with her."

"And even though I'm sure you can go on with a half-dozen more brief—but serious—interludes that you had through college and medical school, the bottom line is that the only *genuinely* serious relationship you've had was with Katie Whitcomb-Salgar."

"You can just call her Katie—I'll know who you're talking about. And you're wrong again. Yes, there have been a lot of on-and-offs with Katie and me but that doesn't mean I wasn't *serious* about anyone in between. The other relationships just didn't pan out. But if they had... Who knows?" he concluded.

"I know I'm sticking with you just having *one* serious relationship," Tanya persisted.

"And I could argue that the relationship with Katie didn't have all the earmarks of a serious relationship itself."

"*That* seems like a stretch."

"Not really," Tate said as he hoisted himself out of the water and sat on the pool's edge beside her.

Tanya's pulse sped up a notch at the sight of him in nothing but trunks, his massively muscled thighs dwarfing hers there on the deck, so much of him bare....

"The *real* bottom line with Katie and me," he was saying, forcing Tanya to concentrate on the subject and not on his magnificent body, "is that we weren't serious enough about our relationship. At least I wasn't. Which is why there were so many breaks from it, why it was so easy for us to *be* on-again, off-again. And, ultimately, that's why we ended it for good this time. I told you, we finally admitted to ourselves that we're more friends than anything else. That it was family pressure—not fate or destiny or any really strong feelings—putting us together."

"Maybe it's fate that keeps urging your families to pressure you and Katie to be together," Tanya suggested, testing him.

"Or maybe it was fate that put you behind the library desk last week...."

"I hate to tell you, but it was families—not fate—that put us together, too," Tanya said, her voice quiet even though she was trying not to let him or his words or the look of appreciation in those eyes get to her. "Remember that you and I only know each other because your mother hired my mother."

Tate grinned. "I didn't think of that. But it doesn't change my mind—I still believe it was fate that brought you back here, now, just when I needed a little color and life and energy injected into things."

"I'm a shot in the arm?" she joked.

"A shot in the arm that I must need because I was hating the thought that today was going to go by without my getting to see you. And then I opened my eyes a few minutes ago and there you were and..." He shook his head as if in awe. "It was definitely a pick-me-up." He suddenly grinned a wicked grin and added, "In more ways than one..."

This time it was Tanya who chose to misconstrue what he was implying. "I'm just glad that you're happier than you were last night."

He bent over and kissed the top of her shoulder, sending little shards of glitter sparkling along her nerve endings.

"Oh, I'm happy all right," he assured her.

"And not because Katie is back in Dallas?" Tanya said, testing still.

Tate leaned farther over and kissed her just behind the shoulder. "I didn't know she was," he said without any indication that he cared.

"That's what I heard," Tanya persisted.

"Okay."

He kissed the top of her shoulder a second time and then the front of it and Tanya wished it didn't feel like heaven. It was just so difficult to deny herself when everything he did made her want him all the more.

"She's always going to be a part of your circle…. Katie is…isn't she?" Tanya felt compelled to say for her own sake, reminding herself.

"It doesn't matter," he assured her in a voice growing more husky by the minute.

Then he slipped into the water again, standing directly in front of her. His hands came around her calves and he pulled her in with him before she even realized what he was doing.

The surprise of it and that initial jolt of cold made her gasp, and she had the impression that a shock was what he wanted to cause.

"I respect Katie. I like her. I care about her as a friend. But as far as anything else goes, she and I are done. So no more Katie," he decreed. "No more Katie in any important way in my life, and definitely not in tonight or anything that has to do with you and me. Got it?"

He was staring down at Tanya intently and with so much heat in his eyes that it was almost enough to wipe away the coolness that she was submerged in to her neck. But still she raised a saucy chin to him and said, "You're laying down the law?"

He smiled and his hands went to her upper arms, clasping them in a firm grip. "That's only the start of what I want to lay down," he said under his breath before he caught her mouth with his in a way that was as if no time had passed between last night and this, as if everything that had ignited in the den then had just simmered below the surface in him until that moment, and at that moment it had bubbled up, demanding to have its day.

Not only in Tate, though. In Tanya, too, she realized as her answer to his kiss was every bit as hungry as his, as her hands went to those amazing pectorals she'd been dying to know the feel of. Her own nipples—already perked up by the cold—now hardened into tiny pebbles instantly striving for his touch.

She struggled against her own inclinations to recall *why* she hadn't let this happen last night.

They'd been in the main house, the McCord house. Tate had had a bad night that had brought up his feelings about his friend's death and she hadn't wanted to just be a diversion from that. Or a diversion he filled the time with when he *was* off-again with Katie.

But tonight...

They weren't exactly *in* the McCords' house and could easily sneak away to the guest cottage nearby.

He wasn't looking for a quick fix for bad feelings about losing his friend.

But could she believe that he was genuinely finished with Katie Whitcomb-Salgar and not only in an intermission?

Maybe she was fooling herself but she had the sense that *Tate* believed it. And if he believed it, didn't that strengthen the possibility that things between Katie and him really, truly, once and for all, were over?

Or do I just want him so much I'm talking myself into it?

Because as mouths opened wide and Tate's tongue came to claim hers and teach it a tango all their own, she *did* want him so much it hurt....

His hands went from her arms to her breasts and the thin, wet layers of her tank top and built-in bra were nothing like the armor that the designer dress had been. It wasn't exactly like having her skin enveloped in his, but it was still good enough to make her nipples strain into his palms as if they only existed for that.

He has to be through with the other woman, she thought. *He just has to be.*

Because tonight, no matter what, Tanya didn't have the strength to say no....

She ran her hands all over him—from the tautness of his lower back up the widening vee to broad shoulders, down impressive biceps, across to a chest where his own nipples were mimicking hers.

And all the while that kiss!

It was open and urgent and enough to drive her out of her mind all on its own....

Maybe it also let Tate know just how willing she was tonight because he took his hands from her breasts, scooped her into his arms and carried her up the pool steps and out of the water. He had to stop kissing her to watch where he was going but even so he didn't ask permission, he merely took her to the guesthouse.

To the guesthouse's bedroom...

Of course Tanya could have objected. But she didn't.

Once they were secluded in his room and she was on

her own two feet again, Tate didn't hesitate to peel off her wet tank top and warm her breasts with his hands first, and then with his mouth. After a moment, he took off her shorts and his swimsuit in quick succession.

Then there they were, and for a brief moment it was almost inconceivable to Tanya that she was actually standing there naked, facing an also naked Tate McCord. But the unreality of it passed almost instantly as wanting him overwhelmed the awkwardness. And from that moment on nothing seemed anything but right.

Tate again whisked her into his arms and laid her on the bed. The curtains were open and moonlight cast a spotlight's glow on him as he stood at the bedside, savoring the sight of her.

She did the same, feasting on the magnificence of a body no sculptor would ignore as that milky light caressed him the way Tanya's hands ached to. And did the moment he joined her, stretching out next to her, lying on his side, his front running the length of her as his mouth rediscovered hers and one of his hands closed around her bare breast once more.

Massaging, kneading, gently plucking at her nipple with agile, talented fingers while mouths again did a sexy reunion kiss that took no time to turn into a randy, uninhibited plundering.

But even a surgeon's hands could only perform so much and Tanya had no complaints when his mouth abandoned hers a second time to kiss a trail from there to the hollow of her throat, to her collarbone, to her breast....

Tiny, feathery kisses were what he placed all around first one nipple and then the other, teasing her, tantalizing her with anticipation before his lips parted enough to draw her between them, and then—at last—to pull her whole breast into the divine warmth of his open mouth.

Tanya's spine arched off the mattress in response to the delights he was unveiling, to flicks of his tongue and tender tugs of his teeth, to his other hand at her other breast, kneading and pressing and—rather than satisfying her— only making her want even more.

She sent her own hands exploring then, boldly, brazenly, coursing all over him again until she found the long, steely shaft that announced how much he wanted her, too.

A low moan of pleasure rumbled from his throat as he draped a heavy thigh over hers. And while his mouth continued its wonders at her breast, the hand that was titillating the other slid away.

With his palm flat against her, that hand traveled down to her stomach, down farther to the juncture of her legs, following the curve of her body to dip between them. And just when Tanya thought she'd been driving him a little crazier than he'd been driving her, he proved her wrong.

Long fingers worked a magic of their own, inside of her and out, raising new levels of need that she hadn't even known she was capable of, leaving her right on the brink.

As if he knew that, he rose above her, recapturing her mouth with his as he positioned himself between her thighs, probing with that portion of him she'd just released. Finding his home, he slipped into her slowly, smoothly, sleekly, until he was embedded deeply within her.

He pulsed there several times. Then he stopped kissing her and dipped to her breast again, sending only the tip of his tongue to the very crest of her breast as his hips began to move—barely in and out in the same slow, measured rhythm his tongue was keeping at her nipple.

But that didn't last for long before his hips picked up speed and force, before his back arched so he could plunge into her, before he devoted himself to those fabulous thrusts that fitted them together flawlessly.

Tanya kept pace, meeting him, matching him, holding tight for the ride that took them up another notch each time he came into her, each time he drew out. Passion, need grew. Bigger and bigger, like a giant balloon carrying her higher and higher until Tanya reached the pinnacle and couldn't do anything but cling to Tate while crystal clear, pristine pleasure held her at the very peak for one mindless moment. One moment when Tate, too, reached the same climax, buried so deeply within her that they were nearly melded together.

And then it began to ebb, to deflate and, in perfect sync, they both slowly drifted back from that shared bliss.

Muscles relaxed and Tate let more of his weight rest on her, his cheek pressed to hers, his breath a hot breeze on her shoulder.

But it was only a few minutes before his arms insinuated themselves around her so he could roll them to their sides, bodies still joined and molded together into one.

Then his lips were on the top of her head, in her hair, placing a reverent kiss there before he whispered, "What you do to me is like nothing I've ever known."

There was a sort of reverence in his tone, too, and all Tanya could do was kiss the marvelous chest she was facing and whisper in return, "Me, too."

That was how they stayed until she felt him beginning to fall asleep. Then he caught himself, finally slipped out of her and laid on his back, pulling her as close as he could to lie alongside him with her head cradled on his shoulder.

His arms around her were still tight enough to let her know he wasn't letting her go. And while she hated the thought of her mother or any other member of the staff finding out about this, she couldn't make herself roll away from him and leave.

As if he knew that was what she was thinking, Tate said, "Don't go anywhere. I just need a catnap. But I don't want this to end...."

She assumed he meant that he didn't want tonight to end yet, and since she didn't either, she merely said, "Okay."

But as she drifted into sleep, too, it did fleetingly cross her mind that he might have been referring to something more than tonight when he'd said he didn't want this to end.

She was too tired and replete herself, though, to explore it, and so she just let herself drift closer to sleep in Tate's arms, feeling more at home there than she'd ever felt anywhere.

And just this once, letting that be all that mattered.

Chapter Twelve

It was four-thirty Sunday morning and Tate was standing in the doorway of the guesthouse watching Tanya leave. They'd bounced from making love to sleeping to making love to sleeping all night, but even though he'd done his damnedest to persuade her to stay longer, she wouldn't. Not and risk that any of the staff—especially her mother—might be starting work early and discover that she'd spent the night with him. She wouldn't even let him walk her home. She'd said that if she was alone and got caught she could say she'd just gone out for an early morning jog.

But Tate had never been so sorry to see anyone go.

As he stood there enjoying the view of her compact rear end in those short shorts, of her silky hair falling around her shoulders, hating it when she disappeared down the path to the housekeeper's cottage, he was also thinking about what he'd said in response to her notion that she was only some kind of distraction for him. He was thinking about the fact that even then he'd told her that she was more than that.

He hadn't been able to define exactly *what,* but now it struck him.

It had already occurred to him that, with Tanya, he felt some of the same kinship he'd felt with Buzz, the same freedom to open up and be himself. After talking to her *about* Buzz, about this last year and a half, he knew more than ever just how true that was.

And when he'd confided in Tanya, she'd altered his view of things. She'd been instrumental in putting so many things that had been bothering him—weighing on him—into focus.

Conscience, not guilt. Replenishing. Striking a balance—those were all things that Tanya had steered him in the direction of. And the more he'd thought about it since she'd said it, the more he'd realized that she was right.

Which meant that she had an insight that not even Buzz had had.

She was insightful, bright, smart....

Not that Katie wasn't intelligent, too—she was. And just as caring and considerate and compassionate as Tanya. But where Tanya was different from Katie was in Tanya's willingness to use her intelligence to go head-to-head with him. Katie *could* have, but in their relationship, with Katie's nature, she just wouldn't do or say anything that might have stepped on his toes or ruffled his feathers. She would have appeased, not challenged.

Tanya, on the other hand, had no compunction about challenging him. Challenging his opinions, his views. Boldly, bravely, without any signs that she cared who he was or what he might think.

And he'd liked that. He'd gotten a kick out of it.

And out of just about everything else he'd done with her.

Oh, yeah, he had fun with her, there was no doubt about that. She was a breath of fresh air. Her energy, her enthusiasm, were infectious. There was just never a moment when he'd been bored or wished he was anywhere else, with anyone else.

And that was all on top of the fact that she was beautiful and sexy. That he could look at that exquisite face until his eyes ached and still not have his fill. That his hands itched to be all over her all the time. That his own body was hard to control the minute she got anywhere around him.

And after these last hours together? He'd meant it when he'd told her that what she did for him in bed was like nothing he'd ever known before.

Maybe, he thought as he continued to look down the path she'd followed, Tanya wasn't merely a lot of things to him.

Maybe she was everything to him....

That was kind of a crazy thought.

And yet, the longer he rolled it around in his head, the less crazy it began to seem.

When he thought about talking through problems, through issues and difficulties, there wasn't anyone he wanted to talk to more than Tanya.

When he thought about going anywhere in the world, at anytime, to anyplace, there wasn't anyone he wanted to be with more than Tanya.

When he thought about sharing the best—and the worst—life had to offer, there wasn't anyone he wanted to share any of it with more than Tanya. There wasn't anyone he knew who he *could* share even the worst with the way he knew he could share it with her.

And when he thought about how much he'd just plain wanted her almost since the minute he'd seen her, about holding her, kissing her, making love to her? There wasn't anyone else.

And more than that, he suddenly knew there never could be.

None of that was anything he'd ever thought about Katie. Not that he would want Katie to know that and hurt her, but it was true. Somehow, from out of nowhere, he'd suddenly found the one person who was everything to him. And it wasn't Katie. It never had been. It was Tanya.

She'd said that he'd finally developed a third dimension, that he'd grown up, matured. And maybe he had. But the truth for him was that *she* was what made him feel complete and well-rounded and grounded and able to take whatever it was that had changed in him and use it to the best advantage. She was the reason he'd come to be comfortable with it.

The truth was that it was Tanya who replenished him. Who struck a balance for him. Who made everything worthwhile.

He'd just been settling before and he saw that now, too. He'd told Tanya that Katie was great and that was true. But Katie had just never made him feel what Tanya made him feel.

And what he felt was a driving need to have Tanya in his life. Not just on the peripheries of it—center stage, starring role, main focus.

But she wouldn't even stay with him until the sun came up....

On the other hand, maybe if she—and everyone else—knew how much she mattered to him, how important she was to him, she wouldn't be so determined to hide what they had together.

He had to hope so.

Because now that he knew that she was the world to him, he couldn't imagine anything without her.

And as soon as that sun did rise and her mother left her alone, he was going to make sure she knew that....

After a night of more lovemaking than sleep, Tanya was snoozing pretty deeply at nine o'clock when a demanding knock on the cottage's front door woke her. And even after she was awake enough to get her bearings and realize what all the racket was, she waited a moment, hoping her mother hadn't left yet and would answer it so she could go back to sleep.

But the knocking kept up and she finally got out of bed.

She'd taken a quick shower when she'd returned from the guesthouse. After that she'd put on a pair of pajama pants and a T-shirt—both concealing enough to go to the door in. She wasn't expecting it to matter so she merely ran her fingers through her hair to push it away from her face and—makeupless—she opened the front door.

To find Tate—freshly showered and shaved, hair neat and clean, wearing jeans and a T-shirt that fit him like a second glorious skin.

"Ohhh, I'm not presentable," Tanya moaned when she glanced blearily into his clear, alert eyes.

Tate merely smiled as if he liked the bed-head look. "I had to see you. I was watching for your mother to go up to the house so I'd know when she was gone."

Tanya was at least grateful for that. Not that she wasn't glad to see him—she was *always* glad to see him. Elated, in fact. She just didn't like being at a disadvantage in the grooming department. And she was a little concerned that he thought they could have privacy here when she knew better.

"You can't...come in. Mama could come back anytime or someone could see you...."

"I want to talk. If your mother comes back and finds us doing that, so what?"

His expression was happy but there was something intense and insistent in his attitude that Tanya didn't quite understand. Still, she supposed if all they did was talk....

"I'm sure Mama left coffee. Why don't you pour two cups and take them out on the patio where we had lunch? I'll be right there," she said.

"Just hurry."

Tanya could hear him in the kitchen and then going out the French doors in back as she rushed through brushing her teeth and her hair, pinching her cheeks and applying a touch of mascara. She didn't waste time doing more than that, however, because she was too curious about what was going on with him. It didn't occur to her until she was on her way through the house to join him that maybe he'd had an early morning phone call from Katie. Or a visit. Or some contact that had rekindled things between them. And that now he'd made a beeline here to tell her....

That put a damper on things and by the time she sat across from him at the patio table she was feeling a whole lot more reserved.

"What's up?" she asked.

His smile made him look very pleased with himself. "A lot that I needed to talk to you about right away."

Because now that he'd made the conquest of the house-keeper's daughter he'd come to say it was Katie he should be with after all and he wanted Tanya to keep quiet?

That seemed too likely to Tanya and her stomach knotted. Which meant that even though she could have used a shot of caffeine, she ignored the coffee because she didn't think she could get it down. And she just kept thinking that the housekeeper's daughter might be who a McCord slept with, but a Katie Whitcomb-Salgar was who ultimately got the man himself....

"I'm listening," she said in response to his claim that he needed to talk.

Tate slid his chair around the table so he could be closer to her and then yanked her chair to face his, leaving them sitting knee to knee. Then he leaned his elbows on his thighs and took her hands in his.

To comfort her when he gave her the bad news? she wondered.

And yet his touch still felt so good, so familiar, it almost made her melt on the spot....

"You've done a lot to open my eyes since we've been hanging out," he said then. "But this morning when you left, they really opened—"

"Katie called," Tanya blurted out what she was so afraid he was going to say.

Tate smiled a confused smile followed quickly by a dazed frown. "No. Why would that have anything to do with...." Light dawned for him. "No, Katie didn't call and it wouldn't have mattered if she had. I told you Katie and I are through. What I realized this morning was that nothing I ever felt for her or had with her could compare to what I feel for you, what you and I have together."

"We don't really have anything together," Tanya pointed out quietly, still worried about where he was going with this.

"We have a lot together," he countered. "Maybe not

friends or life experience or lifestyle or what it was that made it seem like Katie was right for me. But what you and I have is so much more. It's everything...."

He said that with a small chuckle, as if it had a meaning for him that she wasn't privy to.

Then he went on. "That's what came to me this morning—that you're everything to me. Sometimes being with you is like being with Buzz—freeing, calming, relaxing, just fun. Sometimes being with you gives me a break from everything—you're like a tropical vacation. Sometimes it forces me to be on my toes, to keep my debating skills up. It's always the way I think it *should* have been with Katie to ever have considered marrying her, only with you it's even better than I thought it could be—the physical, the emotional, all of it. It's always just great—there hasn't been a single minute of it that I've wanted to end. I hate it when it does, and I want it to start again as soon as I can make it. What all that boiled down to for me this morning is that I just don't want it to ever end. So here I am and I know this is quick and unexpected and maybe a little crazy, but I want you to be my—"

"I'm your housekeeper's daughter," Tanya cut him off, not letting him finish what it seemed he might have been about to say. What she would have liked to hear.

But what if she heard it? Nothing else would be changed, she'd still have to refuse him and she wasn't sure she'd be able to....

"It doesn't make any difference that you're the house-keeper's daughter," Tate persisted.

"Maybe not to you. It makes a lot of difference to me. And to my mother. And probably to your mother and the rest of your family and friends. Your mother, your family and friends not only wouldn't like you being with someone from the back side of the bushes, but they've already picked out who they *do* want you to be with."

"And I tried to go with that and it didn't work. For Katie or for me. What works for me is you."

Tanya shook her head. "You lost your friend. You spent time in a part of the world where awful things are happening. You're adjusting to a lot of changes in your life, in yourself, you've had problems getting back into the swing of things with the people who have always mattered to you. You just think—"

"It's not as if I'm delusional, Tanya. I've known what was going on with me all along but it took you to show me how to deal with it, to give me a new and better perspective. And you aren't only a diversion, either—if that's what you're getting at. Thinking that is selling yourself short."

"Okay, let's say that's true. It doesn't alter the fact that I am who I am, and you are who you are. I might as well be a Foley—I wouldn't be any more welcome or at home than they would."

"Even the Foleys have wiggled their way in here and there—with my mother and now with Penny."

"And you're none too happy about that!" Tanya pointed out.

She also thought about the charity dinner. Yes, his friends and family had been cordial, but none of them had known how to relate to her, how to make more than polite, surface conversation with her. They might as well have spoken different languages.

But more than his family, it was her own situation that held Tanya back. Especially when she thought about Edward the butler bringing her the dress when it was delivered from the designer, when she thought about him learning that Tate would be paying the bill. It had been so awkward. So embarrassing.

And she wasn't even as close to Edward as she was to some of the other staff. To her mother....

"My mother *works* for you."

"A lot of people work for us—"

"She's cleaned your house. *Served* you. She depends on you for the roof over her head."

"So if she was my secretary or my surgical assistant, that would be different?"

"I don't know," Tanya said because she didn't. What she did know was that growing up here had made her well aware that there was a distinct line between the people who served the McCords and the McCords themselves. Between the people who catered to their lives and the people the McCords socialized with and most certainly coupled with. And that she was on the side of the people who catered to them, not the side of the people they socialized and coupled with.

"All I can tell you," she continued, "is that I can't sit at your dining room table and be served by someone I was borrowing shampoo from last week. I can't be chauffeured by the man who used to fix my bicycle, who put bandages on my scraped shins, who taught me to drive. I can't sleep in a bed turned down by my mother's best friend or put my own mother to the tasks she does for your family. I wouldn't."

"So don't. All of that can be worked out. It isn't important—"

"That's right, it isn't important to you. Because what goes on with the staff beyond meeting your needs is their problem, their business. But it *is* my business and it *is* important to me—that's the point."

"But you're talking details that can be sorted out. I'm talking a much bigger picture. I'm talking about your future and mine, about us having a life together."

A complicated life—that's what her mother had said about the life he led. And how he might escape from it for a while with her, but that eventually he would go back to it. Which Tanya thought he could do at anytime now that he seemed on top of what had been bogging him down before. The problem was that he was trying to sign her on for the return trip, and she was too afraid that once he got back in the center of that circle, the fact that she didn't belong there would be their undoing.

And then what?

Her mother would likely be out of a job, for one thing.

But even worse than that, Tanya didn't think she could bear discovering that she honestly couldn't be a part of his world, that he might be ashamed of her, that she might embarrass him. That when the blush of his infatuation with her dimmed, he would take a look at her, a look at Katie Whitcomb-Salgar and realize he'd made a mistake....

"Yours isn't a life I want," she said, holding her chin as high as she could, making it sound as if she was firm in that decision.

"You don't want the life, or you don't want me? Because they're not the same thing."

"They are the same thing. It's *your* life. A life my mother was right to remove me from when I was a kid because it *isn't* my life. It can't be. And I don't want it to be." Not when she was so convinced that she would eventually come up short in it and lose him anyway. Lose him and her mother's livelihood and her own pride along with it all....

"There's just too much at stake, Tate," she said. "Last

night was…" Why was her voice cracking? She wasn't going to cry! She wouldn't let herself.

She cleared her throat. "The last week, last night—it's all been amazing, I won't deny that. But in the cold light of day today, when you're talking about the *future?* You still belong on your side of the bushes and I still belong on this one."

"I'll cut the damn bushes down!"

"That's the point—even if you wanted to do that, no one else on either side would stand for it."

He shook his head firmly. "No, Tanya, I'm not taking that as an answer."

"It's my answer. You can't change it."

"But you can. You want to break down barriers for a living, expose wrongs, change things—start here."

"I don't think it would make any difference here. I only think it would do damage." To her. To her mother. And she wouldn't do that.

"Tanya, I'm in love with you!"

Her breath caught in her lungs at those words that everything in her wanted to hear, wanted to be able to rejoice in.

But as heartfelt as they sounded, she still wasn't sure that whatever he was feeling was real or enduring or anything she should count on. She thought it was more of an exuberance he was experiencing as he emerged from the low point he'd been in. And that wouldn't last.

Tanya swallowed hard and forced herself to breathe again. But the best she could manage was a whispered, "I'm sorry," before she pulled her hands out of his.

"Don't do this," he said. "You're wrong and you're ruining so much for both of us."

But she only repeated, "I'm sorry."

Then she stood and went into the house because she

knew she couldn't keep from crying for much longer and she wouldn't do that in front of him.

She made it as far as the laundry room and ducked in where she knew Tate couldn't see her before she crumpled against the dryer and sobbed.

And that was when she admitted to herself that while she might not believe that Tate genuinely loved her, she was very much afraid that she might have genuinely fallen in love with him....

Chapter Thirteen

"Tate McCord *proposed* to you?"

It was after four o'clock on Monday afternoon. In the midst of last-minute, hectic preparations for the McCords' Labor Day party, JoBeth had hustled into the cottage for a sandwich and, while she was throwing it together, had demanded to know what was going on with Tanya and Tate.

Because her mother was so busy with the party, Tanya had been able to keep a low profile since Tate's visit Sunday morning. *This* morning JoBeth had noticed her lethargy and swollen eyes, but Tanya had said it must be allergies. She'd known her mother was skeptical, but JoBeth hadn't had the time to explore it.

Then, apparently, during the course of the day, JoBeth had overheard the gardeners talking about seeing Tate storm away from the housekeeper's bungalow Sunday. Added to an unusually heated argument between Tate and his brother Blake over Katie Whitcomb-Salgar at lunchtime—during which Tate had apparently shouted that Katie Whitcomb-Salgar was the last thing on his mind—JoBeth had put two and two together. And come home to Tanya for the truth.

Knowing how relentless her mother could be, Tanya had given in without much resistance and told her mother the whole story.

"It wasn't a formal, will-you-marry-me proposal, no," Tanya answered her mother's shocked question. "But I think that was what he was saying, yes."

"And you said no?"

It hadn't occurred to Tanya until hours later on Sunday that Tate could fire her mother out of retribution, and with that on her mind now, too, she could only apologize to JoBeth the way she had to Tate yesterday morning. "Yes, I said no. And I'm sorry, Mama. I don't think it will hurt your job but it's probably better if I get an apartment right away—out of sight, out of mind—just for safekeeping."

While she ate more of her sandwich, JoBeth waved that away, obviously unbothered by it. "It isn't as if I'd have you marry a man just to save my job, Tanya. But by the same token, I wouldn't have you *not* marry someone you want to marry because of it."

"I didn't say I wanted to marry him," Tanya said quietly.

"But you do. Look at you—this is not *allergies*. And I heard you up pacing most of the night."

"Everything with Tate just came out of the blue and surprised me," Tanya said. "Having something serious with him—a *future* with him—isn't something I'd ever thought about." Although she'd thought about almost nothing else since …

"But you do want to marry him," JoBeth repeated.

"It's complicated—maybe that's what happens when you let yourself get involved with someone who leads a complicated life," Tanya said, referring to her mother's past words.

"But you do want to marry Tate," JoBeth repeated yet again.

"I don't know, Mama!" Tanya snapped.

JoBeth let a moment of silence follow to relay her lack of appreciation for having her head bitten off. She didn't say anything about Tanya's outburst, though. Instead, after finishing half of her sandwich, she said, "My position here is not the reason for you to say no if you want to say yes. Either I'm hired help who makes the schedule and tells the staff what to do, or I'm the in-law on the payroll who makes the schedule and tells the staff what to do."

"You don't think it would be weird if you were the in-law who did it?"

"Weird becomes normal if you give it enough time. And I'd certainly have job security," JoBeth said.

"Unless of course I married him and six months down the road he realized that I don't belong with his family and friends, and Katie Whitcomb-Salgar looks good to him again—the way she always has before when one of their breakups ended."

"So my job isn't the only reason you said no."

"It was only one of them—a big one, but only one. You've reminded me yourself that Tate and Katie always get back together. And of course I know how things are— a *McCord* isn't supposed to *marry* the help. And I'm happy with who I am, I like it, I *want* to be in touch with the real world the way you sent me to Grandma and Grandpa to be. I don't want to be a *McCord*."

"Another of the reasons I sent you to spend time with your grandparents was because I didn't want you to want what you couldn't have. But you want Tate. And wanting what you *can* have? I don't know that you should turn your nose up at that, Tanya."

"But like I said, even if I *can* have Tate now, will it last? And wouldn't it be so much worse to have him for a while and then lose him because one day he regrets that I'm *not* Katie Whitcomb-Salgar?"

"What does Tate have to say on the subject of young Miss Whitcomb-Salgar?"

Tanya told her mother all of Tate's claims that he and Katie were nothing but friends and never again would be engaged.

"And you don't believe him?" JoBeth asked.

"It isn't that. But you know how many times they've called it quits and then started up again. I'm sure he believed it was over every time. And it wasn't."

"But he's different now than he was before."

That was true and Tanya couldn't refute it. But did the change in him mean that the back-and-forth with Katie was over?

"He is different," Tanya conceded rather than address the issue of whether or not that was any guarantee that he was finished with the other woman. "But the rest of his family and friends aren't and they have their hearts set on him being with Katie. There's bound to be pressure for that and all the more disapproval of me because I'm standing in the way of that."

"But if it really is over between them Tate won't go back with her because other people want him to. So his family and friends will just have to be disappointed and learn to live with it. And if Tate honestly has changed and doesn't feel as if he completely fits in with everyone anymore, doesn't that clear the way for the two of you to carve out a place of your own that isn't altogether on his side of the fence—so to speak—or altogether on yours?"

"We'd be *in* the bushes?" Tanya muttered to herself, knowing her mother wouldn't understand the reference to what she and Tate had talked about.

Then, to JoBeth she said, "I don't know. I suppose it's possible that we could make a niche of our own. But it still wouldn't take away the risk that eventually Tate might want to be back in the heart of his circle, and not with the housekeeper's daughter at his side."

"So I suppose what you can do is try to figure out if you think this change in Tate is permanent or temporary. And no matter what you think, decide if you want him enough to take the risk on him."

JoBeth glanced at the clock on the wall. "I shouldn't have been away this long on a party day. I have to get back," she announced as she set her dish and the other half of her sandwich in the sink.

But still she hesitated to leave Tanya, looking at her daughter with sympathetic eyes. "I hate to see you so mopey," she said. "And poor Tate, he seems just as miserable. I thought he was down before, but now? This is as bad as he was right after word came that his friend was hurt."

Tanya felt guilty for being comforted and satisfied at hearing that Tate felt awful, too. But she did.

"I know he invited you tonight," JoBeth went on. "Maybe you should come."

"And help you tell the kitchen staff to wash glasses and serve dessert, or hide that you and I are mother and daughter when I'm introduced to the governor?"

"I'll take care of the glasses and the dessert and when I see you with the governor I'll come over and you can introduce me, too," JoBeth said, solving the problem simply. Then she gave Tanya a hug before she headed for the door to leave.

But before she did, she turned back to Tanya and added, "I always wanted you to have more in life than I did, Tanya. I wanted you to have your education, to have a career you chose—not just the best job you could get under the circumstances. You've done that and I'm proud of you. Proud of the person you are and proud of your accomplishments and successes. But most of all, I just want you to be happy. If Tate McCord makes you happy, then… Well, where there's a will, there's a way. That may not be something Tate had to learn, but it's something you did. And don't ever—*ever*—let me be what blocks that way. Or any other people, either."

When her mother left the cottage Tanya sat at the kitchen table where her notes were spread out. She'd been trying all day long to get some work done on her report but today, like Saturday, cataloging information on the McCords didn't help keep her from thinking about Tate.

Plus the sounds of all that was going on on the other side of the bushes didn't aid her concentration.

The day of one of the McCords' parties required full staff in addition to outside caterers, waiters and waitresses, bartenders, decorators, florists and extra gardeners. As a child on days like this, Tanya would have been at the heart of it all. She would have had orders to stay out from underfoot, but she would have been put to work running messages from one place to another or doing small odd jobs. It had always been fun and exciting for her.

And then when the party got underway, she would have kept out of sight in the kitchen, watching from there or from behind the bushes when her mother sent her off to bed and she'd hidden there instead of minding her mom.

But today she was nowhere. She wasn't enjoying the bustle and camaraderie of the staff as they did their jobs. She wasn't getting to see everything come together. And she wouldn't spend tonight in the kitchen or sitting in the bushes to watch from the sidelines.

This time around, she was missing out on it all and that added to the sadness she was already wearing like a shroud.

She was sad and melancholy and lonely and miserable and tied up in knots—that's how what had happened with Tate yesterday had left her.

And yet her mother had been so calm about it....

Was that only an act to make me feel better? Tanya wondered as she stared into space rather than at any of her papers.

She knew her mother well and she didn't think that JoBeth had been hiding her true response to spare Tanya. Her mother hadn't seemed at all upset or worried or even unnerved by this turn of events or what could come of it. And if it wasn't a big deal to her mother, should it be such a big deal to her? she asked herself.

Maybe not *such* a big deal—at least when it came to her mother's job. But the fact that JoBeth could come to grips with the idea of Tanya being with Tate still didn't remove the whole problem.

It would still be strange for me, she thought.

As strange as it had been to be at Tate's country club, at the charity dinner, surrounded by the people who had always been a part of his life, by his family. A family *served* by her mother and other people who were like *her* family. How could she be a part of both sides?

Just thinking about it felt awkward, even if JoBeth *had* taken it in stride.

But it was her mother who had suggested that maybe Tanya and Tate could carve out a place of their own and that caused Tanya to recall something that had occurred to her on Thursday night after that steamy kiss they'd shared—that when they were together it *was* in some kind of no-man's-land between their two worlds.

But even if they *could* carve out a place of their own between the two, there would still be times when she would have to venture into the McCord circle....

Okay, so she'd handled Friday night's charity dinner all right, and while she hadn't been received with open arms and warm hugs, there hadn't been any open hostility or snubbing, either. If it was always like that, would it be unbearable? she asked herself.

It wouldn't be, she decided. And really, as a reporter, she was often met with some reservation. So what if the country-club set didn't embrace her and usher her into their ranks? She didn't want to be there anyway and as long as she wasn't shunned, she could live with aloof courtesy. Plus, socializing with the movers and shakers might even give her inside information here and there that she could use—in that way it could even be good for her career.

But country-club events weren't staffed by her mother and a whole lot of other people Tanya was close to. What about *those* times? Times that were purely personal? When her career wouldn't enter into it?

She thought about that. Thought about her mother's comment about introducing JoBeth to the governor.

Yes, if Tanya met the governor she'd be thrilled to turn

around and introduce her mother. She certainly wouldn't be embarrassed or feel the least bit ashamed.

So maybe when it came to occupying a new position here, it was all in the attitude. And since Tanya felt certain that she would always have the same attitude toward the people who worked for the McCords, then maybe an alteration in roles was just something minor to be dealt with. Something slightly weird that would become normal, the way her mother had said of her own position....

The more she thought about that, the more doable it seemed.

But what *wasn't* only something to be dealt with was Tate himself.

Were the changes in him permanent? Could she trust that he *had* come to the point where he was finished with Katie Whitcomb-Salgar....

The musicians must have arrived because Tanya heard the tuning of instruments begin.

The party would start soon.

Tate would be there.

Katie Whitcomb-Salgar would be there.

And the mere idea of that tightened the knots in Tanya's stomach and somehow made everything she was mentally sorting through feel all the more in immediate need of a resolution.

Were the changes in Tate permanent? Or would he go back to being the carefree, insulated, good-time-Charlie he'd been before?

She'd told Tate that it seemed to her that the changes in him were really only that he'd grown up, matured. She honestly believed that. And those weren't things that were likely to revert.

Plus, she thought that his eyes genuinely had been opened, and to more than his feelings for her the way he'd said on Sunday morning. And now that they were, now that he felt so strongly about what he'd witnessed and experienced, was it conceivable that he would close his eyes to it all again and be able to forget about it, to go blithely on?

She didn't think that *was* conceivable.

What she'd learned about him was that he had a determination to do more, to help more. Yes, he still needed to reconcile his guilt over having so much himself, but to go back to his carefree ways? That just didn't seem like what the man he was now would do.

No, the more she thought about it, the more convinced she was that the Tate who had evolved out of the sorrow of losing his friend, the Tate who had gone to the Middle East to contribute what he could, was also the Tate who had returned home determined to continue to contribute here. And *that* was the real Tate now. The Tate he would be from here on.

The Tate who had impressed her and earned her admiration. The Tate who had won her over.

But there was still Katie Whitcomb-Salgar....

The last thing on his mind—that's what her mother had overheard him yell at Blake.

And how many times, in how many ways, had he told Tanya that his relationship with Katie was over?

More times, in more ways, than she could recall.

And if she tried to plug the new Tate into the old pattern of on-again, off-again with Katie?

Tanya had to admit that it didn't line up.

The old Tate was easily swayed. He'd gone whatever way the wind blew. So whenever the wind had blown him back in Katie's direction, he'd merely gone with it.

But the new Tate was firm in his convictions. Plus it seemed as if he'd gotten to know himself on a deeper level. To recognize things not only about life beyond the walls of the mansion and the country club, but about himself, too.

And one of the things he'd said he recognized was that he and Katie were nothing more than friends. And never would be anything more than that....

Tanya wanted to believe that so much it hurt.

But a breakup of Tate and Katie that actually stuck? That was the hardest for her to bank on when he'd gone back to Katie so many other times....

But he swore it's me he wants, not her....

And the truth was, Tanya wanted him too much not to hang her every hope on believing that, too.

Because if her mother was right, that where there's a will there's a way, Tanya definitely had the will to be with Tate. And if the way was to accept that he meant what he'd said when he'd told her he was through with Katie, then that was what Tanya had to do.

She just had to.

To do anything else was to deny herself Tate.

And more than anything in her entire life, *he* was what she wanted.

And if she could have what she wanted, she should....

That was something else her mother had said and suddenly Tanya was in complete agreement.

She nearly jumped up from the kitchen table and ran for the bungalow's front door.

Then she heard the strains of music coming from the other side of the bushes.

Somewhere in the midst of being lost in her own head, the party had begun....

That's where Tate would be now. And in order to get to him, to see him, to tell him she'd changed her mind, the party was where she would have to be, too.

"So I guess I'm going to my first McCord private party as an invited guest," she said as she took a deep breath to steady herself.

But then she realized how she was dressed.

Her mother had said that the invitations had recommended casual dress, but cutoffs, a tank top and her hair in a ponytail were a little too casual.

Besides, she didn't want to be anywhere near Katie Whitcomb-Salgar without looking her best.

"Just a little while longer," she muttered to herself as she spun on her heels and made a dash for the shower.

Just a little while longer before she could find Tate and tell him that if it wasn't too late—and if he'd really been asking her to marry him—the answer just might be yes....

Chapter Fourteen

Flowered halter sundress. Three-inch high-heel sandals. Slightly less than on-camera makeup. Hair washed, dried and left flowing loosely around her bare shoulders—that was how Tanya left her mother's house and went into the Labor Day evening where darkness had fallen and the white glow of bright party lights lit the night on the other side of the bushes.

Music was playing and the muffled sound of voices and laughter drifted to her as she stepped onto the path that cut through the bushes and trees separating the McCord mansion from her mother's bungalow.

Her shower and party preparations had been tinged with doubts and concerns about everything from the possibility that Tate might have had second thoughts about her by now, to the chance that he *hadn't* been proposing at all and she'd grossly misunderstood him, to the fear that because she'd turned him down he'd already reconnected with Katie.

So as Tanya went along the path she was a bit of a wreck inside.

The closer she got to the McCords' backyard the louder was the music, the voices, the laughter, and the brighter was the glow of light from beyond the path.

That bright glow cast deeper shadows from the bushes and trees and Tanya was startled to suddenly happen upon two people in a small clearing almost at the path's end. Two people standing facing each other, talking intently enough to be unaware of her.

Tanya hesitated. She had to pass by that clearing to get to the party. To Tate. But by then she could tell the people were a man and a woman, and although she couldn't hear what they were discussing, they were very involved in it.

Plus, there was something familiar about the man's broad-shouldered back that gave her pause....

Then the woman moved inches to one side and Tanya caught enough of a glimpse of her to realize who it was.

Katie Whitcomb-Salgar....

And if that was Katie standing in a relatively private cove with a broad-shouldered man....

Tanya held her breath. She thought her heart actually stopped beating as the worst-case scenario flooded through her mind.

Was Tate the man whose back she was staring at? The man with Katie?

Were they getting together again?

Was that what they were talking about?

Frozen now with her own fears, as Tanya looked on, the man took a step forward, closer to Katie Whitcomb-Salgar.

They could just be talking, Tanya reasoned.

But what if there was more to it....

She didn't want to witness it if there was. If it was Tate with Katie.

Should she make her presence known?

Or should she just turn around and go back to her mother's house? Should she forget everything about this last week with Tate? Everything he'd said to her? That he may have proposed to her? Should she ignore everything she'd hashed through this afternoon? Everything that had brought her here to talk to him?

Better that, better that he never know she'd changed her mind, better that she salvage her pride if he was proving that she'd been wrong to decide to trust him. To believe that he really had grown or matured. To believe that he had meant it when he'd said he was finished with Katie....

Hot tears flooded Tanya's eyes and she hated herself for being so gullible....

And then there was another adjustment in the positions of the two people she was spying on. The man shifted and turned, putting him in profile, allowing her to see that it wasn't Tate with Katie.

It was Blake....

It was Blake!

Tanya blinked away her tears, realizing at that moment that she was just being a basket case. She had no idea why Blake would be in a somewhat secluded spot with his brother's former fiancée but she didn't care. The only thing she cared about was that it *wasn't* Tate.

She let out the breath she'd been holding, veered far enough off the path for Katie and Blake not to see her as she slipped past them, and then there she was, at the end of the path, peering into a sea of Dallas's elite and the people serving them.

But there was only one face she was searching for in the crowd. That one face she wanted to wake up to every morning for the rest of her life....

And then she spotted it.

Tate was standing near the guesthouse's front door. Alone, looking out over the festivities, removed from them.

He was dressed in slacks and a sport shirt. He had a drink in his hand, but his expression said he was only going through the motions. And not putting much effort into even that.

Tanya summoned strength with another deep breath and stepped off the path's edge and into the crowd, making her way through it with her eyes trained on Tate.

Please don't let it be too late....

She was several yards away when he saw her coming. His eyes opened wider, his brows arched. But he didn't smile. He just watched her close the distance between them and she knew that repairing things was going to be up to her....

"Hi," she said when she reached him, hating the quavery tone in her voice and hoping he hadn't been able to hear it over the music and the party sounds.

He didn't return her greeting. He merely raised his eyebrows higher, acknowledging her that way but offering no more than that.

"I wondered if we could talk," she said, not knowing what else to do but get right to the point.

"If you're worried about your job or your mother's, don't be. In fact, when it comes to your job, I just talked to Chad Burton—"

"The station owner of WDGN is here?"

Tate nodded in the direction of the crowd of guests. But

Tanya didn't want to look away from him. As important as her career was to her, at that moment it wasn't as important as he was, as what she'd come to talk to him about.

Still, before she'd said anything else, Tate said, "I told him to put you back on the air."

"You did?"

"He thinks there's enough material to stretch out your reports, to start them with family history and go from there. I agreed. I'm just hoping that you won't burn us—that you'll keep any information on the diamond for a big finish only if and when we find it."

He was trusting her. That meant more to her than the fact that she was getting her job back. And it also brought her around again to what she really wanted to say to him.

"Thank you," she said first. "But my job and my mother's job aren't what I came to talk about."

"What did you come to talk to me about?" he asked in a challenging tone.

"I wanted to talk about us...." If there *was* an us... "Could we go somewhere quiet? And private?"

His expression remained blank but he motioned with his glass to the guesthouse.

Tanya's heart was back to beating like a drum as she preceded him to the door. Since it was his home, she waited for him to open it and only went in when he said, "Go ahead."

She stepped into the guesthouse where a single table lamp was the only light and it was actually dimmer inside than it was outside.

Tate came in after her, closing the door behind them, muting the noises. And suddenly Tanya was on the spot without being sure what she was going to say.

She walked as far as the island counter that separated

the kitchen and the living area, turning to lean against it and grab on tight to the granite's edge on either side of her hips as if she needed anchoring.

But before she'd thought how to proceed from there, Tate set his glass on an end table half the room away from her and said, "So there's an *us?* You told me at the planetarium that there wasn't."

"I hope now that there is. Or can be," Tanya admitted.

"It was you who didn't want there to be," he reminded her.

"It isn't that I didn't *want* there to be an us," she amended. "I was just…worried about what it might mean if I let there be."

"But now you aren't worried?"

"Well, less," she admitted with a nervous laugh, thinking that she couldn't in all honesty say she was completely unconcerned after the scare she'd just had on the way here.

"But I talked to my mother," she continued, going on to tell him what she and JoBeth had discussed, how JoBeth's support had cleared the way to rethinking everything else that had caused her stance on Sunday morning.

"You said I gave you a new perspective—but I guess I needed one myself," she concluded when she'd told him the whole thing. "But maybe you should tell me how you see things after having a little more time to think about it."

"There's only one thing I see, Tanya," he said, coming to stand in front of her, taking her upper arms in his hands. "What I see is you and that I want you. A life with you. Close to my family or far away from it—all I want is you. I told you, the details can be sorted out. The only thing that's important to me is that you and I are together."

"In what way, exactly?" she asked quietly, tentatively,

because as good as what he'd said sounded, it still wasn't a proposal.

He broke into a slow, one-sided smile. "What do you think?"

"I think you were asking me to marry you yesterday morning, but maybe not and I don't want to accept a proposal that isn't one."

A wide grin spread over his handsome face and obliterated even the last remnant of the dour expression she'd been greeted with.

"It was a proposal yesterday. It's a proposal today. I love you, Tanya. I want you to be my wife."

"I'd like to be your wife," Tanya said, intending it to sound more lighthearted but instead her voice had come out quietly and heartfelt.

And in response Tate's grin became a soft smile just before he pulled her toward him and leaned to meet her so he could kiss her as if it had been far too long since the last time.

Or maybe that was just how it seemed to Tanya as his arms came around her and hers went around him, and she melted into him, starved for that kiss, for him.

Almost instantly the kiss wasn't only a kiss that reunited them and sealed their commitment, though. It was a kiss that sparked a hunger in them both and ignited a flame of passion.

Passion that quickly had his hands on her eager breasts.

But when he untied the halter from around her neck, Tanya reluctantly broke away, holding her top in place with one hand pressed to her chest.

"The party…" she reminded him breathlessly.

"…can go on without us for a while," Tate finished her sentence before he retook her mouth with his.

Tanya couldn't refuse herself what he was offering in

favor of any party. Or anything else she could think of as her mind emptied of everything but the wonders of Tate's mouth on hers, of his hands on her bare breasts, of her hands unfastening the buttons of his shirt as fast as she could.

The island counter was the perfect height and once clothes had been flung aside, Tate lifted Tanya onto it, making good use of it. Still kissing, and with her legs wrapped around his hips, and hands exploring and tantalizing, nothing penetrated their absorption in each other or the tiny universe of pleasure that surrounded them and carried them away.

Until the pinnacle had been achieved and the sounds of the party in full swing just outside the guesthouse seeped back into Tanya's consciousness.

"I hope you locked that door," she said with her forehead resting on his shoulder as if it were a shelf.

He nipped at her collarbone and said, "I don't think I did."

"So anybody—one of your family—could just walk in any minute looking for you...."

That made him laugh. "I guess they could."

Tanya pushed away from him and crossed her arms over her bare breasts. "We have to get dressed and go out there before that happens."

Tate placed a sweet, sexy kiss on each of her breasts where they bulged above her arms. "I could lock it now and we could take our time..." he offered, sucking lightly on the side of her neck.

"I think it's better if we can slip out of here before anyone comes looking for you and finds the door locked or unlocked."

He took a deep breath and sighed it out in a warm gust that brushed her bare skin. "The voice of reason—how much fun is that?" he said before he kissed her again and gave her second thoughts about having him lock the door after all.

But then he stopped kissing her and lifted her off the countertop. "I suppose I should track your mother down anyway and ask for your hand in marriage," he pretended to concede against his will.

The idea of him asking her mother for her hand in marriage made it Tanya's turn to grin. "Have I told you that I love you?" she asked him when the feeling welled up in her so much she couldn't contain it.

Tate kissed her, a brief peck of a kiss, and said, "No, but now that you finally have, I'll want to hear it at least seven times a day, every day."

"Should we make a schedule?" she joked as they both began to gather their clothes and dress again.

"I think spontaneity might be nicer."

Which he proved when he used the time during which he was buttoning his shirt to kiss her neck again and say, "But I *do* love you, Tanya Kimbrough. More than you'll ever know."

After a few swipes of his brush through both of their hair and a little damage control of her makeup, they shared one more long, lingering kiss before they did as Tanya had suggested and slipped back into the Labor Day festivities.

As they did Blake was in the process of quieting the music so he could take over the microphone at center stage.

When he had, he said, "On behalf of my mother and the rest of my family, we want to welcome everyone here tonight."

Tanya was surprised when Tate moved to stand directly behind her where he wrapped his arms around her, holding her tightly against him and propping his chin on top of her head.

With wide eyes, Tanya glanced around to see if anyone

was looking. But no one seemed to be taking any notice and since it was so nice to be there like that with him, so nice to be publicly claimed by him, she just curled her own arms up and clamped her hands around his forearms.

"…I also wanted to take this opportunity," Blake was saying, "to say congratulations to my cousin Gabby and her new husband, Rafe—who have just come back from their honeymoon in Italy." Blake held up his glass in toast as he went on. "Rafe, we're happy to have you as a part of the family now."

Applause and congratulations went up all around and Tanya was heartened somewhat by the warmth that went with it. The man Blake was so openly admitting into the McCord clan was Rafael Balthazar, who had been employed by the McCords to provide security for McCord's Jewelers and, more recently, as Gabby McCord's bodyguard. If the security consultant and bodyguard could become a McCord without anyone wincing, maybe Tate marrying the house-keeper's daughter wouldn't be so difficult to accept either.…

But as Blake urged Gabby and Rafe to join him on stage, and the crowd chimed in their encouragement, Tanya looked out over the splendor that was the McCord home and lifestyle and knew in her heart that it didn't make any difference if she was ever truly a part of it.

The only thing she wanted to be a part of was what she and Tate would have together. The rest was nothing more than the border around the edges of the bigger picture.

And as she stood there, fitted to him as if they were meant to come together as one, the last of her doubts, of her fears and worries, seemed to float off in the evening breeze.

Because at that moment she knew deep down that nothing he could have ever had with anyone else, nothing thrust upon him, nothing he'd drifted in and out of, could be anything like what the two of them had found with each other.

And that what the two of them had found with each other really would hold them steady through family approvals and disapprovals, through feuds and diamond hunts and lost treasures and financial woes. Through anything that they had to face.

For a lifetime that they had already begun to carve out together.

* * * * *

Dear Reader,

Taking on new challenges is sometimes frightening, always thrilling, hopefully rewarding. Such was the case when we were given the privilege of collaborating with other authors on THE FOLEYS AND THE McCORDS series. Writing as partners, our twosome suddenly became a "sevensome" to develop this series. It stretched our skills and gave us a backstage look at how our fellow authors create. *The Texas CEO's Secret* was—in short—a blast to write.

Watching as the touching complexity of the love affair between Katie Whitcomb-Salgar and Blake McCord developed, we found our own emotions entrenched in their lives and in the lives of the other Foleys and McCords. That's the fun thing about writing and reading romance—living vicariously through characters who, simply put, are merely people like us, with the same loves, losses, joys, sorrows, dreams, hopes and fears we all have. It is with this thought in mind we hope you enjoy the exciting, passionate unfolding of Blake and Katie's discovery that they are meant for each other.

Nicole Foster

THE TEXAS CEO'S SECRET

BY
NICOLE FOSTER

First published in Great Britain 2010
Harlequin Mills & Boon Limited,
Eton House, 18-24 Paradise Road, Richmond, Surrey TW9 1SR

© Harlequin Books S.A. 2009

Special thanks and acknowledgment are given to Nicole Foster for her
contribution to The Foleys and the McCords mini-series.

ISBN: 978 0 263 88831-7

23-1010

Harlequin Mills & Boon policy is to use papers that are natural, renewable
and recyclable products and made from wood grown in sustainable forests.
The logging and manufacturing processes conform to the legal environmental
regulations of the country of origin.

Printed and bound in Spain
by Litografia Rosés S.A., Barcelona

Nicole Foster is the pseudonym for the writing team of Danette Fertig-Thompson and Annette Chartier-Warren. Both journalists, they met while working on the same newspaper, and started writing historical romance together after discovering a shared love of the Old West and happy endings. Their twenty-year friendship has endured writer's block, numerous caffeine-and-chocolate deadlines, and the joyous chaos of marriage and raising five children between them. They love to hear from readers. Send a SASE for a bookmark to PMB 228, 8816 Manchester Rd., Brentwood, MO 63144.

For my partner.

In all our years collaborating as partners, friends and sisters, writing this book was a unique experience. For us to be able to share it made it the best experience possible. Thanks, partner.

Chapter One

It was a lover's night, velvet-dark and sultry, with silvered moonlight and the intimacy of midnight stillness that invited temptation and seduction.

But Katerina Whitcomb-Salgar wasn't with the man she'd professed to love and had intended to marry. She'd left him behind, another woman in his arms, along with the confidence that there were certainties she could rely on, and at the top of the list was that one day she'd be Mrs. Tate McCord.

Instead, she was on her way home with Tate's older brother and wondering what the lingering revelers at the party they'd abandoned were making of that. More strongly, she questioned herself and what had prompted her to accept his unexpected invitation to escort her to her doorstep.

Katie looked sidelong at Blake McCord, covertly

studying his profile in the dim shifting glow of passing cars and streetlights. He and his brother shared the same dark blond good looks, but Blake's arrogance and focused resolve, the qualities she'd defined him by over the years, showed clearly in the lean, hard lines of his features. He and Tate were so different, almost opposites; nothing about him should have attracted her.

Yet here she was, alone with him and conscious of an edgy, almost nervous energy that was both unfamiliar and unsettling.

"You're very quiet," he said, in a low voice that filled the silence in the car and betrayed no emotion except polite concern.

"I'm sorry, it's been a long evening." It had nearly been an evening at home. She'd considered making her excuses about attending the lavish Labor Day party at the McCords' Dallas mansion, especially days after she and Tate had broken their engagement, knowing people would be talking, speculating, asking questions. But backing out simply to avoid a few uncomfortable hours seemed cowardly so she'd put on a little black dress and a smile and walked in alone. Except she didn't remain alone. Blake, oddly enough, had spent the majority of the time at her side, attentive in a way that was almost protective. He'd even made a point of getting her alone for a few minutes to ask for her version of her and Tate's broken engagement and how she was handling it, then made his offer to take her home early.

He briefly glanced her way. "No apologies necessary. Seeing Tate with someone else can't have been easy."

"No, but not in the way you mean," she told him honestly. "It's more my having to make explanations to everyone as to why we broke things off."

"He hurt you—"

"I told you before, at the party, it's not like that." Katie sighed, not sure how to explain her feelings any more clearly than she'd tried earlier. Blake wasn't a man who inspired confidences. Unlike Tate, whom she could easily read, she was never quite sure what Blake was thinking, what emotions lay behind the cool, aloof face he presented to the world. That he was Tate's brother—longtime friend or not—made this whole conversation, their being together at all, strange and more than a little uncomfortable.

She repeated the assertion she'd made to him the first time. "A marriage between Tate and me wouldn't have worked. We've both known it for a while now. I care about Tate, I always will. But there wasn't any… passion between us."

"You were lovers."

Katie felt herself flush, glad for the covering darkness. "It's not the same thing. Neither of us ever felt compelled to be together. There was never anything overwhelming about what we felt for each other."

"That sounds like Tate talking," Blake said tightly.

"You seem determined to blame him. But believe me, it was a mutual decision. I'm just feeling a little… lost, I guess. Tate and I were together for so long. It's the starting over part of this that isn't easy."

She didn't expect Blake to understand. In all the time she'd known him, the women he'd dated seemed nothing more than accessories to him, the obligatory beautiful and well-dressed companions for the social events he attended and, she assumed, casual lovers. Against her long-term attachment to Tate—cultivated by their families from childhood—Blake would have no basis for comparison.

"It may have been mutual, but as far as I'm concerned, he treated you badly. He never appreciated what he had in you. All those years you were together, I wouldn't have called him faithful or even considerate a good part of the time. You didn't deserve that."

The underlying anger in his tone surprised her. She wouldn't have pictured Blake in the role of her defender and yet she had the impression this wasn't the first time he'd voiced these opinions, probably to Tate. It left her more confused about who he was and what she wanted.

The conversation lagged the remainder of the ride and the short walk from his car to the front door of the Salgar estate Katie still called home. Awkwardness took hold, at least on her part, as she hunted for the conventional courteous phrases to release him from any further obligation to her and finally end what had been several taxing hours.

"Thank you for bringing me home," she said. "It was nice of you to take the trouble."

He was looking at her with an odd expression she couldn't decipher. "It was hardly the chore you're making it out to be."

"I appreciate it all the same." She hesitated before adding, "Good night, Blake."

She expected an echoing rejoinder and him leaving. Instead he let several moments pass before reaching out and tracing his fingertips over her cheek.

His touch, gentle and unexpected, hitched her breath. "Blake…"

Under any circumstances, she wouldn't have anticipated him touching her like this, let alone taking it further. But when he did, she couldn't think of a reason he shouldn't. She couldn't *think* at all.

He moved closer and, drawn by the intensity of his gaze, she matched him until they stood lightly pressed against each other. Bending to her, he brushed her lips with his, the barest touch at first. It teased her senses, giving her a taste of the wine he'd drunk, a hint of his heat, the spicy scent of his cologne. She returned the caress in kind, testing the novel sensation of his mouth on hers and finding the scant feeling more enticing than an intimate kiss.

After long seconds, Blake broke the tentative contact to look at her, as though gauging her and his responses. Whatever he saw apparently made up his mind and he slid his hand around her nape, threading his fingers into her hair, bringing her closer at the same time he slanted his mouth over hers.

If he had been aggressively passionate, she would have found him easy to resist. But his kiss, slow and sensual, with a depth of tenderness she never would have guessed he possessed, had her melting into his arms, yielding to a rush of desire so intense that what she'd felt when Tate held her suddenly seemed pale in contrast.

It was impossible. This was *Blake*. They couldn't— and it didn't matter because she was kissing him back, her hands on his shoulders, his free hand splayed low on her back molding her body to his, and her world in that brief time narrowed to him.

She might have given into temporary madness and allowed her feelings to seduce her into inviting more intimacy than a few kisses, but Blake didn't give her the chance. Almost abruptly, he stepped back from their embrace and from his slightly stunned look she knew he'd been as caught off guard as she by the feelings he'd exposed.

He half raised a hand as if to touch her again then let it drop. "Good night, Katie," he said softly.

He left her in the pool of light on her doorstep, watching him stride away and fighting the urge to call him back....

"Katie?"

Slim fingers waved in front of her face, jolting Katie back to the present.

Her assistant, Tessa Lansing, stood at her side, with a handful of papers and the twitch of her lips threatening to become a grin. "I've got the information on those grant proposals you wanted but it looks like you're somewhere else a lot more interesting than here. Whoever he is, he must be somebody special."

"I was just thinking," Katie said quickly, sure her face was as red as Tessa's bobbed curls.

"I got that. But that look on your face begs the question about *whom?*"

Coming from anyone else, the blunt curiosity about her personal life would have been irritating. Tessa, though, was a friend and after eight years of working closely together, helping Katie in her position as administrator of the Salgar's charitable foundation, there wasn't much about Katie's moods that escaped Tessa's notice.

"No one in particular," she said lightly.

Tessa eyed her over the top of her glasses. "Right. I've never seen you look like that even when you talked about Tate. Sorry," she added at Katie's small frown, "I'm sure that's a sore subject right now."

"I am getting tired of everyone assuming Tate dumped me for Tanya Kimbrough or that I left him because he treated me badly and that either way, I'm devastated."

"Oh, I see," Tessa teased. "You're saying you dumped him for the guy that makes you all dreamy-eyed."

"No, and I wasn't all dreamy-eyed. Let me take a look at those," Katie said, taking the papers from Tessa to change the subject.

But the subject—Blake McCord—was no more easily dismissed in her thoughts than he was in person.

Nearly a week had passed since that kiss that shouldn't have happened and she should have forgotten. Except she couldn't forget, and forbidden or not, she couldn't rid herself of the restless, indefinable longings he'd stirred up in her.

If things were different, she would have avoided him until she could sort out the tangled mess that was her feelings these days. But she and Blake were the primary planners for the Dallas Children's Hospital's major annual fund-raising ball, and at this phase of the preparations, she couldn't limit their contact to phone calls and e-mails without compromising efficiency.

In fact…she glanced at her watch. In a few hours, because of the scheduled hospital board meeting, they would be in close company again. She didn't know what to expect, from him or herself. Would he pretend it never happened and nothing had changed between them? Or—and this was the more daunting option—would he want to confront it, either dismissing it as a moment's impulse or acknowledging it was something more?

Uncertain how to answer herself, Katie was less sure which alternative made her more uneasy.

Blake McCord stared at the electronic display of times and dates telling him where he was supposed to be today, not really seeing the neatly plotted schedule, but instead having an all-too-real vision of disaster.

He was fast running out of time. Unless he could pull

off the risky scheme he'd devised to rescue McCord Jewelers, there might be little left to salvage from the wreckage of the family fortunes. There was no question about his determination to succeed. But he didn't like the odds that the entire plot would blow up in his face and leave him with an even worse situation.

Wishing for other options was a waste of time. He'd committed himself to carrying this through, despite the dangers. There was no going back.

"This is becoming a bad habit with you." Seated at the head of the table, Eleanor McCord frowned at the brief glance her oldest son gave her in acknowledgment. "I don't know why you bother coming to meals anymore. It's obvious that business has all your attention."

"I'm sorry," Blake said shortly. He put aside his BlackBerry long enough to finish off the last of his coffee, wondering at the same time why he did bother. This morning, in particular, he should have avoided a breakfast tête-à-tête with his mother in favor of the relative solitude of his office. He had enough on his mind these days without adding family issues to the mix. "I'm juggling a number of things and they're all priority at the moment."

Eleanor didn't respond at once but instead studied him. "You never share your responsibilities," she observed after a moment. "I can't remember a time when you allowed yourself to share the load."

"That would be because they are *my* responsibilities. Besides, It's not like anyone has exactly begged me for the opportunity."

"Perhaps, but nonetheless, I'm concerned about the effect that whatever this latest crisis is having on you. I don't think I've ever seen you quite as irritable and distant as you've been these past few weeks. I'm assuming the situation with the business is worse off than you've been saying. Or is it something else?"

"It's nothing you need to worry about." The lie came out smoothly.

"It's not that, so much," Eleanor said. "I'm worried about you."

"That would be a first," he retorted, immediately regretting it.

Under other circumstances, he would never have let his feelings slip. But things between him and his mother had been more tense than usual since Eleanor had revealed that an affair twenty-two years ago between her and Rex Foley, patriarch of the rival Foley clan, had produced Blake's youngest brother Charlie. That her late husband, Devon McCord, had apparently never known Charlie wasn't his son hadn't made Eleanor's confession any easier for her four other children to accept. What with the weight of being solely liable for the family business's survival or collapse coupled with the knowledge of his mother's betrayal, Blake silently admitted his temper was more than a little frayed. It was straining all his relationships, but particularly those with his family. He and Eleanor had never shared a warm, close bond, but her admission had severely tested the link there was.

Still, he hated his inability to keep his emotions in check. Shoving them aside, he made an effort to backtrack. "Everything is fine, or will be soon. I just need a few more weeks to straighten things out."

Eleanor's raised brow telegraphed her annoyance. "I'm not stupid, Blake. I know there are problems. Your father's spending habits were hardly a secret. Sometimes I still find it hard to believe how much money he managed to go through in a relatively short time. I know he didn't do the business any good, and with the retail market the way it is, McCord's must be suffering."

"If there are problems, I'll take care of them," Blake said, getting to his feet, deliberately ignoring the familiar criticism of his father. He, better than anyone, knew how many millions Devon had squandered on maintaining the lavish lifestyle he thought he was entitled to. "I always do."

"Blake—"

"I have to go. I have a full schedule and a board meeting at the hospital this morning," he explained referring to his seat on the board at Dallas Children's Hospital.

"Will Katie be there?" Eleanor asked.

At the mention of his brother's former fiancée, Blake retreated further behind carefully constructed indifference. "I would assume so. She is a board member."

"You're working together planning the Halloween ball, aren't you?" At Blake's curt nod, Eleanor appraised him in silence for a moment, then gave a small sigh. "It's a shame she and Tate couldn't have worked things out, they were so well suited. Although he and Tanya seem very happy together, so I suppose it's all for the best. I wonder about Katie, though, if she's been accepting of their breakup and Tate becoming engaged again so quickly as Tate claims."

Blake sensed his mother still harbored reservations about Tate's romance with Tanya Kimbrough. Scant weeks had passed between Tate breaking his engagement to Katie and deciding Tanya, the McCord's housekeeper's daughter, was the love of his life. Blake had doubts, too, but he kept them to himself, not wanting to encourage any hopes his mother might have that Tate and Katie would reconcile.

"Katie appears to be handling it well," Blake said dismissively.

On the road to his office a few minutes later, he wished his mother hadn't mentioned Katie. With everything demanding his attention, he didn't need another distraction and yet he found himself too often thinking about the one woman who never should have entered his mind—his brother's ex.

For months now, and especially since the night of the Labor Day party, he'd caught himself watching her, finding reasons to talk to her, thinking about her even before she and Tate split up and when his focus should have wholly been on business.

And that night... The memory still had the power to eclipse all others despite his best attempts to exorcise it and reject it as nothing more than a fleeting impulse on his part.

He had told himself his offer to take her home was a friend's gesture, to help ease her awkwardness at being the center of speculation at the party, the hurt she denied but he had to believe she felt seeing Tate in love with another woman. He could make a case for that up until the moment he touched her. Then he'd kissed her, his fingers tangled in her dark, thick hair, her soft curves pressed against him, and he knew he shouldn't have, but damn it, it had felt too good, too right to stop.

Before, as Tate's girlfriend, then fiancée, she'd been off-limits. He still wasn't allowed to want her, though she was no longer his brother's woman. She was vulnerable after her breakup with Tate and he had no business exploiting it to satisfy his own desires. Katie needed someone who would cherish her, commit to a loving, lasting relationship. In that respect, he was definitely not the man for her, or anyone else.

Despite that, he couldn't seem to control his feelings when it came to her and his lack of control irritated him. It also made him more determined to act the strict professional today at the board meeting. Most likely, she'd decided the same thing. They could ignore what had happened and go back to being friends working together to accomplish a common goal.

He convinced himself of it as he strode into the boardroom, ready for business.

Except, following him inside was an invisible companion that taunted him for his prick of disappointment when he didn't see her among the group, an inner voice that called him a liar and questioned whether forgetting was going to be as easy as he expected.

Chapter Two

Where was she? Blake tugged the white cuff of his shirtsleeve back and for the third time in ten minutes glanced at his watch. Would Katie actually skip the board meeting to avoid seeing him?

It was only a kiss.

If that were true, then why did his insides still turn at the memory of her willing lips? Why did his fingers ache for the feel of her hair twined between them, his senses yearn for the scent of her musky perfume?

"I'm sorry to keep everyone waiting."

The rich melody of her voice brought his eyes up, meeting hers. She stood across from him at the massive boardroom table; their eyes caught and held moments too long. A fact he knew didn't go unnoticed by the other board members.

Katie broke their gaze, glanced quickly around the

room. "I had a last-minute delay," she said, smoothing her black pencil skirt to her slim thighs before taking her seat opposite Blake.

She looked perfect, as usual, he noted, the teal of her silk blouse accenting her dark eyes and hair, the sensual curve of her mouth as she spoke drawing the attention of every male in the room, an observation that made Blake both jealous and proud—though he realized one touch to those lips gave him no right to be.

At the head of the table, the board president called the meeting to order and laid out the agenda. Blake heard him drone on, but only from a distance. He couldn't manage to focus on anything but the woman sitting in silence, quietly stealing his attention, too far away to touch, close enough to capture his every thought.

"Blake, you *will* take care of those paintings for the silent auction, won't you? Blake—are you with us?"

Katie's eyes fixed on him. "Blake," she whispered across the table. "Evan is talking to you."

"Of course I will." Blake turned sharply toward the man at the head of the table and said tersely, "I told you I would a month ago, didn't I?" He hoped his tone would be a save for his embarrassingly distracted state.

"Good. *Sorry,* I didn't think you were listening," Evan Rutherford returned, matching Blake's insolence.

Blake faced Katie. "You and your family know the Kenningtons better than I do. They might be more generous with their donations if you joined me when I go talk to them."

Katie's lashes fluttered once as she blinked back a look of awkward surprise that amused Blake. "I—of course, I'll be happy to visit them with you. I'm quite familiar with their collection."

"Thank you." He'd put her on the spot publicly and after the barest hint of a falter, she'd responded with her usual grace. But the look she gave him now said he'd be hearing about this later.

"Very well," Evan pronounced with typical condescension. "I trust you two will manage to secure a few excellent pieces for the auction. Now moving on to the remainder of the donations…"

Again Blake tuned Evan out. With a flip of his BlackBerry, he could call in favors across the country to bring in a number of high-ticket items for the auction, in addition to the Kenningtons' artworks and he hardly needed Rutherford to tell him how to do it.

What he did need was time alone with Katie. Seeing her again after spending too much time wondering what she'd been thinking, feeling since that night they'd kissed intensified his need to know. Damn this meeting, anyway. It was taking forever. They'd all done these charity events dozens of times before. Why were they wasting his time on details he knew by rote memory, wasting hours he could be using much more productively? He had to get back to the office soon. Deciding to take control of the situation, he motioned to Evan.

"Are we about done here? I have another meeting."

Rutherford cleared his throat loudly. "Well—er…"

"Good." Blake shoved his chair back and turned from the older man to Katie. "May I have a word with you before I leave?"

Again, Katie shielded her thoughts from the rest of the room, allowing for his eyes only a flash of agitation. "Certainly. Will you all excuse me for a moment please? Obviously, Blake is on a tight schedule. As usual."

He followed her out into the hallway of the administrative wing of the hospital. The second he closed the door behind them, she planted the palms of her perfectly manicured hands on the curves of her hips and fixed him with a frown.

"If you weren't a McCord, Evan would have kicked you off the board by now, you know that? He doesn't take well to interruptions or usurpations of his authority. Yet you manage to pull them off at nearly every board meeting."

"Evan can go straight to hell."

"Well, you're certainly in a mood today."

"So I've been told. Is there some reason you've been avoiding me?"

She glanced away, letting her palms slide from her hips down the front of her skirt. "I haven't been avoiding you."

"It's interesting, then, that I haven't heard a word from you since the Labor Day party. We are supposed to be working together on this fund-raiser."

"That doesn't mean we need to be in constant contact, does it?"

"Are you angry about that night?" Blake asked her bluntly. "Angry I kissed you?"

Her eyes brightened, her lips parting for a too-light and casual laugh that sounded forced. "What, that? Oh, Blake, really. I'm not a schoolgirl. It was a simple kiss good-night. Nothing more. We both know that."

His eyes narrowed on her. "You're lying."

"Don't flatter yourself."

"I don't have to. I've known you since you *were* a schoolgirl, remember?"

Her bravado left her then. "Touché." She paused and took a deep breath. "No, I'm not angry," she said softly. "It was…I don't know—nice."

"Nice?" She nodded and he scowled. "I don't think I've ever been told that before."

"Well, I'm sorry if that doesn't flatter your ego, but somehow I think it will survive intact without my stroking it."

Blake found himself taking a step closer. "You think so?"

"I doubt my opinion of you matters," she said levelly, but he noticed the quickened pace of her breath, the slight flush in her face.

"It matters." Gently, he traced his knuckles down her cheek. "It matters a lot."

She looked back at him, her dark eyes pooling with a mixture of emotions, drawing him to plunge in.

Then the schedule alarm on his BlackBerry beeped, breaking the mood. Blake swore under his breath.

"You'd better go or you'll miss your meeting," Katie said.

"I'll call you later today about meeting with the Kenningtons."

"No rush," she returned lightly, renewing the tension Blake had been battling for the last week.

"Just keep your phone on." Irritated and feeling she'd somehow taken control and gotten the best of him, he turned on his heel, determined to ensure the next round with Miss Cool and Collected Whitcomb-Salgar would be his.

When the last trace of his broad shoulders disappeared around the hallway corner, Katie released the breath she'd been holding and leaned against the wall. Had she succeeded in hiding the past week's daydreams, memories, questions, guilt and desire his single kiss evoked in her? Judging from his reaction, she'd have to guess she had. So why didn't it feel more satisfying to know she'd fooled him into thinking that night—that kiss—didn't matter?

She glanced at her watch. She should get back to her office, too, but she'd told the other board members she'd rejoin the meeting. Desperately wanting to escape, she reluctantly went back into the boardroom to face a dozen sets of curious eyes.

The rest of the meeting passed in a blur, her thoughts unresolved, miles away in a different moment and place.

As if the day hadn't been long and difficult enough, Blake's arrival home only added pressure on pressure.

"So I heard you walked out on the board meeting at the hospital today and pissed everyone off, particularly Evan," Tate said as he met Blake in the library of the McCord mansion, drink in hand. "Everyone but Katie, that is."

Blake poured himself a scotch on the rocks. "If our company worked as efficiently as the gossip mill around here did, we'd be thriving instead of drowning."

Tate's brows drew close. "So no progress yet."

"All I can say is the PR campaign had better work miracles, and Paige had better get busy finding the Santa Magdalena Diamond, or we're sunk."

He was relying on his younger sister, the geologist and gemologist, to locate the famous canary diamond as part of his efforts to restore the McCord fortunes. The diamond was supposed to be hidden in an abandoned mine on Travis Foley's ranch, which made the task of retrieving it all the more difficult. Though the McCord family held the deed to the ranch, if the Foleys got wind of what they were up to, Blake was certain they'd find a way to sabotage his plans. He hated having to depend on Paige, but this was one element of his master plan he couldn't pull off himself.

He downed the shot of scotch. It burned slightly as it slid down his throat, but the pain was a welcome distraction from the pain in his head. "Speaking of that, is Paige around?"

"I haven't seen her yet this evening." Tate paused, swirling the ice in his glass. "So what's this I hear about you and Katie whispering in the hospital hallway?"

Blake jerked back a little. "What's it to you who Katie's whispering to? You broke things off with her."

"I did not and you know it. It was mutual—and it was her idea first. Katie's free to whisper to anyone she cares to. But it just looks strange for my brother to be disrupting a meeting to pull my ex out into the hall for a little tête-à-tête."

"That's ridiculous," he said, knowing it was a lie. "Who's been talking to you?" Though he'd rather walk on hot coals than admit he had any interest in Katie, internally he tensed. The truth was he couldn't get her off his mind and a part of him felt oddly guilty because of it.

When he'd seen her today, his first thought was to taste those tempting lips again. His second was to get her alone and taste a lot more than that. That's where he'd stopped himself from mentally drifting any further into fantasies about his brother's former fiancée.

"To me?" Tate was saying. "No one. But Evan called Mom after the meeting and apparently he was pretty put off about the whole thing."

"Evan needs to get a life. And so does everyone else who's trying to make something out of nothing. I had to leave and before I did I needed to make plans with Katie to help me wring a few pricey paintings out of the Kenningtons. End of story. Not that it's any of your business."

"What's none of his business?" Paige asked, waltzing into the room. Blond and beautiful as her mother and her twin, Penny, Paige's eyes sparked mischief as she perched on the edge of an armchair.

"Don't you start, too. Isn't any damned thing private around here?" Blake muttered, refilling his glass.

"Are you kidding?"

"Right. What was I thinking?"

"So, what's the big secret Tate isn't supposed to know?" she asked.

Blake skipped answering her question. "I needed to talk to you. I've got some new information on the mine. It's not much but I thought I'd pass it on in case it helped."

"Really?" Paige asked, looking interested. "What?"

"It has to do with the interior configuration and passages. I have the specifics at my office. Drop by tomorrow and I'll show them to you."

"Sure. I have to run now, though. I want to catch a lecture on a rare Chinese black pearl at the museum of gemology."

"Sounds thrilling," Tate teased.

"Beats the heck out of scrubs, blood and needles," she quipped in reference to Tate's position as a surgeon at Meridien General Hospital.

"Okay, okay, point taken."

Paige waved a hand goodbye and left the room, humming some new tune Blake had heard on the radio but couldn't name. He was counting on his little sister to come through for him and secure the Santa Magdalena Diamond or—or *nothing*. He didn't want to think about the *or* because at this point there wasn't one.

Tate finished his drink and flipped open his cell, punching in a number, smiling when the person at the other end picked up. "Hey, babe, you ready? I'm done here." He paused, listening, then with a "Love you, too," punched the off button.

"How's Tanya?" Blake asked since it was obvious Tate had been making plans with his new love. Though he couldn't resist giving Tate some grief over his treatment of Katie, actually Blake was happy his brother seemed to have found a true soul mate in Tanya.

"Great. Perfect. We're meeting some friends for dinner at that new bistro downtown so I need to get going."

"Give her my best," Blake offered, glad to see his brother relaxed and enjoying his new relationship, despite the pain and awkwardness the whole breakup with Katie had created.

That was in the past and Tate now seemed genuinely satisfied. Katie, on the other hand, seemed conflicted. Suddenly he remembered he'd told her he'd call before the day's end. He checked his watch. Eight o'clock already. Too late to call? Probably, but somehow he didn't care. He wanted to see her as an antidote to the day's tensions, though, through no fault of her own, she'd been a contributing cause.

"Sorry it's so late," he said when he heard her soft voice at the other end of the line.

"I thought you'd forgotten."

"No, just a long day. How about a nightcap?" He threw out the invitation casually, then waited, hoping the long pause wasn't a signal he was wasting his time.

At the other end of the line Katie considered his offer. All afternoon she'd been haunted by confused feelings, conflicting emotions of guilt over the chance that she might be attracted to Tate's brother and excitement over the possibility that Blake might be attracted to her.

Against her better judgment, she finally answered, "Sure. Sounds *nice,*" she teased recalling to him her description of his kiss—which was so much more than *nice* she scarcely dared admit it to herself.

"I have to do something about this *nice* stuff. It's going to ruin my image."

She laughed a little and they arranged to meet at an intimate club situated in town about halfway between the McCord and Salgar estates.

Katie rushed to change into a little designer cocktail dress and strappy heels and to freshen her makeup. Lining her lips in a shimmering pink tone that flattered her skin, eyes and hair, she gazed at herself in the mirror, realizing she'd never before felt compelled to primp for Blake. He was just a friend after all. Now, though…uncertainty washed over her as she imagined a ghost of Tate at her side in the mirror.

"This is ridiculous," she muttered, stuffing the lipstick into her beaded evening bag, reminding herself she and Tate had agreed to move on with their lives and without each other.

Twenty minutes later, after the valet had taken the keys to her Jaguar, she entered the dark club, her eyes adjusting to dim lighting and low tables with black tablecloths and silver candles.

She felt a large, warm hand on her lower back. "You look beautiful." Blake's appreciative remark sent a shiver down her spine only to disappear beneath his touch.

"Oh, you startled me. I didn't see you there."

"I have a table for us." He pointed to an intimate booth in a corner near the elegant marble-topped bar.

"Looks like you had a few to choose from. Small crowd tonight."

"Midweek." He shrugged, motioning her to lead the way.

As she sat down, she saw that he'd already ordered her favorite white Bordeaux. Lifting the glass appreciatively, she smiled. "You've known me too long."

He slid in beside her and as her eyes adjusted she noticed he too had changed from his business suit to a more casual black turtleneck and blazer, a look she definitely appreciated.

"On the contrary, lately I've begun to feel like I'm just beginning to know you."

Her nerves jumpy, Katie took a sip of wine to calm them. "Is that so?"

"Very much. In fact, I'm looking forward to working with you more closely on the Halloween ball. I have the feeling I'm going to see sides of you I've never seen before."

"You make me sound more complex than I am. I'm the same old Katie you've always known."

"There's nothing the same or old about you. It's not really fair, you know," he mused, resting back in his seat, "wearing a dress like that when we're supposed to discuss business. Looking at you, how am I supposed to think straight?"

"Since when do you waste compliments on me? Save them for those supermodels you seem to like to decorate your arm with."

"They're wasted on them," he said in a low voice she almost took for serious.

He couldn't be, though she didn't understand this change in him. He'd always been coolly polite to her, solicitous even, but never flirtatious or suggestive, nor had he ever given her the slightest indication he considered her anything else but his brother's fiancée. This shift in his attentions to her was unsettling because she didn't know how to respond.

Deciding to take control of the conversation, she brought up plans for donations for the ball. Obligatorily, he answered her questions, agreed to her ideas, added a few of his own.

"As a team, I've no doubt we'll bring in more top-dollar auction items than the rest of them put together," he said.

"Ever the indefatigable confidence. I'm glad you have it because I'm concerned this year. People aren't as generous in times like this."

He leaned a little closer. "Katie?"

Wondering at the intensity of his tone, she met his gaze. "Yes?"

"Can we change the subject?"

"I—of course. But I thought that's why you asked me here."

"It wasn't."

Her stomach fluttered and she wasn't sure if she wanted to ask the obvious question. She did it anyhow. "Then why?"

"It was a demanding day for a lot of reasons and the one way I realized I could actually relax and enjoy the evening was to spend it with you."

Now he wasn't teasing. She knew him that well. His honesty touched her, reflected her own feelings about seeing him again tonight. "I'm glad," she said quietly, "because I wanted to see you again, too."

"I'd like to do more of that."

Wanting the same, nonetheless she lowered her eyes. Where was this going? It should stop here, before it really started. She'd ended her engagement only weeks ago; she had no business throwing herself into another relationship so soon, especially a relationship with Tate's brother.

"Isn't there another fund-raiser for your uncle coming up in a week or so?" Blake interrupted her inner debate.

Katie nodded, though his question, seemingly off topic, caught her off guard. Her uncle, Peter Salgar, was making a bid for governor, and the upcoming gala was one of many she'd attended over the last year in support of his campaign. "I can't say I'm looking forward to it, but it's difficult to say no."

"I know you usually end up going to those alone."

"If you mean Tate never went with me, you're right. It would have been rather awkward, don't you think?" That was putting it mildly. Scandalous might be a better description. One of her uncle's strongest supporters was Rex Foley and the McCords had traditionally backed Peter's opponent in this race, Adam Trent.

"Why don't you let me escort you?" Blake offered.

"You?" Katie shook her head. "I couldn't ask you to do that. Your family would disown you."

"You aren't asking, I'm volunteering. And as for my family, whom I spend my time with and where is my business."

"I don't think your mother will see it that way."

"I'm well beyond the age of needing my mother's permission, or her approval." Reaching across the table, he touched her hand. "Say yes."

If it were merely a simple party, the answer would have tripped off her lips easily. She enjoyed every moment they'd spent together at such events as friends. But now, given her breakup with Tate, the fact that most of the Foleys would be at the fund-raiser, and there would be many people there taking critical note of her escort, in addition to the lingering memory of how much she'd enjoyed their one kiss, she felt confused, hesitant.

"I want to go with you and I appreciate the offer but—"

"I understand," he said gently, and she feared he truly did. "I'll have your car brought around."

He seemed disappointed, though his brief half smile exhibited a sincere attempt to hide his feelings.

Without thinking of the consequences, she blurted out, "I'd love to. To go with you," she amended at his confused look. "Thank you. It was nice of you to suggest it."

His expression relaxed and he gave an appreciative nod. "There's that word again. I promise, my intentions are purely to ward off all those people who want to ask questions about you and Tate."

"Thanks, but I can take care of myself. I'll just enjoy not having to show up alone." That much was true. She delighted at the idea of walking into the fund-raiser on Blake's arm. Unfortunately, her mind wouldn't let her enjoy that notion freely, though. It came with weighted strings attached.

"Will you let me bring your car around now?"

"Oh, no need. I valeted." She took her ticket out of her purse and with a slight brush of her lips to his cheek, eased away from him. "Please, stay and finish your drink. Thank you again for the wine."

For a moment she thought he might get up and follow her out, but after moving in that direction, he seemed to think better of it and stayed put. "Send me a text when you get home, okay? Let me know you got there safely."

Turning from him, her mind and emotions locked in internal warfare, she managed a smile and a lighthearted "Will do" before slipping out into the night.

Chapter Three

A dozen important things demanded her attention and there were other places she ought to be, but Katie, desperately needing a distraction or a confidant—she wasn't sure which—had temporarily put them aside for a long lunch with a friend. She hadn't planned on the outing today—on top of everything else, she was hosting a dinner tonight for several potential donors to the children's hospital benefit—but when Gabriella called, Katie had jumped at Gabby's invitation.

Gabby, Blake's beautiful blond cousin, had recently wed Rafael Balthazer, the head of security for McCord Jewelers, and the couple had decided to make their home in Italy. But at Blake's request, Gabby was back in Dallas for a short stay, doing some modeling for McCord's as part of the PR campaign Blake had recently launched.

"Marriage obviously agrees with you," Katie said, after the waiter had left with their orders. "I know it's a cliché, but you're positively glowing."

"Being in love will do that." Setting down her wineglass, Gabby fixed her with a slight frown. "You, on the other hand, are not glowing. Just the opposite in fact. What's wrong? Is it the breakup with Tate?"

"Not really," Katie hedged. "That's been difficult but not nearly as awful as everyone seems to believe." At Gabby' expectant look, she gave in. "It's Blake."

"Ah. I was wondering how long it would take him."

"How long it would take him to do what?"

"Whatever it is that he's done to upset you."

The waiter interrupted, bringing their salads, and Katie waited until he'd left before saying firmly, "He hasn't upset me. But I didn't expect—" She broke off, not sure if she meant to confess about him kissing her, his new attentiveness or her confused feelings.

"I've suspected for a while from things he's said and the way he looks at you that there was something between you two, at least on his part. I'm not the only one who's noticed, either. If it hadn't been for Tate I think Blake would have done something about it a long time ago." Gabby shrugged off Katie's skepticism. "Don't take this the wrong way, but I hope you know what you're doing getting involved with someone so soon after Tate, especially a man like Blake."

"I'm not *involved* with him, but even if I were, what's so terrible about Blake that you feel the need to warn me away?"

"I didn't say terrible," Gabby said carefully. "But Blake is—difficult. He's not exactly a warm, open person. As far as I know, he's never had a serious relationship, which is not surprising considering how demanding he is. I'm not sure you're ready for the challenge."

"Just because he's focused and takes his responsibilities seriously, doesn't make him difficult," Katie responded, with more force than she intended. "And I know I can rely on him. I cared for Tate, I still do, but he was never the devoted type, at least with me," she said, echoing Blake's criticism of his brother. "If I hadn't been raised to believe we'd end up together one day, I doubt I would have stayed with him as long as I did."

Gabby started on her salad. "If I were you, I'd rethink that denial about not being involved with Blake."

"It's the truth. We're friends, nothing else." Inwardly, she winced, aware of the waver in her voice that betrayed her uncertainty. Yet she doubted that Blake had been as affected by their brief encounters, and she was wary of admitting anything she felt was more complicated than a weak moment on her part. He'd made it clear he found her attractive and had, in typical fashion, taken charge and acted on it. She was vulnerable, finding her way in the wake of her broken engagement, and had surrendered to temptation. Why did it have to be anything other than that?

"Whether it's true or not, if people keep seeing you together, they're going to talk about your preference for McCord men," Gabby cautioned her.

Not wanting to admit it to Gabby, Katie found the idea she could be seriously attracted to Blake a little embarrassing. Her friend was right, people would talk, and the gossip wouldn't flatter either her or Blake. She could only imagine his reaction to that. Thinking about it, she was seriously starting to regret accepting his offer to escort her to her uncle's fund-raiser. It was only going to convince some people, like Gabby, that there was more between them than friendship and a temporary working partnership.

"I can't stop people from talking, but I'm not certain what my preferences are right now." Yet even as she said it, she saw Blake. "I've never given any thought to what I want in a relationship and until I do, I don't intend to get too deeply involved with Blake or anyone else. It wouldn't be fair to either of us." She smiled at Gabby, hoping she radiated confidence. It was a sensible speech, a reasonable plan for the future.

But inwardly, Katie thought sense and reason didn't have much to do with desires and it was going to be difficult to stick to her guns when it came to Blake McCord.

Her determination to try, though, carried her through the rest of the day and into the evening, allowing her to maintain a veneer of aloofness when she greeted him in the elegantly appointed living room an hour before the guests were due to arrive.

There were questions in his eyes at her shift in attitude, but he didn't comment and, taking his cue from her, his manner toward her was a shade cooler.

"I haven't had the chance to tell you, but I had a call from the caterer this afternoon. They apparently had a scheduling problem and they've cancelled," she said, handing him a glass of wine. His fingers brushed hers and lingered for brief seconds, as did his gaze on the smooth skin and hint of cleavage exposed by her sleeveless dress. Her breath quickened and she turned slightly aside. "I've found a replacement, a firm your mother recommended. I tried to call you before I booked them, but you weren't answering your cell."

Blake's mouth quirked at the corner in a sardonic half smile. "You don't need my permission to make decisions, Katie."

"I know you're accustomed to taking the lead," she answered with a small smile of her own. "I'm pretty certain teamwork isn't one of your favorite strategies."

"Guilty as charged. But you're quite capable of taking the lead yourself. I'm impressed you were able to find a replacement so quickly. I doubt I could have handled the situation any better."

"It was hardly a crisis. But thank you, that *is* a compliment."

"You sound surprised." Blake moved by her a few steps with the apparent intent of studying one of the large landscapes on the wall, stopping within a hand's distance of her. His focus on the painting, he added, "I do give them occasionally."

"From what I know, very occasionally," she said, softening her tone to a gentle teasing, though she herself had more than once thought him cold and critical of others' opinions or actions, especially when it came to his business. Yet over the years, she'd come to realize that he was most critical of himself, demanding perfection of himself and expecting no less in others. She had never really given it much consideration, accepting it as part of him, but she wondered now what drove him to put so much pressure on himself. It could be arrogance, him believing no one else could do it better than he. Some instinct balked at accepting that simple explanation, though. There was nothing that simple about Blake.

Abandoning his appraisal of the painting, he faced her. "You don't seem to have a very high opinion of me," he said dryly. "I'm guessing that's the reason why we've gone back to being polite acquaintances."

"That's not it at all." Her eyes slewed from his steady gaze to his hands, one clasped around his glass. It was ridiculous to crave a touch, so strongly desire the warmth of a caress; to feel those needs all the more intensely from simply a glance his direction. How could she, who couldn't claim to have ever been swept away by passion, want so much?

"If it's easier for you to pretend that nothing happened—"

Katie raised her eyes, saw an inscrutable expression in the steel-gray of his. "No, I don't want to pretend. But it's…complicated."

"I suppose it is, if we make it that way."

"It can't be any other way, for me." And it troubled her he apparently didn't understand or share her conflicted emotions.

He replied with silence, watching her in a way that made her feel he was weighing her words, judging her honesty. "Then it's complicated," he said finally. "But it doesn't have to be impossible."

"I need to decide that for myself. I've let everybody tell me what's right for me for too long now. It's time I make my own choices."

She half expected he'd take offense, but to her surprise Blake smiled. "Fair enough. But I hope, at least once in a while, you'll give me the opportunity to influence those choices."

Not waiting for her answer, he took a step closer and lightly kissed her, touching her only with his mouth. The lingering caress flushed her with a slow, curling heat and briefly erased every reason she'd given herself that this was a bad idea. If the door chime, announcing the first of her guests, hadn't intruded, she suspected Blake might have convinced her to forget reason completely and act on her desires.

She thought Blake knew that from the almost smug satisfaction in his face and the way he stayed next to her to greet the new arrivals as if they were a couple, hosting the evening together. She liked the feeling he always seemed to be there when she most appreciated having someone at her side; she was unnerved by how much she liked it. More unnerving was how much she liked him touching her.

This shouldn't happen between them, not so soon after her broken engagement, maybe not ever. And yet, putting on the face of hostess, she couldn't shake the sensation that somehow, some way, it had become inevitable.

Never a fan of these sorts of gatherings, Blake found new reasons for his distaste the longer the evening progressed. Most of the guests, the women in particular, preferred hearing about Katie's personal life over her appeal for the hospital. He knew it wasn't the first time she'd had to put up with the whisperings behind her back and the less than subtle probing to her face, but tonight he found it unusually grating.

After dinner, in the middle of making small talk with one of the hospital's bigger benefactors, Blake shifted slightly to bring Katie into his view. She'd been cornered by Selina Harrington and from her stiff posture and the flush in her cheeks, the conversation wasn't going well. Excusing himself, he strode over and slid a hand against her waist, smiling at her when she looked up with a slight start.

"I'm sorry to interrupt, but Parker was asking about the plans for expanding the orthopedic wing. If you wouldn't mind, you're better with those details than I am."

She thanked him with her eyes. "Of course," she said, glancing to Selina. "If you'll excuse me—"

"You two seem very cozy," Selina commented once Katie was gone. Her smile was brittle, a gesture that didn't extend beyond the movement of her carefully painted mouth. "All this togetherness and solicitous concern is so unlike you, Blake."

"Obviously you don't know me as well as you seem to believe," he drawled, the deliberate sardonic cast he put to his words causing her face to tighten. Despite it being three years past, Selina had never forgiven him for turning down her invitation to a casual affair. Selina, former model turned trophy wife, had her attractions but he'd made it clear to her then he never got involved with married women. She, though, had chosen to take his refusal personally.

"Obviously," she snapped. "I thought you had this rule you didn't—how did you so charmingly put it?—take second place when it came to your lovers. Apparently that doesn't include your brother's leftovers." The gibe stung and Selina nodded in satisfaction at his scowl. "So it's true, Katie Whitcomb-Salgar didn't waste any time substituting one McCord man for another. I'd love to know her secrets. Any woman that could convince you to be your brother's replacement must have something special."

He made himself smile, but it was as hard as his voice. "Katie is something special. She's a beautiful, intelligent woman and a friend. But much as I hate to disappoint you and the rest of the gossips who are apparently bored for lack of a scandal, I'm not Tate's replacement and am never going to be."

"Honestly, Blake," Selina said with a harsh laugh, "do you expect anyone to believe that? You spend most of your time looking at her as if you're thinking of everything you want to do to her once you get rid of the rest of us."

Selina's husband coming up to claim his wife saved Blake from a less than honest answer. But rejoining Katie and the conversation of Parker's intended contribution, he couldn't easily discount Selina's observation as pure spite. It made him hyperconscious of his expressions, his gestures around Katie, wondering how much he was betraying without being aware of it.

Even more grating was the idea that he was considered Katie's second choice after Tate. Worse was the unwelcome thought that Katie might look at him that way, as a substitute for the man she loved and desired but couldn't have.

He was still dwelling on it, hours later, when he and Katie said their goodbyes to the last of the guests.

With a sigh, Katie leaned her back to the door. "I always have a hard time enjoying these things. They're too much like work."

"It was quite a success, though. Parker in particular agreed to double his contribution. You should be proud of yourself."

"Yes, that will certainly make a difference," she said slowly. She looked closely at him, frowning slightly. "What's wrong?"

"As you said, these events are too much like work." Aware of the shortness of his tone, he tried to amend it. "It's late and I'm sure you're tired. I should be going."

She ignored his attempt to avoid subjects best left

alone. "Selina said something to you, didn't she, about me taking up with you on the rebound from Tate?"

"She said something along those lines, but it's hardly an issue, is it?"

"Apparently not," she said quietly. Straightening, she turned away from him. "You're right, it's late. Thank you for coming, Blake."

"Katie—"

"I can't stop people from talking." she spun back around. "All I can tell you is they're wrong."

"Are they?"

"Exactly what is that supposed to mean?"

A volatile mix of frustration, banked desire, doubt and anger cracked his facade of indifference and he eliminated the distance between them, grasped her shoulders and covered her mouth with his. He took advantage of her lips, parting in surprise, to kiss her deeply, his tongue sliding along hers in intimate possession. She matched him with a throaty moan that spiked his need and urged him to take what he wanted, what he'd wanted for months, for years but had refused to acknowledge to himself.

He couldn't deny it now. But he hated the idea Katie might be comparing him to Tate; hated more the uneasy feeling that he might not care, that he might be willing to sacrifice his pride if he could have her.

Abruptly, he broke off, breathing hard. "I won't be second-best. Not now, not ever."

Before she could confirm or deny it, he strode past her and out the door, not sure which of them was more shaken by the complete loss of his prized control.

Chapter Four

It was the price they had to pay.

Katie sighed to herself, listening alongside Blake as Pearl Kennington droned on about Katie's broken engagement to Tate and any other tidbit of McCord or Foley gossip she could latch on to. In order to be privy to a showing of possible artworks for donation to the hospital charity ball auction, Blake and Katie were destined to endure luncheon with Pearl. Hal, short for Halbert Kennington, was to join them later.

On her part, she was ready to put up with Pearl for the sake of the children's hospital. It was Blake that worried her. He'd never been easygoing and that he was under pressure was obvious, but she'd never seen him so tense. The way he'd snapped that night at her house had given her a glimpse of the demands he put on himself and hinted at something more unsettling, that he was angry she might compare him to Tate and find him lacking. If he only knew how many times it had been the other way around.

"I simply can't imagine your mama's disappointment, Katie, dear," Pearl was still going on. "I mean after all these years of hopin' and plannin' on your life with Tate. Oh, my, poor Anna. I haven't had the courage to call her. After all, what does one say to a dear, old friend on such a sad occasion?"

"Tate is much happier and so am I," Katie managed, trying to keep the edge out of her voice. "Mother understands that." It was a white lie, but one she had to tell in order to stop the hemorrhaging of gossip and guilt.

"Well, of course that *is* all anyone ever wanted for the both of you," Pearl said with a slight sniff. She raised her delicate teacup, pinky properly uplifted, and glanced absently toward the silver tray of finger cookies.

Blake had sat mostly in silence throughout the ordeal of lunch and dessert. Now, Katie noticed him restlessly drumming his fingers on the arm of his oversize chair. As was the case with every room in the Kenningtons' mansion, furnishings and trappings were overdone. Bigger than life—Texas style—Katie's mother, Anna, had once commented. Anna, who favored elegant understatement in everything from her clothing to the design of her estate, told Katie long ago that the Kenningtons' lifestyle gushed with the same excess as their numerous oil wells did. Nonetheless the two couples had been friends for decades, Anna keeping a polite distance throughout.

A fact that had driven Pearl to near madness. On occasions such as this, she used every moment to go for the social jugular.

"Juanita." She clapped as she called for her maid who stood silently behind them at the ready. "I believe we're finished. Please refresh my guests' coffee so they can take it along on our little tour."

"*Sí*, ma'am." The girl nodded, her eyes bowed.

"I am anxious to view your collection," Blake said, helping Pearl from her chair. "I've heard a lot about the controversial sculpture by that French artist who recently passed away. LeDoux was it?"

"Why yes, such a tragedy. So young. But you know those French…"

Katie scrunched her nose and caught Blake's barely concealed smirk. Standing behind Pearl as she rose, heavy gold bracelets clanking, a serious look swept his expression clear of anything but a studied interest. "Oh, yes, *those* French."

"Precisely," Pearl echoed, satisfied her guests caught her meaning.

Katie fell in beside Blake, who, gallantly, had taken Pearl's arm. They walked, rather nearly crawled, down a seemingly endless corridor, the walls lined with a wealth of paintings to rival a moderately sized city art museum.

Pearl prattled on, shuffling from room to room, describing in tedious detail her proud collection and pointing out a few pieces she might consider donating to the auction. "But, ya'll understand, the final decision is up to Hal."

"Naturally," Blake agreed, continuing to ask politely interested questions while Katie struggled to resist looking at her watch. Then one work in particular caught her eye. She examined it closely, turning to find Blake mesmerized by the same painting.

"This is astounding," she said distractedly.

Blake stepped closer to her and to the painting. They stood in silence several long moments, though within that silence passed a communion of spirit as the painting's effect permeated their hearts and minds.

"It's so simple, yet so profound," Katie said at last.

"I know." Blake's voice had lost it's usual assertiveness, as though humbled by the impact of the artist's rendering of a small child bending to save a lone, wounded duckling from the shore before a rush of water was about to sweep it downriver.

Pearl moved closer to the twosome. "My, my, why, I never would have imagined you two would fancy that little ole watercolor. How odd that you both took to it so."

Katie pried her eyes from the painting to examine Pearl. She found her eyes still piercing, despite the wrinkles that nearly engulfed them. "Why?"

Pearl lifted a thin shoulder and dropped it. "Well, it's simply not that impressive a work to most people. It's by a little-known eighteenth-century Russian painter who died in obscurity."

"And poverty, no doubt?" Blake turned to Katie. "Like most artists."

"Yes, it's hardly fair, is it?"

"Well, this one might have made a living at his work, but he painted so few, even if he had sold them all, he couldn't have supported himself. The ones that survived the revolution are worth quite a bit, however."

Blake glanced at Katie, who knowing what he was thinking, replied with a small nod. "I don't suppose you could part with this one, for the auction?" Charm was layered in his voice, his smile subtly sexy enough to melt a woman's resolve at any age.

"Well, now," Pearl said, eyeing them both speculatively, "it seems the two of you are sharing some private affection—for the painting, that is. I'm sure it has nothing to do with any more than that, now does it?"

Katie bristled. So, lunch wasn't the only price today. If they were to earn their auction donation, they were going to have to pay with inside information. Which of course, she wasn't about to dole out.

"Pearl, Blake and I are friends. I don't know what you've been hearing that might be to the contrary, but I'm here to tell you it's not true. Isn't that right, Blake?"

Blake nodded, letting Katie's eyes only see his fingers crossed behind his back. She swallowed the smile tugging at her mouth.

"Absolutely. Katie and I go way, way back, as you know. That's why we were both drawn to this painting, I'm sure. We're kindred spirits of a sort."

"Hmm…" Pearl replied doubtfully. "Well, as I told ya'll, the final decision is Hal's."

"Now, there's a well-trained woman" came the booming voice of her Texas oil-magnate husband. Hal ambled into the library, alligator boots clicking against mahogany plank floors. "Howdy Blake," he said, beaming, slapping the younger man's back. Sweeping his Stetson aside, he bowed to Katie. "Lovelier by the year. Come on over here and give ole Hal a kiss, girl."

Katie obeyed, knowing Hal to be obnoxious, but harmless. "Good to see you, Mr. Kennington."

That won her a round of bawdy laughter. "I think we're long past the Mr. Kennington nonsense, now aren't we, Katie my girl?"

"I'm sorry. It's my mother's brainwashing."

Pearl cleared her throat to get Hal's attention. "Hal,

they're interested in this little Vladislava work for the auction."

"That scrap? Hell, take it away. You'd be doin' me a favor. Never liked that pathetic little duck hangin' on my library wall anyhow. It's depressin' when I'm sittin' down after a long day with a scotch in one hand and a Cuban in the other. Last thing I want to see is an orphaned kid and a doomed duck starin' at me."

Katie and Blake both laughed. Pearl huffed. "You could have told me and I would have had it moved."

"Wouldn't be worth the grief. Anyhow, take that one and pick out two or three more. I don't give a damn. Got too much stuff in this place anyhow." He waved off the painting. "Now, what I want to know, Miss Katie, is when is that fund-raiser for your uncle Peter? I'll make sure he's the next governor, singlehandedly if I have to."

"He'll be delighted to hear that. It's coming up shortly. I'm sure there's an invitation already in the mail to both of you."

"We can arrange to have the Kenningtons at our table, can't we?"

Katie stared at him. What was Blake doing? Not only did he just give Pearl the best gossip leak she'd get all year, but he was committing them to something she couldn't promise. Was this about the auction items? It couldn't be since Hal had essentially already given them carte blanche. It was as though he wanted to announce he would be her date.

"That would be an honor," Pearl said, hedging. "But I can't imagine you'd be attending that fund-raiser when you McCords have always supported Adam Trent. Will you be escorting Katie?"

"I certainly will."

The touch of pride in his voice was at once complimentary and a little too possessive. Katie was determined to stop the runaway train in Pearl's head before it carried them to disaster. "We're going as friends, just as we've done before to other events."

"Of course, naturally," Blake assured, but she knew him too well to miss the mockery in his tone.

"Sounds like a shindig to me," Hal said jovially. "We'll look forward to hashing over next year's policies and funding at dinner. We oil men gotta keep those regulators under control, know what I mean?"

Blake answered something vague, but Katie was too distracted with her own thoughts to hear it. She managed to move the group along, winding down their other selections and extricating them both from Pearl.

When finally they were off the grounds and on their way to somewhere yet not discussed, she shot Blake a look and let loose with what had been on her mind for over an hour.

"What was that about? I can't promise them a seat at our table!"

"We got five donations, didn't we, including the Russian work?" His tone was too cool, too arrogant. It infuriated her.

She turned in the seat of his car, the leather squeaking under her. "Blake McCord, you know exactly what I'm talking about. You told Pearl deliberately. Why would you do that? You know she's going to be blabbing it to everyone and we're going to get grief even before the fund-raiser. Do you enjoy torture or what?"

"Are you finished?" he asked calmly.

"I'm not sure."

"If you're pausing at least, then I'll explain. The truth

is I can't take being treated like I'm second-best to my little brother. Call me egotistical, but it irritates the hell out of me that everyone still thinks he deserves you more than—than anyone else might. He had his chance and he blew it."

Katie sat in stunned silence. This was not the explanation she'd expected. At all. She'd had no idea Blake felt this way. His seeming possessiveness, his bursts of frustration arose from a sense of inadequacy? That she never would have guessed. Not from Blake. But it touched her somehow, that he cared for her enough to want to be known as someone who was important in her life.

"I didn't realize…"

"I know. And I'm sorry if I was presumptuous in inviting them to your family's table. I just decided it is high time people stop seeing you as my brother's fiancée. You could be with any man you wanted to be with now. And if you choose to go to the fund-raiser or any other event with me, then I consider myself a lucky man and I'm not going to hide that. Gossip or not."

Again, he surprised her, showing a humility she wouldn't have believed he possessed. "Thank you," she said softly, reaching to lay a hand on his arm. "I'm happy you're taking me. To heck with the busybodies."

He smiled over to her. "My sentiments exactly."

His BlackBerry summoned then and with an apologetic glance at her, he answered. From what she could glean, the conversation had to do with McCord jewelry store closings in California. When he hung up he seemed drawn, tired and her heart went out to him.

"Bad news?"

Blake blew out a weary breath. "An omen of things to come, I'm afraid. We've had to close our Boston and

San Diego stores. Unless things turn around soon, this is only the beginning."

"Oh, Blake, I'd heard rumors but I didn't know it had come to this. I'm so sorry."

"Thanks. But I'm not beat yet. I've got a new PR campaign underway and a few other plans in the works. If can pull everything together—"

"I'm sure you will."

"That remains to be seen," he said darkly.

He radiated tension and Katie searched for something to take his mind off business and fund-raisers and gossipy patrons. "We need to find an activity that doesn't involve party planning or politics."

"I might have an idea."

"And that is?"

With a provoking half smile, he turned the Porsche sharply to the right. "Trust me."

In a short while they were on their way up the long, towering pine-tree-lined drive to an exclusive Dallas golf club.

"Golf?" she asked with a laugh.

"Just nine holes. You can still get a couple hours in at the office if you really have to."

"The day is shot. I'll double-time it tomorrow. I didn't know you played golf."

"All work and no play… I'm glad I can still surprise you." He shifted the car to a sharp stop in a premiere parking spot at the formal entry to the club.

"You're surprising me every day lately."

"Good." In one swift move he was out of the car and holding her door open. "Wouldn't want to bore you."

She shook her head. "Not a chance of that."

They strode together beneath the forest-green awning that canopied the entryway. "I don't have clothes," she said, swiping her palms down her tailored suit.

"We can fix that. I have an account in the pro shop."

In no time he and the salesgirl outfitted Katie in an attractive powder-blue golf skirt, white golf shirt, socks, shoes, gloves and hat. They both removed to separate dressing rooms to change and by the time she found him with the caddy, he'd secured her irons and a golf cart.

She caught his approving once-over before she climbed in beside him, noting a bottle of white wine in an icy bucket joined their clubs in the back of the cart.

"You look great."

"Thanks, but fair warning, my golf is somewhere along the lines of my skiing, you know, snow bunny style? I have all of the trappings, but none of the skill."

"We're here for relaxation, not competition. For all I care we can just ride around in this thing and drink wine." With that he stepped on the gas and the cart lurched forward, thrusting Katie nearly out onto the lawn.

"Sorry," he said, taking her arm to right her in her seat. "I drive this thing the way I drive my car. I'll behave, promise."

She laughed. "I didn't know these could go that fast."

"They can't. I had to buy one once because I ruined the engine."

Smiling, she found her tension ebbing. This was a side of Blake she rarely—if ever—had seen. Decidedly, she liked it and secretly hoped to see more of it. The only glitch in enjoying the lighter side of Blake was that it reminded her of Tate. He'd always been the easy-going playboy, the fun one.

"Hey." Blake slowed the cart to a stop beneath a giant old shade tree. "I'm losing you, only this time it's not because you're falling out of the cart."

She swallowed hard. The last thing she wanted to do was to ruin this moment with thoughts of Tate or guilt over being with Blake because of her past with his brother. "No...I'm just enjoying the view," she explained. It was partially true. "That's what I love most about golf courses. They're so scenic, so lush and green. They calm you, you know?"

He nodded. "That's the only reason I even make an attempt to play. Want to give it a go?"

"You first."

They hopped out of the cart, Blake choosing driving irons for them both. Standing behind him, she couldn't help but notice the play of muscle in his back and shoulders as he practiced his swing. Her thoughts wandered in a completely different direction, musing over what it would feel like to run her hands there—

"Well, not too impressive for a first shot. But typical for me." He turned to her. "You're up."

"Hmm? Oh, sure."

"You're really engaged here, I can tell."

She was, but not in the game of golf. She tried to remember the lessons her father had insisted she take in high school, planting her feet the right distance apart, gripping her hands on the club in the right spots, swinging from the back and abs. Still she knew something wasn't right. "I'm hopeless," she said after her first shot dug a nasty hole in the manicured lawn.

"May I?" Blake moved close behind her.

"Please, I need all the help I can get." He pressed

lightly up against her back, wrapping his arms around hers and covering her hands in his.

"Now, just relax and let the feel come naturally," he murmured against her ear.

They swayed together, in a sort of dance that went nowhere. She let her body ease back against his and she could have sworn she heard a slight groan.

"How's that feel?" he asked.

Very nice, she wanted to say. Instead she tried not to sound dizzy and dreamy, the way he made her feel. "It's helping. I think I was just tense."

"Good. Now, let's take one swing together. Ready?"

Letting him do the work, they cracked the iron against the ball and sent it sailing into the air.

"Wow! I can't even see it anymore." Caught up in excitement, she spun and grasped his arm. "That was amazing."

Laughing, he put his hands on her shoulders. "See, you're a natural." His hands lingered, lightly massaging in what felt more like a caress.

"Why is it that I'm feeling like we shouldn't be having so much fun?"

"It's because you're listening to the wrong voices." Gently touching his lips to her forehead, he let his hands slide down her arms to grasp hers. "Try to listen to the one that says it's okay for us to enjoy each other instead of the ones that beat you up for it."

She nodded, knowing he was right, yet wondering if *they* could ever be right.

Chapter Five

A dazzle of lights—the golden glow encompassing the aisle leading to the doorways of the elegant downtown hotel starred with camera flashes—greeted Katie as she took Blake's hand and stepped from the car. There had been no chance they would arrive unnoticed. The fund-raising dinner for Peter Salgar was one of the biggest events of the political season, a glittering display of wealth and power evidenced in the carefully chosen guest list. On name alone, she and Blake were targets for the paparazzi. Tonight especially, with his hand at her waist, his arm lightly pressing against her back in what could easily be construed as a possessive gesture, the stir of interest they created was almost palpable.

Blake seemed oblivious to the ripple of reaction their entrance into the reception area caused among the growing group of guests. "Regrets already?" he murmured close to her ear before they became part of the crowd.

"I should be asking you that question." She stopped, facing him. "I don't think this was such a good idea. You have enough on your mind right now without me adding to it."

"You're not adding to it. I think you know me well enough to be certain I wouldn't be here if I didn't want to be."

"I'm still worried about you," she said, overlooking the clear skepticism, almost disbelief crossing his face. "Rex Foley, and most likely Zane and Jason will be here, too, and—" She shook her head. "I should never have agreed to this."

"We talked about this. It's not as if I'm going to be blindsided. And it's hardly the first time I've been in the same room with the Foleys and I've managed to survive so far." He dismissed her concern but there was a new look in his eyes, almost bemused, as if someone anxious on his behalf was an unfamiliar concept. "Besides, it's too late for you to back out."

"I don't want to back out, but I wouldn't blame you if you did."

"That's the last thing on my mind right now." Blake reached to her and lightly dragged his fingertips over her cheek, his eyes following the motion then quickly sweeping over her. "You're so beautiful, Katie. And in that dress…" His open admiration made her glad that on impulse she'd forgone her usual black for a deep red, in a style slightly less conservative than her custom. "Tate was an idiot to ever let you go."

The husky note in his voice momentarily disarmed her fears. He was distractingly attractive, the black-and-white formal attire accentuating his lean good looks, but times like this, when he gave her a glimpse of warmth and charm behind his cool exterior, were when she found him most irresistible.

They might have been alone in those brief seconds. His gaze, with its now familiar intensity, held hers and she had the disconcerting sensation of falling. That was a novel experience for her. That Blake was the cause made it all the more unsettling.

How it would have ended if it had remained only the two of them, she never knew, because her parents chose that moment to interrupt, breaking the fleeting communion between her and Blake.

"Katerina, there you are." Anna and Benton Salgar walked up to them and though their timing frustrated Katie, she made herself smile. Still a beauty in diamonds and a shimmering silver gown, Anna's seemingly effortless elegance and her greeting to her daughter—a brief clasping of hands and touch of cheeks—were marred by her slight frown as she recognized Katie's companion. "We didn't expect to see you here, Blake. This is quite a surprise."

"Peter will be happy if you've switched sides," Benton said as he shook Blake's hand. "He didn't think he had a chance at an endorsement from the McCords. We assumed Eleanor would continue to back Adam."

"I assume she will, as well," Blake answered. "I'm not representing my family. I'm here for Katie."

"Blake offered to escort me tonight," Katie intervened hurriedly at the surprised looks her parents alternated between her and Blake.

Benton and Anna exchanged a glance before he said,

"You didn't mention that when you turned down coming with us."

"It's no wonder people are talking," Anna said, sounding irritated as she focused on Katie.

"That's going to happen no matter what I do."

"Well, you must admit, it's odd, you two being seen together this often and so soon after you and Tate broke your engagement."

"There's nothing odd about attending a party with a friend." Turning to Blake, Katie put a hand on his arm. "I'd love a glass of wine. Will you come with me?" As soon as they'd excused themselves and were out of earshot of Anna and Benton, she told him, "I'm sorry for that. My parents still haven't given up on the idea Tate and I might get back together. Apparently his new fiancée isn't enough to convince them it's well and truly over."

Blake's face gave nothing of his feelings away. He didn't answer until they'd made their way to the bar and he'd given their orders. "Why do I get the impression that in their eyes, I'm partly to blame for your breakup?"

"They don't. At least …" She accepted the wine glass he offered her, flushing at his outright incredulity. "As my mother said, people talk. We've spent a lot of time together since the Labor Day party and although it's mostly been because of the hospital, you know as well as I do there are some people who just wait to pounce on anything appearing even remotely scandalous. After that fiasco with Pearl, you should have guessed the gossip was only going to get worse."

He ignored the reference to the Kenningtons. "Is that what we are, Katie," he said, the low, suggestive undertone in his voice sending a pleasant shiver through her, "remotely scandalous?"

She could have taken him seriously, fretted over the image they made in a very public setting, questioned her judgment in getting entangled with him to the extent she had when she was trying to find her way after Tate. Instead, she chose to toss him a half smile and to enjoy the surprise that touched his expression. "Probably. Does it bother you?"

"For the most part, no."

Remembering again his forceful assertion that he would never be second-best to Tate or anyone else, Katie guessed that was what bothered him the most about the evening. She also knew he'd deny it if she confronted him. She could consider it arrogance on his part and refuse to pander to his ego. Yet, it was a vulnerability that struck a chord in her because she'd never imagined Blake as anything but completely sure of himself and his abilities and disdainful of anyone who thought otherwise.

"Maybe I'll let them believe it," she said on sudden impulse.

"Believe what?"

"That you're to blame for my being unattached. Who knows—" she teased him a bit "—for a change, a little scandal might be fun."

"If I thought you were serious—"

"Who says I'm not?" He frowned and she laughed. "Oh, for heaven's sake, Blake, of course I'm not serious. You'd never forgive me."

"That depends," he said as he moved a step closer, very nearly crossing the line from polite into personal space, "on whether or not you meant it."

She suddenly lost control of the game she'd started. He was asking her something she couldn't answer, not yet, when she wasn't ready to redefine how she felt about him. "If I did something of that magnitude," she said, forcing a lightness she didn't feel, "I would mean it."

Blake didn't respond in kind; if anything he looked even more troubled. "I think you would," he said slowly.

"Is it that hard for you to believe that I care about your feelings?" That it apparently was difficult for him made her wonder if anyone else ever had. Abandoning her wineglass, she put a hand on his shoulder and brushed a kiss against his cheek. "Thank you for being here. You're the only man I've ever known who would put himself through this for me."

"You don't need to thank me for something I wanted to do," he said gruffly, then, unbending for her, he briefly touched her hand. "You're welcome." They looked at each other and he gave her that half smile of his. "I guess this means we're both staying."

"I guess it does," she said, returning a smile of her own. "Who knows, we might even find something to enjoy before it's over."

"That," Blake said, taking her hand and fitting it into the curve of his arm, "I can promise you."

Blake found it difficult to keep that promise through dinner and speech-making and the hour of headline entertainment that followed. He and Katie were seated at the head table with Peter Salgar, his family, the Kenningtons and Katie's parents, a less than comfortable arrangement. Peter took advantage of Blake's unexpected presence and what he apparently assumed was Blake's attachment to Katie to subtly lobby for Blake's support. Benton and Anna, though making an effort to be pleasant, couldn't completely mask their disapproval of Katie's choice of companion; and more than once,

Blake felt eyes on his back from Rex Foley and his two oldest sons, Zane and Jason, sitting at the neighboring table. If it hadn't been for Katie, he would have told the lot of them to go to hell and been done with it.

"Blake…?"

His name, a softly spoken question, pulled him out of his thoughts and he found himself alone at the table with Katie and looking into her dark eyes.

"For a moment there, I thought I'd lost you," she said, smiling a little.

"I'm sorry, I let myself get distracted."

"That's not very flattering."

"It's just been one of those long evenings. It isn't you."

"You're not very good for my ego, you know." She glanced to their right, where the Foley men were getting to their feet, Zane and his beautiful blonde companion leaving them to join other couples who were moving to the open ballroom floor for the start of the dancing. "I was hoping I could talk you into at least one dance. But I'm sure I can find another partner. Jason Foley, maybe. Considering his reputation and the way he always eyes practically every woman in the room, I doubt I'd have difficulty convincing him."

"If that son of a bitch so much as—" Blake started, breaking off when her lips twitched with suppressed laughter and he realized she was messing with him. "Not nice, Katie."

"It got your attention, though."

"I assure you, you have my attention." He moved his hand to the back of her chair until his fingers slid against the smooth bare skin exposed by the low dip of her dress. "As much of it as you want."

The faint rise of color in her cheeks and her quick

intake of breath betrayed her attempt to appear unaffected by his touch. "I'll need proof of that."

"Then dance with me."

She accepted his invitation by taking his proffered hand and standing with him, her eyes never leaving his.

Their path to the dance floor took them directly past the Foleys' table and though Blake preferred to avoid acknowledging them, Rex Foley made that impossible by stepping up to them. Jason, he noted, hung back, watching them from a few feet away.

"It's nice to see you again, Katie," Rex said, the smile he gave her coming easily, as if to an old friend. "I know Peter appreciates you being here."

"And he appreciates your support. He always has," Katie answered. Her swift sidelong glance his way told Blake she keenly felt the awkwardness of the meeting. "It means a lot to him."

Rex nodded, then looked to Blake. "You being here is a surprise."

"So I've been told, numerous times," Blake retorted coldly.

"I know Eleanor—" Rex gave her name soft edges "—still backs Adam Trent. That puts you in the enemy camp, so to speak, at least tonight."

"I don't always agree with my mother's choices of friends." *Or lovers*, he nearly added but held his tongue. His mother's relationship, past and present, with Rex Foley was the last thing he wanted to get into right now or at all, for that matter. "And my reasons for being here are my business."

From his look between Blake and Katie, it was obvious Rex had formed his own idea of why Blake was here but he only nodded. "I'm sure Eleanor understands." He seemed about to add something but left it unsaid.

"I'm beyond the age of needing her approval. Now, if you'll excuse us—" He didn't wait for Rex's reply but with his hand to her back, gently urged Katie forward.

"That could have been worse," Katie ventured a few moments later. "At least Jason didn't get involved."

"For good reason," Blake said shortly. "He and Penny are apparently seeing each other. He's probably not sure how much I know about it and isn't interested in hearing my opinion."

"Penny? Your sister Penny is *dating* Jason Foley?"

"That's what she calls it. But I doubt he sees it that way."

"I have a hard time believing Jason and Penny—" Katie broke off with a rueful grimace. "I'm sorry, that didn't come out the way I meant it."

"It's okay, I have a hard time believing it, too." Penny was her twin sister Paige's opposite, quiet and shy, hardly the type to be attracted to a brash womanizer like Jason Foley. She wasn't his type, either. "I'm certain Jason is trying to use Penny to get any scrap of information he can about my plans for McCord Jewelers. I just can't convince her of that."

"You could be right," Katie said slowly. "But that's between her and Jason."

They stopped short of the dance floor, facing each other. "If you're telling me to butt out, I can't. Not when it involves my business."

"Give Penny some credit. I doubt she's going to betray any family secrets. I'm sure you hate the idea of anyone in your family in a relationship with a Foley, but Penny has to make her own choices, without your interference."

"I thought you'd be on my side with this."

Katie sighed. "It's not about taking sides, Blake. I understand what it's like to have families meddling in your relationships. Look at Tate and me. I grew up never having to decide for myself what I wanted in a lover or a husband because our families told us we were perfect for each other. Now I have no clue what I want or need or how to have a relationship with someone who isn't Tate. I wouldn't wish that on Penny or anyone else."

"Even if you knew she was making a big mistake?" Blake shot back.

"Even then. It's her mistake to make." Catching her bottom lip between her teeth, Katie hesitated then touched his arm. "I know you think you know best, but this is one time you have to let someone else deal with the situation. If you keep trying to interfere, you're only going to make things worse."

He didn't want to admit she could be right. His mistrust of the Foleys was too ingrained, and Penny's involvement with Jason Foley seemed almost as much of a betrayal as his mother's affair with Rex. "I see your point," he finally conceded.

"But—?"

"But I don't know that I agree."

"At least promise me you'll think about it."

"I promise," he said, unable to deny her appeal with her so close and looking into his eyes. Then she smiled and he knew he was lost. He held out his hand to her. "You promised me a dance."

A new melody started, slow and sensual. As he took her in his arms she yielded, malleable to his touch and the rhythm of the music. Somewhere, at the edge of perception, Blake could hear it, feel the brush and heat of other bodies, but it all seemed removed, as if time had caught them in a suspended moment.

He became very aware of how close he held her, how her hand curved against his shoulder, the other clasped in his. Of how, with her dark hair framing her face, in a dress that shaped her curves, and the movement around them shifting shadow and light against the ivory of her skin, she looked like his fantasies personified. And that, with the slightest motion, a simple slide of hands and bodies, the tensions between them would twist into a different fire that had nothing to do with the evening's frustrations.

Sliding his arm further around her waist, he pressed her closer, his cheek against the silk of her hair, and she leaned slightly nearer, her breath brushing the hollow of his throat. Their coming together wasn't a conscious thing on his part, or it seemed hers, and the fact they didn't seem to have any control over it made it all the more bewildering.

The music came to an end on a soulful, lingering note, leaving them looking at each other for seconds—minutes? hours?—while the other couples moved around them, and the band began another song.

Katie's lips parted but nothing came out and Blake had a pretty fair idea of how she felt. They'd started something but, like her, and for the first time, he didn't have a clue what was supposed to happen next.

"We should go back and mingle, or I should at least," she said finally.

"We should," he agreed, though he made no move to let her go.

"Uncle Peter and my parents will be wondering where I am."

"Probably."

The music wove around them and she shifted closer again. "You're becoming a bad influence."

"Me?" They swayed together and Blake's attention fixed on Katie, making him ignore everything else. "No one's ever accused me of that before."

"Yes, you, and your 'do things your way and to hell with what anyone else thinks' attitude."

"I was in trouble for that a little while ago," he reminded her.

"That was different. Here and now, I like it."

"Maybe you should try it yourself more often."

"Maybe I should," she echoed softly. "Who knows what might happen?"

Blake didn't have an answer so he simply held her, and for a little while, that was all that mattered.

Chapter Six

Blake didn't need to be told there were repercussions from his night with Katie; one look at his mother, Paige and Tate's faces when he walked into the dining room the next evening said everything. He'd managed to avoid any confrontation up until now by leaving the house before breakfast, but that was only a delaying tactic.

Forgoing any usual greetings, Eleanor held out a newspaper section to him, turned to a story on Peter Salgar's fund-raising efforts. The report was accompanied by a photo of Peter and his wife in conversation with a congressman and a high-profile attorney, Katie and Blake standing to the side. "This was an interesting way to start the day. Adam called me to ask what it meant and I had no idea how to answer him. If you were going to put yourself in a position of appearing to support Peter Salgar, I would have appreciated an advance warning."

"It looks more like he's supporting Katie," Paige commented, directing the attention away from politics to a potentially more dangerous topic. She darted a quick grin at Blake, not in the least quelled by the scowl he returned. "What's going on between you two, anyway?"

"Nothing that you're imagining," Blake said, unable to keep his irritation from showing. "We're friends. She needed an escort. I volunteered."

"Yes, that—" Paige gestured to the newspaper photo "—looks very *friendly*."

Blake silently admitted that their pose—his hand curved around Katie's waist, her leaning slightly into his arm—suggested they were closer than friends. It was his expression, though, that clearly betrayed him. The photographer had caught him in an unguarded moment, his eyes on Katie as she smiled at her uncle, and even he recognized the desire and what, in another man, he might have even called tenderness.

Giving the photograph a brief appraisal, Eleanor turned a watchful gaze on Blake. "You and Katie have been spending quite a lot of time together. Do you think that's wise, considering the circumstances?"

"What *circumstances* would those be?"

"The timing—" Eleanor glanced to Tate.

"Doesn't matter," Tate interrupted. "No one can accuse Blake of taking Katie away from me."

"Or of cheating on someone else," Paige muttered darkly.

Eleanor's face constricted but she said nothing in response to her daughter's not-so-subtle reference to her affair with Rex Foley. Paige, like Blake, hadn't made much of an attempt to hide her resentment of what both of them considered Eleanor's betrayal.

"I hate to spoil the perception of drama, but everyone's making much more of this than it was." Blake kept his voice level. "I didn't declare my undying loyalty to Peter Salgar, and Katie and I aren't a couple." No one at the table looked convinced, prompting Blake to deliberately change the subject before he lost his temper and told his family to mind their own business. "Where's Penny tonight? I expected she'd be here."

"She said she was going out," Eleanor said carefully, not quite meeting his eyes.

"Meaning she's seeing Jason Foley."

"I don't know that for certain. But it's likely. She refuses to talk about it with anyone. And it's no use you stating the obvious, that you don't approve." Eleanor went ahead before Blake could say anything. "I'm not sure I do, either. But Penny's a grown woman. None of us can make her choices for her."

It was essentially the same thing Katie had said to him. He didn't like hearing it any more now than he had then. But it was remembering Katie asking him to stay out of it that kept him from arguing his opinion that Jason Foley was using Penny.

It was a relief, less than an hour later, to escape the strained atmosphere that pervaded the remainder of dinner. Blake was on his way to the study, intent on checking some e-mails, when Tate stopped him.

"I hope you know I meant what I said," Tate told him.

"I know it. And—thanks." He and Tate had heatedly argued more than once in recent weeks, mostly over Katie, but Blake appreciated his brother's support.

"I also hope you know what you're doing."

"I always know what I'm doing."

"With business, and probably with any other woman you've known. But Katie is different."

"I don't need you telling me that," Blake snapped, suddenly angry. "I've been telling you all along how special she is. You're the one who let her go."

Tate surprised him by not responding in kind. Instead he studied Blake for a moment before saying, "I don't think you do know what you're doing this time."

"I'm not interested in your opinion."

"Probably not. But I don't want Katie to get hurt."

"And the assumption is I'm going to do that?" The implication stung because Blake knew he could easily do that. He'd never committed himself to any relationship. His expectations with women were as high as his certainty that he would end up disappointed, and consequently he refused to let himself get more than superficially involved. But, irrationally it seemed, he still resented Tate automatically deciding Blake's involvement with Katie would end badly.

"I didn't say that." An aggravated note worked its way into Tate's voice. "I'm just saying to be careful with her."

"Like you were?"

Tate blew out a breath. "I don't want to get into this with you again. We've done it enough over the past few weeks and it's getting old. I'll just add one thing—if this is your way of proving, once again, that you're the best man for the job, then get out now. Like you keep telling me, Katie deserves better."

Not giving Blake time to counter him, Tate swiftly turned and strode away, leaving Blake alone with the unwelcome thought that when it came to him and Katie, his brother might be right.

* * *

In the middle of the majestic ballroom, the sunlight dancing stars on the crystal of the chandeliers set in the high ceiling, Katie half listened to the woman detailing the amenities of the room. The woman's voice was slowly becoming a background drone as Katie's attention kept wandering as she tried to figure out Blake's mood.

He'd agreed readily enough to accompany her here, to the historic music hall where the Halloween ball would be held, to settle some details about the event and the location of various activities within the hall itself. But he'd been tense and withdrawn, cold almost, so very different from the man who two days ago had danced with her, held her close, looked at her in a way that had stirred to life desires she'd barely recognized.

Her name and the words *wine tasting* penetrated her distraction and she gave a slight start, realizing she'd completely missed the last few minutes of conversation.

"I'm sorry," she said hastily, avoiding Blake's sardonic glance in favor of the woman's slightly affronted face, "I let myself get sidetracked imagining how lovely a setting this is going to be for the ball. A wine tasting would be wonderful."

The woman beamed, mollified by Katie's explanation and her apologetic smile. "If you don't mind waiting a few minutes, I'll get that set up for you."

"Lovely, is it?" Blake asked after the woman had gone. He glanced around them, frowning as if he was inspecting the ballroom and it had fallen short of his expectations.

"Yes, it is. Which is more than I can say for your mood," Katie said before she could stop herself. "If you didn't want to do this today, you should have said so. I could have handled it myself."

He stared at her a moment then shook his head and for the first time in the last hour appeared to relax. "So you could have. But I wanted to be here to help. We're supposed to be a team."

"*Supposed* to be…?"

"Okay, we're a team."

"Mmm…considering how much you dislike the whole idea of depending on someone else, that must have hurt to admit."

"A little."

She smiled and drew an answering half smile from Blake.

"Now if you're through forcing me to inflict pain on myself," he said, "maybe you can explain again how we're going to manage nearly a thousand people, a string ensemble, and all these activities in this one *lovely* ballroom."

"There's plenty of room," she assured him. Laying a hand on his arm, she directed his attention upward. "We'll have all the balcony space, as well as the ballroom, and there's seating and standing space just outside by the bar—" Katie broke off when she realized he wasn't following her gestures but watching her face. Her breath hitched and the room suddenly felt warmer but she tried to hang on to her composure. "Don't ask for explanations if you aren't going to listen."

"Balcony, ballroom, outside by the bar," he repeated. He took a step closer and slowly ran his hand over her shoulder and up the curve of her throat until his fingers threaded into her hair. "Got it."

She didn't doubt it but when he leaned in to kiss her she didn't care. Ballrooms, space and wine retreated and she yielded to what she wanted—uncaring of where they were, no space between them, reveling in the taste of him. Maybe it wasn't wise, as everyone around them kept reminding her, but reason had nothing to do with the electric feelings that sprang up between them every time they got within touching distance. Blake didn't deny them, either, forgoing any gentle, exploratory caress and kissing her deeply, pulling her closer when she wrapped her arms around his neck and urged him in that direction.

"We're ready for—oh." The woman's voice broke them apart, although Blake didn't quite release her. "The wine tasting…we're ready—if you…" Waving her hand in the general direction of the door, the woman avoided looking directly at them.

Katie bit her lip against laughing, caught the amusement in Blake's eyes, and had to glance away from him for fear it would burst out anyway.

"We probably shouldn't be doing this before lunch," she murmured half an hour later, when they were nearly finished sampling the array of wines and deciding which they wanted available at the ball.

"Worried you'll get tipsy and I'll take advantage of you?" Blake asked as he leaned back in his chair, eyeing the sample of burgundy he was trying.

"You do that without the benefit of wine," she lightly accused. "And who says it wouldn't be the other way around?"

His brow lifted slightly. "I promise not to object."

"I'll keep that in mind." Annoyed at the warmth that crept over her throat and face, Katie glanced at their checklist. "We just need to decide on the champagne and then we're done."

"You're on your own there."

"You can't tell me you don't like champagne." She affected to look shocked at his shrug. "I don't see how that's possible. Some of my favorite fantasies involve it."

She'd definitely gotten his attention with that one. He straightened, a now familiar glint in his eyes. "Would you care to elaborate?"

"No," she said, laughing, "you'll have to be satisfied with imagining."

"That could be dangerous. I can imagine quite a bit."

"Really? I never took you for the creative type, Blake."

"If you'd like a demonstration—"

Katie studied the list a moment before checking off a selection of sparkling wines she was familiar with and then got to her feet. "Not here. I think we've embarrassed the staff enough for one day. And I really am ready for lunch."

"Then I'll take you to lunch," Blake said, rising with her.

"How about I take you?" She was pleased at being able to surprise him with the offer, pleased overall with the light, flirtatious mood between them, a welcome change from that morning. "It's Saturday, the sun is shining and I don't feel like anything fussy. I have just the place in mind."

"Then I'll let you lead the way."

"You will?"

Putting his arm around her waist, Blake brushed his mouth against her temple and murmured, "Just this once."

Katie chose a small, quaint café on a quiet back-street that she'd stumbled upon one time when searching out a specialty shop in the area. It was a distance from her and Blake's usual haunts—the elegant, expensive restaurants and upscale nightclubs—and they were unlikely to run into anyone they knew, the reason she liked it best.

"This was a good choice," Blake said, settling back in his chair after they'd given their orders.

"You like it?"

He smiled a little. "You sound surprised. Yes, I do like it. It feels like an escape."

"That's exactly how I feel, too. I've always come here alone for that reason," she added.

"Ah, so you don't like to share. How did I rate an invitation?"

"I thought you, of anybody, would appreciate it." She paused for a moment then said, "Everything is so serious with you. You take so much on and you're always pushing yourself. And now all this pressure with your business—if anyone needs a break, it's you. You should do it more often, or in your case, do it period."

"I'm starting to feel like one of your charity projects," he said, but without his usual sardonic sting. "Aren't you busy enough without adding me to the list?"

"Probably, but I can never resist a good challenge."

That made him laugh, and Katie liked the way it changed him. In this setting, forgetting work and responsibility for a while, he looked younger, more at ease, definitely more approachable, and at his most appealing.

"So is this your only way of escaping," Blake asked about halfway through lunch, "or do you have others? Something involving champagne, maybe?"

"You might as well give up. I'm not going to tell you," she insisted. Though with the right persuasion on his part—Katie quashed that thought immediately and hoped the warm rush the idea caused hadn't translated into a telltale blush. "I do have a few others."

"Should I assume they involve shopping or the spa?"

"You should not. You obviously need to change your ideas about what women like."

The expression in his eyes suggested he had several ideas and this time she didn't have to wonder about the blush. "Tell me what you like, Katie."

"I don't think you'd be interested," she said, avoiding looking at him.

"You might be surprised. Come on," Blake coaxed, "tell me one thing, one of your favorites."

"All right, one thing." She considered for a moment. "This is a little silly…"

"I doubt it, but I promise not to laugh."

"Okay, I love Bogart movies. Occasionally, I lock myself in the den with a week's supply of popcorn and spend the night watching my favorites." Feeling slightly self-conscious at her admission, she added, "I've never told anyone else that, so I'm counting on you to keep my secret."

Blake reached out and took her hand, threading her fingers with his. "You can count on me, Katie." And it sounded almost like a vow that had nothing to do with her penchant for old movies. "I promise."

One thing she knew for certain about Blake McCord, he didn't take his promises lightly and knowing he intended to keep this one caused a mixed up mess of pleasure, confusion, desire and uncertainty in her that Katie couldn't begin to sort out.

She didn't try, not now, but allowed herself to enjoy being with him, here in this temporary haven, where nothing and no one else intruded, and to believe it could be the beginning of something she had never expected.

Chapter Seven

"Katerina, it's only for the weekend." Anna Salgar's growing frustration with her daughter was clear as she slapped smooth hands to slender hips. "You need a dress for the ball and I won't have you attending in something from Dallas. It's too risky."

Katie groaned. "Oh, Mother, don't be ridiculous. There are dozens of designer stores here. I'll find something no one else would *dare* wear. I promise."

"That's not what I mean and you know it." Anna turned her back and idly fingered an Italian jewelry box on Katie's bureau. "Tate brought this to you, didn't he? From Florence?"

"Yes, and—"

Anna opened the box listened to a chimed rendition of Tchaikovsky's *The Sleeping Beauty* waltz, closed the box and faced her daughter. "And, since you keep telling me that you and Tate are finished, that means you're single and available. You can't take chances with your attire. You need to dress appropriately and with a singular sense of style."

Katie paced in front of the floor-to-ceiling windows at the back of her bedroom suite. *Single, what is that?* For as long as she could remember she'd been promised to, then engaged to Tate. She dropped down on the edge of her bed and let her face sink into her palms, forgetting any pretense of grace. "Mother, I don't even know what that means."

"Oh, darling, I know," Anna said, moving to sit next to her. "That's why I want to take you to New York, just the two of us, for a mother-daughter shopping trip. I need to show you how to enjoy your new freedom." She brushed a lock of hair from Katie's cheek. "I never imagined you'd face this day, but you have and now we have to switch strategies."

Katie's chin went up. "Strategies?"

"Well, perhaps that's a poor choice of words, but what I mean is that you have to learn new skills, have a new attitude toward men. And yourself."

Thoughts of Blake rose in her mind. She wasn't *with* Blake as a lover, but there was no denying they'd become more than friends. She felt lost, confused, as though in a no-man's-land. Should she heed her mother's advice? It felt that's what she'd always been doing when it came to her relationship with Tate, listening to what others told her was best, never considering if it was what she wanted.

Yet here she was, over thirty and for the first time in her life single. How did one be single, anyhow?

"This sounds ridiculous at my age, but honestly,

Mom, I'm afraid I don't know what the rules are and I'm not sure I really want to learn."

"Of course you do. And I want to help you with all of that. It's important now that you're no longer engaged, that you don't rush into anything—or anyone—else."

Anna's implication was clear, though Katie knew well her mother would far rather avoid a confrontation over Blake, relying instead on understatement and implication than actual honesty, than tell her straight-out to keep her distance from another McCord man.

"That isn't a problem," she said flatly, trying to ease her mother's suspicions.

It was a problem, though. *He* was a problem. She couldn't stop thinking about him, about the time they'd enjoyed together recently, about how comfortable she felt with him. How much she wanted more…

"Good," Anna said, obviously relieved. She patted Katie's leg then stood and strode over to open the double doors to Katie's expansive walk-in closet. "We may need to start from scratch," she said, fingering dress after dress, blouse after blouse, skirt after skirt, her expression mostly disapproving.

Katie followed her. "I like my clothes."

"You have wonderful taste, dear, but we may have to, well, tweak it."

Shaking her head, knowing if she didn't put a stop to it here and now, Anna would take over her closet *and* her love life. "Okay, let's compromise. I'll go to New York to buy a dress for the ball, but only if you promise not to throw out one piece of clothing from my closet until we can talk more about this and go over things together."

Considering, Anna slowed her rapid-fire sweep of Katie's clothing, shoes, purses, belts, scarves. Anna was on a mission now and it frightened Katie. Her mother's will was harder than any diamond in the McCord collection. Anna lingered over a black cashmere sweater-dress, weighing the quality of the fabric between her index finger and thumb.

Katie held her breath and her stance. She wasn't going to give in to her mother this time.

Finally, Anna dropped the piece of fabric and turned to Katie with a conservative smile. "So, we'll start with New York."

Katie's arms were so loaded down with bags when her cell phone rang that she had to drop several of them smack onto the Fifth Avenue sidewalk to grab her phone.

Anna had stopped alongside her, but discouraged her from answering the phone. "Let it go. You can get the message later."

"I can't. It might be Blake." His name spilled out unchecked and she hurried to find an explanation. "We're right in the middle of finalizing auction items. He might need information."

"Hmm" was all Anna would reply.

"Finally." Katie jerked her phone from the bottom of her purse and flipped it open. "Hello," she said breathlessly, the brilliant sunlight overhead preventing her from reading the name on the screen.

"You sound more like you're at the gym than a boutique."

It's Blake, thank heavens, she mused. The New York trip had come up so suddenly she'd only had time to say goodbye over the phone, in a message no less. Because they hadn't spoken she wondered if he might think she was running away, or that she needed a break from him.

"Katie, are you there? All I hear is heavy breathing. Not that, given the right circumstances, that's a bad thing."

Oh, yes, that's what she needed right now, on a busy street, with her mother hanging on her every word—Blake being suggestive. "Um, yes, sorry. We're in the middle of foot traffic on Fifth Avenue. My arms are loaded down and I couldn't find my cell."

"So, it's been a productive venture?"

"Far too much so." Katie glanced at Anna, who huddled her chinchilla coat around herself. "Mother bought out three boutiques."

"I thought you went for one dress."

"Me, too." She heard his deep laughter resonate at the other end and suddenly ached to see the smile that went with it. "I think I've been hijacked."

Though her mother wore oversize sunglasses, Katie knew she was rolling her eyes behind them.

"So how are things there? Any news on those last few donations?" They were hardly the questions she wanted to ask but under the circumstances had little choice. She was tempted to ask him if he missed her, if he'd thought about her as much as she'd thought about him. Spoken in her mind, though, those queries sounded a bit childish, a demand for reassurances he couldn't give.

There was a long silence and then "I miss you."

Her heart jumped. Anna's big black shades were riveted on her. "Yes, exactly, my thoughts exactly."

Again the familiar amusement in his voice. "If I didn't want to see you so much, it would be fun to know you're standing there in the heart of the Big Apple squirming."

"You can be an arrogant jerk, you know that?"

"Yes. But I still miss you."

"Katie, I'm freezing. Can you please continue this little tête-à-tête indoors?" Anna flagged a cab. "Let's go over to the Plaza for a hot toddy."

She nodded to her mother. "Can I call you later? Mother is cold and we need to catch a cab."

"I'll be here. I just wanted talk for a moment. Your message was a poor substitute."

Katie felt a twist in her chest, something between thrilled and frustrated. "It helped me, too."

"Ring whenever you're free, okay?"

"Tonight, um, after—"

"After your mother is asleep?"

"Exactly," she said with a slightly guilty schoolgirl laugh.

"Have fun."

"Thanks. I'll try." She wanted to add that it would be much easier if he were there with her, but instead settled for a soft goodbye.

An hour later, warm and comfortably cozy in their corner of the vast and recently renovated Park Plaza bar area, Katie stared out a giant picture window toward Central Park. At certain angles she could catch glimpses of horses and carriages, couples nestled beneath blankets, enjoying the crisp late autumn air and the golden reflection of waning sunlight—enjoying each other.

She knew it was corny, and Blake would probably laugh at her, but somehow she'd always imagined a horse and carriage ride through Central Park on a starry eve to be hopelessly romantic. Would he even be able to sit still for an hour's ride? So driven, so ambitious and responsible, would he be on edge and miss the wonder of the entire experience?

"If I wanted to keep myself company, I would have come to New York alone."

Katie looked up to where her mother was reseating herself, not even realizing she must have left for the ladies' room. "I'm sorry. I have a lot on my mind right now with the ball and so on. I let myself get distracted."

Anna lifted a crystal champagne glass, pink from the Kir Royal filling it. She must have switched from toddies to champagne when cocktail hour started. Something else Katie had failed to notice.

"Liar."

Katie jerked back. "Excuse me?"

"You've been *distracted* since Blake called."

Sipping her now icy cold hot toddy, Katie winced. "You're jumping to conclusions."

"You expect me to believe you haven't been thinking about him the whole time?" When Katie answered with an exasperated shake of her head, Anna flashed a bright smile that was as false as Katie's denial. "Well, if that's true, then you won't mind entertaining one of New York's premiere residents."

Katie sighed. Her mother was up to something; she'd sensed it from the start but tried to believe it wasn't so. Inwardly counting to ten to calm her anger, she took a deep, soothing breath then confronted Anna. "What are you talking about? I thought this was a girls' weekend."

"Oh, it is, it is, darling. I just thought it might be fun to have a drink—and perhaps dinner—with an old friend's son."

"I can't believe you," Katie groaned. "Please tell me you didn't bring me here to try to set me up."

"How suspicious you are! Oh, there he is—" She shook a warning red-nailed finger. "Now you be nice."

Gritting her teeth, Katie followed her mother's eyes to a tall, dark and attractive man wearing a designer suit cut and sewn to every lean line of his towering frame. He strode toward them with the ease of a man who might well have lived at the Park Plaza. Smiling broadly, a waiter rushed over to him and the taller man bent to give an order in his ear. Before Katie could get up and beat a hasty exit he was there, standing over them, grinning.

"Hello, Anna, stunning as ever," he said smoothly, reaching to brush a kiss to Anna's hand. "And you must be Katerina," he said with a slight bow and an ever-so-subtle sweep of a gaze.

"Katie," she managed as politely as possible.

"Katie, this is Ruth's son, Girard. Remember, Ruth is one of my dearest friends from Wellesley. We were in the same sorority and have been friends ever since."

"It's just a shame you two live so far apart," Girard said, "and that Mother isn't up to traveling these days."

"It is a shame. I'd loved to have seen her. I'll fly up east again this summer for a visit. Dallas is unbearable in July. Oh, my, I'm so sorry, please, do sit down. We've a chair right here."

Reluctantly, Katie scooted away from her window enough to allow him access to the chair next to her. Her mother had thought of everything, even in her choice of table and seating. Typical. She tried to reason that her mother wanted only what she thought was best for her, but after getting past Tate, already Anna was again interfering in her choices in men and in life. It was all Katie could do not to take her irritation out on Girard.

He was catching Anna up on his mother's health when the waiter arrived with a bottle of French wine and a tray of elegant appetizers. He turned to Katie. "I hope you don't mind. I just finished a rough day on Wall Street and I could use a drink and a snack. If you don't like the wine, I'll get another."

"It all looks lovely," Katie said, hoping no sarcasm slipped into her tone. The spread was lovely, the wine was lovely, Girard was lovely, but she wasn't so lovely. She felt quite unlovely actually, since all she wanted to do was to get away from all of this loveliness and go home to Blake. Who at times wasn't so lovely. But somehow, most of the time at least, instinctively, she understood why.

"It looks like your shopping trip has been a success," Girard mentioned, smiling over the heap of elegant shopping bags stacked around them.

"Oh, yes, we've found the perfect dress for the charity ball Katie is organizing. It's simply smashing, made for her. Take it out and show him, Katie."

"No, really, I don't think so," Katie said, trying not to grit her teeth. "This isn't the place."

Girard laid a gentle hand on her shoulder. "I'll take your mother's word for it. What color is it?"

"Midnight-blue," she said softly, managing not to flinch when he touched her, though she found the sensation oddly disconcerting. She realized she didn't want him or any man other than Blake to touch her. When had that happened? Throughout her relationship with Tate, she'd danced with other men, allowed them to put an arm around her now and then, even held a hand or two or accepted a kiss here and there. It had meant nothing. Now she felt a sense of betrayal. It was irrational and ridiculous, yet in an odd sort of way it felt good to know she cared enough about one man not to want the attentions of another.

"It sounds perfect," he was saying.

She thanked him politely and changed the subject.

They chatted pleasantly enough and by the time they'd finished their wine and appetizers, he'd succeeded in convincing them to go to a quaint but elegant Italian restaurant where they worked their way through four courses and a couple more bottles of fabulous Italian wine. When he escorted them back to their hotel, Anna excused herself to the elevator, leaving Katie to say a sleepy and a bit tipsy good-night.

"May I see you again?" Girard asked as he walked slowly beside her to the elevator. It opened, the doorman waiting patiently inside.

"Thank you, but I—" *I'm what? Involved with my ex-fiancé's brother?*

"No problem." He lifted a finger to her lips. "I don't need an explanation." He extended a hand kindly, but with an air of distance. "It was a pleasure to have met you. I hope the remainder of your visit is wonderful. If you need anything at all, your mother knows how to reach me." With a tip for the elevator operator and a gentlemanly nod, he turned on his heel and headed across the marble lobby to the front door.

She watched him walk away, not wishing to follow or that he would come back, but wondering for the first time if what her mother had said had some truth to it. Was she rushing into something with Blake? Should she take more time exploring being single and dating other men before she made up her mind what she wanted?

Logic and reason gave her a definite yes. But her heart stayed silent, steady, Blake's name echoing on every beat.

Chapter Eight

Katie rubbed at her temple, feeling the threat of a headache. "Is there some reason why these grant applications have to be six-dozen pages long?" she grumbled.

Looking up from her notes, Tessa grinned. "I'm sure it's nothing personal."

"Right now, it seems like it. I feel like we've been working on this same paperwork for weeks." She sighed, put aside her frustrations and started scanning the next section of the packet only to be interrupted by the chime of her cell phone. Tempted to ignore it, she changed her mind when the displayed number told her it was Blake. She hadn't seen him since she'd gotten back from New York a few days ago and their phone conversations had been unsatisfying to say the least.

"I need to get this," she told Tessa, who, focused on her paperwork, gave a vague wave in reply.

"Is something wrong?" she asked after their hellos.

"Not that I know of," he said. "Does something need to be wrong for me to call you?"

"Of course not. You just surprised me, that's all."

"Pleasantly, I hope."

"It depends on your reason for calling," she came back lightly and he laughed.

"I wondered if you were doing anything this evening. I thought I might stop by. It's the first chance I've had to see you since you got home."

More than a little curious, she told him, "I don't have any plans. My parents are having dinner with Uncle Peter but I didn't feel up to another fund-raiser disguised as a social event. Is this about the ball?"

"About six, then?" He completely ignored her question. "I'll bring dinner."

"That's fine, but Blake—"

"I'll see you then." And he cut the connection before she could question him any further, leaving her staring at the phone in confusion.

"Wow, it really is true."

Katie looked up to Tessa, her assistant's face avid with interest. "What really is true?" Although she already had a good idea of Tessa's answer.

"You and Blake McCord being an item. He's the last man I would have thought you'd fall for, especially after Tate. I mean he's rich and gorgeous and I'm sure there isn't a lack of women who'd love to get him in bed," Tessa added hastily at Katie's frown. "But I never figured you'd be attracted to the cold, arrogant type."

"You don't know Blake. There's another side to him than the one everyone sees," Katie defended him. "And we're not an item. I like him, we're friends—"

"You're spending tonight with him, apparently just the two of you."

"It's just dinner and talking, and I'm sure it's something to do with the plans for the ball."

"Right," Tessa drawled. "So how long has this been going on? Wait—is he the guy you've been daydreaming about since you and Tate broke up?"

"Tessa—"

"That's the reason you and Tate called your engagement off, because you and Tate's *brother*…?"

"Of course it isn't," Katie said, sounding more defensive than she would have liked. "I told you, Blake and I are friends. We're working on planning the Halloween ball together. That's all there is to it." It was a flat lie, but she couldn't define what she and Blake were beyond that to herself, let alone anyone else. "Even if we were seeing each other, Blake doesn't have anything to do with what happened between Tate and me. Tate and I were over long before then. We just didn't make it official."

"You are seeing Blake, then," Tessa persisted.

Exasperated by Tessa's determination to get her to admit what Katie hadn't decided for herself, she said, "Oh, stop already. Let's just get this paperwork done."

Katie focused on the work in front of her, but Blake and his cryptic call kept distracting her, leaving her wondering, speculating, imagining just what he had in mind for them this evening.

Blake tossed his cell phone on his desk, satisfied he'd successfully convinced Katie to spend an evening with him without the necessity of making an excuse that it had anything to do with the hospital benefit. He wouldn't have resorted to directly lying, but had no qualms about editing what information he did give in order to get his way. If he'd told her his plans for the night, she might have turned him down and he wasn't going to take that chance.

A hesitant tap at his office door interrupted his review of his agenda for the evening and Penny poked her head into the room. "Do you have a minute?"

"What have you got?" Blake asked, gesturing his sister to a chair and accepting the portfolio she handed over the desk.

"These are some of the new designs I've been working on using the canary diamonds. I think you'll like them, at least I hope you will."

"Your work is always good," he told her absently, while looking over the sketches with a critical eye. Perched on the edge of her chair, Penny, her fingers laced tightly together, watched him flip through her efforts. There were a few more modern looking pieces Blake didn't care for, but overall, Penny had used both canary and white diamonds in white gold, silver and platinum settings to give the designs a rich, romantic feeling, as if the jewelry itself was centuries old, yet timeless in its beauty and appeal. He was nearly at the end of the sketches when one ring in particular caught his eye. It was a classic, square cut solitaire set in platinum.

Without taking his eyes off the sketch, he said, "This is something special," and immediately Katie came to mind. He thought she would love this, something unique and beautiful, but not ostentatious, like Katie herself.

"What do you think?" Penny asked and Blake caught the anxious note in her voice.

"That you've done a great job with this, especially these—" He spread out the designs he liked best. "I'm not a big fan of the others, but I suppose it's wise to include them."

"Not necessarily. If you're planning to tie the collection in with the Santa Magdalena diamond, then considering the history behind it, you might want to stick with the more traditional-looking pieces." Looking happier at Blake's praise, Penny started gathering up her sketches. "I like those best, too, so I'll focus more on them."

"Not this." Blake pulled back the sketch of the solitaire ring. "I don't want this included in the collection."

Penny's eyes widened slightly. "I thought you said it was special."

"It is. Which is why I only want one of them."

"*You* want it?"

"Yes, is there a problem?"

"No." Penny dragged out the syllable, eyeing him doubtfully. Blake could see she wanted to pursue the matter, but it wasn't in her nature to push. Instead, she settled for a nod and "All right, if that's what you want." She finished putting her portfolio back together then stood up, readying to leave.

It wasn't the best timing but since he hadn't seen much of Penny lately, and unwilling to let her go before he had his say about a subject that had nothing to do with jewelry designing, he said abruptly, "Are you still seeing Jason Foley?"

Starting, Penny recovered quickly. "I'm not going to talk about that with you." An uncharacteristic defiance settled over her face. "I already know you don't approve. There's no point in us discussing it."

This new show of stubbornness took Blake aback. "Penny—"

"I thought you might understand, at least a little,"

Penny went on, "because of Katie. You should know how it feels when people want to talk about things that are private between two people."

"That's completely different. Katie isn't a Foley."

"It's not different. You just won't see it any other way because of this stupid feud with the Foleys that doesn't mean anything to anyone anymore, except you." With that, Penny turned and almost ran from the room, leaving the door flung open wide behind her and Blake staring at her wake, wondering what the hell had just happened and whether Jason Foley was responsible for this different side of his baby sister.

It was an unwelcome thought. And yet, reluctantly, he could understand how Penny felt having someone dissecting her relationship and telling her it was completely wrong. He wasn't sure where he and Katie stood with each other, but he did resent the attempts by their families, friends and even acquaintances to influence how they felt about each other. He didn't trust Jason Foley; he was sure the only reason Jason was pursuing Penny was because he wanted information about the diamond. On the other hand, maybe his badgering Penny about it was only making things worse by spurring her determination to stick with Jason and prove Blake wrong.

Doubting himself and his certainties made Blake uncomfortable. Katie had more or less accused him of being inflexible and he conceded in some areas, she might be right. When it came to the Foleys, though, he couldn't afford to question himself. Not when he had so much riding on this plan to find the diamond and revive McCord Jewelers.

So for now, he pushed aside his misgivings and

focused his thoughts on the evening ahead and those plans that had more promise of succeeding exactly as he hoped.

Though Blake had made it clear he'd decided the agenda for the evening, Katie determined she'd be the one setting the mood. Blake needed to learn to relax once in a while and she admitted she liked being the one who coaxed him into it. She deliberately dressed casually in jeans and a button-down white shirt, leaving her hair loose, her makeup minimal, and enjoyed his approving look when, promptly at six, she opened the door to him.

"Are you going to tell me what this is about?" she asked, leading him into the kitchen so he could deposit the large hamper he carried. He apparently had been thinking along the same lines as her as far as mood because in khakis and a dark blue shirt, sleeves rolled halfway up his forearms, he looked more dressed down than she'd ever seen him.

"Escape," he answered in a word. "You told me I needed to do it more often."

"And you listened? I didn't know I had that much influence over you." Her lips curved up. "You could be in trouble."

"Be nice. I brought champagne."

"You had an ulterior motive for that."

"And this—" Reaching into the hamper, he handed over a DVD.

It was Bogart's *In A Lonely Place,* one of the few she'd never seen. "If I didn't know better, I'd say you had spies." The smug look on his face stopped her. "How did you—?"

"While you were in New York, I asked your house-keeper to check your collection."

It was so typically Blake, not content to settle for less than perfection in executing a plan, and yet the gesture touched her because he'd cared enough to make the gift and the evening personal to her. "Thank you," she said softly, and pressing her hand to his chest, lightly kissed him. "For all of this. I can't think of a better way to spend the evening."

"Can't you?" His eyes swept over her. "Then I need to try harder."

"I don't think so," she said, quickly shifting the subject from one that evoked dangerously seductive images to one more mundane. Lifting the hamper lid, she peered inside. "What's for dinner?"

"Lasagna and chocolate cheesecake. It seemed like a strange combination but—"

"I know, you talked to the cook, too, and she gave away my secret passions."

Blake laughed. "No, just your favorite dinner."

He helped her unpack the provisions and after a leisurely meal, Katie insisted on carrying the cheesecake and champagne into the den, and having dessert while they watched the movie. She even persuaded Blake to try the combination, giggling at his grimace after one sip. Afterward, it felt natural to sit next to him on the couch, her shoulder brushing his, until eventually, his arm slid around her and she leaned into him.

Katie sighed when the movie ended, stretching as she picked up the remote and switched off the television. "Much better than an evening of politics," she said, sitting back.

"Or business," Blake agreed. He began idly sifting his fingers through her hair, occasionally skimming against her neck, watching the motion as if it fascinated him.

"Blake…" His name came out almost a plea and she wasn't sure if she was reminding him her parents would soon be home and to stop, or asking him to go further than the barest contact he was making on her skin.

He looked up, their eyes met, and later, reliving the moments, Katie could never remember who moved first, only that they were in each other's arms and locked in a kiss that had gone from a tentative caress to sensually explicit so fast it dizzied her. The thought of holding back never crossed her mind. His hands roving her shoulders, her back, made her greedy for every feeling, careless of where they were and who might see them.

Distracted by the openmouthed kisses he dragged along her throat that caused her to arch back, offering him better access, she fumbled blindly with the buttons of his shirt. Finally succeeding in freeing them all, she jerked his shirttails out and spread her hands over his chest, drawing a low groan from him that rumbled against her ear.

She pulled him with her as he eased her down on the couch. Blake claimed her mouth again at the same time he unbuttoned her shirt, pushing it off her shoulders, taking her bra straps with it. The intensity of the sensations felt like a wild slide down a high mountain, an incredible, addictive rush, and so new to her. All those years of being Tate's lover, she'd thought she understood passion. She realized now everything she'd felt before was only a hint of what she could feel, what Blake could make her feel. And she knew Blake shared it from the hungry way he kissed and touched her, as if he'd been holding back for so long and all at once had let go every restraint.

Any inhibitions, any doubts she'd had, burned away.

They'd both lost control of this, if they ever had it to begin with. It was crazy, and exciting, and probably wrong in a hundred ways, but Katie didn't care.

"Don't stop," she murmured in between kissing his neck, along his collarbone.

The sound of her voice seemed to give him pause. "Katie…" Breathing hard, he looked at her and there was something vulnerable in his face, an almost stunned expression. "Are you…is that what you want…here?"

"Yes." She kissed him. "Yes."

His mouth moved hotly against her ear. "Your parents—"

"They're not here."

"But soon…" he muttered at the same time his hand cupped one breast, his caresses becoming more intimate. "I don't want to do this in a hurry."

"Please, Blake." It came out half demand, half begging.

As if he'd come to a decision and it sobered him, Blake straightened, bringing her with him so they faced each other, his hands still gripping her arms. "I want you," he ground out and kissed her hard and fast. "But you deserve better."

For a moment, Katie wasn't sure whether he meant himself or better than a quick tumble on her couch, with the threat of her parents catching them in the act. The thought it could be both quelled her frustration at him stopping and lifted her hand to gently touch his face. "Maybe we both do. But it feels pretty good right now."

"You're not making this easy." Blake groaned, closing his eyes at her touch.

"Sorry," she murmured. She leaned in and pressed her lips to his and he took charge, kissing her slowly, thoroughly, until they were both breathless again, and she was entertaining thoughts of persuading him to throw caution out the window.

Sounds of doors closing, voices and footsteps put an end to that fantasy. They both moved quickly to straighten their clothes and to appear as if the last minutes had never happened. Their attempts, in Katie's eyes, didn't do them much good. Blake's hair was tousled, even more after he ran a hand through it, and he looked ruffled; she doubted she was any better.

"That's probably my cue to leave," he said without much conviction behind it. "They'll have seen my car."

"I guess you should, then. It's late…"

He slid his hand around her nape, pulled her to him, and kissed her, long and deep. "Next time," he promised.

Katie, walking Blake to the door, hoped they could escape her parents notice. She thought she'd gotten lucky when, after a lingering kiss of thanks and goodbye, she saw him off, but her luck ran out almost the moment she turned to retreat to her room.

"It was Blake's car, then," Anna said, coming into the foyer. "I thought you told me you weren't involved beyond the planning for the ball."

"No, you told me we shouldn't be involved," Katie returned. "And as I said before, you're jumping to conclusions."

"Oh, for heaven's sake, Katie, I'm not blind or stupid. It's nearly midnight and you don't kiss a man like that to finalize plans for a ball."

Flushing, Katie stood her ground. "No, but it's time I started making my own choices."

She expected a rebuttal from her mother, repeating all the reasons why Anna thought Blake McCord was wrong for her daughter. Instead, Anna said quietly, "That may be. But are you really sure you know what you want?"

There was no certain answer to that question and for a long time after she left her mother, into the tiny hours of the morning, Katie lay awake, trying to decide if what she wanted from Blake and what she needed were the same thing.

Chapter Nine

Blake found Eleanor in the greenhouse, tending her orchids. It was hard making the trip to his mother's sanctuary in answer to the message she'd left for Blake to find her after work. The last thing he wanted after a day like the one he'd had, having to face the latest reports that McCord's sales were still slipping, was a confrontation with his mother.

But not responding to her would be worse. Then she'd find him, demanding explanations he didn't intend to make.

She looked up from the pot she'd been refilling with the specially mixed fertilizer she used on her prized flowers. "You look tired," she noted, more an idle observation than an expression of sympathy.

Careful not to bump against any of her plants, Blake

stepped a little closer. "I'm fine," he said, brushing her off. "You wanted to see me?"

Eleanor patted the soil with gloved hands then moved the pot she'd been working on from the bench back to its spot on her meticulously kept shelves. She pulled off her gloves and waved Blake to a granite garden bench near her. "Come over and sit down a bit. You've probably been running nonstop all day."

"I have, but frankly, I'd rather relax in the library with a scotch than out here."

"You've never liked my flowers."

Blake rolled his eyes. "That's not true and you know it. I always compliment you on them. I'm just hot in this suit and I'd like to go change and wind down inside."

"I understand, but I wanted to meet with you out here because it's about the only place on this property where two people can have some privacy."

Blake groaned inwardly. He felt a reprimand coming on. And he'd bet the Santa Magdalena Diamond it had everything to do with Katie. "That sounds serious."

"It might be." Eleanor shook out her gardening gloves and placed them neatly beside her little trowel on the workbench. "That's what I want to find out."

"Whatever it is, I'm not sure I can help you. But go ahead."

"I got a call from Anna Salgar." She waited, looking at him as if that said it all.

"And? So what? You two are friends."

"It wasn't about me. It was about you. And Katie."

"Again, my question is, and?"

"I don't appreciate your sarcasm, Blake. You know exactly what I mean."

Blake was not in the mood for what was certain to

soon turn into an all-out interrogation. "Let's be honest. You don't appreciate much about me, Mother."

"That was uncalled for and you know it."

He knew he should have stopped himself but exhaustion, suppressed resentment and a naturally short fuse egged him on. "No, I don't. You've never had any tolerance for my issues, but with Charlie, for example, well, let's face it, he can do no wrong in your eyes."

Eleanor bristled. "I don't see what Charlie has to do with this."

"Nothing, except that if he were seeing a woman you had objections to, you'd still try to find a way to support him."

"This is about you and Katie. It has nothing to do with your brother."

She was partially right and he knew it, but inadvertently she'd opened an old, festering wound in him and this time, maybe for the first time ever, he wasn't going to let her get away without facing it. Katie mattered a great deal to him and he wasn't about to let his mother sabotage what he hoped were the beginnings of something lasting.

"Yes it does, in a roundabout way maybe, but the fact is I know you're going to give me grief about seeing Katie. And, I know if situations were reversed, you would do just the opposite for Charlie. He's half Foley, yet he's always been the golden boy, at least in your eyes."

"He's my youngest," she retorted defensively. "It's typical for mothers to coddle the baby of the family a bit."

"Is it typical that the only time you want to talk to me, it's because you disapprove of something I'm doing?"

Eleanor stood stoically, completely ignoring his accusation. "It's not like you to be petulant."

"I told you, it's been a long day."

"I do appreciate all you do for this family," she told him, softening her tone slightly. "And as for Charlie, this has all been very hard on him. He didn't ask for any of this to happen."

"Neither did I. But then I didn't have much choice, did I?"

Glancing away, Eleanor fidgeted with the leaf of a nearby plant. "Blake, I *am* truly sorry for the terrible stress you're facing now," she said, still avoiding his eyes, until she added, "Don't you think involving yourself with Katie is only adding to that?"

"Look, I don't know what Anna said to you. I probably don't want to know. But for your information and hers, Katie is good for me. She's a beautiful, fun, intelligent woman and I enjoy her company. In fact, unlike most other people, Katie actually helps me relax. She knows how to help me take my mind off business."

"Oh, really?"

"That's not what I meant." Blake balled his fists, struggling to keep his tone from going from sharp to harsh. "I mean she listens and she cares. What the hell is wrong with that?"

"Nothing, of course. If that's all it is. Anna and I are merely concerned about our children's happiness, that's all."

"If that's true, then why don't you both back off and let us live our lives. Neither Katie nor I need you telling us what to do."

"Well, I can see you're not in a mood to listen to me, as usual, so we might as well drop this."

The odd rush of emotion, anger, resentment and frustration from years and years of listening with restraint and respect to his mother's criticisms, corrections, suggestions and demands swelled now in Blake until he thought he would burst into a tirade he knew he would never forgive himself for. Why did her intrusion into his private life feel so much more offensive now than it had ever before?

One word came to mind: Katie.

It was different with her: the way he felt, the need to protect her, them, their privacy, their future. He'd never cared enough about another woman to feel defensive. But now that he and Katie had shifted somehow from friends to whatever they were at present, he wanted nothing more than for his mother, her mother, all of damned Dallas to butt out.

With no small struggle, he banked the worst of his anger and tried to ease out of the conversation and out of Eleanor's space.

"It has nothing to do with my mood. It has more to do with the fact that the only times in my life you've taken a genuine interest in me have been when my decisions might in some way affect or interfere with your life or your plans for my life. By contrast, since Charlie was born, you've always been preoccupied with everything that could possibly help him."

For the first time in as long as he could recall, Eleanor flinched. "That's a horrible thing to say to me."

"I didn't say it to hurt you. I just think it's time for both of us to be honest."

"Well," Eleanor said briskly, now clearly out of her comfort zone, "I promised Anna I'd try to talk to you and so I have. That's all I can do. You've taken this far beyond any conversation *I* intended to have."

"That's the point. If I didn't we'd never have had this

conversation." He turned his back to her. "I'm going to get that scotch now." With that he strode away, leaving his mother to ponder, although he knew she'd never address the issues he raised.

Still, it felt good for once to say what he was really thinking instead of what he knew she wanted to hear. He owed that to Katie, too; she'd given him the motivation.

At that moment he realized he didn't want to have that scotch, or anything else for that matter, without her.

A little concerned but glad to hear from him, Katie wondered at the slightly weary note in Blake's voice when he'd called. It didn't sound at all like him. And asking her to simply take a walk in the park certainly wasn't like him. Nonetheless, she agreed to meet him, wondering what was on his mind.

They found each other at the prescribed spot along the north end of a little known but lushly beautiful park nestled in an unexpected corner of the wealthier Dallas suburbs.

"You're here in time to watch the sun set," Blake said from where he sat stretched comfortably over a wood and wrought-iron park bench, one of several that surrounded a granite fountain and small pool.

"Well, I'd say you look relaxed, except for the pin-stripes and tie."

Blake glanced down at his shirt and suit coat. "I forgot to change." He laughed a little at himself. Something few people ever saw him do, Katie mused. "I just needed to get out of that house."

In all the time she'd known him, Katie had never heard him sound quite like this and it worried her. She walked past the spouting water and sat down beside him, instinctively laying a hand on his thigh. "Hey, what's up? You don't seem like yourself at all."

Blake stared off, mesmerized by the rhythm of the fountain's water show. After a long distracted moment he turned to her. Glancing over her, as though part of him just realized she was there, he said, "You look beautiful."

"In sweats and cross-trainers?"

"Especially."

She couldn't help but laugh. "You do surprise me. I was just getting out of the bath when you called—"

"That's not playing fair, Katie, putting that vision in my head."

"Who says I play fair? I threw this on because I didn't actually know what you meant by going for a walk."

"Sorry, I'd love to walk through the park with you, but after I got here and sat down and started watching the sunset I pretty much forgot about the walk."

Now she was truly concerned. Rather than his usual take-control self, he seemed distracted.

"Blake, did something happen today?"

He laughed ruefully. "Your mom called my mom."

She stiffened. "What?"

"If you're up for drama, we could be Romeo and Juliet except for the fact that we're twice their age and ironically *we* aren't the ones from enemy families. Not to say *that* hasn't happened."

Katie knew he was referring to his mother's affair with Rex Foley. Eleanor herself had revealed to Katie a few details of her past with Rex, and both Tate and Gabby had told her about the brief liaison between Eleanor and Rex, the one that produced Charlie. She suspected Blake was also alluding to Penny's new dalliance with Jason Foley.

"Luckily that's not us," she tried to say lightly. When he kept staring off into the pinks and purples lighting the sky above a fading sun, waning remains of what must have been a trying day, she decided to risk being more direct. "Did you and your mother talk about us or about her affair with Rex?"

He shrugged. "Mostly us, but a little of the other. She doesn't like to go there, needless to say." He sat up from his leaning position on the bench, then turned and took her hand in his, running soft patterns over her skin with the pad of his thumb. "She got on my nerves, it's not an issue and it's nothing new. I just needed to get out and away for a while. I needed to be with you."

Katie's heart swelled. That he had thought of her, wanted to be near her when his heart and mind were troubled made her feel more cherished and needed than Tate ever had.

She smiled, leaning into him to touch her lips to his. With a gentle kiss, she murmured, "Thank you."

"For what?"

"Just being here," she said as a substitute for all the things she could have said. "I needed to be with you, too."

They did end up strolling through the park after sunset, holding hands like old lovers by the light of big round gas lamps lighting the tree-canopied trail. In a dozen lifetimes, Blake never would have imagined himself relaxed and actually enjoying a simple walk in the park. Yet surprisingly, he felt more comfortable revealing his feelings to Katie than he had to anyone previously about his mother, her affair with Rex, the uncertain future of McCord Jewelers and his sense of responsibility for that ultimate outcome.

And Katie simply listened. Something no one else in his life had ever done. She didn't offer correction, guilt, advice or make demands. She merely asked a question to clarify here or there, offered a word of encouragement or support and patiently stayed focused on him.

"I'm sorry. I've gone on about my dramas long enough," he said, realizing with a touch of self-consciousness that he'd scarcely asked *her* anything about how things were going in her world.

She turned and smiled up to him. "Don't be sorry, I like it when you talk to me, really talk to me, like you are now."

The soft pools in her eyes told him she meant it. Pausing on the path, he pulled her close. Nuzzling his face in her jasmine-scented hair, he kissed her neck. "Thank you for listening."

"After all these years of knowing each other, I feel like I'm only now getting to know the real you."

"That could be dangerous."

Now averting her eyes to stare out beyond his shoulder, she admitted softly, "It is. But not for the reasons you might think."

"Worried I'm messed up from my mother's fling with Rex Foley and my family's endless expectations?"

"I wouldn't say that." Cupping his chin in her hands, she kissed him slowly, with a tenderness that melted the edges of what felt like an iceberg that had lodged itself somewhere in his heart so long ago he couldn't remember when it hadn't been there.

Blake wrapped his arms around her and matched her kiss, moonlight drenching them in a soft glow. Pliable and willing, she melded to his chest, her supple body inviting him to touch. Sliding his hands down her back, he nudged her closer and when she responded, he deepened their kiss. As it always was between them, it suddenly became urgent—roaming hands, impatient tugging at clothes, forgetting where they were in their need to get even closer.

He could have kept on kissing her but through the moonlit shadows came the approaching sound of giggling teenagers down the path. She drew back and Blake distanced himself reluctantly, both of them resuming their walk.

Trying to catch his breath through a haze of frustrated desire, Blake attempted to attribute the intensity of his need to mere lust. Katie was a stunningly beautiful, sensuous woman after all. But he knew he was lying to himself. What he felt for her went far deeper, down to a place he'd never allowed himself to go.

"That was close," she said finally, with a small laugh, breaking their long silence.

"Do you think they got an eyeful?"

"I doubt it. It's too dark and they weren't that close."

They were nearing the parking lot but he didn't want the night to end here. He had more to say to her, wanted to feel her in his arms again.

She stopped at a fork in the path. "I'm parked over there. It's been so nice, though, just walking and talking. Peaceful, isn't it?"

After pressing her to him until his arousal ached, Blake's body felt anything but peaceful. And his mind wasn't any better. But he lied, lest he scare her off. "We should do this again. It's still early, though. How about a bite to eat?"

"I'd love to but I can't tonight. I left a stack of paperwork for the charity ball unfinished. I'm falling terribly behind and it's getting close."

Her answer hit him hard, like an out-and-out rejection of him personally, not the simple thanks-but-no-thanks he knew it was. His reaction was unreasonable, caused in part he was sure by his unsettling confrontation with his mother, even if it didn't feel like it at the moment. Well trained in stoicism and buried emotions, he simply shrugged it off. "Another time, then."

"Oh, definitely," she said with a light kiss and a squeeze to his hand. "Thank you again for a really lovely evening."

Her gestures and her words left him worse than unsatisfied. The pit of his stomach went hard, felt suddenly cold and empty.

She held the key to a feeling of intimacy he'd never experienced and wasn't sure if he wanted to continue to feel because when she left him, that feeling wrapped itself around his heart like the platinum watch around his wrist, beautiful, essential to the point that without it—without her—he'd begun to feel lost.

Chapter Ten

"Are you sure I can't change your mind?" Blake asked the question, knowing the answer he'd get from Katie, but reluctant to leave without her. They stood together at the gate leading to his private jet, the close warmth of the small room a contrast to the cool gray mistiness of the early fall morning outside the tall glass windows. She'd driven him to the airport today, though it was unnecessary, but her presence wasn't enough to dispel his doubts about yet another separation. Since he'd made plans, two days ago, to make a quick trip to Toronto to personally complete the purchase of several canary diamonds, he'd been plagued by the uneasy feeling that he was going to regret walking away from Katie at this juncture of their relationship, even briefly. If he could call what they had a relationship in terms of it being more than friendship or simple desire, and that was something he hadn't allowed himself to consider too closely yet.

She shook her head, her small smile regretful. "You know I can't. Between work and finalizing the plans for the ball…I wish I could, though."

"Do you?" He stopped her from answering, lightly shaping her cheek with his fingertips. "Katie—" This time he hesitated, uncertain of what he wanted to say to her, more unsure of his own feelings.

"It's only for two days," she said. "We'll both be busy. And you'll be back by the weekend."

"Who are you trying to convince that this doesn't matter?"

"Both of us, I guess. Is it working?"

"Not at this end," Blake told her flatly.

A faint color stained her cheeks. "Why was this not an issue when I went to New York?"

"Hell if I know. Maybe because things haven't been quite the same since you came back."

"I'm not sure what *the same*—" she gave a slight emphasis to the words "—is with us. Are you?"

"No, but I'd like the chance to define it. I'd like to think that you do, too."

Her hesitation was damning, adding to his overall uneasiness that something had changed between them and not for the better. "I'll take that as a no," he said shortly.

"It's not that." She briefly bit her lower lip before reaching out to smooth her hand over his shoulder, following the gesture with her eyes. "If I could just think clearly around you…"

"The feeling's mutual." And before she could protest, Blake pulled her into his arms and lowered his mouth to hers. Neither of them seemed capable of doing anything by half measure and their kiss deepened while she put her arms around his neck and pressed herself closer.

After what seemed to him too short a time, she eased away, pushing both hands through her hair. "This is what I'm talking about. How can we decide what we want and need from each other, or if there's even an *us* to begin with, if we end every discussion like this?"

"It's not every discussion."

"Blake—"

"What do you want from me, Katie?" he asked, beginning to get frustrated, although he knew his irritation stemmed more from his own unsettled feelings than her questions.

"I could ask you the same thing," she countered.

It was on the tip of his tongue to give a glib answer, the one she probably expected: that he wanted her in his bed, no strings attached, no hearts broken. Except this time, with her, the words he'd said to women so many times before in so many different ways didn't come easily—or at all.

"I don't think either of us has an answer right now," Katie said quietly. "This should wait. We can talk when you get back from Toronto."

Blake wanted to argue but time was short and rationally he knew they couldn't resolve anything here and at this moment. The problem was he didn't feel very rational. He forced a deep breath, reined in his urge to blow off the trip entirely, and kissed her cheek, the chaste caress of a friend.

"I'll call you this evening," he said, "if it's not too late."

She responded with a nod and with what might have been an attempt at a smile and stepped back to let him leave.

Taking that as his dismissal, he turned, intending to board the jet, but barely completed the motion before he spun back around, strode over to her and gave her the kiss he wanted, nothing chaste about it. He didn't wait for her response; instead he headed in the opposite direction, refusing to look back.

It was the next morning when her cell phone rang and Katie, automatically assuming it was Blake calling her to confirm she'd be picking him up tomorrow afternoon, frowned a little when she realized it wasn't him, but a number she didn't recognize.

"Katie, this is Marcus Brent." A voice answered her hello and Katie recognized it as her Uncle Peter's campaign manager.

"Marcus, hello. This is a surprise." No lie there; she scarcely knew him, except from their encounters at various fund-raisers. He was in his midforties, successful and good looking in a sleek, polished way. She'd thought little about him except as a key player in her uncle's campaign and had never had more than a superficial conversation with him, which made her wonder why he was calling her now. "If this is about another fund-raiser, fair warning—I've had my fill."

Marcus laughed. "No, this is personal. If you're free this evening, I wanted to ask if you'd have dinner with me. I realize it's short notice," he went on when, caught off guard, she didn't answer right away, "but this close to the election, my schedule is pretty tight. Everything I do these days seems like last minute."

A vision of Blake crossed her mind, clashing with remembered advice from family and friends that she shouldn't limit herself to one man, and her own uncertainties over her involvement with Blake so soon after Tate.

What do you want from me, Katie? She heard Blake's voice in her mind. Instead of answering him, she'd hedged, throwing the question back at him because she didn't know what to say. That was the problem and it prompted her to impulsively tell Marcus, "Thank you, I'd like that. What time?"

It was only after they'd settled the details and she hung up, that she was hit by a mass of regrets and the feeling she'd just made a mistake she wouldn't soon rectify.

The feeling stayed with her even as she tried to reason with herself that she was doing the sensible thing, not limiting herself to the first man she'd been strongly attracted to, considering for once what she really wanted in a relationship. In a way, she and Blake shared a lack of experience in sustaining anything more long-term or in-depth than a passionate affair, and while it was tempting, she knew it wouldn't satisfy her need for something loving and lasting.

Her private pep talk carried her through the evening's dinner with Marcus and although the date wasn't a disaster, she ended it early, pleading a first-thing-in-the-morning appointment, vague about when she'd be able to see him again. He lightly kissed her good-night and she silently thanked him for not pressing it further because all she felt was a sense of guilt that she carried with her to the airport the next afternoon.

Comparisons immediately came to mind when Blake strode over to where she waited and skipped a hello in favor of a long kiss, except there was really no comparison. She forgot Marcus had ever touched her the moment Blake's mouth covered hers and her nagging conscience caused her to kiss Blake back all the more passionately.

"If that's what I have to look forward to every time I leave town, then I'll have to do it more often," he said, holding her a little away from him.

"I missed you, that's all."

"Did you?"

"Why is that so hard to believe?"

"I don't know." She averted her eyes from his searching look. "Did something happen while I was gone?"

"A lot of things happened," she quipped back, "but none of them were important. Just the usual. Are you ready to go? And am I taking you home or to your office?"

Blake hesitated, watching her a few moments longer, and then picked up the locked case and suit bag he'd set down at his feet before he'd scooped her into his arms. "Home is fine. I can stow these—" he indicated the case she assumed held the diamonds "—in the safe there for the time being."

They were out of the airport and a few minutes on the road when he broke the silence, causing her to start. "Is everything all right?"

"Of course, yes. Everything is fine."

"Are you sure? You seem very tense."

The note of concern that warmed his voice nearly caused her to blurt out her jumbled thoughts. *I cheated on you. That's the way it feels. Except it can't be cheating when we haven't promised each other anything, and it's ridiculous to think of having dinner with another man as a betrayal.* "I have a lot of things on my mind right now," she said and it wasn't wholly a lie. "Work has been busy and the ball is coming up fast…"

"Is that all?" Blake persisted.

"Isn't that enough?" She didn't dare glance his way.

"I suppose it is." He fell quiet again and they were less than five minutes from the McCord estate before he spoke up again. "Will you have dinner with me tonight? There's a new French restaurant on the west side—"

"No." Blake raised a brow at her sharp protest and she quickly amended, "I mean yes, I'll have dinner with you, but not French. I'd rather do something more casual." Marcus had taken her to an expensive French restaurant and the last thing she wanted was to be reminded of it the entire evening with Blake.

"I'd invite you home, but—" His mouth pulled in a wry grimace.

"But that would be weird," she agreed. "Under the circumstances, I don't think I'm quite ready for an intimate family dinner." She'd reached the mansion and pulled into the long drive, stopping near the front. After a moment, she shifted to face him.

Expecting him to reach for her, she was surprised and admittedly disappointed when he didn't make good on the clear desire she saw in his face. "How about an intimate night with me?"

The soft, low timbre of his voice sent a shiver through her. "Are we still talking about dinner?"

"I don't know, are we?" Blake asked and the caress of his eyes on her was nearly as potent as a physical touch.

"I thought we were going to talk," she said, aggravated it came out slightly breathless, giving away her own desires.

"Who said that?"

"We did, before you left town."

"That was you."

"Blake—"

"Okay," he said, holding up a hand. "We'll talk. I'll pick you up at six." He let himself out of the car, retrieved his bags and then leaned back inside and before he let her leave added with that cocksure half smile curling one side of his mouth, "Remember, though— you didn't define the topic."

Blake had accepted Katie's earlier mood, taking her word it was the pressures of work and the upcoming benefit that were responsible for her odd edginess. He wondered, though, as he pulled into the drive of the Salgar estate precisely at six, if her insistence they "talk" had more to do with defining their relationship than work and party plans. She'd seemed happy enough to see him, as willing as he to pick up where they'd left off. But it was also clear something had changed, that she wanted more from him than he'd ever been asked to give.

Knowing that forced him to consider the question she'd thrown back at him and he'd never answered, what did *he* want from her? The answer had become increasingly complex, extending beyond desire, to friendship, caring, warmth—things he'd learned to live without but had come to rely on from Katie.

Halfway through dinner he was still thinking about it, unaware of being lost in his thoughts until Katie's slim fingers brushed his hand.

"Is it jet lag or me?" she asked, the slight curve of her lips making it a tease.

"Neither. I'm sorry, I let myself get distracted thinking of all the things I need to catch up on."

Katie pulled a face. "You're supposed to be relaxing, forgetting all of that until tomorrow."

"I could say the same about you," he returned. He

took her hand, rubbing patterns against her skin with the pad of his thumb. "What's wrong, Katie? Are you having second thoughts about us?"

"Is there an us?" she asked pointedly.

"Do you want there to be?"

"That isn't an answer." She sighed, fiddled with the edge of her napkin. "I want to say yes, but I'm not sure if that's wise."

Blake leaned back in his chair, letting his hand slide from hers. "Because of Tate?"

"Tate?" Her eyes jerked to his and Blake swore he saw guilt flash in her eyes. "No, Tate has nothing to do with this." Her firm denial was at odds with her uncertain expression.

"Then what does—or should I be asking who?"

"If there's a 'who,' it's me. I've never thought about what I want in a relationship and I don't think you have, either. I feel like we've rushed into this blindly just because we're…attracted."

"Attracted?" he repeated with a lifted brow. "I don't think it's anything that tame."

A flush stained her cheeks. "No, and like I said before, it's just complicating things." She took a deep breath, slowly let it go and then squarely met his gaze. "You asked me what I wanted from you. I'm not sure, yet, but I'm worried that whatever it is will be more than you're willing to give me."

She was being honest with him and he owed her the same in return. "I can't make you any promises because you're right, I don't know any more than you how to make this work long-term. I can only say I'm willing to try, if you are."

Looking at him a long moment, Katie surprised him

by leaning over and kissing him. "You must be serious," she said softly, "because I'm pretty sure that's the first time I've heard you admit there's something you don't know how to do."

"Don't let it get around. My reputation will be ruined."

They shared a smile and the mood lightened, lingered the remainder of the evening. It was only much later, when he'd left her at her front door after reluctantly ending their passionate embrace, that he realized that she hadn't answered in kind his offer to work toward a commitment.

Chapter Eleven

Why on earth had she agreed to this?

Seven o'clock on a Saturday, and instead of buried under blankets, taking advantage of the chance to sleep in, she was on the court at the Westwood Tennis Club about to play a mixed doubles match against her ex-fiancé and his new love.

Stretching her back and legs out at the net, she turned to Blake where he stood on the sideline, fiddling with his racquet, pacing, looking anything but relaxed. "Remind me again why I went along with this idea of yours."

"You were the one who decided it would be a good way to quiet the gossips if we were seen socializing with Tate and Tanya," he said shortly. "My only contribution was suggesting tennis."

"I thought we'd both decided." When he only shrugged, his mouth pulled in a hard line, Katie felt a twinge of uneasiness. "If you didn't want to do this, I wish you'd have said something."

"It seemed important to you so I went along with it."

Ready to push him to elaborate on that, Katie was interrupted by the arrival of their opponents.

"Morning all." Tate and Tanya, racquets in hand, waltzed lightly onto the court. Tanya looked fresh and glowing, Tate as handsome as ever.

The foursome exchanged somewhat strained greetings and Blake immediately took control. "We'd better get started, we're running late."

"I have to warn all of you, I haven't played in months," Katie said as they moved onto the court, "and I wasn't that great to begin with."

"Always the modest one," Tate teased, drawing a questioning look from his partner.

When the serve was decided and Blake set the ball in motion, Katie saw the spirit of competition flare in Tanya's eyes. A trait that came in handy in her career as an investigative reporter, no doubt. Inwardly Katie groaned. She'd never been much of a competitor in sports and now playing against her ex and his girlfriend, she felt even more uncomfortable.

"Nice work," Blake praised her when she, surprising herself, caught a ball at the net and killed it before Tanya had a prayer of returning it.

With a graciousness that may have been slightly forced, Tanya echoed the compliment. "If that was any indication of how she plays when she's rusty, we're in trouble, Tate."

Tate shrugged lightly. "Told you."

They volley bantered on at a clipped pace, and Katie began to relax as she realized Tate and Tanya, while strong competitors, were truly making an effort to be supportive and keep the atmosphere as tension-free as possible.

Game after game, she and Blake began to learn more about each other's styles, strengths and weaknesses. She found herself relaxing, working with him as a teammate, enjoying their wins, accepting their losses.

"Match," Tate called out on the final shot. "Looks like we're pretty well tied. Want to call it a day?"

Blake wiped the sweat from his brow, a simple motion that sent Katie's mind to flights of fancy. She found him even sexier with his hair mussed, the muscles in his arms and legs pulsing with power, glistening with sweat.

Tanya caught her staring and smiled a woman-to-woman kind of appreciation. She walked to the net to congratulate Katie on the game and took her hand warmly. "Nice view, hmm?"

Katie couldn't help but smile. "It seems to run in the family."

Tate and Blake shook hands, as well, and Blake put an arm around Katie's waist, lightly holding her to his side. For a moment, it felt awkward, the display of familiarity in front of his brother, but it passed when she saw Tate smile.

"Drinks on me," Blake offered. "Do you two have time for the juice bar?"

Tate turned to Tanya. "I think so, don't you? We aren't due to meet up with Charlie for a couple of hours."

Tanya nodded. "Juice sounds great."

"You have plans with Charlie?" Blake asked sharply.

Tate and Tanya exchanged a glance. "He asked if we could catch up with him for a late lunch."

"I didn't know you and Charlie palled around much."

The edge in Blake's voice was telling. Katie knew

that ever since Eleanor revealed Charlie was actually Rex Foley's son, Blake's relationship with his youngest brother had been strained.

"We don't. He's too busy at the university and with my surgery schedule we hardly ever get to see each other. But…"

"What's going on?"

Katie saw Tanya slide her hand into Tate's. "Honestly, I don't know. All he said was he wanted to talk to me." He stopped, considering, then went on. "He said it has to do with Mom and Rex."

"I see," Blake said flatly. "Well, good luck with that, then." He turned and gestured to Katie. "How about that juice?"

Tension electric between them, the foursome headed toward the front of the club.

The poshly appointed juice bar featured every fruit, basic to exotic, and dozens of add-ons to boost energy, relieve stress or curb hunger. All around them, people sipped icy concoctions in tall, brightly colored glass goblets.

As Katie perused the menu, having skipped breakfast—her stomach beginning to growl—she failed to see the man stride up beside her. She was the last at her table to realize he was trying to get her attention.

Marcus Brent touched her shoulder lightly, breaking her concentration. Her eyes darted upward; her stomach plummeted. She felt all eyes on her and was certain her face had turned a dozen shades of red.

"I didn't realize you were a member here," Marcus said smoothly, turning to the rest of the group. "Hello, Blake," he said, extending a hand. When Blake's eyes looked questioningly at him, he added, "We met at Peter

Salgar's fund-raiser. I'm his campaign manager. It was a pleasant surprise to see you there." He paused. "And to see you here, Katie."

Katie saw Blake struggle to make sense of Marcus's familiarity with Katie. "Right, sorry, it took me a moment to place you," he said finally, taking Marcus's hand.

Marcus turned to Tate and Tanya. "And you must be Tate McCord and the lovely Tanya Kimbrough. I used to see you on the news, now I see your picture in the society column. Neither of them does you justice."

No stranger to compliments, Tanya thanked Marcus graciously. "You did a superb job on the recent campaign ads for Peter. Brilliant, really."

"Thanks, but it was a team effort."

Blake pulled out an empty chair beside him. "Have a seat. We were just getting some refreshments after the game."

Marcus shot Katie an amused glance.

He's enjoying this! she seethed inwardly, wishing she could disappear.

"I'd love to." Marcus took the seat. "But I'll only stay a minute. I don't want to interrupt and I have a game in ten."

"So, have you known the Salgars long?" Blake asked, glancing at Katie.

It was all she could do not to visibly squirm. Instead she focused intently on her mango-raspberry smoothie.

"Not really. Peter hired me after noticing some work I'd done managing campaigns in San Diego and Austin. He made me an offer I couldn't refuse, so I moved here."

"And after this campaign?" Tate asked.

"Well," Marcus said with a little laugh, "I guess that depends on how it turns out." Focusing on Katie, he added, "But I have become quite fond of the Salgars, so it would be difficult to move again."

Reluctantly, Katie pried her eyes from her nearly empty glass. "Oh, yes, Uncle Peter and my parents speak highly of you. I'm sure Uncle Peter would give you an excellent reference—whichever way the campaign goes."

"None of that talk," Marcus teased. "There's only one way for this campaign to end, with a win. But enough about politics. From what I hear, McCord Jewelers is a much more fascinating topic *du jour*."

"I doubt that," Blake said. There was a warning note in his voice that Marcus either didn't recognize or chose to ignore.

"I read in the business journal recently that a couple of stores were closed. I hope everything is okay."

"Reorganization. It has to be done from time to time to cut the fat and raise efficiency. It's routine."

Marcus checked his watch and shoved back in his chair. Standing, he again reached for Blake's hand, then Tate's. "Glad to hear that's all it is. Even long-standing empires hit hard times now and then." Smiling broadly, he offered Tanya a nod and again, touched a hand to Katie's shoulder. "You'll ring me sometime, won't you? We can do dinner again. Maybe Italian next time."

If he hadn't turned and strode briskly away, Katie would have been tempted to dump her smoothie down the front of his sparkling white tennis shirt.

Tanya, bless her feminine compassion, tugged at Tate's arm. Katie avoided both brothers' glares and smiled at Tanya. "If we don't leave now we're going to be late to meet Charlie. And I'm not stepping out into public with this hair and these drenched clothes I've been soaking in too long already."

Taking the not-too-subtle prodding, Tate laid a hand on Blake's back. "Thanks for the game. We'll have to do it again sometime."

Blake nodded absently, his face locked in a hard, stoic frown. "Say hello to Charlie," he ground out.

Katie knew his tone was due in part at least to Marcus's untimely appearance. When Tate and Tanya had left, she had no option but to face him. But what could she say? How could she defend herself for something so minor and meaningless to her, yet so magnified now that it looked like a calculated deception to Blake. Again, murderous thoughts toward Marcus crossed her mind.

"Blake, about Marcus—"

Blake stood, held up a palm. "Save it. I'll go have your car brought around."

At the tense set of his face, a wave of guilt washed over her. And then defensiveness took over. She hadn't done anything wrong. They weren't officially a couple and she *was* officially single and could do as she pleased. Hadn't she convinced herself she needed to give herself time to discover what she really wanted in a relationship?

Or so she'd told herself. The idea she had hurt him, though, quelled some of her rebelliousness. He was the one who'd offered to work toward something long-term; she was the one who'd hesitated and then decided to test the dating waters with Marcus.

"It was only one dinner, when you were in Toronto," she said finally.

"I don't want the details, thanks."

"I don't have that many to give. It's not as if we were lovers. I spent a few hours with him, that's all."

"You're free to see whomever you like." He echoed her own thoughts, but hearing them spoken aloud in his cold, expressionless tone renewed with a vengeance all her uncomfortable feelings. "I need to go. I have to stop by my office. I'll mention your car on my way out."

"Blake—" Katie put a hand on his arm, stopping him from turning to leave. "Can we at least talk about this?"

"What is there to talk about? You decided to date someone else. End of story."

"No, it's not. You're obviously upset about it."

"I don't think my reaction matters one way or the other. You didn't consider it when you chose to go out with Marcus Brent." They locked gazes for brief seconds and then Blake blew out a breath, shoving a hand through his hair. "This is pointless."

"I don't want to leave things like this," Katie said, at a loss to know how to fix it.

"What do you want, Katie? My blessing on your decision to play the field? Sorry—" He pulled free of her grasp. "I can't do that. But you don't need my approval. As you keep pointing out, we're just *friends*."

Not giving her time to respond, he spun around and strode out of the bar, leaving her alone with her regrets.

A last-minute invitation to a fashion show that afternoon in downtown Dallas was unwelcome to say the least. But it was Gabby who'd called to invite her and as they'd been trying for weeks to do lunch or a drink, Katie couldn't possibly say no, even though the invitation included Anna and Eleanor. Still, after the confrontation with Blake, the last thing Katie wanted was to be gently but expertly interrogated by her mother, Eleanor and Gabby.

As they took their seats front row to the catwalk, Katie wished she'd made an excuse to stay home.

"I can't wait to see a sneak preview of the spring Milan collection," Gabby was saying excitedly. "We're so lucky to have gotten in today. It's a small, private showing, but my friend is the designer's cousin. I owe her big-time." She focused on Katie and her grin turned to a small frown. "Are you all right? I know this was last minute. Did I interrupt something?"

"No, it's not that." Realizing she probably looked as if she were sulking, Katie made an effort to brighten her tone. "I'm a little tired, that's all. We played several games of mixed doubles at the club this morning. I haven't played that much tennis in months."

"We? Meaning you and Blake?"

"Against Tanya and Tate," she said, nodding.

At the sound of her sons' names, Eleanor craned her head around to join the conversation. "Did I hear Blake and Tate mentioned in the same breath?"

Katie's stomach tightened, afraid Eleanor would use the moment to quiz her about Blake. "Yes, we all played tennis together this morning."

"Oh…well, that must have been interesting."

"It was fun, actually."

"Look, ladies, the show is starting." Anna pointed to the head of the stage where a glamorous woman with a microphone had appeared from behind the curtains. "That's Margo Hererra. You know her, she's the new designer from Spain."

Gabby smiled. "I told you this would be worth changing your Saturday afternoon plans."

Katie didn't know her or care, but she smiled obligingly.

As all heads turned, riveted toward the stage, the

noise and excitement allowed Katie a welcome respite from conversation. Though appearing to pay attention to the glittering swirl around her, she was in fact miles away. She wished she'd tried harder to convince Blake to talk to her. She hated how they'd left things and wondered if she'd broken whatever bond existed between them.

After a span of time Katie couldn't have recalled, Eleanor leaned toward her. "It's almost over and it's cocktail hour so what do you say the four of us steal away early and grab an appetizer and a martini?"

They shared Anna's Mercedes sedan to a trendy little restaurant nearby and took a corner table near the window where they could people watch and comment on Dallas fashion—or the lack thereof.

"You seem under the weather today, Katie," Eleanor was saying as the waitress handed them their drinks. "Too much tennis?"

"No, not at all. Tanya is a lot of fun and she and Tate are so good together. I'm happy for them."

"What about Tate?" Anna asked.

"What do you mean?"

"Well," she said, stirring the olive around the bottom of her glass with her finger, "it must be difficult for him to see you and Blake dating."

"Why? He's engaged to be married. And anyway Blake and I aren't—" Katie stopped midsentence when all eyes stared her down, letting her know they weren't buying it. "Okay, so we've been seeing each other, but—"

"But what?" Gabby asked, her voice gentle.

Katie hesitated, then, figuring Marcus wouldn't keep it a secret, said, "I don't know how much Blake and I are going to be seeing each other from now on. He found out that I had a date with Marcus Brent while he was in Toronto."

"Oh, Katie, that's wonderful," Anna said, reaching over to pat her daughter's hand. At Katie's disbelieving look, she added hastily, "I didn't mean that quite the way it sounded. It's just dating more than one person is the healthy thing to do, don't you agree?" she asked, directing the question to Eleanor.

"Absolutely. You and Tate were together so long, Katie. You shouldn't limit yourself to one man too quickly."

Gabby listened in silence and Katie felt her friend's empathy. Finally, Gabby politely interrupted the twosome. "Excuse me, but none of us has asked Katie if *she's* glad she dated someone else. Are you?"

Katie's first instinct was to say that it was a horrible mistake and she was worried Blake wouldn't forgive her. Instead she banked that flood of emotions and turned the tables on Gabby. "Did you date anyone else after you and Rafael were involved?"

"I barely looked at another man after Rafael. I was smitten, as they say." She lifted a brow and grinned, catlike. "Not that I let him know that."

Is that the way I feel with Blake? It seemed an almost tame description of the volatile mix of desire, need and communion she felt when they were together.

She turned to Eleanor and Anna. "What about you? Is that the way you felt?" As soon as the words fell from her lips she wished she could have swept them up and away. Of course Eleanor had been head over heels—but for Rex Foley, not Devon McCord.

Anna answered first, rescuing her friend. "In a manner of speaking, yes, I fell for your father the first time I saw him. But it took time to truly fall in love with him."

"I'd be lying if I said Devon and I were ever really in love with each other, even after so many years together," Eleanor said quietly, after a long silence. "All of you know that isn't true. But Rex—I think I fell in love with Rex the first time I saw him. To this day, the thought of him can bring back those feelings. And now, the problem is Blake and the other children know it. Blake, in particular, resents me."

Katie didn't know what to say to comfort her. It was true. Blake had a rigid, hard side she doubted anyone would ever penetrate. "I think he's working on accepting it," she managed, "but with Charlie as a reminder, it's, well, it's going to take time."

"I hope that's all it will take," Eleanor said sadly. "Blake is so angry at me and it's caused a rift between him and Charlie."

Gabby reached out to take Eleanor's hand. "It's a shock, that's all. They're brothers. They'll work it out eventually."

"I hope that's true. But enough about my dramas," Eleanor said, pasting a smile back on her face. "What we want to know is, how was your date?"

Back in the hot seat, Katie sighed. She was with friends; she might as well tell them the truth. "It was fine."

"But?" Anna prompted.

"But he wasn't Blake."

Gabby's smile comforted her. "That says a lot."

"Maybe, but it probably doesn't matter now. We ran into Marcus at the club and he made a point of letting Blake know we had dinner together. Blake didn't take it well." Inwardly, Katie winced at the definite understatement.

"Oh." Eleanor waved a hand. "His ego is just bruised. You know how proud my son is. He'll get past it. And my guess is when he does, now that he knows he has competition, he'll pursue you even harder just to prove he's the better man."

With that all four women lifted their glasses and toasted what they'd managed to turn from Katie's disaster into Katie's accidental victory.

As she took a sip of her drink, Katie wished she could believe Eleanor was right, but the wounded rage in Blake's eyes when he'd left her made it hard to hold on to the hope it was true.

Chapter Twelve

Two pages left to go and Blake was starting to question how he and Katie had managed to get through the past hour's worth of last-minute checklists for the ball without saying more than a few sentences to each other. On the other hand, the strained silence between them spoke volumes.

They hadn't really talked, except impersonally about business or the benefit, since he'd found out about her date with Marcus. Because of that he'd been surprised when she'd agreed to meet him this evening at his office to go over the final list of donations for the silent auction. He hated the distance separating them. It seemed vast, despite them sitting side by side on his office couch, paperwork spread over the coffee table. But he didn't know how to deal with his jealousy or the idea he couldn't dislodge that she didn't place much value on their relationship or consider it serious to begin with. It would be easier if he could simply dismiss his feelings and move on, but he hadn't been able to command his emotions as easily as he did everything else in his life.

"I don't think we've actually gotten this painting yet," Katie said, frowning at a notation on one of their lists. She leaned over to pick up another paper at the same time Blake reached for the same one and their hands touched.

The inadvertent contact froze them midmotion. Their eyes met and Blake saw in hers the same desire that had been tormenting him.

"Blake…" The way she said his name, with both longing and uncertainty, snapped his restraint.

All the pent-up tensions of the past days loosened at once. He pulled her against him and she met him halfway, kissing him back with an intensity that overwhelmed his every other thought and feeling except wanting her closer. Taking control away from him, she pushed gently at his shoulders to urge him back against the couch and they ended up with her half lying on his chest.

He took advantage of the position to slide his hands under her thin sweater and over warm, smooth skin, emboldened by the hum of pleasure she made to drag the material higher, giving him access to rove over her back and the sides of her breasts. Her body and hands rubbing, caressing him, nearly drove him to forget patience and propriety, strip off her clothes and his, and take and give what they both wanted.

It struck him this might be all he would ever have with her. She hesitated when they came too close to deepening their relationship, but she never hesitated in this. And if this was all he could have, maybe he could pretend it would be enough.

"Let's get out of here," he murmured, nuzzling her neck.

Her fingers found their way inside his shirt and teased open the first few buttons. "Where?"

"Anywhere with a bed and no chance of being interrupted." Blake paused his explorations long enough to shift to look at her. "We can take the jet, go somewhere for the weekend and finish this in private."

"Finish this?" she echoed and a wary note crept into her voice. "This, being together—or us?"

Blake sat up, bringing her with him, although he didn't fully let her go. "There isn't really an 'us,' is there? You obviously aren't committed to me in any way."

"And you're committed to me?"

"I'm not the one who decided to see other people the minute you left town."

"It was one date! I needed to—"

"Figure out what you want, so you've told me. But you said yourself our wanting each other was getting in the way, making things more complicated. If we spend a couple of days together we can satisfy it and go back to the way things were before."

"Let me get this straight," she said slowly. "You think a few days of casual sex will fix everything."

The honest answer was he didn't. But he also didn't believe she wanted anything else. "You can't tell me it isn't what you want, too."

For a moment, she stared at him in stunned silence. He waited, expecting her to tell him he was right, that sexual chemistry was all they had and would ever have, and that a weekend in bed would cure them both of the lust that was interfering with their friendship.

Instead, she suddenly jerked out of his hold and to her feet, swinging around to look him squarely in the eye. "No."

"No?" The word caught him off guard. He stood up, halting his step toward her when she thrust out a hand. "Katie—"

"No, Blake. I'm sure you're not used to hearing it, but the answer's no." She pressed a hand to her face for a moment, briefly shutting her eyes, and Blake noticed her trembling, as if she were on the verge of tears.

Only then did he realize he'd made a huge mistake.

"I can't believe, after everything that's happened, that you can be so—" she struggled over the words "—cold."

Blake shoved both hands through his hair, fighting the urge to grab her back into his arms and speak to her with his body, the only way they managed to communicate clearly, it seemed. "What am I supposed to think, Katie? You keep telling me you don't know what you want. But every time I touch you—"

A sharp rap at the office door cut off Blake's sentence. He considered ignoring it or telling whoever it was to leave them the hell alone, but when he looked at Katie to see if she shared his feeling, she made a helpless gesture and turned away.

Cursing under his breath, Blake strode over and yanked open the door, surprised to find Charlie standing there. Hands jammed in the pockets of his jeans, shifting from foot to foot, his younger brother appeared uneasy about his reasons for showing up at Blake's door.

"What are you doing here?" Blake snapped out, letting his frustration speak before he could temper his greeting. "You're supposed to be at school. Did something happen?"

"No, or at least not anything you're thinking. I need to talk to you alone. It's important," Charlie persisted when Blake showed no sign of giving way.

Blake nearly refused, except the determination on Charlie's face told him his brother wasn't going to accept being dismissed before he'd had his say. Blowing out an irritated breath, Blake moved back from the doorway. "Come in, then. Whatever it is, you can say it in front of Katie," he added at Charlie's hesitation at seeing Katie standing there.

"I should go," Katie started, not wanting to be another source of friction between the two brothers. "I need to—"

"Stay," Blake cut her off. "We don't have any secrets from you."

Their gazes locked and after a brief silent battle of wills, she nodded, and sat back down on the couch, her stiff posture telegraphing her awkwardness with the situation.

Shaking his head at the chair Blake offered him, Charlie remained standing, facing Blake, his tension over whatever he'd come to say radiating of him. It gave Blake the unwelcome feeling that whatever his brother had come to tell him, he wasn't going to like it.

"I'm going to meet with my father tomorrow."

Charlie broke the news without any preliminaries and for a few long moments, there was a taut silence, with him and Blake staring at each other like adversaries about to do battle.

Katie fervently wished she'd defied Blake and left when she had the chance. No matter what Blake said, she didn't belong here, witnessing what should have been a very private conversation. She looked between the brothers, knowing from the hardened set of Blake's face he wasn't going to take Charlie's blunt announcement well.

Shifting her glance to Charlie, she recognized the same unshakeable resolve she'd seen so many times in Blake; she also, with new eyes, saw how much he resembled his father. Although he shared Blake and Tate's lean build, he had the dark good looks of the Foley men, and she questioned why no one, herself included, had ever noticed how Charlie McCord stood out like a changeling amongst his own family.

It was Blake who finally ended the quiet. "I assume you're talking about Rex Foley," he said tightly. His hands flexed at his sides. "How can you be sure he wants to meet you, or that he even knows you're his son?"

"He knows," Charlie said. "Mom told him."

The revelation took Katie aback. She wondered if Eleanor had thought about how much angst she'd be causing both families by revealing a twenty-one-year-old truth. If Eleanor had believed it would somehow reconcile the two families, then she had far underestimated how deeply the antipathies between the Foleys and McCords ran.

"She told him," Blake repeated. He shook his head sharply in disbelief. "I don't know why I'm surprised."

"She should have told him—and me—a long time ago."

"She should have stayed away from Rex Foley."

The harsh condemnation breached Charlie's outward calm, leaving him scowling. "And maybe you should have stayed away from Tate's girl, but it doesn't seem to have stopped you."

The cold, unforgiving anger taking control of

Blake's features prompted Katie to her feet and she moved to his side. Underneath the tempering hand she curled over his forearm she could feel the steely clench of muscle.

"I'm not the one who slept with the enemy," Blake ground out. "And you've apparently decided to join them."

"I'm a Foley, whether you like it or not," Charlie countered, not backing down from Blake's fury. "You can't change what happened. Everyone's just going to have to find a way to live with it."

"What do you hope to gain by all this?"

"It's not a matter of gain. I want to know my father. Why can't you understand that?" Pacing a few steps back and forth, Charlie swung on his brother again. "I'm not who I thought I was, all these years. I need to do this."

"So as usual you get whatever you want and damn the consequences to anyone else, is that right?"

Katie gave credit to Charlie for keeping a hold on his own temper, though he looked like he wanted to take a swing at Blake. "I didn't ask for this."

"You don't seem too devastated by it, either," Blake shot back. "Why did you bother coming to tell me? You can't seriously believe I'd approve."

"No, but I thought you might understand. Obviously, I was wrong." Not waiting for Blake's reply, Charlie spun around and strode out the door, leaving it hanging open.

"Son of a—" Turning away from Katie, Blake slammed a fist onto his desktop, rattling everything on it.

Cautious about approaching him in this mood, his angry display unsettled her further. Katie, though, couldn't completely back away from him. "I'm sorry," she said quietly. "This must be hard, especially with everything else going on—"

"What the hell does he think he's doing? He knows how I—most of the family—feel about the Foleys."

"He wants to know his father." She stood up to the glare he fixed on her. "He's right, what happened between your mother and Rex isn't his fault. You can't blame Charlie for trying to figure out who he is and where he fits in."

"I'm sure my mother is encouraging him," Blake said as if she hadn't spoken. "She never could deny Charlie anything."

The harsh bitterness in his voice caught Katie off guard. For the second time that evening, she realized what she'd never seen before: Blake was jealous of Charlie. She didn't fully understand it, but she suspected that part of his angry reaction to Charlie's news had more to do with his family relationships than his dislike of anything to do with the Foleys.

Despite his dangerous mood, she felt compelled to comfort him. Beneath his furious reaction there was pain and it drew her to move closer and slip a hand over his shoulder, gently squeezing. "I know how you must feel—"

"No, you don't." He pulled away from her, deliberately putting distance between them again. "Don't pretend you do or that you care."

Katie flinched, hurt by his accusation. "That's not fair or true."

"Isn't it?" Blake stared a moment out the darkened windows then abruptly said, "I need to get out of here."

She almost made the mistake of thinking he meant that they should go together. But he strode over to the coffee table, focusing on gathering up papers and jamming them back into files, and it was obvious he was dismissing her. "I'll call you tomorrow, then," she said quietly, not about to let him see her upset again. "We can finish up anything we've missed."

Getting only a curt nod in answer, Katie grabbed up her purse and her own portfolio and left him, walking fast to where she'd parked her car to avoid the temptation of looking back or worse, turning back.

On the drive back home, she told herself she should be furious with him for more or less throwing her out of his office without so much as an explanation or apology for his behavior. Yet she found herself more worried than angry. She knew Blake well enough to realize he would never treat her that way, even if he was angry with her, unless he was in some sort of emotional turmoil.

Charlie's announcement had bothered him, but his reaction seemed out of proportion. She couldn't define what was bothering him but it seemed to be all tied together with his mother, Charlie, Rex Foley and the whole mess with his business. Maybe part of it, too, was her.

Looking back, she wished she been a little less adamant about turning down his proposition they spend a weekend together. She couldn't accept, not and feel good about herself afterward, but she also couldn't suppress her disappointment with him.

She'd thought they had something more than a basic physical attraction, that they were truly friends, with the potential to be more.

What they were now—if anything—she didn't know.

Skipping the ice and water, Blake drank back his shot of scotch and poured out a second. It wasn't an answer to the memories, the feelings he wanted to obliterate, it didn't even dull them. But after a lifetime of suppressing his emotions instead of acknowledging them, he didn't know any other way.

He wished he'd picked a better place than his study to indulge his misery, though, or at least had bothered to close the door because he'd just raised his second drink when Tate looked in, brow arching at seeing Blake.

"Charlie must have found you," his brother observed, coming in uninvited.

Blake's reply was to finish off his drink and pick up the bottle to pour another.

"This is something you can't take charge of," Tate said. "You can't blame Charlie for wanting to know his father."

"No, I'm supposed to be understanding and accept he's a Foley and support his decision to switch sides. Have I covered it all?" Leaving his drink untouched, Blake paced over to one of the large leather chairs and flung himself down. He didn't like this feeling, that his life was out of control, and there wasn't a damned thing he could do about it.

"This isn't just about Charlie, is it?" Tate asked, coming to sit opposite him. He waited a moment then asked, "Did something happen with Katie?"

"If it did, it doesn't matter any more."

"You're giving up? That doesn't sound like you."

"You're the one who told me I didn't know what I was doing with her. You'll be happy to know you were right."

Tate shook his head. "When you're through wallowing in self-pity, maybe you'll take some advice. Talk to her," he said, without waiting for Blake's agreement. "Admit how you feel. Knowing you and how you prefer keeping everything to yourself, she probably doesn't have any idea."

"What exactly is it I'm supposed to be admitting?" Blake returned.

"I'll let you figure that one out on your own," Tate said. He got to his feet. "It took me a while, but once I got it, I realized it's been there between you two for a long time." Leaving Blake with that cryptic observation, Tate walked out, closing the door quietly behind him.

For a long time afterward, Blake sat alone, staring at nothing, but seeing Katie, wondering if he was honest with himself and with her, if in the end, it would be enough to repair everything that had been torn apart.

Chapter Thirteen

"Tessa," Katie called out as she saw her assistant pass by her office. "Can you please bring me the final hard copy of the menu for the ball?"

Tessa stopped and took a few steps backward to look in at Katie. "Sure. I was going to take it to the printer this morning. Do you still want me to?"

"I need to look it over once more to make certain the changes are all correct. Last time I looked it over a few of the French words had the accents backward and one of the desserts had been entirely left off."

As the impending ball had drawn near, Katie was glad to be able to immerse herself in work. She needed to work to keep from spending all her time lamenting the state of her relationship with Blake.

Tessa bustled back into her office, menu in hand. "Here you go. You do know about the change, right?"

Katie looked up from her computer screen. "What change?"

"Blake made a last-minute change in the menu."

"When did that happen? It took me weeks to put this menu together and do all of the tastings with the chef."

At Katie's sharp tone, Tessa gave an apologetic shrug. "I'm sorry. He told me you wouldn't mind, so I went ahead and made the change."

"I see." *So much for teamwork.* "Well, from now on tell him you have to run everything by me first."

"I will, I just thought that since you two were seeing each other that you'd have already talked it over."

Shoving back from her desk, Katie stood, turned and stared out her window. "No. We haven't." She didn't elaborate. Rehashing the whole mess with Tessa wasn't going to do any good. "I'll call him about this, though. Looking at this menu, I don't understand why he would change the shrimp scampi to prime rib."

"Are you sure you want to talk to him?" Tessa asked, eyeing Katie doubtfully. "If there's a problem, I can call him and ask about this for you."

Katie sighed. "No thanks, I'll talk to him." Even if he were still angry with her, she missed hearing his voice.

After Tessa had left, she delayed making the call, though, barraged with reminders of the last time they'd seen each other. The scene at his office had been so painful in so many ways, for him in regard to Charlie and his mother and for her because she hurt for him. His sexual proposition had only muddied the waters further, making her feel cheap and disposable, like any other of the women with whom he'd had brief flings. But right now, despite all of that, she was missing not only his voice, but their former closeness.

If only they could go back to when their friendship was on the verge of being so much more.

Shaking herself free of her useless musings, she picked up the phone and dialed his cell.

"Hello, Katie," he answered, all cool formality.

"Um…" For a moment she lost her train of thought. Hearing him sound so distant, so guarded after the closeness and passion they'd shared hurt, momentarily throwing her off balance. Then she glanced to her desk, seeing the menu that jogged her mind back on track.

"I'm calling about your menu change. I don't understand why you would switch shrimp for prime rib. I worked it out meticulously with Chef Bedeaux."

"I changed it because several members of my family are allergic to seafood and a number of other people are, as well," Blake explained.

"Oh, I guess I never thought about that."

"You can change it again, if you want to." There was more in his conciliatory tone than in his words. His voice had gentled, sounding almost weary now.

"No, this will be fine. I'm done with revising this menu. It will have to do."

A long awkward silence followed until he broke it with, "Katie, I don't want us to argue. The other day was rough."

A lump rose in her throat. There were so many thoughts and emotions she'd been banking since last they were together, she didn't dare express them now or she'd fall apart crying. "I know," she said softly. "Let's just get through this ball and then we can try to sort everything else out, okay?"

"Okay. I'm willing if you are."

"Of course I am. I just think we need to get past this event before we can focus on anything personal."

"It'll be over soon enough. I'm buried in McCord's business as usual, but please call me or e-mail me if you need any help and I'll drop what I'm doing."

She longed to tell him she needed help now. Not with the ball. With him. With her. With them. Instead she simply thanked him and listened for the click of his phone that ended the call with a sense of loss and the flat sound of emptiness on the other end of the line.

Shoving the pained conversation with Katie from his mind, Blake forced himself to turn his attention back to pressing matters at McCord's, namely, finding the Santa Magdalena Diamond. He hadn't spoken to Paige recently to check on how her hunt for the diamond was progressing—and come to think of it, he'd seen neither hide nor hair of Penny lately, either.

Dialing on his cell, rather than risking using the office line, he connected with Paige. "I haven't heard from you lately. Anything new on the mine?"

"I didn't want to bother you. With the ball being so close, I figured you were up to your ears in last-minute details."

"I am, but this is far more important. Can you talk?"

"Yes. I'm just driving to Café Zozo to have lunch with a friend."

Blake rocked back in his leather chair and whirled it around to gaze out at the Dallas cityscape. "Sorry to interrupt but I haven't seen much of you lately."

There was a pause and then Paige answered. "Well, it's not like you're around much, either. You're with Katie a lot."

"You're mistaken about that. I've scarcely seen Katie in weeks," he said gruffly. He felt suddenly defensive, unwilling to even broach the subject of Katie, afraid his hurt and frustration might seep into his tone of voice. The last thing he wanted was his little sister probing him about his messed up relationship with Katie.

"I'd ask you what was wrong, but I know you wouldn't tell me," Paige said. "You can ask me about the diamond though."

"Okay—any news on the mine?"

Paige's voice brightened. "As a matter of fact, yes. I was able to get to the mine. That's the good news."

"And the bad news?"

"It's old, rickety, unstable. It's going to be a dangerous venture getting inside and navigating my way to where the diamond is hidden. I'll need to plan carefully and take the right gear with me or I might not make it back out of there."

Silent, Blake considered the risk. It worried him terribly that his sister could wind up trapped in an old collapsing mine. "I don't like the sound of this," he said finally.

"It's okay, really. I'm going to take every precaution. I've been researching how to prepare for and anticipate anything that could happen down there. I've spoken with some old-timers who know the ropes where mine shafts are concerns. They've given me a lot of helpful information."

"Still…"

"I want to do this, Blake. I have to. And I can and I will. For the family."

Blake admired his sister's courage, in fact pride for her welled in him; nonetheless, he wouldn't stop worrying until the whole caper was over and done and she was safely back at home. "We are in desperate circumstances, I won't kid you. We need that diamond if McCord's is to survive."

"I know that. That's why I'm willing to take whatever risk is necessary."

"Promise me one thing."

"What?"

"Don't embark on any of this until you clear everything with me. I want to know every detail of your plan, start to finish. I'll do anything I can to help assure you're safe. Got it?"

"Always the big brother," Paige said flippantly.

"And don't you forget it."

After they'd hung up the phone, it occurred to Blake that Paige wasn't the only one of his siblings that he had lost touch with in the past weeks. He considered a moment then sent Penny a text message asking her to meet with him because he hadn't seen much of her at all. He blamed that on Jason Foley.

I'd love to but I already planned to go to the gym, she wrote back.

Fine. I'll meet you there. We can play a round of racquetball. I'll reserve the court for four.

Penny didn't text back for several minutes. When she did, it didn't sound promising. I was going to do a Pilates class, but I suppose I can skip it today.

Satisfied with his arrangements, Blake arrived at the court on time and began to warm up, pounding the rubber ball with all his might into the back wall. He needed to vent a dozen frustrations over Katie, the family business, worries about Paige, Penny, the elusive Santa Magdalena Diamond, the charity ball, Charlie and his mother.

He slammed the ball again, about ready to give up

on Penny showing. But the door squeaked open and Penny ducked inside, into the white-walled echo chamber of the racquet ball court. Blake caught the ball before it ricocheted off the back wall right at her.

"Wow, that was some serve," she said, hunkering down lest he didn't stop the speeding ball in time.

"You're late."

"I almost didn't come at all."

"Why?"

"Because I have the feeling the reason you asked me here wasn't to play a game." She took her position on the court, rocking from one foot to the other in anticipation of the serve.

A short distance from her, Blake turned to her. "I miss my little sister, isn't that okay?"

"If that's really why you asked me here, of course. It's just not like you."

Avoiding the comment, Blake started the ball in play, and they volleyed some to warm up before keeping score. He knew she didn't have a chance of beating him so he took it easy on her.

"You're patronizing me," she said after winning three shots in a row.

"Would you rather I kill the ball every time?"

Paige shrugged, out of breath. "No. This is challenging enough."

They played hard, shoes squeaking across polished hardwood floors, sweat pouring over Blake's goggles and drenching his shirt. Not realizing they'd run out of time, a pound on the door reminded them their hour was up.

They grabbed their towels, dried off a bit and Blake congratulated Penny on a game well played.

"Thanks for coming," he said. "We don't do enough of this kind of thing together, do we?"

Looking a bit startled, Penny said, "You mean twice a year isn't enough?"

Outside the court Penny started to head for the ladies' locker room but Blake's hand on her arm stopped her. "Come sit with me in the lounge for a minute before we go, would you?"

An apprehensive frown crossed her face, but moments later she agreed to join him. "I've only got a few minutes. I'm scheduled pretty tightly today."

As they walked toward a casual lounge area where guests could watch TV, grab a bite or a drink and chitchat, Blake decided he'd better get to the point quickly before she bolted.

"Seems like you're scheduled pretty tightly every weekend, too. You don't even sleep at home much anymore."

Penny looked away. "I'm an adult. What I do with my time is my business."

Stopping her with a hand to her elbow, he turned her to face him. "Penny, you don't know what you're dealing with in Jason Foley. You don't have much experience and I don't want you to get hurt."

"Thanks, but I can take care of myself. From what I hear, you'd be better off guarding your own heart instead of worrying about mine."

Her words stung sharply but he wasn't about to reveal any emotion in regard to Katie. Instead he merely stared at her, quelling his inner fire.

"Really, Blake, I am sorry but I'm going to be late." She turned on her heel, obviously feeling she couldn't get away from him fast enough. "I have a date with

Jason tonight and I need to go take a shower and start getting ready. We'll do a rematch and have coffee or something another time. Thanks for the game."

Left standing in the foyer of the gym, Blake gave up the idea of sitting in the lounge in favor of a hot shower at home. Now clean, more relaxed and long overdue for a quiet evening, he went to the kitchen to rummage for dinner. The official family dinner hour had passed and with it service from the house staff. He was fine with digging in the fridge and eating in the kitchen breakfast nook, blessedly alone with his newspaper, rather than eating in the usual spot—the formal dining room with everyone hashing over family dramas.

He'd found some leftover roast pork loin and a spicy polenta that smelled too good to be true. Fixing himself a plate and grabbing a bottle of hearty Bordeaux from the wine cooler, he nestled into a window seat to enjoy his solitude.

No sooner than he'd taken the first sip of wine, however, Eleanor padded into the kitchen in her slippers and robe.

Blake groaned inwardly. One night of peace and quiet around here was too much to ask. Tension immediately crawled up his spine and into his head, making it pound.

"What are you doing sitting there eating all alone in the near dark?" she asked, setting a kettle on the stove to boil.

"It seemed like a good idea to me," he said flatly.

"Well, it's not. Not healthy to eat alone. I'll bring my tea and sit with you."

Suddenly the roast pork lost its savory appeal and Blake shoved his plate aside, favoring another glass of wine instead. "Okay."

Eleanor prepared her tea with meticulous ritual,

gracefully carrying the delicate china cup and saucer to the nook where she scooted in opposite Blake.

She bent to sniff the aroma of her brew. "These Asian teas are so fragrant."

"So are these French wines."

Eleanor smiled, glancing at the label. "I recall that vintage." She looked wistful. "It was the year your father and I separated."

Pain rose in her face, tightening her features and hollowing her eyes, making her look suddenly much older. His chest tightened and he realized that if he were ever to forgive his mother for the affair she had with Rex during that separation, he had to understand a whole lot more about her history with him.

There's no time like the present, he heard an inner voice urge. So, bracing himself he acted on it.

"I think it's time you leveled with me. All of this tension, anger and resentment aren't good for any of us. I need to understand about you and Rex Foley. If I don't, I can't even begin to forgive you."

Eleanor gripped her tea cup in both hands, her head dropping as she stared into the steaming cup. When at last she looked up at him again, her eyes were filled with tears.

"I fell in love with Rex when I was sixteen." Swallowing hard, then taking a deep breath, she went on. "We planned to marry," she said, her voice beginning to tremble. "Oh, we were absolutely inseparable for three years, it all seemed so perfect, like a dream come true."

"What happened?" Blake monitored his tone carefully. This was the first time they'd ever spoken of Rex and her past with him and he felt certain it might be the last time she would ever open up. He measured his words. "If you were so in love, why didn't you marry him?"

"It's all so painful," she said. "It all went so wrong. All of our plans…" Bending to sip her tea, she tried again. "One night, after a ridiculous fight with Rex, I was upset. I wanted to punish him for something he'd done that offended me. I can't even remember what that was now. Anyhow, I wanted to make him sorry."

"That sounds pretty typical for a girl that age."

"It was the worst mistake I ever made," Eleanor said grimly. "That night I accepted a date with Devon."

Blake braced himself. The sense that that date changed the course of his mother's life began to settle over him like a shroud.

"Devon had pursued me for months, hoping to take me away from Rex. He saw his moment and he seized it. He made the most of his one chance."

Blake's thoughts turned to Katie, the date she'd had with another man. Had something similar happened? To him, although he was angry, it didn't matter enough to change everything. Had the other man seized his chance with Katie? Right now wasn't the time he could get an answer to that. His mother was about to reveal keys to her past he'd waited a lifetime to have.

"I was very emotional that night, determined to show Rex he couldn't take me for granted, and one thing led to another and, well…" Her eyes turned downward. "Devon and I became intimate." Immediately she lifted her chin, eyes suddenly wide with shame. "I regretted it the moment I gave in. I didn't want it, but it seemed too late. I didn't know how to stand up and say I'd changed my mind. I was still more girl than woman."

Blake reached across the table, briefly touching a hand to hers. "People make mistakes. You should forgive yourself. After all these years, let it go."

Tears began to tumble freely down her pale cheeks. "Blake, that one mistake got me pregnant." She paused, letting the painful truth penetrate him. "In my family, being an unwed teenager wasn't an option. My parents demanded Devon marry me and he happily obliged, in his eyes marking up another victory over the Foleys for the McCords. It was the last thing I wanted but I didn't see any way out of it."

The realization of what she was truly saying began to dawn on Blake and his body went cold. "I'm the result of that *mistake*, aren't I? I'm a mistake."

"Oh, Blake, don't—" Eleanor grasped for his hand and he yanked it back.

"I'm the result of a weak moment on your part with a man you didn't love. While Charlie is the product of your only love." He shook his head. "How could I have been so blind all these years? It makes perfect sense. Everything makes perfect sense now," he said bitterly.

"But I do love you, Blake. Yes, it's been difficult, painful—all that pent up guilt for marrying a man I didn't love, of knowing I ruined my only chance for happiness with Rex in one night." Sobbing now, she couldn't stop herself. "Every time I looked at you…"

"You resented me. I'm the reason you and Rex have been separated all these years." His insides burned, not with anger as much now as with emptiness, loss.

"Blake, please. I tried to hide it, not to take it out on you, but it was hard for me to bond with you, especially since you look so much like Devon. Even now, you remind me so strongly of him and sometimes… Oh, Blake, can you possibly try to understand, to put yourself in my position—to forgive me?"

He stood, unable to bear the sight of her another

moment. It was as if he'd been shot in cold blood but couldn't die. Loneliness, sharper than any dagger's edge, sliced through him. The one person who could help him now, comfort him, the one person he could open up to might have given herself to another man the same way his mother had. He couldn't call Katie. He couldn't talk to his mother or his siblings. All he could do was lock his heart up in a steel cage and toss away the key.

"Don't ask that of me. Not now. Not ever."

Chapter Fourteen

All the months of planning, the focus on each detail, had finally culminated in a perfect evening for the Halloween ball. Katie, standing at the fringe of the crowded ballroom, taking a moment alone to watch the elegant gathering, knew without a doubt that her and Blake's efforts would bring in more funding for the children's hospital than any previous year. They'd sold every ticket to the gala, and the auction sales had far exceeded expectations. It should have been their time to bask in the warm glow of their shared success.

But her smile pasted in place, only half her attention on the conversations around her, Katie's predominant emotion was worry.

"What are you doing alone in a corner?" Her mother's voice pulled Katie out of her thoughts and Katie turned to find Anna at her side.

"After two hours of playing hostess, I needed a break," Katie said lightly. "I think I've managed to talk to every person here at least once."

Anna did a quick study of Katie's face then followed the direction of Katie's gaze, frowning when she spotted Blake. He was standing in a group that included Tate and Tanya, his attention on whatever Tate was saying. "Ah, well, I see…" Anna touched Katie's arm. "I imagine it must be hard seeing Tate with that woman."

"Of course it isn't. Why would it be? I've been telling you for weeks now that you're wrong thinking I'm still pining for Tate."

"Oh, Katie, you've been distracted all evening," Anna said. "I'm not the only one who's noticed. I assumed it was because of Tate and frankly, so has everyone else."

With an impatient shake of her head, Katie dismissed the idea. "That's ridiculous. I'm glad Tate is happy. I wish you would finally give up this idea that I'm in mourning over our broken engagement." Her eyes were drawn back to the group, but it wasn't Tate she sought. Despite her mother's ideas, she'd scarcely noticed him and her gaze skimmed over him now. While her former fiancé and his new love appeared blissful, Blake did not.

She'd been watching Blake most of the evening and he was the cause of her concern. On the surface, he'd played his part of cohost with his usual cool efficiency. At her side, in front of others, he'd openly praised her and had given her the lion's share of the credit for their successes, treating her with a careful courtesy that was minus the warm gestures, the touches she'd grown accustomed to when they were together. He'd made excuses, though, to avoid her beyond what was expected of them as hosts. Despite their agreement to talk things out after the ball, his behavior didn't surprise her, considering the way they'd left things since that night in his office.

But from the moment she'd seen him, she'd known there was something very wrong with him apart from their unresolved issues. Maybe it wasn't obvious to anyone else. To her, though, it was if he were mechanically going through the motions, his mind and heart elsewhere.

"You and Blake are quite the pair tonight," Anna commented with a touch of irritation. "After all the months of work you both spent on this, the two of you are giving the impression you'd rather be anywhere else. I suppose Blake is preoccupied with business," she mused. "All those rumors about McCord's…"

"You should know better than to pay attention to the gossips," Katie told her mother. Whatever was wrong with Blake, she felt sure it wasn't business. Suddenly, she couldn't wait any longer to find out. "I should get back to mingling. I'll find you again later." Quickly kissing her mother's cheek, she headed straight for Blake.

He was alone in the crowd, striding away from the group he'd been a part of in the direction of another. Katie walked up to him, stepping into his path, forcing him to a stop.

"You haven't danced with me," she said without preamble, ignoring the curious glances from bystanders and the surprise that briefly flicked over his face when she clasped his forearm.

"I didn't think I had an invitation," he said, yet there was no emotion in it; it was simply an observation, made absently, as if there were no implications to her asking.

"Now you do."

His lack of question or objections, letting her lead him

into midst of the dancers, increased her uneasiness, though she refrained from saying anything until they were facing each other and pretending to move to the music.

"Blake, what's wrong?" she asked gently.

He didn't meet her eyes, staring at a point over her shoulder. "Why the sudden concern?"

"It's not sudden and you know that. No matter what's happened, I care about you. I can tell you're upset about something. Is it business?"

"I wish it were," he said, so low she almost didn't catch the words.

"What, then?"

She didn't get an answer, not in words. Instead, he looked at her and for brief seconds his mask slipped. Katie caught her breath, taken aback by the pain she glimpsed in his face. She'd never seen him like this, almost vulnerable, as if he'd suffered a crippling emotional blow. It vanished almost immediately, yet left Katie shaken, unable to imagine what had the power to hurt him so deeply.

Avoiding her searching gaze, Blake gathered her closer, his hold tightening, pressing his cheek against her hair.

They finished the dance in silence and as the music ended, Blake released her, taking a step away, his facade firmly in place. "I should get back to—"

"No," Katie said firmly, refusing to let him shut her out this time, "you shouldn't."

"Katie, this isn't the place."

"Then let's find a better place. I'm not above causing a scene," she added quickly, seeing the start of a refusal in his eyes.

Blake looked as if he might challenge her then, his mouth twisting in a sardonic facsimile of a smile, but he relented, sweeping out a hand in a mocking gesture for her to lead the way.

She did, to an isolated nook away from the main ballroom area, in a dimly lit area of the music hall that wasn't being used for the ball. The music and voices faded to a distant sounding hum in the background and she could almost pretend they were completely alone.

Rubbing a hand over his neck, Blake blew out a long breath. "Why are we here?"

"Tell me what's wrong. And don't say it's nothing because I know that's a lie."

"I can't talk about this with you right now."

"Can't or won't?"

"I—can't. I don't even want to think about it. Can you just…" He seemed to flounder for words.

He looked lost and without thinking, Katie put her arms around him and held him close. For a few seconds, he stiffened but, as if he couldn't help himself, then pulled her into a tight embrace.

Katie rested her head on his shoulder and thought about her rejection of his offer to go away, the two of them. Her answer should be the same except right now, Blake needed a friend, whether he wanted to admit it or not. He had no one else in his life willing to offer him comfort and support; certainly no one he would confide in. She wanted to be that person.

Why, she didn't want to admit to herself. It wasn't a lie, telling him she cared. Deep down, though, she knew her reversal was more than that. But she wasn't ready to confront those feelings yet.

Very gently, she leaned inches away from him. "I've changed my mind," she said softly. "Let's go away, just the two of us."

"Katie…" His frown was mixed confusion and suspicion. "You made it clear the other night that isn't what you want."

"It's what I want now. We won't tell anyone, we'll just leave everything behind for a while. Please, Blake—" stretching up, she kissed him, a light press of her mouth on his to stop him from asking more questions "—say yes."

Blake didn't know what to say, let alone think. After all the days apart and the way they'd left things… "Why the change of heart?"

"Because it's something we both need."

"Before—"

"Doesn't matter. We can sort things out later."

Her reasoning didn't entirely satisfy him. In his current state of mind, mistrusting his own judgment, he wondered if the whispers around them were true: that Katie was still smitten with Tate and her attentions to him and her abrupt turnaround was prompted by seeing her former love and his fiancé together.

"I missed you," she murmured, her fingers stroking against his nape. "We both deserve a break, I think."

He translated that to it wouldn't be real; it certainly wouldn't resolve anything. It would be a short-lived fantasy and all too soon they would return to the mess at home. Yet at the lowest point that he could ever recall being, the appeal of escaping with someone he cared about and trusted, even for a little while, was stronger than his reservations.

"Next weekend," he said before he could talk himself out of it. "Gabby's family has a villa on San Vincentia Island. It's private, we'll have the place to ourselves, nothing around but the Mediterranean and a great stretch of beach."

"It sounds perfect." She sighed. "I wish we could leave tonight. The idea of going back in there…"

"I know." It sounded inadequate and the urge to sweep her out a back door, onto his private jet and far away from Dallas to that island paradise was so strong Blake nearly gave in to it. Running away had never been an option for him but at this moment, the temptation to say to hell with everything overrode his dislike of ignoring problems.

Instead of succumbing to it, he took her in his arms again except simply to hold her. It felt like more, though, as if he was holding on to her, grasping at the chance of an anchor in the emotional storm he'd been caught in since his mother's confession. He hated to let go but after a few minutes, aware of the people who had seen them leave and would be speculating about where they'd gone, he gently put her from him.

"We've probably generated enough new gossip for one night," he said.

"Probably. I'm having trouble caring at the moment, though. Blake—" She stopped, opened her mouth to start again, then gave up. Tentatively, she raised a hand, laying it against his cheek, tempting him to lean into her warmth. "Will you be all right?"

It was on the tip of his tongue to say no, but he wouldn't let himself be that weak. "Yes, of course."

By mutual silent agreement, they started walking back to the ballroom, separating almost immediately as they entered the crowd. To onlookers, Blake thought it probably seemed he and Katie were avoiding each other and in a way, at least on his part, it was true.

Exposing his vulnerabilities to her, no matter how briefly, on top of the confrontation with his mother, had yanked his control away, leaving him without a foundation and uncertain how to cope.

He'd never shown weakness to anyone before Katie because he knew it was an invitation for someone to take advantage of him. Yet she hadn't used it against him. She'd listened and held him, and then, inexplicably, she'd changed her mind about them being together.

None of it made sense to him. But he didn't want to analyze anything too closely, for fear the answers he'd get would harder to accept than the questions.

Back amid the noise and what seemed like too many people, Katie wished she'd tried harder to convince Blake to leave the ball, even though she knew it would have been impossible. She wished harder she could have avoided family and friends because it was easier with acquaintances to pretend everything was fine when it wasn't.

"There you are." A well-manicured hand reached out and grasped hers, turning Katie to face Gabby, a beautifully gowned Gabby, sleek in jewel-tone red, but without her handsome spouse at her side. "Back again, I see."

"Have you lost your husband?" Katie asked, hoping to distract Gabby from the questions she was probably dying to ask about her and Blake. She knew it was a vain hope that sharp-eyed Gabby hadn't seen her and Blake disappear together and not return for nearly half an hour.

"He's only very temporarily abandoned," Gabby said easily. "I haven't gotten the chance to talk to you for more than few minutes. So when I saw you standing here all alone—why are you alone, by the way?"

"I don't think being surrounded by a thousand people counts as alone."

Gabby gave up on her attempt at subtlety and asked point-blank, "Where's Blake?"

"Mingling somewhere, I assume," Katie said, at the same time hunting around for a safer topic. Committed now, she was nonetheless starting to second-guess her impulsive decision to go away with Blake. More daunting was her fear that she agreed not out of concern or caring or friendship, but because she'd fallen in love with him.

She'd fallen in love with him....

She loved him.

"It's true, then. You two are together."

Katie looked at Gabby and her friend smiled knowingly.

"Did you just figure it out?" Gabby asked.

"It's not what you're thinking."

"Oh, I think it's exactly what I'm thinking."

"Honestly, do you think between my past with Tate and all the other complications we would ever end up— together?" She had wavered so much, afraid of making a mistake, unsure of what she wanted. She didn't believe Blake was dedicated to exploring any possibilities with her beyond friendship and a casual brief affair—at least not any more.

"It doesn't matter what I think, or anyone else, either," Gabby said. "This is between you and Blake."

"Whatever *it* is."

"I did warn you any relationship with Blake wouldn't be easy."

"Maybe it wouldn't be so hard if I had a clue what I'm doing," Katie blurted out. She pressed fingertips to her forehead. "I sound about seventeen."

Gabby laughed. "No, just confused. Love will do that to you. If it's any consolation, Blake has no clue what he's doing, either. My advice is the two of you should get out of here and work on trying to figure it out."

It was so near to what she and Blake did plan on doing—at least the escape part—that Katie wondered if Gabby somehow knew. Considering Gabby's talent for ferreting out information, it wouldn't surprise her.

"Speaking of getting out of here," Gabby said, "it's time I got back to my man and let you find yours."

Katie let Gabby leave without correcting her; Blake wasn't hers and wasn't likely to be anytime soon. But she couldn't deny she wanted him; in some ways it felt as if she always had.

That didn't stop her from anticipating and fearing a broken heart. She loved him and this weekend away was as likely to turn out badly, as it was to fix anything between them.

Yet she wasn't ready to give up the time she and Blake could spend together, no matter how brief. It had been too long, if ever, that she'd allowed her emotions full rein and damn the consequences. She wasn't going to let the opportunity slip away, not when it meant so much.

Not when there was a small hope that, despite everything, there was still a chance for them.

It was nearly two when Blake let himself into the McCord mansion, feeling the weight of too many sleepless nights, the long drawn-out evening, and his own thoughts in the stiff set of his shoulders and neck. He almost hated coming back here, having to live with the pervading tension between him and his mother, though they'd done a good job of staying out of each other's way the past week and even tonight. His only solace was in a couple of days, he could escape with Katie, at least for a short time.

Shedding his jacket and tie as he went, he started toward his room, only to be stopped by a quiet voice.

"You're finally home." Eleanor stood in the archway of the living room, still in her formal gown.

"I couldn't leave until everyone else had," he said shortly, adding, "What are you doing up?" though he guessed she'd been waiting for him.

"I wanted to talk to you."

Blake scrubbed a hand over his face. "Tonight? Can't it wait?"

"If we wait, we'll both continue to find some reason to avoid it." Eleanor gestured toward the living room and Blake, too weary—emotionally and physically—to argue, followed her in.

He tossed his jacket and tie on a chair, unfastening the first few buttons of his shirt, but stayed standing as his mother took a seat opposite him. "I don't need to ask what this is about."

"I can't tell you how many people came up to me tonight and asked if there was something wrong with you," Eleanor said instead of answering him.

"Am I supposed to apologize for that?" Hearing the bitterness in his voice, he shook his head sharply. "It's easy enough to tell them it's business. It's even partly the truth."

"That's not the point. Blake…" She half raised a hand then let it drop. "I don't want to leave things like this between us. Despite what you may think of me, I care about you and I hate seeing you in pain and knowing I'm the cause."

"I don't want to leave it like this, either, but frankly I don't know how to fix it." He didn't add that he wondered if it could be fixed. There was no way for his mother to take back her confession, no way for him to forget it. "I'm going away for a couple of days," he said abruptly.

Eleanor's brows raised. "On business?"

"No, it's not business."

"I see," she responded, although she sounded doubtful. Yet she didn't press him for an explanation. "It's not like you just to leave. I can't recall you ever taking a vacation."

"I need to get away." There was a long silence between them and then Blake blew out a breath. "This isn't going to be resolved tonight. When I get back— we'll talk then. Maybe…" He tried to think of a compromise, a way he could learn to live with knowing there was a time she'd wished he'd never been born. Nothing came to mind and he settled for "Maybe a few days away will help me clear my head."

"I hope, for your sake, that it does," Eleanor said. She rose to her feet and after a moment's hesitation, came up to him and touched his arm. "Blake…"

The open concern in her face was almost as difficult to take as her admissions because part of him wanted to believe it was honest, while the hardened side of him rejected it as guilt. "I can't do this right now," he said repeating what he'd told Katie. "I— I'll talk to you in a few days."

He turned on his heel and quickly left the room.

Chapter Fifteen

Blake stood on the patio of the elegant villa—the late-afternoon sunlight glittering on the clear blue of the Mediterranean, blazing against the sky, the air perfumed with sea and lush clusters of bright red bougainvilleas—and was unmoved by the vista of paradise. It seemed a lifetime ago he'd wanted this, days isolated with Katie in a sensual hideaway. Bringing her to San Vincentia should have fulfilled one of his fantasies. Instead, he felt detached from it all, unable to shake off the shadows of Dallas.

A whisper of sound turned him from the view and Katie walked over to him, leaning her hands against the low railing to look out at the sea. Barefoot, she'd changed into a sleeveless white dress and the light breeze molded the thin material to her curves, taunting him by revealing she wore little underneath. When she stretched and turned her face up to let the sun kiss her skin, Blake decided paradise was overrated. The view couldn't compete with the vision of Katie.

"It's beautiful, isn't it?" she said, taking in a long breath. "This is definitely one of your better ideas."

"Do you want a drink?" he asked abruptly and was already starting inside before she answered.

She glanced at him, brows slightly raised, and shook her head. "No, thank you. Not now."

He was being a bastard and he knew it, had been since they'd left Texas and the whole of the plane trip to Italy, the boat ride to the island, and up to this moment. Though he didn't deserve it, Katie had put up with his moodiness and hadn't pressed him for an explanation. Pouring out a generous portion of scotch, Blake drank it back, taking the second one with him out onto the patio.

Katie didn't comment, but the look she slanted him told him she wanted to. Finally, she moved to his side and slid her hand up his arm to the crux of his neck and shoulder, very lightly massaging the tight muscle. "It's good to be away from everything."

"Yes, for as long as it lasts."

"Blake—"

He looked at her and seeing the determination in her eyes, knew she wasn't going to accept cryptic answers and rebuffs from him anymore.

"Be honest with me," she said. "I know something is wrong and it's more than our issues. I want to help but I can't do that if you won't talk to me. What happened, before the ball?"

For long seconds, he balked, thought about the things he'd have to tell her to fulfill his promise to be honest. "I'm sorry for the way I've been acting," he substituted.

"It's not been fair to you. But it has nothing to do with you, I promise."

"Then what does have to do with?"

Blake nearly refused to tell her; it meant dragging out the memories again and they were too fresh to be painless. The gentle encouragement in her voice, though, broke his resolve to guard his feelings. They were alone and if there was one person he could trust to understand, it was Katie.

"Do you know who I am?" he asked. He gripped the railing hard enough to leave marks, his knuckles whitening with the effort. "I'm the reason my mother and Rex Foley have been separated all these years. I was never supposed to be a McCord, or to be at all, for that matter."

Her fingers tightened on his shoulder. "I don't understand."

"I didn't, either, until recently." He told her then, all of it, not gilding it with emotions or his mother's excuses, but reciting it starkly. When he was done, he waited, expecting her surprise, questions, or worse, pity. What he didn't anticipate was the flare of anger in her eyes.

"How could Eleanor say those things to you?"

"I suppose she felt compelled to explain, or maybe justify what she'd done." Blake pushed a hand through his hair. "Hell, I don't know."

"There isn't any justification for telling your child he was unwanted and resented," Katie said hotly.

"At least I understand why I was never her favorite son. It explains a lot of things."

"It doesn't make it easier to accept," she said in a voice suddenly very quiet.

She made to put her arms around him, but Blake quickly shifted out of her reach. "This was a mistake. I shouldn't have brought you here, not like this. Not because I don't want to be with you," he added quickly, seeing the hurt flash into her eyes. "You don't know how much I want that."

"Then why—"

"As my mother pointed out, I'm too much like my father. I wanted you and I didn't bother to consider your feelings when I asked you to go away together. I assumed you'd say yes. I convinced myself that's all we'd ever have together, that you weren't any better than any other woman I've known." There was more he had to say and it felt like the hardest thing he'd ever done. Exposing his vulnerabilities was almost as painful as reciting his confrontation with his mother. "I always thought you were too good for Tate. But you're too good for me, as well. I can't believe I could ever be the kind of man you deserve."

Katie's eyes were shining with unshed tears. "What about what you deserve?" She didn't give him time to come up with any good answer for that. "Success and ambition are poor substitutes for loving and caring."

He knew that, didn't he?

"You expect too much of yourself," she began, closing the space between them, slowly, as if she were afraid he'd bolt if she got too near. "I don't need perfection, Blake. And you aren't your father, you never could be."

"Then I'm doing a pretty good imitation."

"Not even close." Katie ignored his move to evade her and laid her palm against his face, her caress warm and tender. "You're so much better than that."

It was tempting, so tempting, to grasp her close, satisfy a base desire as a poor substitute for a deeper emotional need. She would be willing. But he didn't want her offering herself like a consolation prize. A few days of being her lover wasn't going to be enough.

The slight pressure of her fingers recaptured his gaze. "Blake, what are we doing here? I thought I knew. But now—I'm not sure."

"I don't think either of us has ever been sure of what we were doing."

"No, but I need to know."

If the circumstances were different, if his defenses hadn't been lowered and he'd been in control of his emotions, he would have given her the easy, glib answer. He couldn't. Compared to the possibility of another rejection, lying to her suddenly seemed the worst he could do.

"When I found out about you and Marcus," he started slowly, "I didn't expect to feel like you'd betrayed me. But I did."

"I felt the same way, but it wasn't like that."

"I know. Even if it was, I didn't have the right to be jealous, of him—or Tate."

That startled her. "Tate?"

He took her hand, guiding it down from his face but lacing their fingers, unable to stop touching her. "It was hell, watching you with him, knowing you loved him—and wishing it was me."

"You? But…you never—" She shook her head as if what he'd admitted didn't make any sense. "Why didn't you ever say anything?"

"What was I supposed to say? That I'd fallen in love with my brother's fiancée? That all those nights I knew you were with him, I wanted to be the one in your bed?"

"If I had known—"

"Then what? You were making wedding plans, Katie. You said you were in love and that you were happy. I doubt you would have thanked me for telling you I thought you were making a mistake." Letting go of her hand, he fisted his hands over the railing again. "You keep telling me you're not sure how you feel or what you want. If I'd said anything then, it would have caused complications none of us was ready to deal with."

"Maybe that was true then," Katie confessed, "but not anymore."

"Isn't it? It's still complicated."

"Probably, although right now, it doesn't feel like it. Blake…" The softly spoken request implicit in her voice compelled him to face her. "I love you. I've never been more certain of anything."

He could have argued or questioned except she stepped up and pressed her mouth to his and in that instant, swept aside his doubts, leaving him with the fantasy turned reality of having Katie where he'd wanted her for years: in his arms and in love.

It happened so fast, a dizzying rush of sensation and emotion released by his admission, that Katie could only hold tightly to Blake and let it overwhelm her. It was as if all these years she'd been blind and suddenly she could clearly see everything they both had denied for so long.

Since that first forbidden kiss after the Labor Day party, she'd known, though she'd refused to admit, that Blake wasn't simply a friend. He was the man who'd always been there for her, waiting, though for the longest while all she'd seen was Tate's older brother, not a would-be lover. Now, she didn't want them to waste any more time avoiding their feelings, arguing, talking and pretending it wasn't inevitable they'd be lovers.

Leaning into him, she let her lips tell him how much she needed him.

Blake eased his arms around her, returning her kiss but his was more tender than passionate—an affirmation of love rather than desire. The care he took touched her yet she sensed he was deliberately holding himself in check. Accustomed to him taking the lead, his hesitation, lack of confidence almost, concerned her but she thought she understood. He was afraid of repeating his father's sins, taking advantage of her vulnerabilities to get what he wanted.

She was determined to convince him the difference was love.

"Are you going to make me beg?" she teased with a brush of her lips against his ear.

Instead of returning her light tone, he shifted a few inches back, looking troubled. "Too much more of this and it'll be the other way around. But we don't have to take this any further if you're not sure it's what you want."

"What does a girl have to do to convince you?"

"Katie—" Framing her face in his hands, Blake looked into her eyes, his reflecting an intense emotion that both excited and humbled her. "I love you. I should have told you a long time ago."

"Show me," she urged. "Please, Blake." And spurred by the open desire on his face, she began unbuttoning his shirt. "This is right. I know it is."

Her certainty overpowered his hesitation. He gathered her to him, kissing her in an imitation of how she wanted him to love her and she moved restlessly in his arms, wanting to give him everything, craving what only he could give her in return. The low hum of pleasure he made deep in his throat intensified the feeling, sharpening the edges of her need for him.

He honed it further, exploring the hollows and curves of her neck and shoulders, his mouth replacing his hands as he pushed down the thin straps of her dress.

Katie encouraged him, spreading open his shirt, splaying her fingers over his chest, suddenly greedy for the hard press of his body against hers. She ached, in a way she never had before with Tate or anyone. From their first kiss to now, being with Blake was all heat and need; there was no room for thought other than she wanted more.

As though she'd asked aloud, he granted her wish, re-claiming her mouth, his tongue sliding along hers at the same time he ran his hands over her back, up her sides, until his fingers brushed her breasts. His thumbs grazed the sensitive tips through the thin cotton of her dress and her breath caught, released as she breathed his name.

She felt, rather than saw, his smile, and he continued to stroke and tease her a little longer before murmuring in her ear, "Let's go inside." His arm was around her waist and he'd made a motion in the direction of the door before he realized she wasn't going with him.

Katie glanced around them. The patio was on two levels overlooking the sea, the steps leading down from the upper level where they stood to a swimming pool, tiled all around in a bright mosaic. A small smile curved her mouth and she took Blake's hand. "Let's not."

"If this is another one of your fantasies," he said, fol-lowing her down the steps to the pool's edge, "I like it."

"There is one problem." She pretended to frown.

"And that is…?"

"I don't have a swimsuit."

"That's okay." His gaze swept over her, hot enough to make her flush. "Neither do I."

Blake cut off any further words by kissing her, long and deep. Without breaking contact with her mouth, he eased down the zipper of her dress, sliding the material off her body until it pooled at her feet and left her wearing only a lacy white thong. Halting to look at her, the almost dumbstruck expression in his eyes had her smiling to herself.

"I don't know if you've heard this enough," he said huskily, "but I guarantee that in my lifetime, I won't stop telling you. You're the most beautiful thing I've ever seen." Watching intently, he lightly dragged his fingertips over her lips, tracing a path down her throat, to the valley between her breasts.

Then, as if the feel of her skin under his broke his patience, he dropped to one knee, teasing her with nibbling kisses on her stomach as he drew down the thong. Tossing it somewhere behind him, he slid his hands back up her legs, shaping her thighs and hips, the caress of his hands and mouth becoming more intimate as—giving this self-appointed task the same focused, meticulous attention he gave anything he considered important—he discovered what she liked and what she needed. Pleasure spiked in her and she gripped his shoulders, gasping at the riot of sensation.

He made her tremble and burn and forget there was ever anyone else before him. Finally, knees weak and threatening to buckle, she traced the line of his jaw, drawing his eyes to hers and took one small step back toward the pool.

In answer to her silent invitation, he quickly stood, shedding his shirt at the same time he slanted his mouth over hers. Somewhere in between kisses he managed to strip off the rest of his clothes, but he only gave her scant moments to appreciate the subtle definition of muscle and long, lean lines of his body. Scooping her off her feet, he carried her into the pool and braced himself against the side before drawing her to him.

The sun-warmed water complemented the sensuous slide of skin to skin. Breath ragged, his mouth hungry on hers, Blake's hands roved over her back to her hips and in one fluid motion, he lifted her up, her legs wrapped around his waist and her arms around his neck. Their gazes locked and she shifted her hips to meet his thrust, pushing forward to take him even deeper inside.

Maybe it was cliché, and maybe it was simply love, but for the first time in her memory, a sense of completion swept over her. This was what she'd been missing, the overwhelming combination of desire and pure feeling that she'd dismissed as a romantic ideal. With Blake, it was vividly real.

They made love to each other, partners in this, too. Blake set the first slow stroking rhythm, loving her with a passion so interwoven with emotion it brought her to tears. Then he let her lead and she tried to give him back the same, to warm the cold places in him and replace painful memories with ones of her willingly yielding heart and body to him. Finally, close to the edge and teetering there, the ache of anticipation prolonged by his skillful touch, she fell, crying out his name.

And as he always had been, he was there to catch her.

A slender leg hooked over his and slim fingers trailed over his chest and stomach, twitching down the edge of the sheet that barely covered them both.

Without opening his eyes, Blake turned his head to kiss Katie's temple and murmured, "Were you planning on eating and sleeping this weekend, or is this the only activity on the agenda?"

"Are you complaining?" A few more inches of sheet retreated at the nudge of her hand. They'd made love twice in the pool before moving indoors, promising each other a shower and dinner. Hours later, they'd yet to even glance in the direction of the kitchen.

"No," he assured her, "just contemplating my odds of survival."

She laughed, the rich, happy sound vibrating against his skin. "I have faith you're up to the challenge. We have a lot of lost time to make up for."

Blake shared that sentiment but he was still trying to work out how he'd ended up with her in his life. Making love with Katie had been so much more than he'd expected or ever experienced; being in love with Katie and her loving him was unbelievable. Unbelievable and daunting. She was the first person he'd let behind his walls and now that she'd gotten under his skin and lodged in his heart, he didn't dare imagine what it would be like without her.

"I don't want to lose this," he said, unaware he'd voiced the thought aloud until she propped herself up on her elbow to look questioningly at him.

"This—" she inched her hand lower on his body "—or..."

"You. I don't want to lose you." In a sudden motion, he rolled toward her so they were face-to-face. "I can't believe I almost messed this up. What scares me is that I know I could screw things up again."

"I'm scared I could do the same thing," she confessed. "I guess there aren't any guarantees. But I love you, Blake, and I'm willing to take that chance."

"Me, too," he said softly. Very gently, he drew his fingertips over her cheek, relearning the curves and the texture of her skin. "What amazes me is you've seen the worst of me and you're still here."

"You're forgetting something."

"And that is?"

Katie tugged the sheet completely aside and fitted her body to his. "I've seen the best, too."

Unable to resist even if he'd wanted to, Blake bent and kissed her and for a long time afterward, his world narrowed to a bed in paradise and loving her.

The planned four-day retreat stretched into six, and then ten and it wasn't until Blake realized that it had been almost two weeks since he'd bothered to check his messages or e-mail or even thought about his responsibilities that he reluctantly brought up the subject of leaving. They were sitting together on the beach, watching the sunset, the surf lapping at their feet, and Dallas seemed a million miles away.

"I imagine by now your family and mine are convinced we've disappeared for good," he said. He rested his forehead against the tangled silk of her hair, breathing in the mingled scent of wind and sea and her musky perfume. "I suppose we should have called at least once."

Katie's sigh echoed with longing. "I wish we could stay. Knowing what's waiting at home..." She left it unsaid but Blake all too well understood her desire to make their escape permanent.

"It's tempting—"

"But we can't." Leaning her head back on his

shoulder, she lightly kissed the side of his neck then fixed her eyes on the horizon where the last of the day's sun had painted the sky in pink and orange. "I just don't want things to change."

"They won't," he said, the edge to his words betraying his own worries that once they were back home, the love she professed for him wouldn't be strong enough to withstand reality and his bubble of happiness would irreparably burst. "Not unless you want them to."

"No," she said softly and twisted to face him, "I don't. Do you?"

"No," he repeated and it was a vow. He punctuated it with a brush of his lips to hers.

"Then I guess we're going home."

The finality in her voice convinced him to act on a sudden impulse. "What would you say to playing hooky for a few more days?"

"Here?"

"In Paris." He'd succeeded in surprising her and he smiled. "There's a private dealer who has a collection of canary diamonds I'm interested in buying. We could stay a few days there—" he slowly traced his fingertips along the edge of the cotton camisole she wore, rewarded by the faint flush coloring her fair skin "—combine business with pleasure."

She smiled back, her eyes alight again with the happiness he'd grown accustomed to seeing in the last two weeks. "If I didn't know you better, I'd say you were making up this whole story about buying diamonds just to get me to say yes."

"Is it working?"

Her arms snaked around his neck and right before she kissed him, she murmured, "Oh, yes."

Chapter Sixteen

Katie peered out of the window of the jet, hoping to catch her first glimpse of the Eiffel Tower. Her fingers were laced with Blake's and she gave his hand a quick squeeze. "Isn't it funny that as much as I've traveled in Europe, I've never been to Paris?"

"Apparently your first time was supposed to be with me."

She turned away from the window. "Was it?" she asked, reading a double meaning into his words that she wasn't sure he intended.

"Never doubt it."

"Are we still talking about Paris?"

"I don't know," Blake said, leaning in to nuzzle her neck, "are we?"

The look of disbelief she put on wasn't entirely false. "Are you telling me that Blake McCord, the man who thinks he can control everything, believes in destiny?"

"Only when it comes to you. But don't tell anyone. It'll ruin my image."

This side of Blake—loving, teasing, content to forget about responsibilities, *happy*—made Katie fall in love with him all over again. At the same time, she wondered if she was deluding herself by believing they would last once they were back in Dallas. They hadn't talked about the future beyond Paris except in vague terms. He loved her, she knew, and he'd promised her things between them wouldn't change. But did that mean he wanted her permanently in his life and if he did, as what…his friend, lover, or—

She stopped herself. No matter how much she liked the sound of forever, she couldn't assume Blake felt the same. For now, she determined to treasure their time together, however long it lasted, and face reality when she had to.

"Have I lost you?" Blake's voice, a little husky, pulled her eyes to his.

"Of course not," she returned lightly. "I was just thinking of all the ways we could enjoy Paris." Finding his lips, she gave him a slow, thorough kiss. "Thank you for bringing me here. I can't think of a better way to extend our escape."

"The pleasure's mine," he said. He searched her face and she expected questions about her distraction. Instead, he nodded to the window. "You might want to look out again. We should be almost right over the city."

She ignored the outside vista, her view of him more tantalizing. "The most romantic city in the world."

"So I've heard—" and as he said it he gathered her into his arms "—we'll have to put it to the test."

He drew her into a kiss, opening her mouth under his, and Katie forgot about Paris and her doubts. She was on the verge of suggesting they start their testing while they were still in the clouds, but the sounds of footsteps stopped her.

The flight attendant, the only one aboard Blake's private jet, approached to check that their safety belts were fastened for landing. Katie was thankful that for most of the trip the woman had stayed discretely invisible as it was clear she and Blake preferred privacy.

"We'll be landing at Charles de Gaulle in a few minutes. Your car will be waiting in the usual place, Mr. McCord. Jean-Paul will be your driver, as you requested."

"Excellent," Blake said, his arm still around Katie, "and thank you."

The pretty young blonde ducked away and Katie, regretting the interruption, resumed her search out the window for landmarks she might recognize. "I'd hoped to see Notre Dame from up here. I've wanted to see it since I was a little girl."

"You won't, but you will see it from down there. We're staying in the Latin Quarter. The cathedral is close by. I opted for a small, elegant Parisian boutique hotel over one of the overblown tourist draws."

Katie laid her head on his shoulder. "Mmm…sounds perfect to me."

The plane landed smoothly and like clockwork Jean-Paul was on hand to gather their luggage and whisk them into the limo. On the drive to the hotel, Blake held her close to his side, pointing out historical and architectural markers, punctuated here and there with a kiss or an intimate touch, making it difficult for her to keep her mind on Paris.

"They drive here like they do in Rome," she said as they swung around a roundabout and she landed halfway onto Blake's lap.

"Ah, but there can be benefits to that." He took the opportunity to graze his fingers over her thigh, fully bared when her skirt followed the car's sharp turn.

"Is this why you asked for Jean-Paul?" she asked, pretending modesty by putting a few discreet inches between them, "because you enjoy the benefits of his driving skills?"

Blake laughed. "You have to admit, it makes the drive more interesting."

"I can tell I'm not going to be seeing much of the city," she teased, laughing herself. She glanced outside at the passing scenery. One after another, each more charming than the last, the small, quaint restaurants were just beginning to show signs of preparing for the evening service with waiters, clad in dark clothes and white aprons, changing table linens and candles, putting out handwritten menus for passersby to peruse. "This is a maze of streets. I could never find my way out of here."

"Good. Then I know if I decide to keep you here forever, you're stuck with me."

She answered with a nod, the implication of *forever* one she didn't want to contemplate right now.

"Here we are." Blake nodded ahead to a stone building several stories high, each level boasting colorful window flower boxes and royal blue awnings. "Hôtel Saint-Jacques, one of my favorites."

As Jean-Paul organized the luggage, a liveried servant greeted Blake personally. He introduced Katie and the concierge bowed. "We are at your service, *mademoiselle*. Anything you desire, you have but to ring down for me."

Katie smiled at the dashing older gentleman who stood about four inches shorter than she. *"Merci, monsieur,"* she said, then complimenting him on his charming-looking hotel, delighted him with her perfect French.

"I didn't know you spoke French," Blake said as they followed a bellman to the front desk.

"Part of a proper lady's education, or so my mother insisted."

He leaned close to her ear. "I'd like to be your teacher for an *improper* education."

Her lips curved in a seductive smile and she murmured back, "Who says it wouldn't be the other way around?"

"If it involves learning about your champagne fantasy," he commented just as they were about to step into the elevator and loud enough for the bellman to overhear, "then you're got my complete and undivided attention for a lesson."

The bellman smirked and Katie shook her head at Blake, although her heart wasn't in the reprimand. Instead, she had a sudden explicit image of them together and all the creative ways she could change his mind about not liking champagne.

The heat between them flared as they squeezed into the tiny elevator, her breasts pressed to his chest, the two of them, the bellman and their luggage barely fitting as the ornate iron door closed. By the time the bellman opened the door to their top-floor suite, the passion between them was palatable.

"Oh, Blake, this is wonderful," Katie breathed, taking in the lavishly appointed rooms, decorated in rich jewel-toned fabrics and priceless-looking antiques. She walked over to the window. "And look at the view, the river— I can't imagine anything more beautiful."

"I can." The bellman gone, Blake strode to her side and pulled her to him, running his hands over her body as though he'd been starving for her.

"You'd think we've been waiting for weeks for this," she said, already yielding to the delicious pleasure.

"It feels like it. I can't seem to get enough of you." Cupping his hands on her bottom, he lifted her until she wrapped her legs around his waist. Her skirt scrunched up, revealing black lace thigh highs and slender legs. Blake carried her to the master bedroom, kissing her feverishly as they moved.

Gently he bent and laid her back on the bed, long legs partially spread where they met his thighs. "You're just too beautiful," he said, his expression almost reverent as his gaze swept her body.

"I didn't know that was possible."

"Neither did I. Until I saw you like this."

Katie started to sit up, to touch him, but Blake bent over her, and taking her wrists in his hands, carefully opened her arms at each side and laid her back onto the comforter. "No, let me." Sliding off his jacket, he moved over her and with torturous deliberation, unfastened each button of her blouse, kissing every new appearance of skin as he went.

Her instinct was to reach for him, for his shirt, follow his lead, but again, when she lifted her arms to do so, he took her wrists and pressed them back onto the bed. "Not yet."

Heat tingled through her, an excitement in letting herself be guided by him, of giving herself up to his explorations, unable to respond or return his touch. It was a delicious frustration, growing by the moment as his hands found her waist and pulled her blouse from her skirt, exposing her breasts to him. With a slow, teasing tongue and skillful teeth, he drew back the layer of satin and lace covering one breast, giving him access to her soft flesh. At the same time, he stretched out his arms, laying his hands atop hers, palm to palm and lightly pressing them to the bed.

Katie sucked in a ragged breath and he moved to lavish her other breast with similar attention. All the while, his body hovered over hers, just out of reach. His thighs against the end of the bed kept her legs separated, in a position that left her craving more, aching for him to lie fully on her and take her to heights she knew they could reach together.

But Blake was determined to continue his now wonderfully agonizing seduction. Unclasping the front fastener on her bra, he inched his way with light flickering kisses, across and around her breasts, down her chest and to her belly, where he paused to take longer tastes of her skin.

She moaned in anticipation of what he would do next. "Are you trying to kill me?" she managed, gasping as his tongue flicked a particularly sensitive spot.

"Don't worry," he promised with a wicked smile, "I won't let you die unsatisfied."

Lifting himself farther from her, he released her hands, then cupping his hands beneath her back he brought her off the bed far enough to remove her shirt and bra. All that remained were her skirt, shoes, stockings and underwear and she itched to sit up to rip them off.

Blake, however, made it clear he intended to do that for her. Easing his palms down her hips and thighs, to raise her skirt up so he could remove her stockings, he continued all the way to her feet. There he bent and knelt at the foot of the bed, carefully slipping the straps off her black heels, one by one, then removing first one shoe then the other and tossing them with exaggerated finesse to the side of the room.

Katie laughed and so did he. But when she began to rise off the bed to wrap her arms around him, his hands found hers, entwining their fingers and pressing her back down slowly, softly into the comforter. "Didn't they teach you that patience is a virtue?"

Her body sensitized now to his every movement, each brush of his hand or lips, she felt herself softening for him. "There's nothing virtuous about you, or this. You're not playing fair," she said breathlessly as he slipped one stocking down her thigh, tracing after it with his tongue.

As he flung the stocking out to land on a nearby chair, he smoothed his hands slowly along the length of her leg, from her toes, feet, ankles, calves and thighs all the way under her skirt to lightly grasp her bottom. Repeating the ritual with the other stocking and leg, this time when he reached her backside, he continued on to find the zipper of her skirt. In one fluid motion, the skirt fell open and slid from her body, leaving only her black lace thong to cover her.

He stood over her, an appreciative but hungry look pooling in his eyes. With painstaking slowness, he unbuttoned his shirt, pulled it from his waist and tossed it aside. She lifted her head to look at him, marveling once more at the ripples in his chest and abs, yearning to clasp his arms and pull him down onto her.

But, then again, Blake's game did have its rewards, and watching him as he started stripping off his clothes was definitely one of them. When he'd finished, he surprised her, moving back a step, and taking her thighs in his palms, switched places, opening his legs to move hers together between his thighs. He pressed her legs close as he again began a taunting exploration, with lips and this time hands, of her breasts, belly and below,

"I am going to die, you know," she panted, unable to stop herself any longer from squirming with desire. Still, he held her legs closed, anchored between his.

She reached for his neck, trying to pull him down to her, but he flattened her palms to the sides at the same time unexpectedly, he suddenly reversed his legs, moving one knee then the other between hers to open her thighs to him. All the while, the rest of his body balanced above her, just out of reach.

He stayed there, obviously enjoying her pleasured torment, until finally leaning close enough for her to feel the intimate brush of him against her wet heat.

"Now, Blake, please—"

He ignored her, toying with her, going no further than a teasing touch, drawing back and repeating the motion.

"You're going to pay for this."

"Is that a promise or a threat?"

Lifting her legs, she wrapped them around his waist and, locking them, pulled him to her with all of her strength. "Definitely a promise."

"Touché," he said, with a sexy laugh and finally, he gave them what they both wanted, joining them together, loving her with the passion that had been building since they stepped onto the jet hours and hours ago.

The tension between them, stretched to the breaking point by Blake's sensual play, found release in their lovemaking, and when she finally fell apart in his arms, calling out his name, Katie decided an eternity in Blake's arms wouldn't be enough.

* * *

When he awoke, tangled in the sheets, clothes strewn everywhere and forgotten, their room was dark. Sounds of laughter and the glow of gas lamps and restaurant lights filtered up to their window and Blake had to remember where they were.

"Paris," he whispered to a still-sleeping Katie, "the city of love."

With a tender kiss to her cheek, he brushed a curl of dark hair from her beautiful face and watched, smiling, as she sighed and snuggled closer, marveling at how she'd changed him. She'd saved him from himself and loving her was no longer enough. He wanted more. He wanted her with him, not for a few stolen weeks, but always.

They were in Paris and in love, the ideal circumstances to convince her they belonged together. He'd pulled off plans against stiffer odds. And he'd never been more determined to succeed now.

Katie stirred, her eyes fluttering open, her lips rounding into a contented smile as she focused on him. "Good morning," she murmured.

He smiled back, bending to kiss her. "Actually, it's good night."

"Guess I lost track of the time."

"Me, too, but my stomach didn't. I'm starving. How about you?"

"I'm not awake enough to know yet, but I'm sure once I get up I'll feel it."

"What do you say we throw on some clothes and go grab dinner while they're still serving?"

"Well…" She stretched languorously. "That would involve moving from this bed."

"And—?"

In a quick motion that belied her seeming lack of motivation, she sat up, sliding a leg over him so she straddled his hips. "And I've decided I'm hungry. If you're still serving, that is."

"For you, always," he vowed and for a long time, dinner was forgotten.

The next morning, though, Blake promised himself he wouldn't let anything—Katie included—distract him from his plans. He wanted everything to be perfect for her.

He called for room service and they finally abandoned the bed to breakfast at a small café table near their window, people watching below as they ate croissants and cheese and fruit and drank espresso.

"I thought we'd visit a few landmarks today," he said as they were finishing. "Notre Dame in particular, since that's first on your list."

"Weren't you supposed to be here on business?" she reminded him, her eyes bright with mischief.

"Tomorrow," he said, dismissing work in a word. "Today I want to spend with you." He leaned across the table to briefly touch a kiss to her lips. "Everything I want to show you is pretty close by and we could take the limo, but you'll get a better feel for the city if we walk and take the trains. Unless you'd rather drive."

"Now I'm getting worried." Katie eyed him over the rim of her cup.

"Worried?"

"Yes, because I think I left the real Blake McCord in Dallas. It's been two weeks, you haven't cared about business, and I'm pretty sure if I asked, you'd agree to stay here indefinitely. Not that I don't like the change, mind you," she added and he could tell from the twitch of her lips and the light in her eyes she was teasing him, "but I'm wondering what brought all this on."

He didn't have to wonder. "I love you," he said simply.

All the amusement went out of her expression and she looked directly at him and pronounced softly, "I love you, too."

That brought him out of his seat to take her in his arms and kiss her, slowly, a caress layered with passion and tenderness and the promise of many more to come. When it ended, he held her close for long moments before at last she tilted her head back to smile at him.

"If we're going to do all this sightseeing, I'm going to take a shower. No, you don't," she warned at his motion to follow her. "If you go with me, we'll never get out of this room today."

"If that's a threat, I'll take my chances."

Laughing, Katie pulled out of his grasp. "Later," she said, and with a kiss that promised a private sightseeing tour for later, disappeared into the bathroom, leaving him almost regretting making any plans that included leaving their bed.

Paris. Flowers in every window box, posh little cafés lining cobblestone streets, stylish people bustling to and fro, unforgettable works of art and architecture at every turn, ancient towering cathedrals and historic stone arches, the Seine river meandering through the city, smells of freshly baked pastries and aromas of expensive perfumes wafting through the air—all of it lived up to and exceeded Katie's expectations.

And all of it paled next to the sheer happiness rioting through her because she was with Blake. It felt like a dream, so flawless and wonderful she was afraid to examine it too closely for fear she'd wake and find it couldn't possibly be true.

Hours after they'd started their explorations, Blake stopped at a street corner on a busy intersection and took her hand. "There it is," he said, pointing in the distance to the most gigantic cathedral Katie had ever seen. "Notre Dame."

"Oh, I never imagined… It's amazing."

"Come on." He tugged her and she joined him running across the street to avoid the onslaught of tiny, speeding cars, scooters and bicycles. "I want to get there at sunset."

Just as they approached the entrance to the gothic cathedral, a wedding party began to flood out. They stood aside to watch the spectacle of gorgeously dressed guests, a dozen or so bridesmaids and groomsmen and finally the bride and groom. Blake wrapped an arm around Katie's shoulder and drew her to him.

"She's stunning," she said, captivated by the dark French beauty wrapped in a flowing alabaster gown.

"Not as stunning as you." Lifting her chin with his index finger, he smiled into her eyes.

A warm glow touched Katie's heart and she kissed him sweetly. They stayed there holding each other, exchanging a kiss now and then until the wedding party found their way to the waiting limos and the sun had begun its hazy, saffron descent.

She couldn't help but wonder, as she watched the bride and groom sneak a kiss, if she would ever be that woman in a white flowing gown, married to the man of her dreams. A little sigh escaped her, and she inwardly smiled at her romantic musings. She was with the man of her dreams and she wanted to savor every moment, instead of focusing on what might or might not be.

Resting her head on Blake's shoulder, she turned her thoughts to watching the cathedral transform. Earlier, she'd been awed by the magnitude of the imposing mass of gray towers, huge round stained glass windows, spires, flying buttresses and portals. But now, softened by the glow of the magic hour of dusk, the entire cathedral lit up in reflected gold beauty created one of the most deeply profound visions she had ever seen.

Blake moved to stand behind her, his arms around her waist, his breath close and warm on her neck. "See why I wanted to get here by sunset?"

"Oh, yes, it's unbelievable," she murmured, leaning back into him, mesmerized in thought and vision as together they watched the spectacle of dimming rays of sunlight create magnificent shadows that recalled lifetimes of history, countless loves lost and found, centuries of pain and moments of glorious triumph, all reflected in the unyielding majesty and spiritual prowess of this unequalled monument.

When a shimmering tapestry of changing light encompassed all they could see, church bells began to ring throughout the city, creating a magical fantasia and wrapping them in an ethereal aura of timelessness, Blake gently turned Katie in his arms and backed a step away.

"Blake, what…?"

"I've never been this happy as I have these last two weeks," he said, taking her hand in his. "I don't want it to end once we go back home."

Unexpectedly, he dropped to one knee in front of her and her heart fluttered with surprise and tremulous expectation. He couldn't possibly mean—could he…?

"Katie, I love you," he said, his voice deep and brimming with emotion. "Will you marry me?"

Chapter Seventeen

It was the last thing she'd expected to hear from him today and the single thing she'd wanted to hear for weeks now. "Oh, Blake, I never thought—yes." She looked into his eyes and repeated it, savoring the word and all that went with it. "Yes."

He was on his feet then, sweeping her into his arms, kissing her passionately, mindless of the glances they were getting from passersby. Parting at last, he gently touched her face. "When we get back to Dallas, I want you to pick out an engagement ring," he said. "I have something in mind, one of Penny's designs, but I want it to be your choice."

"I'm sure I'll love it." Stretching up, she kissed him. "I love you."

"Let's celebrate," he said. "I think they may be holding a reservation for us at Chez René."

"Why do I get the feeling you planned this from the moment we got off the plane?" Katie asked as they began walking hand in hand away from the cathedral.

He flashed a smile. "You know me. I don't like to leave anything to chance. I wanted to make it hard for you to say no."

"I wouldn't have said no." And she knew it was true, no matter where and when he'd asked her to marry him.

The rest of their brief stay in France passed in a whirl, with Katie scarcely registering anything of it that didn't directly involve Blake. She didn't have time to think about the implications of the commitment they'd made to each other or the reaction from friends and family. The overwhelming happiness she felt made thinking impossible. Even the flight home, with Dallas growing nearer by the minute, couldn't daunt her joy.

Blake didn't give her any opportunity for contemplation, either. Practically the moment the jet landed, he ushered her into the waiting car and less than an hour later, Katie found herself at the McCord Jewelers flagship store, gazing at the ring Blake had handpicked for her appraisal.

"This," she said, touching a fingertip to a flawless square-cut diamond set in platinum. "This is perfect."

"Then it's yours." Blake picked up the ring and led her back to his office, closing the door against the curious looks and whispers of the store staff before slipping it on her finger. "I promise, no matter what, I'll always love you," he vowed, punctuating it with a tender kiss.

Katie's eyes in turn filled with tears. "Why am I crying again?" she chided herself. "I've never been happier."

"Don't all women cry when they're happy?"

"If you're going to make comparisons—"

"Never. And even if I did, all other women would come up short." He put his arm around her, lightly kissing her temple. "I'm not quite ready to face real life yet. Why don't we put off telling anyone we're home until tomorrow? We can spend tonight alone, deal with everything else in the morning."

"That sounds really nice. Real life is bad enough but facing my parents isn't going to be easy."

Blake frowned a little. "Why? It's not as if you need their permission."

"Of course not," she said. "It's awkward, that's all, so soon after—" She let the sentence die but not quickly enough.

"After Tate, you mean," he said flatly.

"Okay, yes, but it's not only that." Splaying her hands over his chest, she brushed her lips against his. "Let's not worry about all this now. As you said, it'll be easier to deal with in the morning."

She could see he wanted to press the issue, but with a nod he accepted her delaying the inevitable. "How about dinner, then?"

They settled on a small out-of-the-way Japanese restaurant, and to Katie it felt like an extension of the last two weeks. She wanted to convince herself jet lag was responsible for her growing sense of unreality. But in truth, everything had happened so fast and she'd started to question whether or not she'd let herself get caught up the romantic whirlwind that had been San Vincentia and Paris.

"I think I'd better take you home and put you to bed," Blake commented, signaling the waiter for the check. "You look like you're wilting."

"I'm sorry, I guess the jet lag is sinking in.'

"No reason to apologize. You deserve to be tired,

after all the excitement and travelling the past few days."
He reached over and took her hand, his fingers idly
rubbing the ring he'd put on her finger. "Don't worry,"
he said, "everyone will get used to the idea, and if they
don't, to hell with them. All that matters is us."

"You're right," she said softly. "That is all that
matters." And her love for him and the love in his eyes
made it easy to believe.

The next morning, though, waking up in her solitary
bed, her only tangible reminder of the time spent away
her engagement ring, Katie was slammed by doubts. It
had all happened so fast. Had she rushed into her relationship with Blake, heedless of the consequences?

She didn't have answers but told herself she had to
put the questions aside, for at least the day, needing to
concentrate on getting to her office and catching up on
everything that she'd left undone in her absence.

Work, though, didn't turn out to be the distraction
she'd hoped.

Tessa, in the process of handing her several files,
suddenly stopped midgesture, staring wide-eyed at
Katie's left hand. "Oh, my gosh. Is that what I think it is?"

"Yes," Katie said, seeing no point in denying it, though
she would have preferred her and Blake's families had
been the first to know. "Blake and I are engaged."

"I didn't believe it when you kept denying you were
involved, but I never expected…" Tessa stopped, looking a little flustered, and then put on a smile. "Well, congratulations. It looks like you're going to be Mrs.
McCord after all."

Katie flushed at the implication that she'd traded one
McCord man for another, but then hadn't she expected
that reaction? She didn't have time to come up with a

response because her cell rang and she recognized Blake's number. Tessa left with a silently mouthed, "Talk to you later," as Katie picked up the call.

"I'm hoping you can meet me at home this afternoon, say about four?" he said. "I thought we could decide on the best way to tell the families about us."

Tension gripped her but she tried to sound casual, pleased even. "Yes, all right. I should be finished up here by then."

There was a pause and then Blake said, "Is everything all right?"

"It's been a long morning," she hedged. "Tessa managed to pile my desk with paperwork while we were gone and I'm trying to sort through it all."

"If that's all—" He gave her a moment to reply and when she didn't, he said, his voice dropping to that low, husky pitch she'd learned so well, "I miss you. I know it's been less than a day, but I've gotten used to us being together."

"I feel the same way," she said.

She heard a muffled buzz at his end and Blake's exasperated sound. "Damn, I've got another call. I'll see you this afternoon. I love you."

"I love you, too," she murmured.

The way he'd opened up to her, how easily he expressed his feelings to her now, quelled Katie's doubts, at least until the late afternoon, when she was on her way to the McCord mansion. Then, determined to defeat them, she kept reminding herself that they loved each other, and that Blake was right, it didn't matter what anyone else said or thought.

Yet the closer she got to the mansion and Blake, the more she worried it was a battle that her heart wouldn't win.

* * *

Blake met Katie at the front door, stealing a quick kiss, before whisking her out to one back wing of the house, facing the gardens. He'd chosen the Florida room because it was least likely they'd be interrupted there. Closing the expansive sliding glass doors behind them, he turned and drew her to him and kissed her again, this time passionately, telling her with his embrace how long the hours had seemed without her.

When they parted, breathless, he smiled. "Sorry for the cloak-and-dagger entrance, but I wanted us to have time alone before we're discovered. No one ever uses this room, unless my mother has her lady friends for tea."

"It's fine." Gently disengaging herself from his arms, she walked over to stand near the windows, looking out at the landscape that was glazed with the last of the afternoon sun. "You said you wanted to talk."

Something in her tone and the stiff set of her shoulders made him uneasy. He went over to her, putting his hands on her shoulders and gently turning her to face him. "What's bothering you, Katie? And don't tell me it's been a long day or it's jet lag," he said before she could give those excuses again. "I know that's not it."

"Tessa knows we're engaged."

"And that's a bad thing? In a day or two, so will everyone else."

"It's not so much that she knows," Katie said, glancing away from his searching gaze. "It was her reaction. She said it looked like I was going to be Mrs. McCord after all."

"I don't see—"

Katie pulled away from him. "A few months ago I was engaged to your brother. That's what everyone is going to say, that I couldn't have Tate, so I settled for the next best thing."

A cold hard knot settled in his gut. "Is that what you did, Katie, settle for second-best?"

"You know that isn't true."

"Do I? I thought I did. I'd convinced myself that this wasn't about you being on the rebound from Tate. Now, I'm not so sure."

"This has nothing to do with Tate. It never did. I never loved him the way I love you."

"Then what is it about?" Blake gritted out, trying hard to keep a leash on his frustrations.

She looked at him a long moment and he could clearly see the struggle in her eyes to put her feelings to words. "Those weeks in San Vincentia and then Paris," she began, "they were…like a dream. I went there with you, not expecting it to last, and then—everything happened so quickly. I didn't have time to think about what we were doing."

Pacing a few steps away from him, she glanced at his ring on her finger. "I've never loved anyone like this, even Tate. It's so overwhelming that sometimes it feels like it can't be real." Her eyes lifted to his, begging for his understanding. "I never really committed to Tate—I was just raised to believe we were meant for each other. And you've never been in a long-term relationship. I can't help but wonder if either of us knows what we're doing. I'm worried we rushed into this blindly without knowing if what we have is strong enough to last a lifetime."

"You're saying we—you—made a mistake." Blake faced away from her to grip the back of a chair. He couldn't have guessed it would hurt like this, to hear all over again someone telling him—Katie telling him, that once again, he was somebody's mistake.

"Blake—no," she said, the anguish in her voice making him turn to her again, "that's not what I meant. Please, I…I never wanted to hurt you like this, for you to think that I regret loving you. I'm just—" In a jerky abrupt motion, she tugged off her engagement ring, and quickly coming up to him, took his hand and pressed the ring into his palm, closing his fingers around it. "I can't be what you need. You deserve so much better than this."

She spun around and started for the door, her sudden action freezing him in place for several seconds. But the sight of her leaving him spurred him to action and he outpaced her and grasped her wrist, keeping her from walking out of his life.

"Blake…" Tears filled her eyes as she looked at him.

For a moment, he told himself he could let her go, save himself additional grief and heartache by ending it now. It would be the simplest way to resolve things and he nearly made that choice to go back to what he was before, alone, armored against caring, substituting ambition and success for love.

But he couldn't go back. And he'd never before taken the easy way out.

"What do you want, Katie?" he asked. "I can't promise you perfection or that we're never going to have to face any obstacles. I can't stop people from talking. All I can promise is that I'll always love you, and that if you feel the same way, then we will be strong enough."

Opening his hand, he offered her the ring. "Your choice this time. I've made mine."

He held his breath as she searched his eyes and it felt she was searching his heart and soul. After a minute that lasted an eternity, when he'd nearly resigned himself to inevitably losing her, she smiled and held out her left hand.

"Will you put it back on?" she asked softly. "For the last time?"

Blake didn't hesitate. He slid the diamond onto her finger and then pulled her into his arms, sealing their future with a kiss that vowed forever.

Two days later, Blake returned home on a Saturday morning, having spent the past nights with Katie. Her parents were in Austin, celebrating Peter Salgar's recent election as governor, and they had the Salgar estate to themselves. They'd spent their days at their respective offices, but their nights alternated between making love and talking. Today, they planned to begin breaking the news of their engagement, starting at lunch with his family.

First, though, he had some unsettled business with his youngest brother. Katie's insights had made him realize that he was still wrestling with lingering demons and he needed to settle things with Charlie, and his mother, as well. She felt strongly that Blake should be at peace with his family before they could begin thinking about having a family of their own. And he had come, reluctantly at first, finally now, to agree with her, at least where Charlie was concerned.

That was why he'd asked Charlie to come home from college for a weekend to talk. When he saw the wariness written in his little brother's eyes as he stepped into the breakfast room, though, he felt a pang of guilt. His bitterness and anger had caused that look.

Now it was up to him to make it go away.

"Good morning," he said, hoping to ease the tension

with the mundane greeting. "I hope you got a good night's sleep."

"It was fine," Charlie returned with a shrug. "We missed you at dinner last night. Mom said you've been gone a lot lately."

"I'll tell you about that later. Right now, I want to talk about something else. Let's go out back."

There was a chill in the air, and they both pulled on coats. Blake pretended not to notice the sidelong looks Charlie kept slanting at him, knowing his brother was probably confused by his complete turnaround in attitude from the last time they'd met.

"What's on your mind?" Charlie asked when they'd walked a distance from the house.

"A lot. But I'll try to simplify it." He took a breath. "I wanted to apologize."

Charlie looked straight ahead. "For what?"

"For the way I acted when you told me you wanted to meet Rex. For resenting you all these years." Charlie's eyes snapped to him and Blake smiled a little then sobered. "It wasn't fair of me to blame you for what happened between Mom and Rex and my father all those years ago."

"It wasn't fair the way Mom treated you," Charlie muttered. He shifted his shoulders, staring at the ground. "I felt guilty for always being her favorite. I never knew why, which just made it worse."

"None of it was your fault. I think it's time we both put it behind us." He laid a hand on Charlie's shoulder. "You're a great guy and you deserve the love of both your parents. I hope you can get to know your father. You both deserve a chance to make up for lost time."

"Thanks, Blake, really, this means more to me than I can tell you. I never expected this from you." He paused then added, "Rex and I are making headway. It's weird, but we have a connection."

"You'll always be a McCord, too. I hope you remember that." Reaching out, he pulled his brother into a hug, for the first time he could remember since Charlie was a child. Charlie returned the embrace and when they backed away, Blake pushed a hand through his hair, clearing his throat against the lump there.

Yet he suddenly felt lighter, the heaviness of guilt and resentment receding, replaced with a warmth and closeness he'd missed between him and Charlie.

"So are you going to tell me what the big secret is?" Charlie asked as they started walking back toward the house.

"Big secret?"

"Come on, Blake. You disappear for a couple of weeks and when you do get back home, nobody can find you. And coincidentally, no one's seen Katie in all that time, either."

Blake smiled at Charlie's not so subtle probing. "Looks like you get to be the first to know—Katie and I are engaged."

"Engaged? Seriously? That's great!"

"You think so?"

"Why wouldn't I?" Charlie asked. "I never thought she and Tate were right for each other even though everybody kept pushing them together. What, are you worried about what Mom's going to say?"

"It doesn't matter what she or anyone else says. We love each other and that's not going to change. So—are you going to join us for lunch and take our side when we make the big announcement to everyone else?"

Charlie flashed him a grin. "I wouldn't miss it."

* * *

Katie sat next to Blake that afternoon, trying not to let her face give away the riotous happiness that threatened to burst out. Eleanor, Tate, Tanya and Charlie had joined them and Katie could see it was all Charlie could do not to burst out grinning.

Blake reached for her hand under the table, brushing his thumb over her fingers. Inwardly she smiled, feeling both joyous and nervous, sure there would be mixed reactions, also knowing she no longer cared.

All that truly mattered to her now was that her fiancé sat next to her, her hand in his, his ring a symbol of their love and the commitment they had made to each other for the rest of their lives. She had, for the first time in her life, made her choice, and it was Blake.

They were nearly finished with lunch when Eleanor put down her glass and looked pointedly at Blake and Katie. "This has been nice, but it's not like you, Blake, to arrange a family meeting without some purpose. Are you going to tell us?"

Exchanging a glance with him, Katie let him bring their clasped hands into view, drawing everyone's attention to brilliant diamond on her hand.

"Katie and I are getting married," he said simply.

There was a brief silence in which Eleanor stared and Tate frowned, while Tanya and Charlie broke out in smiles.

"We love each other," Katie said softly, looking directly at Eleanor. "I know you can understand that."

They shared a moment when Katie felt Eleanor weighing the sincerity of Katie's declaration and then Eleanor nodded. "I do understand."

"Is this what you want?" Tate asked.

Blake tensed, but Katie squeezed his hand and smiled at Tate. "It's everything I want."

"Then, congratulations," Tate said, his expression lighter. He lifted his glass and the others followed suit, though Eleanor was the last. "May you be as happy as Tanya and I are."

Katie's gaze went to Blake and he focused only on her and promised, "We will be."

Heedless of their audience, this time it was she that drew him into a kiss, knowing without doubt that with Blake, she'd truly found forever.

* * * * *

MILLS & BOON®

are proud to present our...

Book of the Month

Proud Rancher, Precious Bundle
by Donna Alward
from Mills & Boon® Cherish™

Wyatt and Elli have already had a run-in. But when a
baby is left on his doorstep, Wyatt needs help.
Will romance between them flare as they
care for baby Darcy?

Mills & Boon® Cherish™
Available 1st October

Something to say about our Book of the Month?
Tell us what you think!

millsandboon.co.uk/community
facebook.com/romancehq
twitter.com/millsandboonuk

All the magic you'll need this Christmas...

When **Daniel** is left with his brother's kids, only one person can help. But it'll take more than mistletoe before **Stella** helps him...

Patrick hadn't advertised for a housekeeper. But when **Hayley** appears, she's the gift he didn't even realise he needed.

Alfie and his little sister know a lot about the magic of Christmas – and they're about to teach the grown-ups a much-needed lesson!

Available 1st October 2010

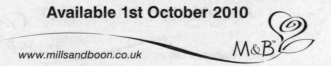

2 FREE BOOKS
AND A SURPRISE GIFT

We would like to take this opportunity to thank you for reading this Mills & Boon® book by offering you the chance to take TWO more specially selected books from the Cherish™ series absolutely FREE! We're also making this offer to introduce you to the benefits of the Mills & Boon® Book Club™—

- **FREE home delivery**
- **FREE gifts and competitions**
- **FREE monthly Newsletter**
- **Exclusive Mills & Boon Book Club offers**
- **Books available before they're in the shops**

Accepting these FREE books and gift places you under no obligation to buy, you may cancel at any time, even after receiving your free books. Simply complete your details below and return the entire page to the address below. You don't even need a stamp!

YES Please send me 2 free Cherish books and a surprise gift. I understand that unless you hear from me, I will receive 5 superb new stories every month, including two 2-in-1 books priced at £5.30 each, and a single book priced at £3.30, postage and packing free. I am under no obligation to purchase any books and may cancel my subscription at any time. The free books and gift will be mine to keep in any case.

Ms/Mrs/Miss/Mr _____ Initials _____

Surname _____

Address _____

_____ Postcode _____

E-mail _____

Send this whole page to: Mills & Boon Book Club, Free Book Offer, FREEPOST NAT 10298, Richmond, TW9 1BR